As danger swept across the burning ~~...~~
of Egypt,
they lit the fires of heroism
and desire.

BEN-HADAD—Proud inheritor of the Mark of the Lion, his desperate search for a cherished friend leads him toward danger . . . and unexpected love.

BENU—Fierce rebel leader in Egypt's occupied lands, he is called "The Phoenix" because he has returned from the dead to seek a ruthless vengeance.

TUYA—Beautiful orphan girl of the streets, her beloved thinks her only a child, until desire makes her a woman able to love—or kill—with passion.

MEREET—Loyal daughter of Egypt, she learns a secret that can bring the pharaoh's downfall . . . or the tragic loss of the husband and children she loves.

JOSEPH—Young Israelite sold into slavery by his jealous brothers, his vision foretells a nation's future . . . and his own fate in the land of the Nile.

THE LION IN EGYPT

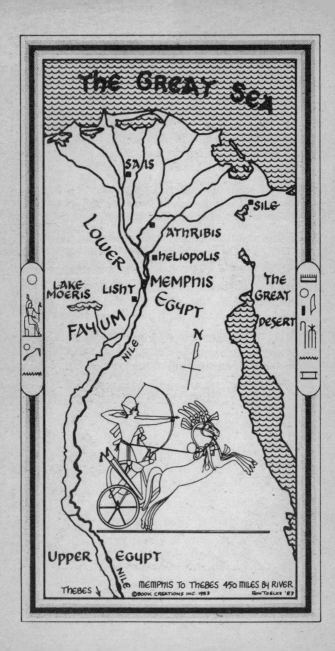

THE GREAT SEA

SA·IS

SILE

ATHRIBIS

HELIOPOLIS

MEMPHIS

LOWER EGYPT

LAKE MOERIS

LISHT

FAYUM

THE GREAT DESERT

NILE

N

UPPER EGYPT

NILE

THEBES

MEMPHIS TO THEBES 450 MILES BY RIVER.

©BOOK CREATIONS INC. 1983

RON TOELKE '83

Other Bantam Books by Peter Danielson
Ask your bookseller, for the titles you have missed

CHILDREN OF THE LION
THE SHEPHERD KINGS
VENGEANCE OF THE LION

VOLUME IV

THE LION IN EGYPT

PETER DANIELSON

Created by the producers of
**Wagons West, White Indian,
Saga of the Southwest, and
The Kent Family Chronicles** Series.

Chairman of the Board: Lyle Kenyon Engel

BANTAM BOOKS
TORONTO · NEW YORK · LONDON · SYDNEY

THE LION IN EGYPT

A Bantam Book / published by arrangement with
Book Creations, Inc.
Bantam edition / June 1984

Produced by Book Creations, Inc.
Chairman of the Board: Lyle Kenyon Engel

PRINTED IN THE UNITED STATES OF AMERICA

O 0 9 8 7 6 5 4 3 2 1

PROLOGUE

All through the long day the blazing devil-winds men called the sharav had howled their way across the baked desert, bringing with them tension, agitation, and madness. Now, as night came on, the winds ceased for a time, and tempers cooled with the cooling earth. Friendships sundered by day were now mended beneath the healing rays of the moon; man and wife, enemies only an hour before, broke bread together in love and restored harmony. The children, their hunger sated and their energy on the wane, nestled up against their parents' legs before the campfire. The coals glowed; smoke drifted upward in curling tendrils. . . .

"He's here," someone said.

And then they all could see him, far beyond the fire's lit circle—the Teller of Tales, tall, thin, gaunt-faced, white-haired, his tattered robe stirring softly in the evening breeze. A murmur spread through the gathering as they watched him approach, stop, and look around, search every face before him with those deep-set eyes, and, at length, spread his long arms wide, the sleeves billowing about him. His voice, beginning as a whisper but carrying easily as he spoke, was soothing, the words growing louder as his half-musical chant began:

"In the name of God, the merciful, the benevolent . . ."

The children cuddled closer against their parents' drawn-up knees. All sounds from the near-silent camp

1

ceased; all faces turned up toward the old man's tall, striking form, which seemed to tower over the dying campfire.

"You have heard," he said, "of the coming of the Shepherd Kings, nomadic warriors without number, and of how they slashed their ruthless way across peaceful Mesopotamia and Canaan, bringing death and destruction wherever they went.

"You have heard," he said, "of the brothers Shobai and Hadad, arms makers of the Children of the Lion, and of how Hadad died at the hands of the traitor Reshef, while saving his blinded brother and his city—and of how Hadad was at last revenged by Shobai and the Egyptian woman Mereet."

Here women as well as men leaned forward, eager-eyed, remembering the tale of the great love between the blind Shobai and the beautiful Mereet, daughter of an Egyptian lawgiver and widow of the brave warrior Baka; remembering how Mereet, marrying the blind giant, had borne him twin Children of the Lion, a boy and a girl. . . .

Raising his voice, the tale-teller continued. "Hear now," he said, "of the son of Hadad, friend, like his father, of the Canaanite patriarch Jacob, blood brother to Jacob's son Joseph, and of how Ben-Hadad followed his kidnapped friend to Egypt, hoping to bring him home to his father's land."

Now it was the turn of the younger listeners to lean forward attentively; Ben-Hadad's was a popular story.

"Now hear of the brave and beautiful Tuya, orphaned girl of the streets, and of her great love for Ben-Hadad, and of how they joined the fight against the hated invaders. Hear of the black giant Akhilleus, and of his quest to the headwaters of the Nile for men to fight the invader and ore to feed Shobai's forges in the ceaseless war against the foreign conqueror. Hear of how resistance grew and flourished in the occupied lands, under the very eye of the all-powerful enemy.

"Hear," he said, his voice falling from its crescendo pitch, "hear of the Children of the Lion, and of their adventures in the land of Egypt. . . ."

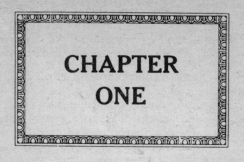

CHAPTER ONE

AVARIS, THE NILE DELTA

I

Silently, unnoticed, the two assassins slipped through the crowded, bustling streets of the half-built city of Avaris.

On all sides, chaos reigned. Oxcarts bearing fresh mud-bricks contended for passage space with bullock-drawn carts bearing dressed wood for the carpenters of the city. These, plus shoppers, merchants, thieves, guardsmen, slaves, ragged or naked urchins, whores, procurers, and the ubiquitous, richly dressed, arrogant, universally detested Asiatic soldiers who, gathered in threes and fours, clogged every corner and passage—all fought for the right to pass, with elbow and knee and fist. In such a boiling stew of humanity, amid a deafening din, the two professional killers moved easily and purposefully toward their destination, attracting no more attention than would a pair of scorpions on a mud-brick wall.

Out toward the fringes of Avaris, the streets no longer followed straight lines or, indeed, any pattern at all. Beyond the ceremonially ordered center of the city, where the architects' graceful geometric designs had been enforced

3

with dictatorial rigidity, the quarters of the city relegated to the common people had, by time-honored Egyptian custom, been left largely to chance. Miserable, squalid one-story dwellings, made of earth or unbaked brick covered with a layer of mud, abutted one another at crazy angles that ignored symmetry and the rules of geometric precision. Through this chaos, the narrow, crowded streets lazily followed meandering paths that might well have been laid out by the bullocks themselves, or perhaps by the winding route of water runoff after the infrequent delta rains. Out here on the fringes, the graceful temple towers that had begun to rise above the city's center seemed far away.

It was easy to get lost here. Even at midday the confusing network of streets and alleys could lead the most experienced traveler astray, into unfamiliar and often dangerous territory. And after dark, when torches of pitch-soaked reeds, hung in metal holders above the major intersections, provided but meager illumination, only the streetwise or the unwary ventured forth. Such was the unwritten law of Avaris.

The city of Avaris had risen from the rich earth of the Twentieth Nome, where only two years ago there had been nothing but farmland. The city's rapid rise bore witness as much to native Egyptian industry as it did to the iron will of its founder, Salitis. Born a prince of the fierce Shepherd Kings in the wild mountains north of the Assyrian kingdoms, Salitis had inherited much of the forcefulness and sagacity of his chieftain father, Manouk, under whom the nomadic Shepherd Kings, en route to the rich Egyptian delta, had conquered half the known world.

Forced from their homeland many years ago by a severe drought, the fierce Shepherd armies had sliced across northern Mesopotamia all the way to the borders of the Hittite kingdoms before encountering serious resistance. Then they had turned south, laying waste to Carchemish and the coastal cities before their advance was slowed, then stopped altogether before the walls of the fabled city of Ebla.

The siege of Ebla, although successful, in the end had weakened the Shepherd Kings' armies, and after the fall of the city, the nomads had avoided battle all the way to the edge of the Sinai desert, honoring treaties made by Manouk with the Canaanite king Jacob. Then the terrible trek across the harsh wasteland had not only destroyed the nomads' gigantic herds, but also left the Shepherd army a fraction of its former size when at last it reached the Egyptian borders at the ancient fortress of Sile.

Sile, however, had fallen after fierce fighting, and the Shepherd Kings had marched into Egypt, taking advantage of a chaotic interregnum that had followed the end of the mighty Twelfth Dynasty. With the Egyptian kingdom splintered into many warring factions, the Shepherd Kings, even in their weakened state, had been strong enough to prevail. They had driven the last of the formal armies of the old Egyptian kingdom from the delta, to as far south as Memphis, cutting them off from foreign trade as well as from the agricultural bounty of the silt-rich delta territories. From Memphis to the sea, only small but stubborn pockets of armed resistance remained, and soon these, too, were eradicated or driven underground.

In part because of the tenacity of this underground resistance, the son and heir of the Shepherd chieftain Manouk had decided that he could not effectively reign over the conquered territories without first winning the hearts of the people. To this end, he had forbade mention of his former name—Avedis—and, assuming the god-king status of a true ruler of the kingdom, had declared himself Salitis, pharaoh of Egypt. His first official act had been to call for the creation of a new city, a capital, from which to reign. Thus, from the bare plain had risen Avaris, key city of the new kingdom, its civic center a conjunction of Egyptian grandeur and Shepherd oriental taste, its outer edges denying all this with the inevitable boomtown chaos: shapeless, lawless, vital, dangerous—a place to make or lose a fortune, to rise or fall overnight, to kill or be killed, almost without hindrance from the supposed forces of law and order. . . .

As the winding street broadened into an irregular square clogged with the normal business clutter of a noisy and squalid lower-class marketplace, the leader of the two assassins suddenly stopped, turned, and motioned his companion to a halt beside him. "Onuris!" the first man whispered into his friend's ear. "We're in luck! Look—by the well."

The man called Onuris followed with his eyes where his crony had pointed. "Where? I don't under—"

"There, you fool! The soldiers! See?" His hand clawed at his friend's bicep impatiently.

"But, Zosar, I don't—"

Then his eyes widened and he half smiled. "You're right," he said. "What good fortune! Not just one of his personal guards—but both of them! And from the looks of them . . ."

Zosar's grip tightened on his arm. "From the looks of them, they've already had half a jar of palm wine apiece. See—the big one's reeling. He can hardly stand up. Come on—this is too good an opportunity to waste!" And, not looking back, he steered a hasty course down a side street away from the two Shepherd soldiers, brushing Onuris so closely that his friend could feel the hard pommel of the dagger belted inside his garment. Hurrying forward through the winding streets, Zosar led his companion a spirited chase, which ended before a stout door made of imported oak. A door that—Onuris's heart leaped at the thought—the drunken soldiers had left ajar.

Inside, on a slanted bed, on none-too-clean sheets, Hovsep, commander of an elite troop of Shepherd cavalry, sat up, naked, addled by palm wine, an equally bare dancing girl on his knees embracing him. In the corner of the uncluttered room two girls in transparent robes, their breasts bared, played the six-stringed Egyptian lyre and the double reed pipe, while a slim girl dancer, wearing only the woven wig of the prostitute and a girdle of faience beads, capered lasciviously, kicking her naked and hennaed feet high over her head. Sinuously weaving, the dancer advanced, then retreated seductively, evading the long reach of the army officer by little more than a finger's length each time. Once his fingertips brushed her bare rump, and she smiled tantalizingly as the musicians, responding to her mood, picked up the already brisk tempo of the dance tune.

"Come here, you little vixen!" the officer said, slurring his words, his lurch forward dumping the nude girl from his lap. The dancer spun gaily away, her breasts swaying temptingly. The officer stood, weaving drunkenly back and forth, and reached out for her, his clumsy steps bringing him close to the curtain that framed the door of the room—

"*Ahhhh!*" he gasped suddenly, clutching his naked belly, then staggering backward.

The music faltered.

The officer turned—and his hands framed a terrible, gaping, red wound.

The dancer screamed. The music stopped.

"No!" one of the girls said. "Please! Not us. We were just—"

Out of the space behind the curtain stepped first one man, then another. Both held knives; one knife dripped red. The taller of the two smiled, bowed sarcastically. The officer's legs gave beneath him; he fell in a heap. From his naked, aging body, a pool of red began to spread.

"Please . . ." one of the girls said again, her hand covering the vital places on her body. "Not me. Don't . . ."

"Relax," the tall one said, wiping his bloody blade on the curtain. "We've done what we came to do. Well, most of it, anyway." He looked down at the dying man at his feet. Then he turned the officer over onto his stomach, using his foot. "Ugh! It pains me to touch scum like this. The things one has to do for one's country." And swiftly, with a scribe's sure hand, he guided the sharp knife in a few deft strokes, tracing a series of elaborate curves on the officer's bare back. The girls stared, rooted to the spot by fear, as the bloody figure of a heronlike bird appeared on the officer's mutilated flesh.

The naked dancer gaped, her hands held to her breast. "Benu?" she said, unbelieving. "The Phoenix?"

The knife-wielder's face creased in a cold smile. She would remember it forever: a hawk's face, as sharp-edged as the weapon he still held in his hand, with a thin knife-blade of a nose and unreadable, almost black eyes, the lip curled in bitter derision.

"The Phoenix?" he said. "Me? No such luck. He's safe, far away from here. But where my hand lands, gutting such poisoned fish as we see here, it strikes with the weight of the Phoenix's arm behind it." He bowed again, still smiling sarcastically. "So when the guards come—and they will—you *can* tell them that you've had a little visit from Benu himself. It won't be stretching the truth too much."

He was obviously playing it up for his captive audience. His friend pulled at his sleeve, eager to go. "I'm coming," he said irritably. "But—you, girls." His eyes leered at the two nude dancers, as their hands went protectively to their secret parts. "If I were you, I'd think twice before whoring with an Asiatic again." His smile was lopsided, insulting, unpleasant; the girls shivered, cringing back against the wall. He wiped the knife again and bowed even more elaborately than before. "You never know when a servant of the Phoenix may be lurking behind a door. And some of us haven't my—"

"Come on!" his companion said. "There's no time!"

In the blink of an eye both of them were gone. And the only sign of their passing was the now-dead man on the floor before the bed. Flies had begun to gather at the edges of the dark pool of red.

Zosar and Onuris walked quickly down the street. Onuris hurried to pull even with his companion. When he did he was shocked at the gleam of excitement—of almost sexual ecstasy—in the taller man's eyes.

"You—you *liked* that," he said. "It wasn't enough to kill the man, as we were commanded to do. You had to maim him, to stand over him and mock him. To threaten those girls, when they were doing only what—"

"Bah!" Zosar said, spitting the word out. "Bitches! Sluts! Bedding down with the worst of the worst like that! Pandering to the foul tastes of slimy Asiatic swine! I should have cut off their—"

"Keep your voice down. And I've told you before—we

joined to fight for freedom, to do what we can to expel the nomads. We didn't join Benu to—to kill for sport."

Zosar's long legs increased the pace. "In the name of all that's holy, will you shut up? You're turning into a sniveling milksop, grieving over the rights and dignity of the enemy, while—"

"No, I'm not! You can't say that—you know it isn't so!" Onuris's hand closed on Zosar's arm, spinning him to a stop beside him. Onuris pulled the taller man into an alleyway to shove him back against a bare wall. "I'm as committed as you are, and you can't look me in the eye and deny that, can you? Well, can you?" The other man did not answer, and he went on. "I just happen to think there's nothing to be gained by—by playing with them the way you do. Kill them quick, I say, and no standing around to humiliate them while they're dying." He shook his head angrily, reaching for words that would not come, frustrated at his own inarticulateness. "Besides—you're going to get us killed, or caught, hanging around afterward like that."

Zosar shook off his friend's grip, his eyes still full of black rage. His hand went to the butt of his dagger at his side . . . and then came away empty. "Very well. You're right. It is dangerous. But I do hate these vile-smelling oriental pigs so."

He allowed himself to be led out into the narrow street again, just as two men no older than themselves brushed past them at the corner. Zosar's rage rose again. "*You!*" he said in a terrible voice. "Watch where you're going, you clumsy oaf!" He reached for his dagger again as one of the men ahead half turned and looked at him and, not even bothering to break stride, shrugged and continued to walk away, lost in conversation with the short young man beside him.

For some reason, being ignored aroused Zosar's anger even more. He sprang forward with an oath . . . and stopped abruptly, as a third figure, no more than half his own bulk, jumped in front of him, barring his way. Where had the newcomer come from? He couldn't have said, then or later. But now the little creature was blocking his path. And there was a wicked blade pointed straight at

him, the noontime light glinting on its razor edge . . . and
the hand that held it seemed to know how to use it.

A boy, half-grown? Or—?

The girl spoke, settling the matter. Zosar gaped at
her, not knowing whether to laugh. How had he failed to
recognize her? "Tuya," he said, his hands falling to his
sides. "What in the name of sixty-five heathen devils are
you doing here?"

"None of your business," the girl said. She remained
in a crouch, the knife weaving before her. Zosar stepped
back, respectful; the little guttersnipe's skill with a knife
was legendary in the Thieves Quarter. "And you stay away
from him! Do you hear? He's mine! You touch him and I'll
cut your ears off! Worse—I'll cut off your—"

"Now, now," Zosar said, suddenly seeing the humor
in it all. This would make a good anecdote to tell back in
camp. He looked at the girl, at her thin face, the slim
hands and feet, at the lithe body in the shapeless garment
she wore. "Don't you worry—I'll leave your boyfriend
alone," he said, chuckling, turning his head for a moment
to smile at Onuris. But his companion had disappeared.
"Now, where can he have gone to?"

"He took off the way you'd better do," the girl said,
her dark eyes flashing. She shook the long knife at him.
"And you'd better remember, Zosar—leave him alone.
He's mine, and I'll kill anyone who lays a hand on him.
Understand? Touch him and I'll cut your throat! I'll slip
up in the dark and do it, when you're sleeping! And don't
think you can hide from me, either. I'll find you. I have
ways."

"All right, all right," Zosar said, laughing, sheathing
his knife, and making conciliatory gestures with his hands.
"If he means that much to you . . . what do I care? I don't
even know him. I didn't even notice his face. Who *is* this
paragon you're so taken with? I have to know whom to
stay away from, don't I? If I'm to avoid your displeasure,
that is."

"His name's Ben-Hadad," she said.

The knife was still at the ready, and anger was still in
her eyes. She actually looked rather beguiling this way, he

was thinking; clean her up a bit and put her in a decent robe and—

"He lives in the quarter, and he plays senet for a living in the Bazaar of the Olive Tree. Everyone knows him." She gestured with the knife as she spoke. "You'd better pass the word along to your friends, Zosar—if you have any friends. Anyone who tries to harm Ben-Hadad— rob him, beat him up, whatever—has to deal with me. You understand? He's mine."

But he had already turned and, laughing, was retreating down the narrow street, his shoulders shaking with uncontrolled mirth. She put away the knife and stood, hands on narrow hips, looking after him, her little bare feet planted wide apart in the dust.

She sighed, and as she did the anger went out of her, to be replaced with a dark and brooding melancholy.

Whom are you trying to fool? she asked herself. Do you really think you're fooling anyone other than yourself? *He's mine*, you tell everyone. Everyone but Ben-Hadad himself.

And he? He hardly knows you're alive.

II

In the Bazaar of the Olive Tree a sizable crowd had already begun to gather around the roped-off platform set up before the front door of the tavern. Now, as one of the two players approached, striding through the crowd, smiling, his shorter partner almost jogging to keep up with his brisk pace, a hum of excitement swept through the watchers. "The foreigner!" a woman's voice said from the rear. "The foreigner beloved of the gods!"

A second voice, male this time, echoed her. "Ben-Hadad!" it said. "Ben-Hadad!"

The crowd parted to let the pair through, and the round-faced, merrily smiling young gamesman climbed onto the platform. After taking off his sandals, he bowed to the crowd, then sat down cross-legged next to the senet board already set up on a low table beside him. His companion waved the crowd to silence.

"Friends!" the smaller man said, holding his two hands high. "Today we have something extraordinary for you. Ben-Hadad, champion of the six bazaars, beloved of all the gods, master of senet and the game of the palm tree, will play today—"

"Whom? Whom will he play? I didn't hear—"

"Quiet! Quiet, please!" the smaller man, his deformed face set in a perpetual arrogant sneer, waved his hands angrily, his voice rising almost to a shrill screech. "I'm getting to that. Today Ben-Hadad will play against the great Khensu of Sile, champion senet player of the border marches—"

The noise of the spectators again rose to engulf his words. Impatient, angry, he glared at the crowd. His champion, the foreigner Ben-Hadad, sat placidly on the carpeted platform, smiling at the faces around him, his powerful young arms folded nonchalantly across his chest. As the noise faded slightly his partner announced the odds. "Now, my friends! Who will wager with me on the favor of the gods? Who will cast lots with me? Who . . . who, I say, will give me six rings to win five? Who will—?"

"Six to five?" a burly man in the front said incredulously. "Six to five *against*? When Ben-Hadad hasn't lost a match in six waxings and wanings of the moon? What sort of fools do you take us for? Even money, or nothing!"

From the low roof of a building that abutted the Tavern of the Olive Tree, Wenis the merchant gazed down at the spectacle below. "How long has all this been going on?" he asked, more than mild curiosity in his tone. "From what this fellow in the front row says, six months at least. But—"

Hedjri, his servant, waited until his master's voice had stopped, leaving the sentence hanging. Then he said, "Over a year, sir, that much I do know. I think the boy arrived not long after the first buildings began to go up on the edges of the civic center of Avaris. He came here as an unproved apprentice metalworker, but when the Shepherd overlords placed restrictions on foreigners working at the skilled trades, the boy was put out of work. What I heard in the bazaars was that he was nearly starving when he discovered how good a player he was at the games of the city. He began with the palm tree game and quickly graduated to senet. In both he has won consistently."

"*Hmmm*," Wenis said, a thin smile on his patrician features. "At both games, you say? That's interesting. Very interesting. But do go on."

"Yes, sir," Hedjri said. He looked down as the boy's partner waved before the crowd a long dowel half covered with copper rings, the principal medium of exchange in the bazaars, calling for any takers for his wager. "It seems to have been around this time—probably no more than six months ago—that the boy met the fellow down there with the stick, the one with the ugly face."

"Yes?"

"Well, sir, up to this time the boy had played mainly for room and board. The tavern keeper paid him in that way to keep people coming to his inn. But when this one who touts the matches, this Anab, struck up a friendship with him, it all changed."

"Anab, eh? I'll have to make a note of that name. Go on."

"There isn't much to tell, sir. Anab and the boy, Ben-Hadad—he's said to be a Canaanite, I believe—they went partners. Anab makes all the arrangements, places and covers the bets, keeps distractions away. This frees the boy to do nothing but play. And—well, you heard, sir. He hasn't lost a match in six months. Best two of three, he always comes out on top. Sometimes he goes a week or two without losing so much as a game. There are those who say he'd never lose a game except that Anab makes him do so from time to time, to keep the odds down."

"Do you believe this?" The merchant half turned, a cynical smile on his thin lips.

"No, sir. The boy's just not a dissembler. It's not in his nature. And . . . I think, sir, that if he were, the gods would not so favor a foreigner, an unbeliever."

Wenis grunted. To be sure, this *would* be the explanation that would occur to the superstitious. Senet—the word meant "passing," short for "passing through the netherworld"—was an ancient game of luck and skill, having to do with the passage of a recently deceased spirit through the many traps and pitfalls of the next world, en route to eternal peace. In fact, to many, senet was much more than a mere game. The contest was said to begin at the moment of death. Each player had seven pieces—dancers, they were called—deployed in the alternate spaces—houses—of the thirty-square board. Through these houses each of the two players moved his seven dancers toward the perils of the last five houses, guided by the random falls of four throw sticks, each separate permutation of which called for a differently numbered move. Some of the play was based on pure skill, particularly the complex moves of the end game, in which a player attempted not only to move his own pieces into favorable positions, but also to block the other player from making similar moves. . . .

Wenis stared down at the curly-haired, round-faced young metalworker's apprentice, at his broad brow, his stocky, powerful young body, his patiently squared shoulders. . . .

But there was more to it than this, of course. Only part of the game involved skill. The rest was luck, or—to those of a religious turn of mind—the favor of the gods. A man who consistently moved his dancers through the complex terrors of the end game to reach eternal rest before his opponent did must quite obviously be enjoying some special favor, since many of the major gods and goddesses ruled various squares of the senet board.

And imagine, Wenis told himself, the thin smile breaking out again—imagine the effect on the popular mind of having the favor of the gods rest perpetually on the shoulders of a foreigner, an unbeliever, a heathen! No wonder the boy was famous in the bazaars, a byword wherever the common folk gathered and gossiped. No wonder he was a hero to them.

Wenis leaned over to watch as the boy's opponent, Khensu of Sile, entered the irregular little square below, trailing hangers-on and retainers. He watched as Ben-Hadad, barefoot and clad only in a loincloth, stood up to bow to his opponent courteously. He noted the powerful muscles of the boy's back and shoulders, the large biceps and forearms, the air of quiet confidence he exuded.

"Hedjri—" Wenis spoke to his servant without taking his eyes off the scene below.

"Yes, sir?"

"Run next door to the inn and fetch me something cool to drink, would you? And a chair, too. I don't want to miss this."

On the edge of the crowd below, little Tuya climbed atop the well, bracing herself on the shaft of the stunted olive tree for which the bazaar had been named. "Anab!" she said, calling the tout through the crowd. "Anab!"

Though not more than four paces away, Anab kept his eyes on the clay tablet in his hand, figuring as he spoke. "Don't bother me now, Tuya, for heaven's sake. Can't you see I'm trying to do sums?"

"Money!" the girl said. "That's all you think of. How is he? Is he in a good frame of mind?"

"Of course he is," the tout said. He stopped and looked up at her, the tablet idle in his hands. "And I want him to stay that way, do you hear? Don't you go bothering him or calling out encouragement, the way you did last week. It distracts him."

"But, Anab, he needs me! He needs me right up there beside him! I'm his luck! Didn't you hear him say so? He says—"

Anab's ugly face twisted in an angry grimace. "I don't care what he says. You stay clear of him, do you hear me? I'm trying to make him some real money for the first time in his life, and that means getting his name known before all the swells here in town. How can I do that with a ragamuffin like you scampering around always in plain sight, ruining the impression I'm trying to—"

But there was a vast sigh from the crowd just then, and Anab turned, startled. "Gods!" he said. "The game's begun! I haven't placed all my bets! I haven't . . ."

Tuya ignored his words, jumping down from the well and squirming her way into the crowd. She was so small and skinny—she stood hardly higher than a normal-sized man's chest and weighed scarcely more than a child of ten—that she was able to find her way to the front of the crowd with a minimum of bother and unpleasantness. Even the people behind her tolerated her presence since she did not stand high enough to block their view.

"Ben-Hadad!" she said. "I'm here!"

On the platform the boy hesitated, the four throw sticks in his hand. Then he spotted her, and smiled. "Tuya," he said, his tone as gentle as if he were speaking to a child. "Come on over here by me. I need all the luck I can find, playing a master like Khensu of Sile." He nodded courteously at his glowering opponent. "I'm sure a famous player of senet like Khensu won't mind my having a good-luck charm like you at my side when I pit my meager knacks against his superior skills and expertise."

Khensu's face bore a flash of hot anger for a moment; Ben-Hadad headed off trouble with further soft words. "Besides, the mighty Khensu has at his own side his collection of scarabs and amulets to ward off evil fortune, and I have only you. I'm sure he won't mind. Could someone please make a place for her up front? Up here beside me?"

A hole opened in the crowd, and Tuya, her heart pounding fit to burst, slipped through the packed people to a spot beside the carpeted platform. And it was through happy tears that she watched him toss the four sticks on the carpet, sharply, and look down at his score.

All four sticks had landed marked side up! Five houses' advance, and an extra turn thrown in for the bargain!

Ben-Hadad smiled at the crowd before moving his dancers around the corner and into the next row. "See? She's my luck. Where would I be without her? Particularly against such an opponent as the famous Khensu of Sile?"

Tuya beamed. But she also noticed, as did many others, how the young man took his next throw before moving, then broke his two moves into several, as the rules of the game allowed, and craftily moved one of his pieces to block off an important space, leaving Khensu with hardly a viable move of his own. Luck? Tuya asked herself miserably, the wind suddenly going out of her sails. Luck had nothing to do with the skillful use he made of his throw. As she surreptitiously wiped her eyes, all the joy vanishing from her expression, she realized that he was just being kind. He didn't really care about her. He'd have done the same for virtually anyone.

She turned to go . . . but knew she couldn't. For what if she really *were* his luck? What if she were wrong? What if he *did* care?

Her heart sank, and she kept her place. *Here I am,* she thought, *hopelessly in love with him, and he probably doesn't care about me at all. And I have to sit here and take it. Because I haven't anything else in the world, have I? Table scraps—no more than table scraps. And here I sit, glad to get even that.*

On the roof, Wenis had not taken his eyes off the senet game, and he did not fail to notice, along with many in the crowd below, that Khensu's moves had begun to take on a desperate look. "Gods!" he said. "Do you believe that? He can't lose now! Six moves and the game's as good as over! And look—Khensu's spotted it! He sees it!"

"Yes, sir. It's quite amazing. I keep forgetting that this is the first time you've seen him. I could hardly believe my eyes at first, either, sir. And—mind you, sir, this Khensu was the champion of the entire border marches. He's a famous name among the followers of the game. There's a stela in Sile, erected by the merchant Shashank, showing Khensu playing senet. One of the water bearers to the Shepherd army told me—"

"This is *that* Khensu? Gods! Shashank told me about him before he died. He said this senet player of his made him more money in a month's play than six caravans could bring in in the same time, draining the bazaars of Ebla and Damascus alike! And here I'm watching a young man thrash him soundly. He makes it all look easy!"

"Yes, sir," Hedjri said. He leaned closer to his master's ear, and his tone became quiet, diffident. "I'm sure you've noticed, sir, that as a partner, as a protector, the boy has nothing more than this weasel-faced fellow, Anab."

"Ah, yes," Wenis said, watching the two men on the platform below set up the board again after the startlingly quick first victory Ben-Hadad had posted. "Anab. Tell me about this Anab. Ugly piece of goods, isn't he?"

"Yes, sir. It's a bit unfortunate. He's a bastard, a foundling raised by thieves. When he was a scrawny child, they used him to climb up the drains of rich men's houses and slip inside to open the door so they could get in and steal the owners blind. And his face—well, he can't have been a pretty child to start with, but during one of the robberies, he ran into a servant left behind by the house's owners, and there was a scuffle. The servant had a knife. He slashed the boy's face—and ever since, part of his face won't move. It gives him something of a demon's visage, sir. Even the grimiest, filthiest whores in the bazaars won't touch him; they think he's bad luck. He's bitter about it, as you can imagine. He's never allowed anyone too close to him, except the boy Ben-Hadad. He fastened himself onto Ben-Hadad like a leech back in the beginning, and now he's the boy's shadow. Keeps everyone away from him. Yet—"

Wenis turned, half interested. "Yes? What were you going to say? Eh? Get it out, man."

Hedjri's face took on a thoughtful aspect. "Well, sir, I had a brother once, with a harelip. He was about as ugly as this Anab, in his own way. It soured him, made him gruff and grouchy. He wouldn't let anyone near him, either—nobody but me. I was little and didn't threaten him in any way. I suppose there was nobody in our town but me who ever saw the way my ugly, bad-tempered brother would cry himself to sleep nights. Sometimes it would take hours. Of course he never knew that I was awake listening, and I never let on."

But as he turned to gauge the expression on his master's face, he could see that Wenis had not been listening. Instead the merchant was again bent over the roof's edge, staring down with fascination at the second game. "Gods!" the trader said. "Will you look at that, now! Boxed in! Boxed in already! And the game isn't six moves old! This is amazing, truly amazing! Look, Hedjri . . . set up a meeting for me with the boy, will you? A private get-together at my villa, away from that ugly chap. Don't let *him* know anything's going on. Make it as soon as possible, but keep it quiet. Mum's the word, eh? There's a good fellow."

Hedjri's face went neutral again. He bowed formally. "Your word is my command, sir," he said in a courtier's polite voice.

III

The end came, quick and sure. When it did, the watchers could not tell with any certainty whether it had come about through Ben-Hadad's skill, his luck, or the ill fortune of his opponent. Not that it mattered in the slightest. The crowd gaped, astonished, as Ben-Hadad, with two pieces left on the board to Khensu's one, came from behind to win.

Khensu's fine middle game and promising end game were wiped out in two ill-favored casts of the throw sticks. With his last remaining dancer favorably situated in square twenty-six, the House of Beauty, and Ben-Hadad's two dancers occupying squares twenty-eight, the Hall of the Two Truths, and twenty-nine, the House of Re-Atum, Khensu's first cast of the four sticks left three of the finger-shaped markers with the decorated side facing up and the fourth with the blank side showing.

The crowd let out an echoing sigh around him. The throw gave the Egyptian player an advance of one house, leaving him in square twenty-seven, the ill-favored House of the Waters. Here his dancer could drown, ending the game. However, the throw carried with it an extra cast of the throw sticks, and the player was not obligated to move a piece until his second cast had been completed. Those who had bet on Khensu sent up fervent prayers to half of the pantheon. There was one chance left. . . .

Khensu, holding the sticks before him, glanced at his opponent, sitting placidly across from him. Then he closed his eyes in a moment of silent communion with himself.

Then he cast the sticks.

Two houses; end of turn.

Khensu swore with rage. "Blocked!" he said. *"Blocked!"* He looked across at the quietly smiling Ben-Hadad. Then, with an angry wave of his hand, he swept the pieces from the little board, forfeiting the game immediately. He rose, glowered down at the winner, and said, "I don't know how you did that, you foreign scum. But I've been smelling witchcraft ever since I first heard about you! And I'm going to get to the bottom of this, if it's the last thing I do!" He pointed an accusing finger in Ben-Hadad's face, his hand shaking with rage. "You watch your step! You're a move or two ahead of death by impalement!"

Ben-Hadad did not speak. There was a roar of disapproval from the gallery. Bad sportsmanship was not tolerated in the bazaars. Angrily shoving his way through the crowd, Khensu left to a chorus of hoots and catcalls. Anab, his eyes bright, a fierce smile disfiguring the mobile side of his face, reached up to take down the standing dowel full of copper rings that the bettors had lost in their wager on Khensu's luck and skill. "Friends!" Anab said, raising his thin voice above the din. "That's all for today, but next market day we promise you a match with the brilliant and famous champion of the Fifth Nome, Wenamon of Saïs. . . ."

"Wait!" Ben-Hadad said suddenly behind him, standing up to wave the crowd to silence. "Wait, my friends! May I have your attention, please?"

Anab turned, frowning. The senet player, on his wooden platform, towered over the crowd. His young body glistened with a golden light from the film of sweat on his broad chest and wide shoulders. His face bore a carefree smile, and his eyes showed his affection for the crowd that still lingered around the platform. "Friends!" Ben-Hadad said.

There were several answering calls from the gallery. "What do you want now?" one man said. "You've already got my week's salary."

Ben-Hadad winced. "That's what I wanted to talk to you about. Anab—how much did we make today? What's my split of the day's winnings?"

Anab scowled. He did not answer aloud; he knew better. Instead, he held up the dowel bearing the rings.

His hand marked the halfway point. He saw Ben-Hadad purse his lips, figuring. And he thought: *Oh, gods of the firmament, let him not be thinking what I know he's thinking. . . .*

Ben-Hadad, however, confirmed his worst fears. "Innkeeper!" the boy shouted. "Innkeeper! Someone call the innkeeper for me, will you, please?"

"No, for the love of heaven!" Anab whispered. "Don't do it, you fool!" But his words did not carry—and he knew it wouldn't have made the slightest difference if they had. As he swiveled his head around to look at the crowd, he saw the innkeeper's ruddy face towering above the other eager faces.

"Here I am, Ben-Hadad," the man said. "What do you want?"

"There are perhaps a hundred of us here," Ben-Hadad said. "And I'll bet they're all as hungry as I am. Could you feed the lot of us—bread, sausage, cheese, wine—for . . . *hmmm* . . . fifty rings? Fifty copper rings?"

"Why—why, yes, but—"

"Well, then, back to the kitchen, my friend! It's a beautiful day, I've just enjoyed good fortune, and I want to share it with my friends here!" He laughed at the innkeeper's openmouthed astonishment. "Come, let's waste no time! Off you go! The best in your house!"

Anab groaned—but his protests were lost in the rousing cheer that rang through the marketplace.

With her bowl precariously balanced so as not to spill a drop of the fresh spring water she had drawn from the well, Tuya was backing through the solid wall of people, fanning her elbows wide to make room. Now, at the crowd's edge, she cautiously turned. "Ben-Hadad," she said, "I brought you some—"

But as she turned and looked up, she saw him take a bowl of palm wine from the innkeeper's assistant and lift it to his lips. "Thank you!" he said, but not to her. And as she stood watching, someone in the crowd jostled her arm and spilled her precious water all over her dress. She stepped back, spluttering. "Why, you—" But the person was already gone, and probably hadn't even noticed her—any more than Ben-Hadad had.

She scowled and let out a quiet, ladylike curse. Just as she did, Ben-Hadad noticed her. "Tuya!" he said. "How did you get so wet, on a dry day like this?"

"Why, I—I . . ." she began, but could not continue. She scowled again and put the empty bowl down on the platform.

"Here!" he shouted. "Plenty of food and drink for everyone! Help yourself!" And, smiling the same smile for her as for everyone else, he turned to speak to a latecomer. "You, sir—food and drink on the house for everyone! My compliments!"

Tuya turned away—and then turned back to look at him. *Isn't that just like him?* she thought. *Always squandering on everybody else his money, his friendship, his love—*

She let out a large, disgusted, yet wistful, sigh. Well, that was Ben-Hadad, wasn't it? Wasn't that part of the reason that she loved him so—the very naiveté of his concern for others, his good-heartedness, his unselfishness?

She bit her lip and sat down on a packed-earth abutment of the inn, feeling a little morose. *There's one way I wish he'd change,* she thought. *He could stop spreading all that big-heartedness and love and generosity around half the known world . . . and maybe send some of it my way, in a more concentrated fashion.*

She sighed. She let her narrow shoulders slump. If only he'd wake up and notice her! If only he'd look down and see her there, see her as the warm and loving woman she'd grown to be. *Woman, Ben-Hadad, not child!*

But that was the way of it when you had grown up in the bazaars, without parents or protector since your tenth birthday, when your uncle had been seized and taken away to rot in prison by the Shepherd soldiers, and you'd done all your growing up right there in the street in front of everybody. They all tended still to think of you as a child, as an urchin living off what you could steal from the fruit merchants and the bakers when they weren't looking. That was how they all viewed her, including Ben-Hadad.

No matter that she'd been a woman, in all the ways that counted, for two or three years by now. . . .

Well, no, that wasn't quite true. A woman in all ways but one. So far she'd defended her virginity with pride and passion against all would-be takers and users, wielding her wicked long-bladed knife with speed and skill, keeping the more aggressive males of the lower-class quarters at arm's length. Let one of those scum touch her? Not a chance! When she let a man make love to her he would be a hero, a prince, a man of stature. . . .

She sighed bitterly. What was the use? She knew who it was she wanted to be the first man to carry her to bed, to lie with her and love her. Ben-Hadad, of course. Since virtually the first moment she'd laid eyes on him, he'd been the standard by which she'd judged all men— and all of the rest had been found sadly wanting.

But now, at the fringe of the gathering, she saw Anab, his strange half-face twisted in a grimace she could not decipher, take the arm of a man, a stranger, and draw him aside, down a narrow alley. Her curiosity, honed by her years in the bazaars, got the better of her. What was he up to?

She moved swiftly to the alley's edge, trying to judge where they'd gone. Then, with a tiny shrug, she decided in favor of practical action. Fingers and bare toes searching for chinks in the earthen wall of the corner house, she quickly made her way to the roof. Once atop the row of houses, she scampered along nimbly, following the faint sound of voices. In a few moments' time she found herself peering down from a dusty rooftop onto the heads of the men she'd followed. She turned her head to one side, inclining her ear to catch the conversation.

The other man, she quickly learned, was Renefres of Bast. A speculator from another district of the city, he was typical of the better-off class of opportunists who had descended upon Avaris when its construction had been decreed by the Shepherd ruler Salitis: the type who would not kill, but who would hire a killer; who would not steal, but would employ others to do the stealing for him; who would, in short, connive at any crime, but would not willingly soil his own delicate fingers. She could not see his face now but could picture it: bland, almost expression-less, the eyes curiously empty, but the hands always busy. . . .

What were they saying now?

". . . know what you could do with a bit of capital, of course. Why should you be content with a small-time operation like this? Playing for olive pits in the bazaars, when you could . . ."

". . . can't understand what *you* plan to get out of this. After all, if I sell you a share of the proceeds, a percentage of his winnings—"

"Oh, come now. Let me indulge myself for a change. I have plenty of money; it's the excitement, the glamour, that attracts me. I think sometimes that, intent as you are on using the boy's . . . uh, talents, or whatever they are, for financial gain, to claw your way up out of the pigsty you live in down here—"

"Watch your tongue!"

"Well, I'm sorry, I suppose. Very well, I take that back. But I do think you miss some of the *drama* in it. I mean, after all, dear boy, we're dealing with something that has a vast potential for exploitation. And you're doing none of this. When I think of how one of these little senet duels of yours *could* be staged, *could* be performed, *could* be promoted . . ."

"I'm not doing so badly!" Anab snapped defensively.

"No, you're not. I mean, considering you've no train-ing in the art. But imagine—sell me half your interest in the boy and I'll have you wagering on his prowess not with paupers and thieves, but with generals! Rich merchants! Shepherd overlords!"

"I'm not so sure. It all sounds very good, but . . ."

"Well, don't take too much time. I may lose interest." The speculator turned to go, a little haughtily, flouncing down the alleyway, his fat hips swaying like a dancing girl's.

"Wait!" Anab said. "Don't go away yet. Don't do anything hasty, now. . . ."

*   *   *

When the stranger had gone, and Anab was counting the new rings on his dowel—gold ones, she noticed, not copper—Tuya dropped down from the low rooftop, landing beside him. Anab started and shrank back, his free hand going for the knife under his garment. "T-Tuya!" he said. "Where in the name of sixty devils did you come from? Don't scare me like that!"

"Anab," the girl said, "I'm ashamed of you. You sold half of your interest in Ben-Hadad to that dandy. Without even consulting him."

"Wh-wherever did you get a crazy idea like that?" Anab said. "We were settling a bet, that's all."

"A bet? Since when do you have the money to back a bet for—what was it, now?" Her eyes scanned the dowel in his hand. "Twenty gold rings? *Twenty?* Is that this week's price for selling out one's friends, Anab? Has it come down to that?"

"None of your confounded business!" Anab said, shrinking away from her, trying to cover up the dowel with its precious cargo. "And don't you go telling anyone that I've got this much money on me. As it is, I'll be lucky if I make it alive to the money changer's, to put this on deposit. Do you want to see me get my throat cut?" He started to slink away, backward.

Tuya stepped toward him, her little hand moving toward her own knife. Anab stopped and looked down at the hand, annoyed. Her expertise with the weapon, her fast and accurate hand, were legend in the quarter, and he had no mind to test the truth of the legend.

"Look," she said, "I think a lot of people around here have you pegged a bit wrong. I think they look at you once and decide you're a treacherous little swine, and they give up on you. I, however, think there's good in you. Well, some, perhaps. I think so far you've never done anything really bad, really rotten. You've thought about it, toyed with it, but until now . . . Anab, if you do this thing—"

"For heaven's sake, leave me alone, Tuya! Don't go prating to me about right and wrong. I don't want to hear it. I have my own life to lead, and—"

Something in his whining, defensive tone annoyed

Tuya. Angry, she stepped forward and grasped him by the hair, slipping the long knife from beneath her single shiftlike garment and laying its razor edge up against his neck, right beside the artery. "Look, you!" she said through clenched teeth, her dark eyes menacing. "I tried to tell you nicely—now I'm telling you in the language I should have used from the first, and you'd better listen and remember, Anab. Listen and remember."

"Y-yes?" he said in a strangled voice, his eyes rolled down to look at the sharp blade at his throat.

"Hear me, then. It's not too late to return the money that painted boy-lover gave you, and call the whole deal off. Under common law a bargain not witnessed isn't yet valid—but you do have to return the earnest money he gave you. You do that and I'll leave you alone. But nobody's going to sell off a portion of Ben-Hadad's life this way, without his permission and approval. Do you understand me? Nobody! Not you, or—"

"P-please," he said. "You—you're hurting me. You've broken the skin. I'm bleeding. I'm—"

"No, you're not. But you will be, if I hear tomorrow that you haven't canceled the deal with that popinjay. *And* given his money back. Do you hear?"

He gulped, nodded weakly. "Y-yes, Tuya," he said.

After she had left, Anab gingerly put a hand to his neck and, to his great surprise, found it did not come away red with his own blood. He stood there in the alleyway, his knees weak, his heart still beating rapidly.

Give the money back? How could he do that, without loss of face, without . . .

He shook his head and swore angrily. The trouble was that he knew she was right. He knew how his stomach would punish him if he did not do as she said—cancel the deal and do away with the evidence of his betrayal of Ben-Hadad. He'd be up all night with cramps, with terrible gas pains that yielded to no physic. He knew he'd toss with the cold sweats until dawn, hating himself, cursing the moment he'd yielded to temptation, to the restless voice inside him insisting that they were all his enemies and had been since his birth, that anything he did to them in retaliation for their rejection, for their laughter, their insults, was all right. . . .

They. Always they. And who were they, these people who had made his life unendurable, left him alone and miserable, perhaps the ugliest and loneliest man in the whole world?

Everybody. They were everybody. Everybody who'd ever looked at his ruined face and turned away, who'd ever crossed the street, seeing him coming, to keep from having to walk too close to him. All the women who'd said no in bitter disgust. All the ones who'd laughed. All the ones who'd thrown stones to keep him away. Who'd refused friendship, refused love. Who'd created between him and the rest of humanity an impassable gulf that he could see across but not traverse himself . . .

He put his hands over his deformed face, trying to blot out the vision, but to no avail.

See across? Yes! See them finding partners, lovers, friends, pairing off, making love, having babies together. Everyone, everyone except him, Anab! How he hated them! How he envied them! How he wanted to revenge himself upon them! All of them—

But the other voice in his soul said, *"All of them? Does that include Ben-Hadad? Who trusts you? Who's never done you any harm? Who looks you in the eye without flinching at your ugliness? Is he one of them?"*

Then the stomach cramp hit, and he doubled over in pain, clutching his gut. It was many moments before he could straighten himself, stagger to an alcove, and vomit up his meager lunch. And when, weak-kneed, he found his way back to the little square, the party had broken up. The innkeeper was sweeping up the mess before his tavern, humming a merry tune.

Anab, hoarse, weak-voiced, his face pale, asked after Ben-Hadad.

"Oh, he left a long time ago," the innkeeper said.

IV

Avaris, the raw young capital city of the Shepherd Kings, might be ill-formed and sprawling, new and uncultured, but the lands around it had been occupied for many centuries. The villa of a rich man like Wenis, who had been born to wealth and power, was laid out according to the old rules, which aimed at formal symmetry, lavish but understated display, and an air of gracious ease.

Ben-Hadad had never seen such a place in all his young life. In Sile, the only other Egyptian city he knew, the villas of the rich had long been sequestered by the Shepherd overlords, and riffraff from the streets, common people like himself, were seldom allowed near enough even to catch a glimpse of their tree-lined walls.

Now, as the servant Hedjri led him through the unguarded outer gates of the vast properties his master had inherited from his merchant-prince father, Ben-Hadad gazed wide-eyed at the pruned, controlled beauty of his surroundings.

The main entrance was through a formal garden, in which flowering shrubs—oleander, jasmine, and syringa—framed a shallow reflecting pool whose clear waters mirrored the imposing facade of the main house, with its tall, brightly painted lotus-bud columns. Rising above the low shrubs were long rows of sycamore figs; above these, tall date palms rose, swaying slightly in the light breeze.

"My master bade me bring you to the entrance hall," Hedjri said. "He apologizes for not accompanying you home from the bazaar. He had urgent business here, and had to leave immediately after witnessing your victory."

"I thank him for his concern," Ben-Hadad said as the two of them climbed the stairs to the high-roofed front veranda of the great house. "And I confess myself unworthy of the notice of a great man like the noble Wenis."

Hedjri smiled. The young foreigner's command of Egyptian words and ways was impressive. It was hard to believe that he had been in Egypt for only two years. "However that may be, sir, you *have* attracted his attention. In fact, it's been quite some time since I saw him get this excited about anyone."

Ben-Hadad followed the servant into the great entrance hall. "What a place!" he said appreciatively. Then, quickly resuming a more formal tone, he added, "I'm grateful that your master has taken notice of me, though I don't quite understand why. What interest could a rich and powerful man like the noble Wenis have in a comparative nobody like me? I'm no one special, just a—"

"No one special!" said a voice to his right. "Listen to the young man, Hedjri."

Ben-Hadad wheeled to see a portly Egyptian nobleman approaching. He was dressed in expensive robes, and his distinguished features were fixed in a benign smile.

"Sir," the man said, "you're too modest. But—I do have the right person, don't I? You *are* the same young genius I saw giving that amazing exhibition today in the marketplace?"

"Yes, sir," Hedjri said. "The senet player Ben-Hadad of Canaan, sir. My master, the noble Wenis." He bowed to each in turn, completing the formal introductions. Ben-Hadad also bowed, then waited for the merchant to speak.

"Come, my young friend," Wenis said, leading him through an open door and into the main hall of the house. In the center of the room stood several ornate couches surrounding low tables on which figs, cheeses, and wines were attractively displayed. Wenis indicated these, but Ben-Hadad politely declined. "Well, I'm sure you've the right idea," he said. "I'm rather too attracted to the delights of the table myself. I should emulate your moderation. Hedjri—remind me to do so."

"Yes, sir." But the servant had caught the note in his master's voice, and moved away through the open door without further words.

Wenis turned to his guest. "Sit opposite me here, if you please." The two took seats before the long table. "Now, you'll be wondering why I asked you here. I'll come right to the point."

"Yes, sir."

"Well, young man, I've heard of you for some time now. You have quite a name around the bazaars. And there's no bazaar west or south of Sile that does not have one or more stalls in it manned by a representative of the house of Wenis."

"I know, sir," the boy said respectfully.

"They've all spoken of you, of your marvelous—some say miraculous—prowess at the game, of your magnanimity in victory, of your equanimity in defeat—though, as I understand it, you are not defeated often. In any case, I had to see for myself, and I did today. The gods favor you, young man. My friends spoke truly. But it is also equally obvious that the favor is well deserved. I saw your gesture in calling for a feast at your expense. An act of nobility. I say this in all sincerity, knowing that acts of nobility are indeed rare in this benighted, barbaric age."

"You do me too great an honor, sir."

"Nonsense! The bazaars know how miserly I am with compliments. When I praise you, you've deserved it many times over. But—may I ask you, please, to tell me something of yourself? You're a foreigner, I take it?"

"Yes, sir. I—I've only been in Egypt two years. I . . . it's a long story, sir."

"I'm also little known for patience, my boy, but I am exercising it now. I am at your disposal."

"Yes, sir. Thank you, sir. I—I'm . . . well, I was born in Canaan. But my parents were from Padan-aram, and I've at least one Egyptian ancestor, my great-grandmother Shepset of Sile. M-my father died in the siege of Haran. My mother escaped to Canaan to enjoy the protection of a local king named Jacob, a close friend of my father's."

"Yes—Jacob; I think I've heard of him."

"Anyway, sir, I owe Jacob my life. And when his favorite son, Joseph, was kidnapped and brought to Egypt in a slave caravan by Ishmaelite traders, I went after him. I've not yet found him, nor any trace of him."

Reminded anew of his failure, Ben-Hadad lowered his head and gazed emptily at the floor. Wenis, after a long moment, coughed impatiently.

Ben-Hadad looked up in embarrassment, then hurried on with his tale. "For a time I found employment as a metalworker's helper, sir. I'd apprenticed to the trade in Canaan, thanks to Jacob's generosity. But then the lord Salitis decreed that foreigners could no longer work at the skilled trades without a permit—which his people were unwilling to give in my case—and I found myself at large in Sile, with no means of support."

"This was when you learned Egyptian games—learned of your aptitude for them?"

"Yes, sir. It was a miraculous discovery. Without it I'd have starved. I might even have done quite poorly regardless, if it hadn't been for my friend . . . my partner, Anab, who took me in hand and began managing my affairs."

"Ah, yes. I was going to get around to him. I take it he makes all the arrangements, books your matches, handles the proceeds?"

"Yes, sir. I've no mind for money matters myself. Without Anab I'd be—"

For the first time Wenis interrupted him. "Yes, yes. But—well, I'd like to talk to you about certain . . . well, certain arrangements I would like to propose to you. I think you're aiming too low just now. And I think there's a way I can help you to change directions. Tell me, is senet the only game you play?"

"No, sir. I started off in the game of the palm tree. But Anab switched me over to senet. He thinks there's more interest in the bazaars in—"

"Oh, there is. And not just in the bazaars. There is extraordinary interest in the Shepherd circles of money and power. Particularly now that Avedis—Salitis, that is, pardon me—has assumed the status of god-king and decided to establish a formal court here."

"Salitis, sir? You mean he intends to act as though he were the pharaoh Dedmose himself and this were Memphis?"

"He intends someday, my boy, to *reign* in Memphis. And as for Dedmose"—Wenis's scorn was evident—"*he* certainly won't be the one to stop him. In any case, while the war continues, Avaris will be the center of Shepherd affairs. And . . . well, I'm sure someone like yourself, new to the city, doesn't know just what extraordinary influence the fine art of gamesmanship has always had in the Egyptian court."

"No, sir."

"Then let me ask you before we go on. Have you ever tried your hand at the game of twenty squares?"

"Twenty? No, sir. Thirty, yes. Senet has thirty, but—"

"No relation, let me assure you. No relation at all. But it's no surprise that you've never heard of it. The people in the bazaars are still resentful of Salitis and his people, whom they see as barbarian invaders usurping the rightful power of the Egyptian kings. Fools! The wise man doesn't dispute power; he learns to use it to his own advantage. Well, now, where was I?"

"The game of twenty squares, sir."

"Oh, yes. It is the national game of Salitis's people. They brought it all the way from their ancestral homeland, up in the high mountains above Lake Van, far to the north of Assyria. If there's a single national passion—other than fighting, that is—among our friends the Shepherds, it's the game of twenty squares. This was true even when the Shepherd Kings were still nomadic, traveling with their herds across Mesopotamia. Like our own generals, they always found time, even in the middle of a campaign, for an evening round of the game. And now that their nomadic days seem to be over, they have become even more obsessed with the game."

"What is it like, sir?"

"Well, for one thing there's less luck involved than in senet. Oh, don't get me wrong, my young friend. I don't mean to downgrade in any way your remarkable skills at senet. But you yourself know, I think, that while an astute player creates much of his own luck, the rest is often in the lap of the gods."

"Well, yes, sir. For some reason I do seem to have their favor; however—"

"My point exactly," Wenis said, leaning forward enthusiastically. "In addition, of course, you have an extraordinarily quick mind, one capable of thinking out a problem on the board both from the tactical and the strategic points of view, and equally capable of switching from the one mode of thought to the other instantly, as the situation demands. I think you'd make a splendid player of the game of twenty squares."

"Perhaps, sir . . . but—"

"Please—hear me out. I was going to get around to why I called you here today. I think you have a future. And I think that, with a certain amount of guidance, you could have an even greater future than you can imagine. Ben-Hadad, I'll be frank with you. I have ambitions. Ambitions concerning the court here in Avaris—ambitions which involve, also, the new court that will follow this one, when Salitis's forces have successfully established themselves in Memphis at the head of a new Egyptian government."

"Then it's certain that the Shepherd Kings are going to win? That the Egyptians—?"

"Oh, I don't think there's any doubt. I think it's generally agreed that it's just a matter of time. After all, the Memphis nobles are cut off not only from all foreign trade by our—by the Shepherds' possession of the entire delta, the two mouths of the Nile, but from the agricultural riches of the area as well. They're asking the Fayum—no more than a glorified oasis, mind you, for all its productivity—to feed their entire people. They can't last forever at that rate."

"I see. I didn't know that. I thought there was still hope for—"

"Hope? Are you taking the losers' side of the argument? Well, that'll change. You're too smart not to know, sooner or later, which way the wind is blowing, and to modify your actions accordingly. But we're getting far afield. What I was going to say is this: Ben-Hadad, how would you like to come work with me? Here, at the villa? Learn the game of twenty squares, little by little, at my expense? I'd hire for your tutelage several of the former masters of the game. You'd be well compensated during your training, mind you—to the point of lavishness. You'd have your own apartments here at the villa, and separate accommodations in the best quarter of Avaris, plus servants to do your bidding and to take your mind off the more mundane aspects of life. And when you're ready to play at court, to play for me, representing my interests—well, then you'll be playing not as a salaried employee, but as a partner in a great enterprise. One to which, I can say in some confidence, there is literally no limit."

"Me, sir? But—"

"Now, don't be hasty. Think it over. Make your decision at your leisure. But remember—it's your future we're thinking about, as well as mine. As I rise, you'll rise with me. Your talents, I'm sure, will give me access to circles within Salitis's court that cannot otherwise be reached by anyone not of Shepherd blood. And where I go, you'll go."

"But, sir . . . I must tell you something else. My father was killed—murdered—by the Shepherd Kings. And though I may not be of noble blood, I do belong to a proud and ancient line—one that, because of the Shepherd Kings, has been made almost extinct. I can't practice the trade to which I was born, the trade that all my forefathers have followed for centuries. Sir, I'm not a senet player by profession. I'm an armorer—a Child of the Lion. Even if I haven't completely finished my apprenticeship, I—"

"Pardon me. Child of the what?"

"Child of the Lion. When I was playing you must have noticed a red birthmark I bear, on the lower back. It's shaped like the paw print of a lion. It's been a family trait for many centuries now. It breeds true in the male side of the family. Among my father's people there is an old story concerning the two sons of First Man. Cain, the elder, killed his brother Abel in rage, and was marked by the One God with the red mark. It was a blessing and a curse combined. We, his descendants, were gifted with a great talent for the working of metals to make weaponry. The mark identifies us and allows us to pass all borders to practice our trade with impunity; the curse is that the armorer is always on the move, with no permanent home of his own—a wanderer forever."

"But is that the life you desire?"

"It's not a matter of desire, sir. We are born to carry on the tradition; it is in our blood. I went for years not knowing who my father had been, sir, who my ancestors had been. My mother didn't want me to follow in their footsteps. But I found out that my father was a great man, a hero. He was small, crippled, yet he went alone into the camp of the Shepherd Kings in the hills above Padan-aram and, by his own cunning, saved his home city—and gave his life for it—and also saved his brother, Shobai. My grandfather, Kirta, their father, was the first man south of the Hittite kingdoms ever to work the black metal they call iron. The secret may have died with him. He was a great man, as great as my father was in his own way. And *his* father was Ahuni, the finest bronze worker of his age, a man who was once personal armorer to Sesostris of Egypt. And Ahuni's father was Belsunu of Babylon, the greatest artisan ever to work metal since the world began. This is why, for me, senet, or any other game, will never be more than just that, a game—at most a way to feed myself while circumstances keep me from finishing my apprenticeship and practicing my trade. You see, other than my blind uncle Shobai, I'm the only male Child of the Lion left."

His speech finished, the boy blushed, apologized for his long-windedness, then tried to smile reassuringly. Wenis watched him closely, silent for a moment, then he took a deep breath and spoke.

"Very well," he said. "But what if, in addition to the rest, I were, ah, subsequently to pay for the completion of your apprenticeship?"

The boy blinked. "But, sir—the license . . ."

"Leave that to me. I have friends in the court already, even if they're not as highly placed as the ones I expect to make with your help. But remember—I said that you shouldn't make up your mind too quickly. Sleep on it. And think of what it would be like, eventually finishing your apprenticeship under the tutelage of the best armorers Egypt's delta lands have to offer!"

"Yes, sir. I will. But you say 'eventually,' and I've—"

The boy stopped dead, looking past his host at something behind him. Wenis turned his head and saw the girl standing there. He looked at her, then looked back at the boy's expression of unabashed adoration. Then he smiled.

Well, heaven knows she is pretty enough, he thought. *It's cost me a small fortune to keep her looking like that.* His gaze returned to the girl, this time carefully appraising her. Her simple household gown, with the sunlight behind her, might as well have been totally transparent; it hid no detail of the finely tended young body inside it. Her eyes stared unblinking from below dark locks. She wore no jewelry at forehead or neck, but the gold in her wristlets and anklets gleamed in the sun, obscuring their lush insets of amethyst, turquoise, carnelian, and lapis lazuli.

Wenis spoke softly. "My daughter, Tamshas," he said simply. Then he raised his voice. "Come over here, my darling," he said. "I have someone I'd like you to meet."

V

"What do you mean you didn't return the money?" Tuya said incredulously, her eyes flashing fire. "You heard my warning to you, didn't you?"

Anab slouched over a bowl of wine in the tavern's back room. His face twisted terribly. "I—I tried to, Tuya. Believe me, I feel as badly about this as you do. It would be like selling a member of my family, if I had one. No, worse. Family doesn't mean any more to me than it does to you." He wrung his hands miserably; his narrow shoulders drooped with dejection. "It's as if—as if I'd betrayed the only friend I ever had. I can't remember anyone who's treated me as well as Ben-Hadad has."

Tuya's eyes searched the ruined face, trying to interpret the anguished grimace. "Then for the love of all that's sacred how could you? How could you sell him out to—?"

"I didn't! I just sold a portion of my own interest in his earnings. And I *did* try to buy it back! I did! But Renefres wouldn't take the money. 'A bargain's a bargain,' he said. 'Even if it hasn't been properly witnessed.' "

"That's a lie!"

"Y-yes. I know. B-but he set one of his friends on me—a big fellow, with arms like a bullock's thighs, with fists of solid rock. He—he picked me up and shook me, as if I were a kitten! He said he'd break my arms and legs one at a time, slowly, if I . . ."

Tuya swore softly; the gutter words rang oddly against her melodious voice. "I know that one, although I can't remember his name. And, yes, he'd kill you in a moment, if told to. Confound it, Anab! Why did you have to get yourself into this mess? Don't you see how vulnerable you've made Ben-Hadad to these people? He doesn't know what's happened at all—and as far as they're concerned, they own a quarter of his earnings, and have the right to tell him whom to play, and where, and for how much—"

"I know," Anab said miserably. He sank into the gathering darkness of the tavern's back room. "If I could only see a way out."

The innkeeper approached their table, his long horse-face impassive, his hands busy drying a drinking bowl. "Anab," he said, "I don't ordinarily butt in where I'm not asked, but . . . Ben-Hadad did me a big favor today with that impromptu feast of his. And I suppose I owe you something too, by extension, for all that it was his idea. After all, you scheduled the match in my patio and not somebody else's place, and—"

"What is it?" Tuya said. "If you've bad news for us, get it out!"

The innkeeper scowled at her. "I don't know what your interest is in all this," he said. "I was speaking to Anab." He addressed Anab: "I couldn't help overhearing a conversation a little while back. I went up on the roof to lay out some tablecloths to dry in the sun, just after the senet match. And—does either of you know a merchant named Wenis?"

"Wenis . . . of the house of Wenis? Gods!" Anab said. "Yes, of course. What about him?"

"He was up there watching the match with his servant. 'Amazing.' says he. 'Look here, my man, why don't you go speak to this Ben-Hadad fellow for me and tell him I'd like to have a little conversation with him, just him and me, and what the fellow with the face doesn't know won't hurt him.' " He looked at Anab apologetically. "Don't take offense, now. I was just quoting what this Wenis fellow said to his servant."

" 'Conversation'?" Anab said, leaning forward, a note of tension in his voice. "What kind of conversation?"

"Well, I couldn't hear all of what they were saying," the innkeeper said. "But I'd be willing to wager they were talking about Wenis's wanting to take over the boy's contract. You know, to manage his affairs, that sort of thing."

"Manage his—?" Anab said, horrified. He and Tuya exchanged anxious glances. "B-but . . ."

Tuya shook her head. "This doesn't sound good, Anab."

"No," he said miserably. "Wenis is big enough to have me squashed like a beetle underfoot if I'm in his way. Even if I do nothing, there's the matter of the quarter interest I've already sold and can't get back. If Wenis takes over and freezes Renefres out, Renefres will sic that big ox on me. Either way I'm doomed."

"Unless Ben-Hadad says no," Tuya said. "That's your only chance. If he says no to Wenis you're halfway off the hook. And there are ways around Renefres. I'm not without friends in the bazaars of the Thieves Quarter, and some of them are twice the size of that ape Renefres carries around with him. And some of them owe me favors. But . . ." The resolve, the determination went out of her for a moment. "But if Ben-Hadad lets Wenis talk him into some kind of a partnership . . . well, Wenis is too big to cross. He draws a lot of water around here. He's even thick with the Shepherds."

Anab scowled. "I know—the treasonous, two-faced—"

"There, there. Not that I don't agree with you, but this isn't the time for calling people names. It's time for some fast figuring." She bit her lower lip. "Confound it! If only I knew how Ben-Hadad had decided. . . ." Suddenly she pounded her little fist on the table. "Anab, you stay here. I'm going out to look for Ben-Hadad. I'll be right back."

"You'd better take care," the innkeeper said. "It's almost dark. A girl like you isn't safe on the streets after dark by herself—"

"Don't worry about me," Tuya said confidently. "I'm so small people usually don't even notice me. And"—she patted the dirk under her garment, its hilt jutting out conspicuously—"I've got something that usually persuades men to leave me alone." Her smile was a glimmer of white teeth in the dim light, and then, in one blink of an eye, she was gone.

Anab, squirming miserably in his seat, looked up at the innkeeper. "I—I can't stay here," he said. He reached

for the long dowel with its garland of copper and gold
rings. "I've got to get this to safety. I've got to think—"

"But the girl told you to stay put," the innkeeper
said. "She said she'd be right back. If you go off now—"

"I—I don't care." Anab stood up, tucking the dowel
into his loincloth under his short robe. "I can't just sit
here. I'd go mad. Gods! Why can't I lead an ordinary life,
like other people?" He shook his head, shot one tormented glance at the innkeeper, and went out into the
night, his movements as jerky, as angular, as Tuya's had
been fluid and graceful.

For a moment the innkeeper stared after him. "Poor
ugly little gnome," he said, half aloud. But that was life,
wasn't it? Life wasn't fair. One man was born to wealth
and ease, the next to unhappiness, poverty, and loneliness.
And what had either done, in the egg, to deserve it? One
man's touch turned everything to gold, while the other's
touch turned everything to so much dross. All too obviously the hand of some demon was on this boy, denying
him happiness, spoiling his life. . . .

The innkeeper shuddered and made the sign against
evil. Better to keep away from anyone as ill-starred as this.
Who knew if ill fortune wasn't catching, like the croup or
the pox?

Anab's hands shook as he hurried down the darkening
alleyway to his wretched hovel of a home. His eyes darted
right and left, seeing robbers and murderers in every dark
close, behind every stunted tree. He should have gone
home earlier. Now he'd have to use a tallow candle to find
the little hiding place where he kept his money. And
whose eyes might see that candle's flame? What hostile
person might be watching as he unloaded the dowel and
carefully effaced all trace of the hidden hole in the wall
where he kept everything he owned in the world?

He shuddered and hurried forward, keeping against
the wall, away from the long shadows. The moon had
already risen, and the sun was down now. Only a narrow
strip of light gleamed in the western sky. Soon, very soon,
it would be pitch dark. In this section of town the lamp-
lighter was likely to be drunk in a corner somewhere,

waiting for someone to rouse him and send him on his way through the treacherous night streets. There'd be no counting on him, no counting on a light to guide his, Anab's, footsteps through the dark alleyways, the rabbit-warren complexities of the nocturnal streets of the city. He shivered with fear at the thought. Even one of Renefres's bravos, tall, well built, and physically confident, would scarcely be safe by himself after night fell in this quarter. And a small fish like himself? Particularly one bearing half a year's wages under his garment, and in negotiable coin?

He froze, suddenly hearing voices up ahead. He flattened himself against the wall and listened, immobile, his heart pounding furiously. What were they saying?

". . . cut the guts right out of him! Left him there in his own blood, as bold as you please!"

". . . even had the nerve to identify himself to the whores who were standing there watching the whole time! 'The Phoenix did it,' he says, brazen as they come. 'Tell them the Phoenix did it!' "

Anab held his breath in the darkness. The voices were speaking the Shepherd tongue. Yes! He could see two men now, in the shadows, where the alley met the main street. Off-duty Shepherd soldiers, and apparently they'd already had a few drinks. . . .

"Phoenix? Who the devil is the Phoenix? I never heard of—"

". . . rebellion of some sort. Said they were holdouts, probably runaways from that army we smashed up over in the West Delta. Damned fools think they're going to drive us out of the . . ."

Anab, cowering against the wall, was so intent upon listening to the interrupted scraps of conversation ahead that he failed to notice a third Shepherd soldier coming up the narrow alley behind him. Suddenly a heavy hand fell on his shoulder. A loud voice spoke, close to him, close enough that he could smell the sour palm wine on the man's foul breath. "Here! Who's this?" the voice said in the Shepherd tongue.

Anab struggled—and the hand clamped down on his collarbone. "Stop!" he said. "Please! You're hurting me!"

The faces down the alley turned his way. "Who's

that? Garabed, is that you?" Feet pounded in the alley. In a moment they had dragged Anab into the street, where the light of the pale moon could shine down on his frightened face. "You!" one of the voices said roughly. "Who are you? What are you doing skulking around here like a rat? Speak up!"

"I—I was lost," Anab said weakly. "I was trying to f-find my—"

It was as if he hadn't spoken at all. "Huh! Ugly piece of work, isn't he?" Hard hands took his shoulders, shook him, shook him. . . .

. . . and as ill fortune would have it, the damnable dowel full of rings started to jangle. And ring and jingle, like the bells on an Egyptian chariot of state.

"Eh? What's this? He makes a lot of music for an ill-fed little river rat, doesn't he? Let's have a look there!"

"N-no, please," Anab said, trying to cringe back, his hands protecting his middle. They were roughly snatched away, and heavy Shepherd hands probed his clothing. Probed—and found the precious dowel, with its irreplaceable burden! "No! Please! Don't—"

"Well, look *here*," the first soldier said. "Look at what I've found, will you? Money!" He held up the dowel. The pale rays of the moon shone first on the dull copper—then on the gleaming gold. "What's this? Gold? *Gold?*"

"Please . . . it's not mine . . . I was carrying it for . . . uh . . . for the noble Wenis, a merchant. He's a friend of the commander of your garrison, an important man. . . ."

But the improvisation, inspired or not, did not carry the ring of authenticity. The Shepherd soldier laughed harshly. "Wenis? A likely story. What would someone like that want with a dirty, ugly little guttersnipe like you? Do you think I'm some kind of drunken fool?" He laughed again. "Well, perhaps I am a drunken fool, at that. But I'm not so drunk that I can't tell gold when I see it. And I'm not so much of a fool that I can't recognize a stinking little sneak thief when I catch one. Well, little man, we'll just relieve you of this, and you run along and steal some more."

"No! Please!"

The soldier took hold of Anab's garment and ripped it across, leaving him shivering in his loincloth and cheap papyrus sandals. "Get out of my sight, you ugly little bastard."

Now one of the other soldiers stepped forward and, backhanded, swung his heavy arm. The blow smashed into Anab's face, driving him to his knees. "Did you hear the man?" the soldier said. "Get away! Don't make us dirty our hands on a toad like you!" With a curse, he kicked Anab sprawling. Anab's head hit the side of a building and he fell dazed on his face. As consciousness ebbed, and waned for a sick moment or two, he could hear the soldiers chortling drunkenly as they swaggered down the darkened street, his lost coins—and his only chance of buying back Renefres's purchase—jingling merrily in their larcenous hands.

He got to his knees—and his already weakened stomach gave way. He vomited again, bent double by the pain in his gut. He'd lost! He'd lost again! It didn't matter what little security he tried to store away against the days of famine and want—they always managed to take it from him in the end! *They!* The ubiquitous, malevolent they! What was the use of trying? What was the use of struggling against fate? He'd always lose.

Tuya met Ben-Hadad at the city gate. She'd been waiting there for some time, and now her heart leaped up at the first sight of his round, handsome young face . . . and seemed to stop beating altogether as he recognized her immediately and smiled broadly.

"Tuya!" he said. "What are you doing out at night like this? Here, let me take you home. You've no idea what kind of ill can befall a girl alone out in the streets after dark!"

He took her arm—as if she were a great lady!—and guided her steps forward into the night streets of the city. She was beside herself with delight. . . .

"Oh, Tuya!" he said. "You've no idea where I've been! It was the most marvelous place you've ever seen! A great villa, with a beautiful garden outside and more rooms than I've ever seen in one dwelling in all my life! And I may be going to live there soon, if everything works out. There's this rich man, you see, and he has plans for my future. He wants me to come stay at his house. I'm to study with the master gamesmen of the world and learn the game of twenty squares. But that's not all. . . ."

Her heart turned icy at the core. *Oh, please,* she implored every god in the Egyptian pantheon, *please don't let him say what I think he's going to say. . . .*

"I—Tuya, I met this girl. She's more beautiful than the sun and moon and all the stars, and—and I think she likes me. At least, that's what her father said, after he introduced us. . . ."

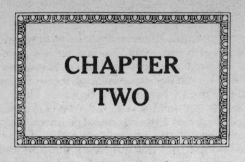

CHAPTER TWO

MEMPHIS

I

For all the imposing height and immense size of the spacious palace of the great king, the Lord of Two Lands, and the equally grandiose ostentation of the various temples that the legendary kings of the past had reared to various gods, the first impression one received of Memphis, the oldest and largest city in the known world, was of the number, size, and whiteness of its walls, walls hedged in the homes of the gods; they separated from the rest of the city the quarter containing the gracious houses and gardens of the wealthy and powerful; they kept apart from the common mass the towering palace in which the great king lived and in which his court transacted all business.

Guards, heavily armed, stood at the gates to each of the walls that partitioned quarter from quarter, admitting to the various sanctums of the elite only those who could show valid evidence of reason to pass. Yet, somehow, rumor and gossip flew over each wall as easily and freely as did the thousands of birds the great city harbored. For Memphis was a city of intrigue, and had been such since its founding, in the bygone days of the great Menes. It was Menes who had raised the first dike to protect his infant settlement from the seasonal floodings of the Nile, so that his son Athothis could complete the laying out of the first city proper.

Now, as the war between entrenched Egypt, driven back into the Red Lands, and the hated Shepherd invaders, who had taken over the fertile Black Lands, stretched into yet another year, the rumors flew with unusual agility, spreading from the closely guarded confines of the royal palace into the other quarters. Dedmose, the great king himself, was said to be little more than a puppet of Madir, his all-powerful vizier. The levels below Madir were said to be fragmented, splintered, a nest of intrigue as various factions schemed to displace one another and insinuate their way into Madir's favor.

Worse—some of the schemers were said to be ruthless and conscienceless. Some of the schemed-against were said to be no more than a matter of days away from violent death. Several aborted assassination plots had been broken up in the past months, and the failed assassins were languishing in Madir's dungeons, awaiting trial at the convenience of Uni, chief of the royal prison and perhaps the most feared man in all Memphis. The friends and family of the prisoners had doubtless given them up for dead, so widespread was Uni's reputation for pitilessness and craftiness. By the time Uni was done, the culprits would beg for the quick death that lay at the end of the headsman's ax. The alternative was impalement.

Nor would a suspect's proven innocence spare him from grief. He might in fact go free, but even the ghost of a suspicion, once lodged against a man's name, marked him for life. This was the way of things in Memphis. It tended to make the average citizen shy away from affairs involving the higher castes, the circles of power. It tended to reduce the number of petitioners who came to the palace on the days when Madir, in his capacity as chief magistrate, held divan, adjudicated disputes, rewarded merit, and punished error.

Thus, on the day of Madir's divan, the guards at the south gate of the palace compound registered surprise when a woman presented herself, asking for admission. The more so as she looked calmly up to meet their stern gaze, and revealed beneath her head-covering a face of uncommon beauty and almost regal bearing. "Yes, ma'am?" the guard in charge said. "What can we do for you?" His tone carried a note of deference, and his stance was cautious. She looked important, after all—yet she wasn't a familiar face to either of them.

"I am Mereet, wife to the arms maker Shobai," she said simply and with dignity. "Daughter to Indi, former magistrate of the Fifth Nome of Lower Egypt. Later adopted daughter to Shashank of Sile."

The guards stiffened noticeably. These were mighty names, or had been once. Indi had been adviser to three of the kings who had reigned briefly in the interregnum between the accession of Sebeknefrure, the queen who had married a commoner and thrown the Egyptian succession into chaos, and the arrival of the Shepherd Kings. Shashank's name had been known at court as well, and Shobai, the blind armorer, was well known throughout the city. There was new respect in the guardsman's tone when he spoke again. "And your business, ma'am?"

"I must speak with Madir. I'm told that my request to give my husband a week's holiday in the Fayum requires his seal."

She looked again from one man to the other and smiled. "My husband hasn't had a day off in a year," she said. "In that time he's armed the whole city, and most of the army. Why, your own weapons bear his mark, I'll wager." Their eyes remained fixed on her, and she spoke again. "See? The mark on the hilt—that's one of his. And yours has it, too. I'm sure you both know of my husband. He isn't the sort to admit to himself when he's tired, overworked. The only way I can get him to take time off is to get an order for him to do so—but it requires Madir's permission and his seal. Probably I won't even have to see Madir himself to get it; it can be handled by one of his retainers. I won't take up much of anyone's time."

The guard in charge glanced at his companion. "Well . . . you ought to have permission to get in, ma'am. But seeing you're who you are, I suppose I can waive the permission. Pass."

His companion started to speak, but was silenced with a nudge. They watched the young woman walk away, dignified, hips swaying. "Imagine that!" the second guard said in a low half-whisper. "And wasted on a blind man."

"Oh, shut up!" the first guard said. "Can't you tell a lady when you see one?"

Coming through the marketplace, Shobai raised his head high above the unseen faces around him, his nostrils flaring to savor the many exotic and familiar smells of the little square: the sharp, briny smell of the fishmonger's stall, the pungency of the freshly cut onions in the greengrocer's booth, the rich, smoky aroma of lamb roasting on a spit over hot coals. Around him the busy traffic of the city square swirled; voices called out to the buyer, the passerby.

"Fans! Fans and bellows for cookery!"

"Sandals! Finest sandals of the softest leather!"

"Perfumes! Exotic perfumes from the four corners of the world! Ointments for the softest skin! Come sample my wares. . . ."

Something stayed Shobai's steps. His hand, which had rested lightly on Hori's forearm all the way through the square, pressed more heavily now. Hori's steps faltered. "Yes, Shobai?" the young subaltern said, turning to look up at the face of the blind man towering a full head above his own. "Do you want to stop?"

The blind man nodded. "Yes," he said. "I'm curious. The perfume merchant—could you lead me back to his stall, please?" And, looking like nothing so much as a tame bear and his trainer, the blind man and his companion wound their way through the crowd to the proper stall.

The merchant wasted an unseen obeisance on the blind man. "Shobai!" he said. "My pleasure, sir, my very distinct pleasure. How may I serve you today? Unguents from faraway Crete, perhaps, for your charming wife?"

The blind man smiled, skeptically but with a certain indulgence. "From Crete, you say, honest Ibu? From Crete, when you and I both know that the last time a boat

from Crete sailed this far upriver was more than two years
ago, before the Shepherds took the delta?" But there was
no more than gentle raillery in his tone as he spoke, and
the merchant did not take umbrage.

"Ah, Shobai," Ibu said in admonition. "In the best of
all possible circumstances, my friend, there would be as
much truth as poetry in the spoken effusions of a poor
merchant trying to lure the tightfisted customer to his
stall. But these are difficult days, as indeed you well
know." He lowered his voice conspiratorially. "If you must
know," he said softly, "the stuff's from Dilmun, and the
Assyrian perfumes are from Punt instead, brought across
the desert from the sea by my caravans. But the formulas
have been copied exactly by my suppliers, and only the
pedigrees of the substances leave anything to be desired. I
assure you that whatever you purchase at my stall for
your gracious lady's beautification and enjoyment will please
her quite as well as anything that had come directly from—"

"Enough, enough," Shobai said, laughing quietly. "I'm
quite aware of the quality of your goods, my friend. But I
confess myself unable to resist teasing you a little, if only
to provoke your well-known eloquence in defense of your
product." The merchant began to protest, but Shobai waved
his words away. "Two jars of the 'Cretan' unguent, please
. . . and if I might sniff the perfume from Punt—I mean
from Assyria . . ."

The merchant sighed and, a wry smile on his face as
he exchanged glances with the subaltern Hori, held the
little vial to Shobai's nose and, for no more than the blink
of a sighted man's eyes, uncorked it. "There," he said.
"Did you smell it? Isn't it just what I said it was? Delicate,
yet pungent as—"

"All right," Shobai said. Reaching inside his garment,
he handed Hori his purse. "My friend? If you'd be so kind
as to count out the proper amount for me. . . ."

The voices of merchant and subaltern blended into
the rich background noises of the bazaar as Shobai, his
scarred eyelids closed over empty sockets, let his great,
leonine head turn away, savoring the sounds and smells of
the bazaar. His face relaxed in a satisfied smile as he

wandered a few paces from the stall, the better to enjoy the delightful smells of the little marketplace. . . .

Suddenly an alien hand touched his arm and held it. He stiffened, drawing away. "Who's there?" he said, pulling his arm free.

"Shobai?" a cautious voice said at his side. "Shobai of Haran?"

"Yes," the blind man said. "But who—?"

There was no answer. Instead Shobai could feel someone press something into his open hand and close his fingers around it. "What—?" Shobai began. But no sooner had he begun the word than he could feel—palpably *feel*—that his visitor was gone. He cut the question short and said nothing more.

Instead he fingered the object in his hand, turned it over in his palm, and touched it with the other hand. A baked clay tablet . . . and, from the feel of it, with writing on it. His fingers traced the regular indentations. Cuneiform writing? The writing of his home country, far to the north?

"What's the matter, Shobai?" Hori said at his side, holding the depleted purse. "I have your purchases here; I'll carry them for you, if you like. But—you look as though something were troubling you."

Shobai's hand closed tightly around the tablet, and he abandoned, for no reason he could easily have explained, all thought of sharing his experience with the young soldier beside him. "It's nothing," he said reassuringly. "Let's go home now, please. I'd like to surprise my wife."

Hori left him at the door, his words of parting respectful and deferential. As his footfalls echoed away down the narrow street, Shobai turned, his hand on the door handle, and started to go in. Then he paused as, inside his garment, his fingers once again closed softly around the little tablet. He bit his lip, wondering.

Heket, Mereet's maidservant, met him at the door. "Welcome home, sir," she said. "Madam's out now. She was supposed to be back more than an hour ago, but . . ."

"Perhaps she had some shopping to do. Are the children up?"

"No, sir. They're napping in their room. Could I fix you a cup of—?"

"No, thank you," the blind man said, his hands finding his favorite low, backless chair at his feet. He sank gratefully onto the cloth-covered seat. "Heket?"

"Yes, sir?"

"It seems to me I remember a scribe in the Bazaar of the Dry Well who knew the languages of the North. If he's still there, could you be so kind as to bring him here? Offer him whatever the going rate is. Plus . . . oh, say an outnou of copper for his trouble. Could you do that for me, please?"

"Oh, yes, sir. As soon as I take your supper off the fire." She turned and padded away.

He sat lost in thought for a moment, until the high-pitched voices in the next room reached his ears. He smiled and, standing, walked to the door. "Children?" he said. "Are you awake?"

His answer was two shrieks of delighted laughter. "Father!" the two-year-old twins said, and ran to embrace his knees. Beaming, the blind man picked them up as if they weighed no more than rag dolls, holding them to his bosom and kissing their foreheads.

"Teti! Ketan!" he said, calling their names one by one, the girl's first. "How good to be back with you! Are you glad to see me?"

Their answers, a high-pitched babble, canceled each other out. He hugged both of them happily once more, and sat back down in his favorite chair, a child on each knee. "Now, tell me—what have the two of you been up to today?"

"They have been *arguing* all day," Heket said, pausing on her way out the door, speaking before the children could answer.

"Arguing? About what?"

Again she spoke first, silencing the children with a stern glance. "Their birthmarks, of all things! Teti says hers means one thing, while Ketan insists that his means something else. I told them to wait until you got home, sir, and you'd explain, but little good it did. The cat pays more attention to me than they do!" With that she turned and, sighing loudly, left on her errand, a look of exaggerated exasperation on her face.

Shobai kissed each of the twins again, meaning to scold them for their disobedience, but before he could say anything, Teti interrupted him by shouting that her mark meant she would one day be the bride of a lion. Ketan started giggling furiously, saying that he had never heard such a silly idea. Their father hastily broke in before the good-natured teasing turned nasty.

"Now, you two, listen carefully," he said. "I'm going to tell you, just once more, exactly what my father told me and my brother, Hadad, a long time ago. This time I want you to remember—do you understand?"

"Yes, Father," they both said, and waited with intense seriousness for the familiar story.

"There is an old legend in our family, a legend having to do with the ancient and venerated parents of us all—the parents of all the people on earth. Now, the First Man and First Woman, as they were called, had two sons, the elder of whom was a farmer, who, for fun, liked to work with metal. The younger son was a herdsman. . . ."

The children snuggled closer to their father's massive chest, listening intently as he spoke.

"The older boy, whose name was Cain, was very jealous of his younger brother, Abel, because he felt that Abel had been favored by their God. One day Cain, while in a fit of rage, struck and killed his brother! It was a terrible thing to do, and, as punishment, their God said that Cain would forever after have to wander among the tribes of the earth as an armorer, making weapons for killing. His descendants, as well, would be armorers of great skill, and they would be instantly recognized by all men of the earth by the mark of Cain on their backs—a birthmark in the shape of a lion's paw. . . ."

Shobai suddenly realized that the twins were extremely quiet. He gently stroked their nodding heads, their breathing coming in a steady rising and falling.

"Would they always know such peace," he said with a sigh.

*   *   *

The sleeping children were still on his lap when, a long while later, a knock on the door broke his reverie. He heard it open, and Heket's voice announced her errand: "Shobai? The scribe Sahu's here, as you requested."

Shobai sent Heket off to the children's room with the twins. Then he turned to the unseen scribe and said, "I've been told you know the written tongues of the North. Can you read this?" He held out the little tablet.

The scribe took the tablet and was silent for a moment. Then he spoke, in a voice at once puzzled and curious. "Well, yes, sir. Of course I can read it. But . . . it hardly makes any sense."

"Never mind the sense—just give me the words. The language—it's that of Padan-aram, isn't it?"

"Yes, sir . . . but not written by a native. Someone's taken the trouble of learning to write this way to get his message across. But he's got a terrible hand. I gather you know the language, sir. See if you can make head or tail of this." He read the syllables from the cuneiform marks. "There, sir. Do you see what I—"

But the scribe stopped speaking when he saw the expression on the blind man's face. "Sir?" he said. "Is something wrong?"

Shobai mastered himself. "No—not at all. You've done well. Ask my maidservant for your fee. Tell her I said you've earned the bonus I promised for good work."

"But—"

"You may go now. Thank you." Shobai sat, the little disk back in his hand again, his face impassive.

The message had been simple but enigmatic: "The foolish coney slept in the absent leopard's lair. The returned leopard dined on coney meat."

Shobai's hand shook, opened. The little disk rolled on the floor by his feet.

"Then it's true," he said in a hoarse whisper. "He's alive. Baka's alive." Getting to his knees, he scrambled on the floor with both nervous hands, his movements jerky, ungraceful. When he found the tablet he hugged it to his chest, his hands still trembling.

And somehow he knew, knew in his heart, that the scribe hadn't misread the message. Rumors had circulated

as early as two years ago that Baka, the famous Egyptian
commander, had not died in the Shepherd prison after his
capture, that he was alive and well somewhere. But the
general Unas, Baka's former colleague and now Shobai's
good friend, had dismissed them as just that—wartime
rumors. Baka, Unas had insisted, was too feared an opponent for the Shepherds to spare—and the Shepherd commander who had captured Baka was not the type to take
prisoners.

Shobai nervously turned the tablet over in his hands.
If he himself had not been convinced that Baka was dead,
he would never have taken Baka's widow as his wife, no
matter how deeply he loved her. He had never met Baka,
but had heard so much about him from Mereet and Unas
that he felt he knew him. And one thing he was sure of, as
sure as he was of his own heart: Baka had loved Mereet
fiercely.

And if it were true? If he were still alive?

Shobai's big right hand clutched the message tightly.

It was a death sentence. It served notice that death
would strike, could strike at any time, out of the universal
darkness that surrounded him. He, Shobai, was marked to
die at Baka's hand.

II

The guards stood to the right and left of the young
man, each with a hand on one of his arms. Their manner
showed their impatience. Yet Potiphar, chief cook to the
inner court of Dedmose, the Lord of Two Lands, held
them for a moment more, unwilling to let them take the
young man away. Hot tears flooded his eyes, as they had
done several times that day, even before the guards had
come. His voice broke as he spoke. "Is—is that all, then?"
he said. "You're not sorry for what you've done to me?
You've no penitence for abusing my trust, my confidence
in you?"

The young man's face remained serious and, somehow,

strangely serene as he spoke. There were in his eyes great hurt and much affection for his master. "Sir, I've done nothing. I've abused nothing. Someday you'll come to realize this. I've served you as faithfully as I could, with love and respect—"

"Faithfully?" Potiphar said. "Is it faithful to try to seduce my wife, whom I've left alone with you? To force your lustful attentions on her while I—"

"I repeat, sir," the servant said, "my noble lady has her own reasons for making these accusations. I don't presume to examine them. I wish her nothing but good. But I say what I have said and will continue to say: I have never approached her in the way she says. My respect for her, as well as my respect and love for you, sir, would never allow me to—"

"My wife says you did!" the chief cook interrupted, his voice tight with anger and confusion. "And my wife doesn't lie!" But there was doubt in his eyes.

"Your honorable wife, sir, is distraught of late. It is not for a servant to say why. When the mind is laden with deep thoughts or fears, the imagination often plays tricks, sir. I'm sure she thinks everything she said was true. I'm only sorry to have been the object of her thoughts when they ran in this direction, sir. I attach no blame to her for—"

"Blame?" the cook said, livid. "You stand there and talk to me of blame? You who—confound you, you've betrayed my good faith! I'll never trust anyone again!"

The young man bowed his head deferentially. "One is either the kind who trusts people or one is not, sir," he said. "Your heart is a good one, generous and wise and open. If I have let you down in any way, I apologize. But I stand firm in my denial of wrongdoing." His Canaanite accent was very slight by now; the honeyed words came out with a courtier's fluency. Somehow the fact only irritated Potiphar all the more.

"Enough!" he said, his voice breaking again. "T-take him away!"

But when the guards had led the young man away, Potiphar stood staring after them for many minutes, wringing his plump hands, one thought running over and over through his mind: *What if she'd lied? What if he'd been telling the truth all the while?*

"Oh, Joseph, Joseph," he cried, half aloud.

The trouble was, he'd never had a better servant, not in a pampered lifetime spent first in a house full of obedient slaves, then at court, where servants outnumbered their masters twenty to one. The boy, landing in Egypt as a slave purchased from Ishmaelite traders, had picked up the language with admirable speed and skill. And he'd had the knack of anticipating almost every command, even every desire, stated or unstated, of his masters. The other servants actually believed he had the diviner's gift. Whatever the reason, he'd become Potiphar's right arm, indispensable and utterly reliable. But . . .

But the trouble, Potiphar thought now, *is that he's so damnably handsome. And my wife* . . .

There was no doubt about it. She was growing older. She could very well be at that time of life when women began to doubt their charms, to look for wrinkles in the mirror, to spend a small fortune on unguents and creams for their aging skin. It was the time when they began to test their attractiveness, to flirt, however insincerely, with every handsome man who came their way.

He shook his head angrily. Something in his heart did not want to believe it. Something made him want to trust the lad when he said that he was innocent and that his mistress's accusations were the result of her own imaginings.

He mastered himself, and slipping his feet into the expensive leather sandals he customarily wore at court, he hurried down the corridor from his apartments toward the great room where Madir, vizier to the Lord of Two Lands, held council these mornings. But purposeful and businesslike though his gait appeared, inside his mind and heart were the same conflicting thoughts and emotions that had tormented him for the last hour.

In the great anteroom, an open, atriumlike hall flanked on both sides by dwarf palms, he ran into Eben, a courtier in exile from the Shepherd-held delta, and the priest Hapu. "Greetings," he said, his tone polite but distracted. "Madir is in, I hope?"

"Yes," Eben said. "He's dealing with civil matters

only today. He should be done with the present litigants by the time the sun reaches . . . oh, about there." His sandaled foot marked a spot on the tiles that was now in deep shade. "What draws the noble Potiphar here today?" Eben shot an unintelligible glance at the priest, then smiled at the chief cook. "Perhaps there's something we could do for you, while you're waiting to see the esteemed Madir?"

"Well, no, thank you. It's just routine business—another spoiled shipment of olives from the Fayum. But—"

Eben, a little more forward now, took his arm, steering him to a corner of the great room, near the dwarf palms. "I'd been meaning to talk to you for some time now, my friend. Our common acquaintance, the distinguished general Harmin, speaks well of you as a man of substance, of intelligence, someone who can be trusted, in whom a person might repose some confidence. . . ."

From the middle of the room the priest Hapu watched them, an enigmatic smile on his face. Potiphar glanced at him once, then held up one cautionary hand. "I . . . I'm afraid I've rather weighty things on my mind today, Eben," he said. "I'd be no good to you just now. I'm trying to deal with some . . . some distracting problems that have come up, which I won't bore you by talking about." He shook his head, waving away whatever it was Eben wanted to talk over with him. "Later, perhaps. When I've a clear mind."

"Certainly, my friend. I'll just—"

"No, please. Don't be offended. It's only that . . . well, if what you want to talk about is of real importance, perhaps you could come to dinner next week and talk it over."

"You're too generous with your time. Could we say rather . . . a private meeting, at my own apartments? Sometime when you're not busy?"

"Yes, fine. Now—if you'd please excuse me. I'll come back tomorrow. You said Madir was hearing only civil matters today. By your leave, my friend, noble Hapu . . ." He bowed slightly and left, the worry still showing on his face.

Hapu approached, the sun gleaming on his shaven pate. "A slender reed," he said. "I wouldn't bother."

"Don't be so hasty," Eben said. "A chief cook—one we can trust—could become a valuable source of information. People tend to forget the cook is there, you know, and they say the most amazing things in front of him. No, he could be very useful. One wouldn't want to tell him too much about what's going on, of course."

"Well, perhaps you're right," the priest said. He looked around, making sure no one was nearby. "What happened at the meeting last night?"

Eben broke into a conspirator's smile. "We decided what to do with Unas." He made a cutting motion across his throat with his hand.

"You don't mean it!" the priest said. "And Harmin was there, his own general?"

"Harmin was the one who suggested it. With Unas gone there'll be virtually no one left in the upper levels of Harmin's command who opposes our withdrawal to Thebes, to more easily defensible ground. Ah—now you see why I'm smiling so broadly."

"As well you might. You own—you and Harmin—much of the real property in Thebes. If we relocate there, half the people in Upper Egypt will be your tenants. And if anyone manages to leave Memphis or the Fayum with enough money or negotiable property to want to buy a place of his own—"

"—he'll have to pay our price. But don't you worry. As a holy man, a priest of—"

"I understand." The priest's thin-lipped smile was as cold as the Nile after the winter thaw. "How did Harmin propose we do away with Unas? You remember, this is the hero of the battle of Saïs we're talking about. He's popular not only in the court, but in the streets as well, among the common herd. Having him openly killed would—"

"Don't worry. There are always ways. He could wind up getting killed in battle by a stray arrow from one of his own men. Or he could get his brains knocked out and be left behind in a retreat, for the Shepherds to find. Imagine what they'd do to Unas, after the humiliation they underwent at his hands at Saïs."

The priest smiled again. "I'm sure the matter's in good hands. And what did the Council decide to do about the big black? What's his name, now? The one who's leading the expedition upriver to enlist mercenaries for our fight against the invaders?"

"Akhilleus. He'll be taken care of. But *after* he's managed to do us some good, not before. He'll be allowed to make deals for ore first, in Nubia—deals a man of lighter coloring might not be able to make, mind you. The Nubians remember the warlike Sesostris and the string of forts he built along the Nile to keep blacks out of his territories. This Akhilleus, or whatever his real name is—"

"It sounds Greek."

"The islanders gave it to him when he was a slave, I heard. But he's Nubian born, or perhaps from a place above even Nubia—no one seems to know for sure; he was taken away by the slave traders when he was a child. But he's obviously black enough to satisfy the Nubians' distrustful hearts, and so is his wife. She *is* Nubian, born and bred, and speaks the languages of the desert lands above the fourth cataract. It'll likely be she who negotiates the treaties. She was the widow of one of the Nubian captains at Sile and knows the language of treaty terms and negotiations."

"So they'll be allowed to go southward and hire troops?"

"Yes, but don't worry—he'll be taken care of after all the deals have been struck, after we've wrung whatever advantage we can out of his mission."

"An assassin?" the priest said, his tone matter-of-fact.

"The best," Eben said with satisfaction. "Quiet, efficient, reliable. And virtually undetectable. He signed on with the expedition as an interpreter. None of them has any idea who he is. By the time the worthy Akhilleus is ready to return at the head of this mercenary army of his, our man will have neatly wormed his way into his confidence. Then, when no one suspects—*kkkkkk!*" He made the slicing sound through his teeth as once again he made the throat-cutting sign with his hand. "And *he* comes home at the head of the mercenaries, instead of Akhilleus. He's to dispatch the woman, too, and anyone else in the original party he thinks is in any way unreliable."

"Splendid. I gather this whole plan was your doing?"

"I'm flattered and reassured that you can recognize my hand in the matter. But don't worry—your own interests are being looked after most carefully."

The priest gave him a flinty look, and the ghost of a smile on his thin lips never reached his eyes at all. "As well they should," he said. "We're all in this together, you'll remember. And each of us knows enough about the others to lead to a virtual bloodbath at the hands of Madir and the Lord of Two Lands, if any of us were to speak out of turn."

"I see we understand each other," Eben said with an acknowledging nod. He moved closer to Hapu and lowered his voice to an almost inaudible whisper. "Let's hope, however, that our friend Yusni soon gets a chance to bake up his special treat for Madir, as he's promised. Something that won't sit too well on the vizier's delicate stomach. Then *all* our worries will be over." He clapped his friend on the shoulder. "Come, let's drink to our success—and to Madir's demise—with a beaker of palm wine. I'll buy." And, arm in arm, priest and courtier walked away, their footsteps echoing lightly within the great anteroom.

For a long, long moment there was no further sound or movement. Then, timidly, a look of utter horror and abject fear on her face, Mereet, wife to the blind armorer Shobai, stepped soft-footed out into the sunlight in the middle of the great room. She looked right and left, reassuring herself that she had in fact been the only listener to the astonishing conversation. Then she removed her head covering and pushed her jet-black hair back from her ears, nervously putting a hand to her perspiring brow. Though she was not sick, she felt intensely hot and uncomfortable.

She was not sure she could believe what she had heard.

Treason?

Conspiracy to commit murder? No—two murders, and maybe more. She couldn't be sure—she hadn't caught most of the last whispered sentences. And—worst of all— the victims were good and faithful friends of hers and Shobai's.

That was the most amazing part of it. How could anyone want to kill Unas—perhaps the most able officer in the Egyptian army? And what sort of person would want to kill Akhilleus? The black giant was the warmest, most generous-hearted person in the world. She'd have sworn that he didn't have an enemy anywhere. To be sure, his outrageous bragging had landed him in a few duels over the years, when he'd offended the few men whom his great bulk had not frightened away. But in most of those cases the duel had ended after a thump or two, with both fighters then repairing arm in arm to the nearest tavern to drown their remaining enmity in wine—always at the black giant's expense.

And Ebana, his Nubian wife? Why would these people think of killing her? Mereet had never met a kinder, wiser person, or had a better or more faithful friend. For anyone to want to murder Ebana . . .

She sat down on a stone bench, trying to catch her breath, trying to think calmly. Why, the conspirators—they intended to force the abandonment of Memphis altogether! Not only Memphis, but the Fayum, the last reliable source of food the Upper Egyptian forces had left, now that the enemy held the delta!

And the conspiracy was on the highest level—only Madir and the king's family themselves stood higher! Imagine . . . Harmin, the general! Hapu, the high priest!

What in heaven's name could she do? Tell Madir? He'd never believe her. Word that she'd told would get back to the conspirators, and . . . sooner or later, some dark night when there was no one but poor blind Shobai to defend her, they'd send another of their assassins after her, just as they were sending one after Akhilleus and Ebana. Since he'd be in disguise, she'd never know who he was until it was too late.

What could she do?

Should she tell Shobai? She shrank at the thought. By no means was she eager to be the one to add anything to his worries. Besides, what could he do? The court surely would be more disposed to listen to her, the daughter of a nobleman and ex-magistrate, than to Shobai, a foreigner— and a blind man.

Mereet bit her knuckles to try to keep her hand from shaking. Whom could she turn to? Whom could she trust?

III

Uni, chief steward of the royal prisons at Memphis, shook his head as he examined the young prisoner. The boy—he was hardly more than that—stood straight and unafraid, with none of the hangdog look of a guilty offender. His manner was reserved, deferential, respectful. Tall and thin, with reddish hair, he didn't look like the usual sort of slave at all. He looked more like a . . . a what? A king's son. Rather more so than some of the kings' sons he had known in the perilous days of the present interregnum.

Uni scowled. Interregnum? Well, that was what it was. The present Lord of Two Lands, Dedmose, who despite all his trappings of power managed to hold on to no more than the Red Lands—leaving the much more fertile, much more valuable Black Lands of the delta in the hands of the hated Shepherd invaders—had held office for only a few years, no more, and his bloodlines were hardly of the order that had produced god-kings, pharaohs, in the great days of Egypt. Stack this Dedmose up against the fabled Sesostris—any of the three kings of that name—or one of the Amenemhets, and he just didn't seem there at all.

But look at *this* boy. You could put him up on the wall in one of the royal friezes, and he'd look perfectly at home. Yet there wasn't so much as a drop of Egyptian blood in him. "You, my young friend," he said at last. "Would you turn around for me once, please?"

The boy, naked except for the narrow loincloth of a house servant, managed to do so with some dignity, and without insolence. He stood patiently, awaiting further orders.

"*Hmm,*" Uni said. "You haven't been beaten, I see."

"No, sir," the young man said. "Nor have I done

anything that deserved beating—or, for that matter, being imprisoned as I am today."

Uni looked at his prisoner sharply. The boy had more to say, but wisely withheld it. *Better to wait until someone asks.* Good. This showed sagacity, an ability to play the game. "Ah, yes," he said, "everyone who comes here has the same story. You're all innocent, every last one." He paused, looking at the boy, waiting for the expected expostulation. Again none was immediately forthcoming. Patiently the boy waited. A good sign. There was something in the boy's manner that suggested he was not keeping silent because he had something to hide.

Uni crossed his arms over his broad chest. "Let me see your hands, boy." The prisoner obediently extended his hands, palms up. Uni examined them. "No calluses to speak of. How long have you been a slave?" he asked. "I'll wager you weren't born one." He waited, still half expecting the usual tale of woe: *ripped from my mother's arms, sir. I'm nobly born, sir; please restore me to my former state.* "Well?" he said after a moment. "That's your cue to start spouting sad stories at me."

"I wasn't going to, sir," the boy said. "Unless you asked me. It isn't my place to volunteer information of a kind that must surely bore you every time you hear it."

Uni chuckled. "Well put, my friend. But I *am* asking. Who are you? How came you to Egypt? You're not Egyptian born, that I do know. From somewhere up north, are you?"

"Yes, sir," the young man said in the same unruffled voice as before. "My name is Joseph. I'm the eleventh son of my father, Jacob, a king in Canaan." He thought for a moment and added, " 'King' doesn't mean the same where I come from as it does here. My father is what you would probably consider a wealthy pastoralist who also happens to be a magistrate and a priest of the God of our people."

"A distinction well observed," Uni said approvingly. "Go on, please. How came you here?"

"I'm the first son of my father's second wife," Joseph explained. "My father loved his second wife better than he did the first, and my half brothers could not fail to see this. They resented me in particular, as the son my father favored over them, when they, by custom, should have had his favor."

"I see," Uni said. "The laws of primogeniture flouted. So your brothers got rid of you, did they?"

"Exactly, sir. Although I think that they acted in a moment of unthinking anger and lived to regret it. I was made a slave by Ishmaelite traders passing through our country and was sold to one master, who then sold me to another. The price I brought always rose."

"It could just have been the decline in the value of our currency," Uni said. "On the other hand, you give evidence of being a useful sort. I can see you'd bring a decent price in the current market, if I were to put you up for sale." He stopped, noting the tiny rise in the young man's eyebrow when he said this. "Oh, don't worry. I've no intention of doing so. As you probably know, it would be illegal anyhow. The charge brought against you is not of sufficient seriousness." He saw the boy's face relax once more, and went on. "Suppose you tell me exactly what happened to cause the noble Potiphar to have you sent here."

The boy cleared his throat. "My lord's wife"—his face twisted slightly, in embarrassment and distaste—"my lord's wife conceived a passion for me. When I did not respond, she denounced me for trying to rape her." His mouth did not want to frame the last words of his brief speech. "I could not defend myself to my lord without telling all, and telling all would have meant the end of what peace my gracious lord enjoys with his wife. The choice was between silence and this place in which I now stand, or speaking out and ruining my lord's peace. I have chosen as you see."

"How terribly noble," Uni said. "And you expect a medal for your deed, I suppose? Am I supposed to reward you for your act of self-sacrifice?"

"I would not presume to tell you, sir, what you are supposed to do," the boy said. He put a slight emphasis on the word *supposed*.

Uni caught this immediately. "I see," he said. "So you're a diplomat, too. And—what are some of the other things I've heard? Are you the servant of Potiphar's who's supposed to have some sort of diviner's gift? Some gift of prophecy?"

"Sometimes, when the God of my fathers wills it, sir, He helps me understand things. Sometimes it comes to me through a dream of my own. Sometimes it's by way of a dream someone else had, which our God gives me to understand." He shook his head a little sadly. "Often I can interpret another's dreams yet fail to understand my own. But the matter is always in the hands of my God."

Uni pursed his lips and walked around the boy, deep in thought. Then he half smiled. "Tell me, then—if your god will give you the words—what am I, as chief steward of the royal prison, going to do about you right now?"

Joseph looked him in the eye, and for a moment Uni saw the ghost of a twinkle in the boy's gaze. "I speak no divination, sir; the spirit of the God is not upon me. But I speak with the native wit He gave me in saying that you will in all probability treat me justly."

"I will, eh?" the jailer said. "Go on."

"If I understand the terms of your office correctly, you cannot free me without an order from above. But you have great personal discretion as to how I will be treated in prison. And you have already noticed, sir, that I haven't the bulk for heavy labor. I'd be totally wasted in that capacity, and you'd be out one slave very soon."

"Accurate so far, my diviner friend. Proceed."

"On the other hand, sir, my former masters trained me in various household arts. I can write, keep records, draft letters. Before my first master's death, I administered a household of thirty slaves and sixteen bond servants, had full power to assign work, and rendered an accurate accounting of my stewardship."

"And you were with this first master how long?"

"A year and one month, sir. Then he died and I was sold with the estate when the heirs broke it up among them. I—"

"A year and one month? And you rose that high? I'm impressed. You're a quick learner."

"So my first master said, sir."

Uni thought for a moment. "Well, it's evident you don't belong among the criminals. And you've a good deal of intelligence; any fool can see that. Perhaps I can use you. You seem to be a good judge of men. . . ." He stared, unblinking, at Joseph. "You are, aren't you? Damned good?"

"Yes, sir," the slave said. "It is as the God of my people wills it. And, sir, I am not mistaken in you, am I?"

Uni smiled, fairly broadly this time. "No, you're not, my young friend. You'll get justice from me. And if you help me with one particularly touchy matter, you'll get better than simple justice—you'll get preferential treatment. Better quarters, better food, a job with a bit of responsibility."

"I am at your service," Joseph said.

"Very well. Sit down, boy. Sit down here beside me." The two took places on a long bench, Uni partially facing Joseph. "Look—there's been a bit of unpleasantness in the court. It seems there was an attempt on the life of none less than the Lord of Two Lands himself."

Joseph's eyebrows raised infinitesimally. "And no one has heard of it?"

"We've done what we could to hush it up. But—there are two suspects. The king's cupbearer, Ameni, and the chief baker, Yusni. Traces of poison were found in food. The taster died horribly, as the king would have done if he had not insisted, contrary to his usual custom, that all his food that day be tried out first on the taster of foods." Uni leaned closer and lowered his voice. "Madir was also present at the dinner—and though he won't admit it, I have reason to believe that the poisoned food may in fact have been meant for him, not for the king." He shrugged, as if the information he had just imparted was of little consequence. "In any case, we've narrowed the suspects down to the baker and the cupbearer. Whoever tne intended victim, either could have done the deed, and neither has an adequate alibi. They've both been arrested; we're taking no chances. But both are virtually unshakable in their denial of any knowledge of the attempted murder. Now, *I* think I could extract a confession with torture, but Madir says no. Both are distant relatives of his wife's, and he doesn't want any trouble with his in-laws just now."

Joseph pursed his lips. "And you're going to put me

in with them, sir? To see if I can get evidence as to who
was guilty?"

Uni smiled. "All your denials to the contrary, young
man, you've a touch of the diviner about you. Either that,
or you're the smartest damned foreigner I've ever run
into. Because that's exactly what I intend to do with you.
If you can get information for us to go on, by whatever
means, well, as I say, you can look forward to the best life
a man can live here in prison. That's the most I can
promise you."

Joseph did not speak for a moment. Then, in his
politest courtier's tone, he said quietly, "I repeat, sir—I
am at your disposal, now and in the future. I will do what
you say, as the God gives me strength and wisdom to do
so."

In the night Mereet, sleepless, sat up in a chair by
the bed, a warm robe draped over her nakedness as protection against the evening chill, her mind a thicket of fears
and worries. She watched Shobai, his great body nearly
filling their bed, his fitful sleep disturbed by violent dreams.
His great bulk tossed and turned, and from time to time
he would groan, as if a terrible pain were wracking his
body. Now the bright moonlight, spilling into their bedroom through the open window, shone on the cold sweat
of his troubled face.

Mereet shivered and pulled the robe more tightly
around her, so that only her bare toes protruded from
beneath it as she huddled, knees up, in the chair beside
their bed. She looked at him, and her heart was fit to
burst with love and compassion.

She'd thought these fits of anguish were over. He'd
gone so long—over a year now—without a single nightmare.
He'd told her again and again how happy he'd become in
his life with her, how her love and the children's presence
had brought him something he'd never known in all his
days.

And she herself could tell the difference. In their first
days together there had been a deep tension in him;
seldom had he been able to relax. She'd cared for him and
comforted him then, trying to reassure him, to tell him

the terrible days of fear and worry were over. It had taken time, a long time, but his trust, his respect for her had grown, had deepened. As he had opened up to her, she could feel, day by day, the warmth, the strength of his love for her, growing, becoming more powerful. . . .

And now? Now the fears, the sleeplessness, the nightmares all were back, as fearful as they'd ever been. Even in the daytime, when the dreams could not reach him, the tension was there—in the tight muscles of his shoulders, in the stiffness of his touch when he reached out to her, caressed her. It was there in his distance from her, in his self-absorption, in his terse answers to her questions.

And now, when more than ever before she wanted, needed desperately to be able to confide in him, to tell him her own deepest fears . . . now she *couldn't* force herself to lay open her heart. Not for anything!

How could she? He had such worries of his own. How could she add to them?

Yet her secret knowledge was becoming unbearable. And the longer she kept the secret, the greater grew the danger to the entire city—as well as the danger to Unas, their old friend who'd come up with them all the way from Saïs after the battle there, when he'd made a name for himself. Unas, who'd known Baka, and who'd been one of the most gallant defenders of the Black Lands from the hated invaders! Unas's life was in danger!

And Akhilleus's as well.

The plot against him and Ebana had to be stopped at all costs, before it was too late. Even Musuri, the old Moabite mercenary who commanded their military escort upriver, would be hard put to prevent a trained assassin from carrying out his mission . . . or would he?

She bit her lip, recalling what Shobai had told her about his old Moabite friend, of how Akhilleus and Ebana would be safe in his care. Musuri, Shobai had said, was a battlewise soldier of wide experience, with a good instinctive knowledge of human nature and a sharp eye. If anything—

"*No! No, please! No! Stop!*"

She sat up straight, her eyes wide with horror. Shobai's great body writhed on their bed, his huge, helpless hands clutching the air, flailing away, trying to keep something from him. Suddenly he sat bolt upright.

"No! Don't!"

She went to him, letting her robe fall, her warm nakedness pressed comfortingly against his feverish, sweaty body. "Shobai, darling . . . it was only a dream. I'm here, darling. . . . It's all right. Everything is all right, my dearest."

But even as he began slowly to relax in her arms, as she felt the tension draining out of him, she knew in her heart that her words of reassurance were lies. Nothing was all right now, nothing at all. Both their lives were going awry, their happiness vanishing, and she didn't know what she could possibly do about it.

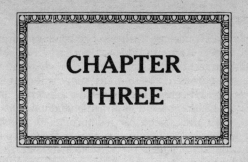

CHAPTER THREE

THE NUBA MOUNTAINS

I

For perhaps the fortieth time since they'd left the track along the river, Musuri of Moab pulled off his helmet to mop his dripping brow. It wasn't a particularly hot day. There was a cooling breeze that broke whatever heat the direct sunshine brought with it. But the pace of their march had increased as the expedition had begun its trek toward the distant mountains and the headwaters of the Nile. Musuri, old soldier and seasoned campaigner though he was, was beginning to feel his age.

Gods! How did Akhilleus and Ebana keep it up, day after day? Akhilleus, like himself, was no longer young and had begun the great journey south rather overweight for a man of his towering height. And Ebana was a woman! Musuri wasn't used to women who could outmarch a professional soldier like himself, particularly in mountain country.

But there you were. Something had happened to the two of them once they'd left the confluence of the two arms of the Nile and struck out roughly westward into the scrub-covered semidesert. Instead of growing weaker, they'd grown stronger. And also odd was the fact that, although they'd discharged their last native guides when they'd left the Nile, it seemed that Akhilleus knew where the devil he was going. His great strides set the blistering pace of the caravan. Ebana, beside him, had abandoned the sedan chair in which she'd been carried through the desert on the first leg of their journey and now walked, strong and confident, beside her gigantic consort, matching his every stride with two shorter ones of her own. Indeed, both of them marched as though this country were second nature to them. Yet Musuri knew that Ebana had never been farther south than Kerma, capital of Kush, the city where she and Akhilleus had made peace with her Nubian compatriots some months before. Musuri, the helmet still dangling from his left hand, used his right to scratch his bald pate. It was an enigma, a most puzzling one.

The peace treaty at Kerma had been a brilliant stroke, to be sure. Akhilleus and Ebana had bargained together, realizing immediately that it would take both his native sagacity and her knowledge of Nubian custom to break down the tribal leaders' reluctance to make peace with hated Egypt. It had been Egyptian armies that had driven them ever farther south in the terrible Nubian wars of Twelfth Dynasty days, when Sesostris III in particular had built forts on both sides of the Nile "to prevent any Negro from passing, by water or by land"—great L-shaped edifices, heavily fortified and perfectly situated on forbidding, unscalable cliffs, with towering thirty-foot walls of sun-dried brick, fifteen to twenty-five feet thick. Soldiers from the forts bearing the ram's-head standards of the Regiment of Amon had enforced the ban on blacks heading northward along the river for a century or more now, and the pitched battles and small sorties between the entrenched soldiers and Nubian raiders had been bitter, no-quarter engagements.

And in one stroke Akhilleus and Ebana had made peace with the tribesmen that the Sesostrises had battered so ruthlessly within living memory! Akhilleus also had made mutual defense pacts with each of the Nubian tribes, which traditionally were at war with one another. He had reopened trade along the Great River, assuring the king's coffers of an unimpeded supply of gold from the quarries of Kush as well as copper and other minerals scheduled for Shobai's forges. They'd even promised ample supplies of tin for Shobai's bronze smelters, and rumor had it that new deposits of the black metal, iron, had been located above the fifth cataract, where the river Atbara joined the Nile waters.

No doubt about it: Akhilleus and the woman, insufferable though each could be at times—he with his bragging, she with her sharp tongue—were indispensable. They'd already accomplished in this trip what no other living person could have done for the failing Egyptian cause. And he, Musuri, was almost beginning to believe that that cause had some chance of surviving now—even prevailing. Thanks to these two alone!

Still, he shouldn't have been surprised. He had known the big black devil for a number of years now. He'd seen him, time and again, driven to the edge, his back to a wall, his resources apparently exhausted, the adversary—whoever that happened to be at the time—apparently victorious. Yet Akhilleus would somehow manage to come up with that unexpected something that saved the day. And this was before Ebana had joined forces with him!

Look at Akhilleus's uncanny instinct for navigation. With perfect confidence, he'd taken a devious and dangerous route southward. Instead of trying to follow the Nile's tortuous course, they'd struck boldly out into the desert. Once there, they'd learned quickly to rely on Akhilleus's almost infallible nose for an oasis or a well in the barren, waterless country. They'd followed a long, semicircular line of flourishing oases at first. Then, acting fearlessly, Akhilleus had ordered a march southward, following an ancient track. And when he'd finally called for a sharp cut back eastward, they'd come out—just as the giant had predicted—directly above the third cataract, within a half day's march of Kerma. Musuri, a veteran in these matters, had marveled. And the miracles had just begun there!

Small wonder that when, with the peace concluded at Kerma, Akhilleus had proposed extending the expedition all the way to the Nile headwaters, he, Musuri, had found it easy to go along with him, despite all his experience and

judgment. Akhilleus had succeeded brilliantly thus far.
Why not let him have his head? Even if the mission
seemed patently insane on the face of it. . . .

Musuri, his tired old legs aching, his upper body now
drenched with sweat, looked down at the helmet in his
hand and thought twice about putting it back on again.
This far away from the garrisons, with a ragtag force by
now largely composed of hired Nubians and a few interpreters from the Upper Nile they'd signed on back in
Memphis, the precise functions of military discipline had
begun to elude him. Up here the banners of whatever
king one was serving didn't seem to mean very much.
Neither did the king's uniforms. . . .

Up ahead, Akhilleus looked back and saw his old
friend and, slacking his pace, dropped toward the rear of
the column with Ebana. "Your helmet's in your hand, not
on your head," he said as he joined Musuri. "I take it
you're beginning to question the usefulness of it."

"I am," Musuri said. "That and all this damned harness.
I'm sweating like a pig."

"Throw it away," Akhilleus said.

Musuri thought about it for a moment; then, with a
shrug, he did so.

Akhilleus grinned. "Soldiers think they have to maintain garrison standards when they're far from home. But
there's another way of thinking, my old friend, which I
recommend to you right now. Adopt the customs of the
country. They're usually better suited to that country
anyhow."

"And just what customs, by your way of thinking,
should I be adopting?" Musuri replied. "In this country
none of us has ever seen before, how the devil am I to
know what the customs are? When I've yet to lay my eyes
on so much as a single denizen?"

"Then you haven't seen them?" Ebana said, her smile
mocking him gently. "The old soldier hasn't spotted them?
I'm surprised at you, Musuri. They've been watching us
for most of the afternoon. I must have spotted fifty of them
myself, one at a time."

Musuri frowned. "I told you, I'm getting old. I should
have retired five years ago. I should be vegetating in a

little kitchen garden somewhere in the Fayum, with a slave girl or two to feed me and bring me cooling drinks under the shade of a date palm. Instead, here I am on this wild goose chase, with you two idiots. You say you've seen them? What are they like?"

"Well," Akhilleus said, matching his steps to Musuri's, slowing the caravan's pace considerably in consideration for the old soldier's evident fatigue, "they seem to have the good sense to abandon clothing altogether in this climate. Curious," he said. "I seem to remember that. There's something about this area that's familiar. Perhaps somebody took me through this country once, when the slavers captured me and sent me downriver into captivity. I seem to know the land in my bones. And seeing these people, even from a distance . . ."

"You're sure you couldn't have come from these people?" Ebana said. "They're as big as you are; you'd fit in with them well, I would think."

Akhilleus shook his grizzled head. "No. You saw several of them fairly closely, back there. You saw the ritual scars they give the young men when they attain manhood. I don't recall anything remotely like that."

"You've certainly no such scars," Musuri said. "I've seen you on board the boats, bathing in seawater. But still, didn't you say that they took you away before you'd reached manhood?"

"A good point," Akhilleus said. He looked down at his own sweat-soaked robe with some annoyance. "Why am I wearing this sodden cloth?" he said. "Adopt the local customs. More comfortable anyhow." He held up one hand, halting the long column that stretched across the brush-covered foothills behind them. And, lips pursed in disdain for the sopping garment he wore, he suddenly reached down and ripped it across. His hands then ripped it longitudinally, and thrust the rags from him. Now he stood as naked as on the day of his birth, his giant body that of an old lion, sagging here and there, but still powerful and vigorous. He stretched, spreading his arms wide, filling his giant chest with huge lungfuls of the fresh foothill air. "There," he said, "that's a lot better. *And* more appropriate." He chuckled. "Everyone used to joke with

me over my vanity, over the fact that I spent a king's
ransom on clothing, on adornment. Well, my people are
vain. They'll do anything to show off. But it doesn't mean
everything to them. They like fine clothing, for show, but
they can do without it just as easily. I spent ten years with
my bare behind polishing a rower's seat on a galley, own-
ing not so much as an earring. Later I spent enough
money on clothing to feed a village for a year. It doesn't
mean anything. It doesn't matter." He shrugged. "Join me
if you like."

Musuri thought it over for a moment, then stripped
to his only undergarment, a narrow white loincloth. He
kept his sword belt but abandoned everything else. "My
customs aren't quite yours," he said. "I have the habits of
a lifetime to break. But I agree!" He pointed at Akhilleus.
Grins broke out in the column; most of the bearers and
interpreters were soon as naked as the black giant.

Musuri turned back to his friends—and was astonished to see Ebana standing next to her husband, as naked
as he, her tall, erect body, high-breasted, long-legged,
gleaming in the sun. They looked remarkably like statues
of the gods, it suddenly occurred to him. Or a king and his
queen.

Without thinking, he bowed his head slightly, as one
might to royalty. Ebana, understanding, returned the obeisance graciously, regally. And Musuri thought: They are
royalty of a sort. Only one couldn't see it through the
inappropriate dress.

He smiled and ordered the column forward. And
now, in the periphery of his vision, he could begin to see
the natives of the area, coming out of the brush one at a
time, watching them pass. All were naked and stood as tall
as cranes, lean, well-muscled, magnificently fit. He looked
one of them in the eye, kept his own face noncommittal,
and held the pace, casual, unhurried.

As the track entered the mountains and wound up the
side of the gentle slopes, with reddish and gray granite
slabs towering above them, they could look down into the
valleys and see fields planted in what looked like millet.
Akhilleus called back to two of the interpreters he'd hired

in Memphis. Both had claimed to come from the country south of the Sudd, but neither seemed to know the other.

The pair joined him at the head of the column. Obwano, the bigger of the two, stood almost as tall as Akhilleus himself; he'd adopted the same lack of costume as had Akhilleus and Ebana and, long-muscled, had the body of a runner. His companion, Uranga, who had kept his loincloth, stood half a head shorter and looked like a semitamed bear, with a thick neck and broad shoulders.

"Where are we?" Akhilleus said. "I would guess that when we've passed the mountains, the Sudd is hardly more than a day's march away, and that we'll reach the marsh country a couple of days after that."

"I don't know," Obwano said. "When I came north I followed the Nile. Perhaps Uranga can say."

Uranga didn't speak for a moment, then said, "You guess right. Give or take a day. But how do you remember so much? You told us you were no more than a child when you came through."

Akhilleus smiled cagily, then led them aside, just off the trail, through a narrow break between two large slabs of granite. From where they stood they could look down into a valley, with a stream running through. A village stood on the flats; there were strange, fortresslike houses, each composed of five turret-shaped buildings arranged in a neat circle, with conical grass roofs. The houses were sturdily and symmetrically fashioned, with stone foundations, and had no windows.

"This *is* amazing," Akhilleus said. "As you say, I was hardly more than a baby. But perhaps there's a kind of memory the senses bear when all else is forgotten—the kind of memory most of us know only through our dreams."

There was a child's look of wonder on his black face. "For instance, I . . . I *know* I've been in houses like those. The five cells cluster around a central court, where everyone cooks, and there's a place to bathe near the cookstove."

Uranga's expression did not change. "What else do you remember?" he said stonily, apparently unimpressed with Akhilleus's seeming clairvoyance.

"Well . . . the rooms open only to the court, not to

one another. That much I remember. Each house has a separate function within a single family. One house holds grain, another beer and water. There's a place for the adults to sleep." He grinned again. "I was a child. Children slept in a room with the animals. Children and dogs, perhaps a goat."

"Look," Obwano pointed. "Someone is coming out to meet us." Akhilleus strained his eyes in the direction indicated. "Yes," he said. "From the looks of him, and the fact that he's got several bodyguards with him, I'd say he must be the chief here. Now we'll see if I remember the proper manners for a meeting. Uranga, stick close by and help me when I falter. My memory still has big holes in it."

Akhilleus was welcomed as a fellow chieftain, a man of standing. There was a festive dinner, and the local chief, Aleppo, sent messengers to the neighboring villages to call the tribes together for a *sanda*—an intertribal jamboree of feasting, dancing, singing, and wrestling, the favorite sport of the tribes of the Nuba Mountains. The women of the village immediately went to work brewing immense quantities of *marissa,* a beer made from millet, the main grain crop of the mountain tribes.

Akhilleus's people settled in happily for the coming feast, making themselves easily at home. To everyone's delighted laughter, two young unmarried girls, stark naked, their slim, high-breasted bodies crisscrossed with patterned cicatrices their peers had given them for beauty's sake, attached themselves to old Musuri, following him around, feeding him, fawning upon him. They were twins—Kosse-Gogo and Rumbe-Gogo. Musuri tried to shake them off, brushing them away like deerflies, but they stuck to him all the closer, as Musuri bore up patiently under the raillery of his men. At evening's end, Aleppo, as *mek* of the tribe, ordered the girls to Musuri's bed. Akhilleus explained to the vainly rebellious Musuri that to refuse would be a major offense—whereupon Musuri reluctantly let himself be led away. From the hut to which the girls had taken him delighted giggles could be heard through most of the night. Heads shook unbelievingly at the sound. Perhaps Musuri was not quite as old and infirm as everyone had thought.

Deep in the night, the assassin opened his eyes. Wakeful, he slipped silently out of his bed, feeling the cool air on his bare body. In the dark village no life stirred. In the bare hills above he could hear an animal's high-pitched cry.

He looked at Akhilleus's borrowed house, and he thought: *I could do it now. I could slip inside and slit his throat, and the woman's, too. I could leave evidence on another, and inform against him. . . .*

Then he thought: *But no. As Eben advised, I shall let him go where he's going, make the treaties, hire the army. And as his interpreter, I shall be at his side all the while. Only when he is ready to return to Egypt shall I strike— and then I shall take over the expedition and return to Memphis at the head of a large and powerful force.*

Yes, I shall wait. The time is not yet right.

But soon, he thought. *Soon. I will strike quickly, and without regrets.*

II

Musuri awoke early, to see, through the door that led to the interior court of the house, sunlight streaming down onto the packed mud floor. The sun was high! He'd slept late, for the first time in years!

He sat up, feeling the aches and pains of age all over his body. But no—they weren't the usual aches. They were from the bedroom athletics he'd indulged in the night before. He looked around suddenly. The girls were gone. *Ah, youth,* he thought. No trouble for a man of experience to keep up with them, perhaps, romping about like that. But . . . confound it, they did recover a bit more quickly. It was afterward that one's age began to show.

He stood, yawned, stretched, and, feeling the cool

morning air on his body, shivered a bit. This was mountain air, after all, thin and chill. He stepped for a moment into the bright sunshine through the open door and immediately felt the sun's warm rays on his body. That feels so good! he thought, and stretched again, letting the sun soak in. Perhaps these people had the right idea about apparel. They knew what worked best down here, where the sun shone the whole year round. Obwano even said there was no winter here that one could recognize as such; people could go around this way all year. . . .

He looked through the courtyard door to the outside and saw people beginning to arrive for the promised feast. Some of *them* wore clothing, now. But what they wore seemed entirely for adornment, not for concealment. Take that fellow, for instance: He's probably spent his entire wardrobe budget on a hat! Musuri smiled and shook his head in disbelief.

When he returned to his bed and reached down for his loincloth, however, his hand hesitated for a moment. Loincloth? Here? He'd only look silly. Or would he? Nobody would care, most likely. Musuri pondered the matter, and at length came to a conclusion: If nobody gave a hang what you wore or didn't, the only person you had to please was yourself. He shrugged . . . and put on his loincloth and sword belt, no more. Habit was strong in a man his age, and he knew he'd feel more comfortable with a bit of cloth between him and the world.

He stepped into the sun again and immediately was greeted with shouts, laughter, and cheers from his bearers, gathered outside. Some of the locals joined in the laughter. "Here he comes!" one bearer shouted. "The Lion of Moab! Two girls aren't enough for him in one night—tomorrow they're giving him three!"

Musuri scowled. All of the bearers were naked as shucked oysters. Confound it! Ordinarily he would order their superior to call them to attention. Now, with the distinctive garb of rank abandoned, he couldn't tell which was the leader and which the led. "Surely you drones must have something better to do than stand around and tell jokes," he said gruffly.

"But, Musuri," one of the bearers said, "it's a festival

day, and these are the friendliest people in the world. Surely we can relax today."

Musuri scowled at him. "Look around you. Some of the people you see are the locals, our hosts. Some are not. Look at the patterns of cicatrices on their skins. Some of them are familiar, some not. By the time the festival you're talking about is under way, both we and the locals will be greatly outnumbered by people who may be friendly—or who may not. What do we know of local customs? How can we tell what one tribe around here feels about the next? What if some of the guests here decide they want to kill the foreigners—that's us—and eat them? Eh? Have you given a moment's thought to that?"

He saw by their puzzled faces that they had not. "Where are your weapons?" he snapped. "I don't give a hang whether you cover your bare behinds or fail to. As Akhilleus says, it makes sense to dress as the locals do—or as they don't, I should say. But that doesn't mean leaving your sword belts behind. Next time I see you, the lot of you, I expect you to be wearing them. Just because these people feed and house us and give us girls to fool around with doesn't mean they've adopted us. I've soldiered in lands stranger than these, even before some of you were born, and I can tell you I've seen people who fattened you up today because they intended to cook you for supper tomorrow."

The hard, angry glint in his eye transfixed them, but to himself Musuri made the sign against bad luck. Most of his speech was a damned lie, of course; he'd heard of cannibals from older soldiers, but had never laid eyes on one—at least not yet.

"Now get those damned belts on, will you? And stay alert! You don't have any idea what the people around here are up to."

While Akhilleus and the local chieftain, Aleppo, conferred on matters of state under a baobab tree, with Uranga between them to interpret, Ebana wandered around the village, satisfying her curiosity. She'd already begun to pick up a word or two, sometimes an often-used phrase, just from listening to random conversations and the children's shouting.

The feel of sun and fresh air on her bare skin was, now as before, a delightful surprise. She was really quite pleased with her earlier quick decision to follow Akhilleus's lead when he had adopted the undress of the country. Not only was it a pleasant sensation simply being naked among other naked people, but she was sure, as well, that it brought her closer to the tribe, made her almost one of them.

Yet there was still more to it than that.

She'd spoken with Akhilleus about his decision during the night. For him it had been more than just the casting aside of a style of dress inappropriate for this country—he had likened it to the casting aside of a whole way of life.

"It is mysterious, Ebana," he'd said. "Something's happening to me, and I can't quite explain it, even to myself. As we go farther and farther south, I can feel a change. It's almost as though I were a worm who'd crawled into his cocoon and didn't know what he was going to be when he emerged from it. It's as though I'd spent my whole life being something I'm not, and now I'm beginning to get a glimpse—a dim glimpse—of what it is that I was born to be.

"It's as though . . . well, I've *been* here before. Not to this village, perhaps, but one like it, somewhere in these mountains. But the memories . . . I can get only pieces of them, a little at a time."

"As you did when you remembered how the houses are laid out here?" she'd said.

"Yes. Perhaps the slave traders stopped for the night in the Nuba hills, taking us northward to market. But it's *more* than that kind of memory. Ebana, I had a dream last night. I dreamed I was walking through a dark and forbidding forest, along a narrow path, with all sorts of unknown horrors lurking behind every tree. Down the long path I could see a glowing light, warm and inviting, beckoning to me. I knew, somehow, that when I reached the light I would learn a wonderful secret—the secret of life and death, perhaps, or the secret of wisdom. But as I approached the light, the unknown terrors of the forest grew closer around me, and unseen, clawed hands reached out for me, trying to grab me, to impede me. Yet the closer to the light I came, the stronger I became, the more confident, the more wise. . . ."

His eyes had fairly glowed when he'd told her of this. And it was true, in a way—she'd noticed a great change in him as they'd entered the Nuba country. The years had fallen away from him; he'd grown younger, stronger. He'd also lost weight on their long trek, until now he was hardly heavier than Aleppo. He looked strong and fit and had somehow acquired, as the strength from this magical land flowed into him through his very soles, a curious personal dignity he'd never really had before, not even when he was Akhilleus, the fabulously rich trader she had first met—a man who could buy and sell whole cities.

And he was right: When he had cast aside the clothing of the northern countries, he had cast aside his old life—*all* his many lives in the years he'd spent away from central Africa. He'd cast aside the life of a nameless slave; the life of a shackled galley rower the Greek sailors and pirates had called Akhilleus, after a mighty hero of their folktales; the life of a pirate; the life of a trader; and finally the life of a merchant prince. And with all these he'd cast aside the habit of clowning, of mocking himself and his own pretensions. There was now a great inner core of seriousness about him, and it filled her with awe and satisfied her in a way she'd never have been able to predict.

She thought about his remark about the worm and the cocoon, and wondered what the real Akhilleus would be when he'd emerged from the silken prison of his earlier life. She thought of his words to her: "My *name*, Ebana. What's my real name? It isn't Akhilleus; that's the only thing I do know. And I keep thinking that I'll find out one of these days. And when I discover my real name, I'll know who I am. There's magic in names, Ebana. There's powerful magic in what you call things or people or animals. Perhaps that's what I saw in my dream, in the light at the end of the path through the dark forest. My name. And with it the secret of my being, of who I am and what I'm here in this world to do and to be."

*   *   *

Breakfast was a hot, steaming mush made of millet flour and water from a mountain spring and flavored, surprisingly, with a tart sauce made from sour fruit. To this one added hot peppers, washing the whole down with the ever-present *marissa*. Musuri was surprised to find how much he liked the combination. It woke up the palate and the senses and cleared the cobwebs from the mind.

Now, like Ebana, he wandered through the village, and as he did he took note of the wide variety of activities the villagers were engaged in: One man's deft hands shaped a clay flute, for sale at the festival; another carved sandal soles from prepared leather, much as the Egyptian cobblers did so many days' march northward. He did raise one eyebrow upon seeing a woman fashion a light, tough little bowl from a mixture of white clay and cow dung. He'd eaten from just such a bowl an hour before.

Reaching the top of a small rise, he could look into the great ring below and see the wrestlers preparing for their contests, with a crowd of women looking on. Thus juxtaposed, the two sexes looked so different from each other as to appear different species. The women and girls, shoulder to shoulder along the periphery of the wrestling ring, wore their festival finery—beads, belts, and coats of glistening butter and sesame oil on their otherwise naked bodies. The men, by contrast, had smeared their bare bodies with white ashes, the better to give the wrestler's hands some purchase in the ritual fights.

The men were naked except for this coating and for braided leather belts decorated with cows' tails. Many also sported clay calabashes hanging from the small of their backs. These gourdlike spheres at first puzzled Musuri, until he observed a playful practice bout, which made their function abundantly clear: A man who, at day's end, still wore an unbroken calabash could prove he had not been thrown.

As Musuri continued to watch, the bouts began in earnest. The first pair of fighters circled warily, eyeing each other menacingly, hissing and flicking out their tongues like snakes. One of them lunged, and they engaged each other, grappling. The rules were quickly apparent to Musuri:

The first fighter to touch the ground with any part of his body except his feet was the loser. As the opponents grew more daring and the fight became more exciting, the crowd pressed forward below the tribes' distinctive banners on their long poles overhead, and the wardens of the fight waved them back with long-handled leather paddles.

Musuri drew closer. The fight was really like a stylized oriental dance. The opponents repeatedly whirled, shook arms and legs, feinted, and backed away. Finally they engaged each other again and spun, each trying to throw his opponent to the ground. Far back in the crowd musicians practiced their drums, tuned five-stringed *benembenes*, the native citharas. Tonight, he knew, there would be dancing, more feasting, and then, for the tribes not native to this area, a leisurely march homeward under the full moon.

It all seemed so . . . well, *primitive* was not the word. It seemed so simple. A simple life lived in these non-threatening hills, under the stars, in weather one could predict with some safety through most of the year, broken only by the spring rains. So peaceful, so at harmony with the spirit of the land.

Then why did he feel a strange foreboding?

Why did the back of his bald head itch, as it always itched whenever danger was afoot?

He scratched his pate, scowling, and, bowing to the general mood of the festival day, dismissed his cavils for a moment. *You're just being a damned suspicious old curmudgeon,* he thought. *Loosen up a little. Don't be so distrustful. What is there to worry about here, anyway?*

"Plenty," he said to himself in a low, irritable mutter. "We're out here, farther away from the home country than any Egyptian expedition has been in fifty generations, surrounded by people we know nothing at all about, and with no one to call upon for help if we get in trouble." He scowled at a pair of his bearers, passing by arm in arm with a pair of equally naked native beauties. "You!" he bellowed, suddenly annoyed. "Get your damned sword belts on! On the double! Right now!"

He watched them scramble away, abashed, the girls in tow. And he scowled all the worse, as much at himself

as at their improvident ways. *Whom are you trying to kid?*
he asked himself in silence. He knew what it was that he
feared. And it wasn't danger from without, the kind that
could be guarded against by pulling the group together
into a tight, disciplined little ball, with the spears facing
outward, defending itself the way a porcupine defends
itself. It was danger from within. *Something's wrong, deadly
wrong, with this expedition,* he told himself. *You've known
it for days now. That old sixth sense of yours has been
trying to tell you, to warn you. And you've been ignoring
it, like a damned fool.*

He frowned and shook his head exasperatedly. What
could you do? Instinct was instinct. And this instinct, this
extra sense, had saved him many times before in his long
career as a mercenary soldier. Every time he'd disobeyed
it, he'd suffered.

"Damn!" he said, and hailed a passing soldier of his
troop, a man who—he noticed with some satisfaction—
wore nothing at all but a good Egyptian sword, hanging
from a good Egyptian leather belt. "You! Get the men
together! I want to start posting guards. We're going back
to some sort of military bearing around here, bare fannies
or no. Tell them I said to assemble immediately. I'll be
waiting. . . ."

From the shadow of one of the cone-topped houses
nearby, the assassin watched, his scowl matching Musuri's.
He watched the soldiers assemble, then saw Akhilleus and
Ebana, arm in arm, stroll into view.

"I'd better join them," he told himself, silently. "And
I might do well to watch my step. Musuri knows. He
knows something. But how? How?"

The assassin's eye fixed on the middle of Musuri's
battle-scarred old back, at the point where a blade, striking hard and swift, would do the most damage.

"Soon," the assassin told himself. "He'll be the first to
fall . . . and soon."

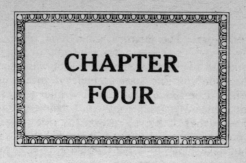

CHAPTER FOUR

THE NILE DELTA

I

"Oh, no you don't!" Akaba, the olive vendor's wife, said in her sharp voice. Striking like a snake, her strong bony fingers closed on the small brown hand that had appeared from behind a shopper's back and grabbed up three of her choicest olives.

She yanked hard on the hand—and a small brown body came out of the crowd with it, dressed in a ragged tuniclike garment. Dark eyes regarded her with exasperation. "Tuya!" Akaba said. "I should have known. I recognized that hand. Good heavens, girl, don't you think I know every wrinkle of that fist of yours by now?" As she increased the pressure on the thin wrist the hand relaxed, letting the olives, bruised now, fall back into the bin.

"They're no good anymore," the girl said. "You can't sell them. Tell you what," she said with a calm confidence that annoyed Akaba to no end, "I'll trade you some information for them."

"You're in no position to trade," Akaba said. "I've got

you red-handed. The guards are no more than a shout away. If—"

"Guards?" Tuya said, smiling. "That was what I was going to trade you information about. If you bring them over here it'll be too late for you. The information I have won't do you any good if they come before I give it to you." She let her dark eyes rest on the ripe olives in the bin. "You have the best olives in town, Akaba," she said. "It would be a shame to lose a stall like this, or groves like the ones that produced these. . . ."

She let the words hang tantalizingly. Akaba scowled, keeping a tight hold on the girl's hand. "Lose? Who's going to lose anything? What are you talking about, you little devil?"

"Do we have a deal?" Tuya said with a demure smile. "Look, I'm getting hungrier by the moment. Throw in a dozen of those day-old olives over there in the corner and I'll tell you right off. Before the bailiffs arrive."

"Bailiffs? What bailiffs?" the woman said with alarm, drawing the girl closer. "Keep your voice down, will you? There are people all around who—"

"Do we have a deal?" the girl said. "You're hurting my arm."

Akaba released the girl's hand. Tuya rubbed her wrist, in no hurry. "Goodness, Akaba. How do you expect me ever to find a suitable husband for myself if I'm bruised all up and down like a ruined melon?"

"We have a deal," the woman snarled angrily. "Take the olives. But first tell me what you're talking about. What bailiffs? Why?"

The girl busied herself counting out olives into her hand. Every third olive went into her mouth, somehow leaving the count undisturbed. "Do you remember that piece of land you sold the Shepherd general, half a league out of town?" She paused to chew, swallow. "*Mmmm. Tasty.*"

"Yes! I remember the land. What of it?"

"It seems there was a problem with the title. And the general says that if the matter isn't settled to his satis—"

"Title?" Akaba's eyes went wide. She held one hand

over her mouth. "Oh, that husband of mine! He forgot to—"

"—to pay the taxes on the last quarter. In which case the property may revert to the crown. And if it does, the general's out whatever staggering sum he paid you for that waterless, infertile piece of—"

"Oh, that thoughtless fool! I knew it! I knew he was going to land us in trouble one of these days!"

"Mmmm-*mmmm!* Delicious! Look, Akaba—I can't let such groves fall into the hands of the Shepherds. I can't let you and your husband risk impalement and—"

"Oh, dear. Oh, me. Oh, what has he done? Tuya—" She grabbed the girl's arm again, but gently this time, imploringly. "Is there anything I can do? You said you were telling me in time to do something. Surely there must be something. . . ."

"There is," the girl said. "Really, you folks in the bazaar ought to take up a collection every month and pay me to keep my eyes and ears open around here. Usually I know more about your business than the lot of you do."

"What? What can I do? Please! Tell me now, before it's too late!"

Tuya looked at her and, the olive count long complete —fifteen olives spread out before her and half a dozen extra already inside her thin little body—she reached casually into the as-yet untouched bin and selected three more of the ripest and finest. "Well," she said, still unhurriedly, "it could all turn out to have been someone's harmless mistake. The scribe in charge of registering deeds could suddenly find that the taxes had, after all, been paid on time, but that he'd mislaid the scroll temporarily. What he's, uh, mislaid, let's say, could suddenly turn up. The property would be unencumbered once again, the general would have a valid deed—everyone would be happy." She paused, sucking on a particularly succulent olive. "But of course the taxes would have to be paid. And the scribe would have to suddenly discover that he had inherited a one-percent share in the yield of an olive grove down by the river." She gazed up, as ingenuously as a child, and smiled blithely at the vendor. "Akaba, think of it this way. You've eight such groves. One percent isn't much. *Two* percent wouldn't be too much to pay, would it, if the alternative was to find yourself decorating a sharpened stake out at the city dump and providing a week's feed for every hungry crow in the delta?"

Akaba, aghast, stared at her. "Tuya! How can such an innocent-looking little mouth shape such words?"

Tuya's expression changed suddenly, growing dark. "Innocent?" she said. "Well, yes, in the sense that no man's got to me yet. But while you and yours were growing up cushioned by family money, Akaba, and family land, with warm houses to keep out the cold, I was out in the street, living off what I could steal or grub for. And not one of you ever took it upon himself to make it any easier for me, did you? Not for me, or for any of the other street children."

It was all too evident that Akaba's own thoughts had never taken this direction of their own accord. "Nobody ever talked to me like this," she said, sounding slightly offended.

"I'm sure they haven't," Tuya replied. "But look around you. There's a whole world you don't see, just because it doesn't come up to your waist. It's full of starving children, children without parents. They wind up dead before they're sixteen, most of them, their throats cut, perhaps. Or they starve to death, or die of the cold in winter. And all you people can think of is to have the guards sicced on us when we steal an olive or two. Look! Look at that little devil over there—the one with the withered arm. He just stole a handful of dried dates. Ordinarily, Akaba, you'd see it and call the guards, and if they could catch him . . . well, he wouldn't last long. If he were prettier they'd throw him to the boy-lovers among the guards, and he'd last maybe a week before they were through with him and threw him over the wall to die. But he's not too pretty. He'd last an hour at most—"

"Tuya! Please!"

"Now, me, I'm smart, as street people go. I've lasted this long in one piece because I've got my wits about me, because I've learned to keep my eyes and ears open, because I'm quick with a knife and have a ready tongue for arguing folks like you out of having me killed. But that little urchin there, the one with the bad arm, all he has is the one hand that works. And with it he supports not only himself, but three others even smaller than himself. Bastards, foundlings, the worthless refuse that the carefree younger sons of your caste tend to father, and then toss away to die."

"Tuya, if I'd only known . . ."

"You wouldn't have done a thing, would you? Be honest with yourself for a change, Akaba." She looked directly in the merchant's wife's eye, without insolence, one woman to another—and reached into the bin for more olives. "I'm going to help you salve your conscience, Akaba, while you're rushing out to the scribe's apartments to pay the bribe. I'm going to tuck away another dozen of these olives of yours in my dress and take them down to a hovel by the city dump and share them with those children. They're little and skinny, and this will buy them another day or so of life. They'll stare out of their wretched little window while they're eating and watch the guards executing felons. Felons, Akaba, who committed crimes such as trying to swindle Shepherd generals. Of course impalement on a stake is not a pleasant sight, but they're used to it. It might trouble rich people to view such things while they dine, but these little ones have strong stomachs, Akaba. They have to, given the kind of horrors most of them have seen by the time they're six years old—if they live that long."

She smiled and popped another ripe olive in her mouth, chewed, swallowed, and spat out the pit. "It's been nice talking with you, Akaba," she said. "If I were you I'd go back home and scrounge up some money to pay off the scribe. Get along, now. I'll mind your stall for you. . . ."

When the merchant's wife was gone, Tuya stood by the stall for a moment, examining its somewhat depleted stock, and shrugged. Sated with her own impromptu luncheon, the best she'd had in days, she looked around for the boy with the withered arm, finally spotting him. "Hey!" she said in a loud whisper that carried well through the low-pitched natter of the marketplace. "Hey! Come here! *Psst!*"

The boy at first tried to shrink back into the crowd. Then, recognizing Tuya, he hesitated. "Come here, I said!" she insisted. Biting his lip, he gazed up at her wide-eyed, wary, a little skeleton, the withered arm hanging useless at his side. "Come on!" Tuya said. "I've got something for you!"

He approached cautiously. "Where's the woman who minds the stall?" he said.

"I shooed her away," Tuya said. "It's a festival day, especially for us. Nobody else allowed. I'm going to close up the stall, cover up the bins. But first I've got something for you and the others. But you've got to promise me you'll share with them. Because if you don't, I won't give you anything at all."

He promised. Tuya had never seen eyes so wide before. A ghost of a smile trembled on the urchin's lower lip and threatened to curl upward. But the smile never reached his unbelieving eyes.

Alone again, she covered the stall with a rough cloth and walked slowly away through the little bazaar. The peak crowds were beginning to thin out, and some of the vendors would be closing up soon. She saw two of them stifling yawns.

Somehow, her little coup complete, she felt a curious melancholy coming upon her. That was strange—she should be feeling quite pleased. She'd fed herself and perhaps half a dozen needy children for the day, and for nothing but fast talk. Why, then, did the gloom descend upon her? Hadn't she just proved her independence, her ability to get by without help, indeed, without anyone—family or friends—to look out for her?

At the thought, a pang of loss, of loneliness, ran through her and nearly took her breath away. Her steps faltered. Weak for a moment, she had to lean against a wall to recover.

But I don't want to be independent, she thought, feeling totally forsaken, her heart empty.

Oh, Ben-Hadad! Why? Why a rich man's spoiled daughter? Why not me?

She closed her eyes, blinking back the tears. Since the rich Wenis had taken Ben-Hadad away from the bazaars, away from her and Anab and all the many friends his generosity and honesty had made for him, she'd seen him no more than twice. True, his greeting for her had been warm—but no warmer than all the other greetings he'd bestowed on all the others he'd said hello to, coming back through the streets. It was as if she'd meant no more to him than anyone else, than a beggar met twice and no more, than a fruit-vendor helped in the public square, than a near-stranger.

And lately rumors had begun to drift back into the city from the fabulous estate where Wenis had taken him. Rumors that, coached by experts, Ben-Hadad had defeated the greatest names in senet in all the Black Lands, including men of such lofty standing that they would never have condescended to play him in the bazaars, the way Khensu, who needed the money, had done.

What else had they said? Ben-Hadad was now apparently being coached in secret by palace experts in the complex moves of the Shepherd Kings' favorite game: the game of twenty squares. Obviously Wenis had ambitions extending far beyond mere gambling. No doubt there was, in new Avaris, capital of a rapidly changing Shepherd empire, much to be gained if one could manage to work his way into the innermost circles of Shepherd power.

And that wasn't easy, not now or at any time. To the Shepherds, Orientals to the bone marrow, blood and nationality were all-important, and any foreigner desiring to gain favor at court would require some special sort of entrée—and such favor, once earned, was extremely precarious. Take the outsider Reshef, whom the entire marketplace, even the Shepherd soldiers, had called the Snake, everywhere except to his face. If any one outsider had seemed to have the Shepherds' ear it had been he. He'd been a close associate of Salitis's father, the nomad leader Manouk; he'd held rank just short of the generals' level as far back as the siege of Ebla, and had held a variety of other high, trusted positions. Yet when Salitis

had declared himself god-king, after the death of his father,
and begun the slow process of forcibly changing the once-
nomadic Shepherd people into farmers, tradesmen, bureau-
crats, overlords of a conquered nation, Reshef had found
himself out in the cold. He'd been given an unimportant
command on the frontier, doing the kind of work it is hard
to look good doing. Just one more outsider, not of Shepherd blood, doing the work underlings, foreigners, did.
And when the Snake had died in the battle of Saïs (some
said his death had come, ignominiously, at the hands of a
woman), his burial had been that of an outsider, a nobody.

She pondered the matter, walking slowly through the
thinning clumps of people in the streets. Ben-Hadad's rich
patron had it all planned out, it appeared. And not badly,
if she were any judge. Word had come down, filtered
through servants of the overlord invaders, of the Shepherds'
insane devotion to the game of twenty squares—a devotion that had already been well-known to outsiders in the
nomadic days when the Shepherd armies were advancing
through Mesopotamia, en route to the delta of the Nile,
and which had reached the point of mania now that the
Shepherds were nomads no more, and had less to do with
their time.

And now Ben-Hadad was being groomed to be the
rich man's key to the inner circles of Shepherd society.
Wenis had all too clearly decided that the best way to the
Shepherds' hearts was through the game board, as, rumor
and tradition had it, had been the case with senet in
earlier dynasties of the legitimate Egyptian succession.
Wenis would train Ben-Hadad, binding him fast in partnership on every level, and would rise with him.

She frowned as the empty feeling threatened to overwhelm her again. Partnership on every level! This was
why Wenis was waving his pretty, expensive, spoiled little
tart of a daughter under his protégé's nose at every turn,
from all one heard. A convenient marriage would bring
patron and protégé together all the more tightly. Once the
game of twenty squares had established him securely in
the Shepherd court, Ben-Hadad might otherwise forget
how he had risen. But if the two partners were in fact son
and father, by marriage . . .

Tuya stopped in the street, so abruptly that a woman behind her, unable to stop in time, ran into her. Tuya stumbled to one side, her eyes full of tears. If this was true, if everything happened as she feared it would, why, she'd lost him! She'd lost him forever!

II

As Tuya wiped away her tears and her eyes refocused on the passing people in the street, she spotted Anab. He was walking slowly, with heavy steps, into an adjoining alley, his thin shoulders bowed in dejection. "Hey!" she called sharply. "Anab! Wait for me! Where are you going?"

He neither turned nor answered. She pushed through a clump of people and set off after him. "Anab! Wait up, will you? It's me, Tuya!"

He slowed, stopped. His ruined face turned toward her, and the half of it that moved and registered emotion bore an expression of such utter depression that she instantly forgot her own troubles.

"Tuya," he said. "Some other time . . ."

"Some other time?" she said. She stepped before him and put her small hands on his skinny arms. "Anab, what on earth is the matter? You look just awful."

He tried to turn away, but her strong little hands dug into his arms, holding him. He would not look her in the eye. "I—I've got some business to attend to," he said. "I can't talk about it now."

"The devil you can't," she said. "I know that look. You can't fool me. This is Tuya, remember? I can even read the part of your face that won't move." She pulled him closer. Limp in her hands, he offered little resistance. "Anab—where did you disappear to? I looked all over for you that night you were supposed to wait at the tavern."

He tried to pull away, but she held on firmly.

"Anab, are you in trouble of some kind? Maybe I can help. Just tell me." She looked around, though, and prudence gained the upper hand. She quickly steered him away from the open second-story windows and into a dark courtyard beside a closed-up, condemned building whose mud walls had withstood the fire that had gutted it. "Nobody can hear us here," she said. "Get it out now, Anab. You can trust me."

"B—but that's just it. I can't trust anyone. Not now."

She let go of him and stepped back. His whole body, every aspect of his posture, spoke of his distress. "Wait a minute," she said in a low voice. "Was that you I saw last night, at the tavern? I wasn't sure . . . but now . . ." She frowned. "It *was* you. You were with Zosar. Yes, and with his fellow cutthroat, Onuris. Good heavens, Anab, what business could you possibly have with a couple of—?"

She stopped, suddenly remembering some of the rumors that had begun to circulate about Zosar. Dangerous rumors. Before last night, she had not seen him in the bazaars for a long time—not since their run-in in the alleyway.

"It's a plot, isn't it?" she said. "Those two are mixed up in some sort of political plot, aren't they? Look at me, Anab!" She let out a deep breath in an angry sigh. "Don't be a fool! Political matters aren't for the likes of you and me. Those people think of us as so much dirty rabble—as animals to be used and thrown away afterward. Look, Anab, I don't know how far you're into this, but—"

"Too far," he said miserably. "Too far already. Please, Tuya, leave me alone. It's hard enough. . . ."

"What are they up to? What have they dragged you into?"

"I can't—" But then his voice failed him and broke. His eyes filled with tears. He glanced at her angry face and his lip quivered—half of it, anyway—and he blinked. A tear ran down his face. "You can't understand," he said. "You can't b-begin to know."

"Try me," Tuya said simply, standing her ground. "I'm your friend. I won't rat on you. You have my word on that, and I don't give my word very often."

His hand clenched and unclenched in spasms. "Tuya," he said at last, in a broken voice, "I killed a man last night. I . . . I haven't been able to sleep since. I've been wandering the streets, trying to think." He held up one grimy hand. "I—I did it with this hand, Tuya. The knife went in so easily. He cried out—"

But then his sick stomach gave way. She helped him stagger to the cluttered corner of the little courtyard, where he lost what remained of his previous night's supper. Afterward he stood weaving, head still bent, his skinny body racked with dry heaves. . . .

In the hour that followed she dragged it out of him sentence by sentence. Confused, bitter, and frightened over the turn of events that had taken Ben-Hadad away from him, he'd drifted from one marginally legal occupation to another. Nearly destitute—only an unexpected stipend from Ben-Hadad had kept him from having to beg in the streets—and expecting at any moment to be caught by Renefres's bullyboys, he'd been ripe for the new movement, and the protection it offered. When its propagandists had approached him, they hadn't done so precipitately. There'd been a slow mating dance of sorts, as they had descended gradually into the little world in which he moved. Then, one night, they'd talked to him until early into the morning. They'd told him of a new organization that had been formed to harass the Shepherd overlords, to assassinate their leaders one by one, along with the home-grown traitors and sympathizers who had forsaken their country and their neighbors by going over to the Shepherds' side. With bitterness in his heart, Anab had thought of Wenis and Ben-Hadad. And he had said yes, he'd like to meet this Benu, this one they called the Phoenix. . . .

But it hadn't been that simple. One didn't meet the Phoenix so easily. One had to be committed—"blooded" was the word they'd used—before one laid eyes on the elusive bandit leader for the first time. Anab had yet to meet him. That was to follow last night's episode. And last night—

"Who was it?" Tuya said. "Some Shepherd higher-up?"

"No. A . . . a traitor. Someone who'd become a sutler to the Shepherd armies. He'd opened a brothel in which innocent Egyptian girls had to lie with the hated Shepherd invaders. That was the way they explained it to me, using words like those. It all struck me as rather strange. I mean, if I had the money, I'd open a bordello myself, I suppose, and if the Shepherds happened to pay better than the locals did, why, all the better. I'd stock Shepherd drink in the tavern downstairs, and I'd seek out good advice as to what kind of women the Shepherd customers preferred. But these people didn't see it that way. Especially Zosar. He's hot-tempered and likes to order people around. He told me either the whoremaster would die last night or I would, at *his*, Zosar's, hand. It appeared I'd committed myself, in their eyes, the moment they'd laid down their guard enough to talk about it with me."

"So you're one of them now?"

"Yes. I have little choice, I'm afraid. Tuya, there are hundreds of people here in the city on their side, from what they tell me—perhaps more. The Shepherds, back behind their front lines, are weak. If an enemy nation were to attack them now from without, either by land at Sile or up the river mouths to the port cities, the Shepherds would be in real trouble. They've committed almost their whole army to the area around Memphis, where the Black Lands end and the Red Lands begin. They want Memphis, and they want it bad. Last month a soothsayer told Salitis he might take Memphis but that he'd never conquer it—whatever that means—and Salitis had the man beheaded on the spot! They also told me there's been disease in the Shepherd camps—and that's not all. Word's come that the Assyrians, in the lands north of the Valley of the Two Rivers, have a new leader who's led them northward all the way to the ancestral home of the Shepherds. Travelers reaching the delta cities have seen towns laid waste that Shepherd swords once protected. They've seen the Assyrians setting great grass fires across the plains, burning up precious graze in Shepherd pastoral country. Rumor has it that some of the Shepherd-occupied cities, lightly garrisoned, have risen against their overlords and overthrown them. Mari's one. So is Carchemish, which the Shepherds rebuilt with their own fortifications."

"Then . . . they've convinced you? That they can win?"

"Y-yes, Tuya. But . . . last night . . ." He swallowed

hard, his voice hoarse. "Last night I had to prove myself. I had to kill the man. The knife, it went in. . . ."

Tuya pursed her lips, shook her head. "Poor Anab," she said, compassion mixed with irony in her tone. "Poor former Shepherd sympathizer, whom Anab had to kill. Poor wife and family of the dead man. Poor everybody. What a dreadful time to be living in." She patted his still-quivering shoulder, feeling the tension in him as she touched him. "And what now, Anab?" she said. "I take it that, being 'blooded,' as you say, you can't leave them. If you tried they'd cut your throat, right?"

He nodded miserably.

"That's what I thought. So—what's next? I gather your people are the ones who've been raiding the garrisons. Come to think of it, wasn't there a Shepherd officer murdered, some time back, in a brothel over in—?" She stopped, her eyes wide. "Why, I was right there! And so were Onuris and Zosar, for that matter! I even had a little run-in with Zosar in the alley!"

"Yes," Anab said. "That was their work. They appear to pick their targets at random, but in fact it's in a prearranged pattern that the Phoenix has devised. Acts against the Shepherd army alternate with acts against civilian traitors. And next time—" His eyes turned toward her imploringly and he started to speak, but he faltered and said nothing.

"Yes? Go on. Get it out!"

"Well, Tuya, I don't know what to do now. Striking against an outright traitor is one thing. I can learn to live with my conscience over that—although it's hard, I tell you, really hard. Afterward I feel dirty. I feel slimy all over. But this . . ."

"But what? Who's next? Tell me, Anab!"

He spoke quickly, almost inaudibly. "The next strike is against Wenis and his household. And one of the people I'm supposed to help kill is Ben-Hadad."

She looked at him, at his terrible, tragic face, and saw the hurt, the horror in his eyes. Only little by little did the full shock of what he had said begin to come through to her.

A long moment passed. Then, thinking fast and

decisively, she said, "I've got to go with you. It's the only way for me to help him."

"B-but they won't let you."

"The devil they won't. In times like these they can use every extra hand they can get."

"Tuya, there aren't any women in the group—"

"There's one now. Besides, Zosar knows me. He knew me enough to back down once when I drew my knife on him. He knows I'm a faster hand than he is."

A stranger approached down the narrow alley and passed the entrance of the little courtyard. They waited until his footsteps faded, then Anab said, "Tuya—I know you've got a quick hand. But could you strike? Could you kill someone?"

She glanced over her shoulder and then returned her gaze to his face. She pulled him a little closer and whispered, "Anab, don't you tell anyone what I'm about to tell you or you're a dead man. I'm not kidding."

"I won't. But—"

"Anab, I've already killed a man."

"You've what?"

"Killed a man. If you call the Shepherds men. I'm not sure what I'd call this one. Anab, I know how you feel. I've gone through the same thing." She let out a long breath, slowly. "It was a Shepherd soldier, a captain of horse, I think. He tried to rape me. If I hadn't put a knife in under his ribs he'd have done it, too, and thrown me into the alley afterward, not giving it a second thought. He certainly wouldn't have felt any pangs of conscience. To them we're not people, just animals of a lower kind. I know—I found out afterward that the same man had raped half a dozen girls in my quarter. He'd killed one of them, too, when she threatened to complain to his superiors. No, Anab, I've got over my bad conscience."

Anab just stared at her openmouthed for a moment. "Tuya! I never knew—"

"Nobody knew," she said. "And thank heaven, otherwise I'd be food for the crows by now. So I'm in your hands now. If you ever tell on me—"

Anab shook his head violently from side to side, and there was a new earnestness in his voice when he spoke.

"No, never. I'd never tell. But, Tuya, they'll still not let you—"

"They'll have to," she said. "I'll barge right in. I'll make them accept me. Just you watch. I'm very persuasive when I care to be."

She stood, hands on narrow hips, feet apart, almost a caricature of the tough-minded little street-orphan she was. Her smile was disarming. "And look, Anab," she said, "I take back what I said about your telling on me. I know you won't. You're not really the back-stabbing little turncoat people would like to think you are. You've had a rough deal in life, and sometimes you're tempted to try to get back at people for their stupid thoughtlessness. But I know there's a decent streak in you, even if nobody else does." She grinned. "Don't worry, I won't tell anyone. I realize you survive by making people afraid of what you might do. But I know it's mostly a pose."

"Pose? Get along with you."

"Not a chance, my friend. You're stuck with me now. Do you think I'm going to let you out of my sight anytime before the raid on Wenis's house? No, Anab. I'm going with you, and I'm going as a member of the Phoenix's little band, whether they like it or not."

As she spoke, she could feel a new presence near them. Something touched her leg, and she looked down to see Ben-Hadad's little Canaanite dog, the one that had come with him across the desert all the way from the northern lands. "Lion!" she said, reaching down to pet the little animal's shaggy head. The dog danced delightedly around her, showing his obvious affection for her. She smiled; she'd cultivated the dog's friendship from the first, hoping to ingratiate herself with his master. "Lion, what are you doing out on the streets? You know what the Shepherds think about stray dogs."

"Ben-Hadad left the dog with his landlady," Anab said. "Otherwise he would have followed him to Wenis's place. Ben-Hadad gave her some money to feed him, but the moment he was gone, she turned the dog out." His hand reached down and ruffled the dog's fur. "He follows people that he likes. It seems he's latched on to you now."

Lion danced away from him, but did not bark. The dog stayed just beyond arm's reach.

"What a rotten thing to do," the girl said. "I know her. She's a mean, ugly old pig. Just you wait. She could wind up having a little accident. Slops poured on her head, say, as she walked down the street in her festival finery. . . ."

"Best forget about it," Anab said. "You can take care of the dog now."

"So I can," she said, crouching next to the animal. "Although I think Lion's a lot like me: He doesn't need too much caring for—but he likes it when he can get it, nevertheless. Isn't that right, Lion?" The dog wagged his tail. "He made it all the way across that awful desert between Sile and Canaan, and that's the worst country in the world, the soldiers from the fort used to say. No oases for days and days. Lion must be able to live without water or food for as long as a camel can. Isn't that right, fellow?" The dog nuzzled her like a cat and danced back, full of energy.

Tuya looked up at Anab, the confident smile back on her face. "All right, Anab. Lead me to those friends of yours. You're about to get a lesson in persuasion."

III

"I still don't like it," Zosar said. He scowled back over his shoulder as he and Onuris walked side by side down the high road to the rendezvous. "We've never had a woman on a raid before, and everything has worked perfectly well up to now without one."

Onuris's voice was reassuring, soothing, a peacemaker's. "It'll all go just fine," he said. "And we can use all the competent help we can get. Besides, Tuya isn't like most women. Remember how she faced us down in the alley? You certainly stepped back when she waved that knife of hers. You could tell that she knew how to use it. I'm not saying you backed down—don't get me wrong. But you knew enough to act prudently."

"That may be," Zosar said peevishly. "But what if she's caught, for example?"

"From what Anab says, and a few others I talked to who know of her, there's nobody—not even Benu himself—who's less likely to talk under pressure."

"Confound it, I still don't like it."

"You don't have to. I'll keep her at the other end of the action, if you like."

Zosar glanced over his shoulder again. "And what about that stupid dog?" he hissed. "Why on earth is a damned dog coming along?"

"The dog belongs to the boy Ben-Hadad. She's going to use it to find him."

"It'll bark. It'll alert everyone."

"That's a Canaanite dog. It's a good breed, if you like dogs. They don't bark much, so they don't attract attention."

"Ah, when I think what Benu is going to say when he hears what we've brought along with us!"

"He'll probably approve, if we pull off this raid. He's a realist above all else. You know that."

The raiders did not travel as a group, but walked in small clumps of people, looking like shoppers returning from market. Two groups back, Anab walked with Tuya and the dog, Lion. "Are you sure you want to go along with this?" Anab was saying, for the third time since they had set out.

Tuya sighed in exasperation. "Listen—I know too much," she said. "I can't back out now, Anab. If I did, Benu would have to kill me to shut me up. And that's the way I want it."

Anab shook his head. "You must love Ben-Hadad very much, Tuya. Perhaps too much for your own good."

"What do you mean?"

"I . . . well, think about it, Tuya. He's never returned your affections. He went off and didn't give any of us, his friends, a second thought. And rumor has it that he's more than half promised to Tamshas, Wenis's beautiful daughter. If the marriage goes through—"

"Enough. You don't have to rub it in. If you'd ever been in love, you'd know that it isn't something you have much control over. I can't help myself. Really, Anab, I tried to look at it reasonably. I tried to dismiss him as out of my reach. I even tried to hate him. But all the while I knew that if he were to call me, I'd still come running, panting like a deer." She sighed. "Might as well be honest with yourself, at least."

"As you please. But, look—that should be the rendez-vous up ahead. Isn't that one of Akaba's groves?"

"Yes, I'm sure of it. Anab, there's no chance we'll meet this Phoenix fellow tonight, is there?"

"It's highly unlikely. He wouldn't waste his time. Zosar said this is only a minor mission, harassing the turncoat class."

"Minor? It may be to you. It certainly isn't to me." She smiled as she strode beside him. Somehow the mere fact of being allowed to come along on the raid had relieved some of her abiding sense of loneliness, of emptiness. She felt strong, confident, in control.

In the west the sun prepared to go down; the sky was full of lovely muted colors. There was a soft fragrance of evening in the air, and overhead, as the benevolent and fertile delta lands prepared for the coming night, small birds flew in low, swooping arcs, seeking the insects that came out only at dusk. The air was deliciously cool; soon low fogs would hang on the knolls and highlands.

Late in the night, by the light of a pair of tallow candles, Ben-Hadad studied his game problem. He sat, legs crossed, before the low table on which the little game board stood, pieces in place where his mentors had put them.

He raised his hand—and then lowered it. "No," he said. He looked down at the astragals again, lying where he had thrown them. It was curious, he thought, how his luck tended to pick up when he used the knucklebones instead of the four wooden throw sticks. Was it because they were once part of a living animal? He couldn't explain it. His luck also seemed to improve when he used the ivory "fingers," or *djebao*, instead of those made of wood or stone.

Again he thought over his move. He'd thrown twice: The first throw netted him one house and an extra throw, and the second had read "two houses, end of turn." As the rules of the game permitted, he could put his moves to any of a number of uses. He could, for instance, move any of his dancers the combined total of three houses. Or he could move any piece two spaces and another piece one space. He surveyed the board carefully. His mentors had set up a difficult end game problem for him, one in which a man, they had said, might with luck and skill crush his overwhelmingly favorably situated opponent in no more than four casts of the knucklebones. Or—they'd said this while exchanging knowing smiles—he might get stuck in a ghastly trap from which it would be impossible to extricate himself; a single move, made wrong, could end the game in the opponent's favor.

"Ah," he said, suddenly reaching forward. His hand closed on the lead dancer, in the House of the Towrope. He started to move, feeling confident, his mind swiftly racing ahead, thinking out the possible permutations of moves his opponent could make. . . .

And then he stopped again. He put the dancer back down where it had been. He looked back at his next dancer, sitting on the House of the Ba, and frowned, scratching his head. If the second dancer moved only one space, to the House of Spitting, and the dancer behind it, on the House of Life square, moved forward two squares to the House of Mut . . .

He sighed very deeply and let his shoulders slump. It was very late; his two candles were probably the only lights burning in all the sleeping quarters of the great villa. He remembered what Wenis had told him: "Now, don't stay up late again. You need your sleep." And it was true: He was tired, very tired.

On the other hand, sometimes when you were very tired, so tired that you had passed the point of exhaustion and your mind would not work in the usual channels, something else took over—some power that you hadn't been able to draw upon during the normal waking day.

When this happened, sometimes the moves would have an unconscious, uncontrolled brilliance you could never have achieved otherwise. It was, he guessed, something like what had often happened to his old friend Joseph, back in Canaan, when he'd go to sleep and have a dream that would somehow tell him with great accuracy what was going to happen in the future. . . .

Joseph! he thought. *What has happened to you? Will I ever see you again? Will you ever be returned to your homeland, to the father who loves you so?*

He sighed regretfully. *Not at my hands,* he thought. *What a fool I was! I've failed both Jacob and myself. Who was I to think that I could come all the way here to this strange land by myself, without a friend in the world but Lion, and find you and bring you back?*

His mind had begun to wander, though. Lion! Dear old Lion! He'd hardly had time to think about his dog for days, he'd been so busy studying. They'd scarcely given him time between game problems and lectures on theory to eat and sleep, much less to think about his friends. . . .

A pang of regret went through him. How he missed his many friends: Anab and Tuya and . . . But no, it was probably those two he missed most, them and dear old Lion. Did they miss him, now that he'd been spirited away to this cold, half-empty palace where he never had time to do anything other than tangle with one game problem after another and play people who'd been brought here to compete with him?

He wondered if they had forgiven him. Anab had seemed so hurt when he'd learned that Ben-Hadad was leaving for Wenis's house to study senet playing. It hadn't even been possible to mention the further tutelage he'd been receiving in the game of twenty squares, the Shepherds' game; Wenis had sworn him to silence on this. He'd tried to cushion the blow to Anab by sending him money from time to time. It was only fair, since Anab had lost his income when Ben-Hadad had left him. Still, it wasn't at all like seeing a friend or talking to him.

After all, you didn't make genuine friends often in life. He himself had hardly had a friend in the world before Lion had come along. Of course there'd been Joseph.

But who else? Only Anab and Tuya. And now? There were no friends to be had here in this chilly manor. Even Wenis, despite his many assurances of friendship, was more like a partner—a coldly manipulative partner—than a friend.

And Tamshas? Ben-Hadad shook his head in disappointment. They might have become friends, actually, if there hadn't always been present the undercurrent of her father's increasingly obvious plans for the two of them. She wasn't a bad sort; she'd probably make a marvelous wife over the years. Not only would she bring to a marriage her own startling beauty, her fat dower, and her family's power and influence in the kingdom, but being her father's daughter, she also had a good mind for business, for protocol, for all the little intrigues that went on at this level of the world. She was an astute judge of people, too, and could help a man thread his way through the treacheries of court life without making fatal missteps.

It was just that . . . well, why did he sit here thinking about her as if she were a prize racehorse he was considering buying? Or, more precisely, some racehorse Wenis was considering buying for him, whether or not he happened to ride, to like horses, or to want one of his own just now? If Tamshas were really the model among women that she seemed to be, why did he feel as though he was being rushed into marriage headlong? Why did he begin to feel within himself the first stirrings of resentment about the whole arrangement?

It had happened so fast! Wenis had sprung the idea on him so swiftly and deftly, that he'd hardly had time to say yes or no. In any case, he wasn't too good at saying no to people in the first place. So here he was doing Wenis's bidding, getting ready to play matches Wenis had arranged for him instead of those Anab would otherwise have arranged for him. What an extraordinarily agreeable fellow he'd been, letting himself be manipulated this way! What had happened to the Ben-Hadad who had abandoned a promising apprenticeship and journeyed to Egypt with one aim firmly in mind—to find his friend Joseph?

He absentmindedly fingered one of the dancers on the board and longed, suddenly and deeply, for the old

days, and the old Ben-Hadad, and for his old friends: for
the faithful Anab, and Tuya (his luck, wasn't she?). Why
couldn't he have brought her along? Wenis could have
indulged him a bit. He missed the streets, the bazaars,
the friendly greetings on every streetcorner from all the
people who knew him and liked him. He missed dear old
Lion! How many days had it been since he'd been awakened in the morning by Lion's licking of his face? How
long had it been?

He looked up from the board. His eyes came into
focus. He blinked, gazed at the open door, then blinked
again.

"I m-must be dreaming," he said. "Lion? Lion, is that
you?"

The little dog stood splayfooted before him, his tail
wagging furiously. He hesitated, then took a few steps
forward. Always prudent, always cautious. *Lion!*

Ben-Hadad opened his arms, and the dog jumped
into them. "Lion!" he half shouted, hugging the dog close,
forgetting himself for a moment. "Lion, how did you get
in here? For heaven's sake! How did you get away from
my landlady? Didn't she treat you well? Did you come all
this way to see me?"

But then he noticed a figure standing in the door. His
gaze swept rapidly upward from the brown bare feet on
the stone floor. He started. "*T-Tuya*—" But her fingers
went to her lips, shushing him.

"Quiet," she said. She entered the room and pulled
the door shut hastily behind her. "Be quiet, please. You're
in terrible danger."

"Danger?" he said, in a full voice. "But—"

"Please!" she said, again making silencing motions.
"Keep quiet. It's absolutely essential that nobody hear us.
Including the people I came here with."

"People you came here with?" he said. "I don't understand, Tuya. What are you doing—?"

"For goodness' sake, Ben-Hadad, some people have
come here to kill you. You and Wenis and that daughter of
his. Everyone in the whole household except the slaves.
The only way I could save you was to come along with
them, once I'd learned about it."

"But, Tuya—why would anyone want to . . . ?"

"Oh, for goodness' sake, Ben-Hadad. Sometimes I wonder if you've got your head sewn on properly. Haven't you ever heard of a man called Benu? The Phoenix?"

"Yes, I have. He's that fellow who's been raiding the outlying Shepherd posts and assassinating Shepherd officers in the city. But what has that to do with—?"

"Listen to me," she said, growing impatient with his obtuseness. "He's also after people who, according to him, have betrayed their country by going over to the Shepherd side. People who've cooperated with the new regime and wormed their way into favor with the Shepherd overlords. Do you get me? People like Wenis. Wenis is to be killed tonight. This place will be burned to the ground. By morning there'll be nothing left but a burned-out ruin full of dead bodies. Wenis's. Tamshas's. Yours, Ben-Hadad, if I can't get you out of here first somehow!"

"But—"

"Don't talk. Just listen, will you? I don't have much time. I heard about it through Anab. He blundered into this group and couldn't get out when they told him he had to come here and help kill you. When I learned what was going on, I joined him. It was the only way to get here and try to save you. I didn't know where your room was, so I brought Lion along, knowing he'd lead me to you. Now we have to find some way of smuggling you out of here before someone sticks a knife in you."

"But—your friends. What will they do when they find you've let me off?"

"I'll think about that later," she said, looking small but feisty in the flickering light of the two candles. "Do you have a sword here with you? A knife? A weapon of any kind?"

"I've a sword I made back in Canaan," he said. "Why?"

"Can you use it?"

"Yes, I think so. But—"

"Then get it. Forget everything else. There's no time—"

Through the open outside window they heard a scream, then another. In the hall there was the sound of scuffling. Someone shouted, "Here! You! What are you doing?"

Metal clashed against metal. And there was a new scent in
the night air: smoke.

"Come on!" Tuya said in a loud whisper. "Let's get
out of here!"

IV

Out in the hall there was fighting—and flames leaped
from the doorway of the great end room. Silhouetted
against the fire they could see a large man—Wenis's slave,
who guarded the patio entrance—battling two of Benu's
people. "Come on!" Tuya said. "This way!" And with Lion
dancing at her bare heels, she took off in the opposite
direction.

Ben-Hadad brought up the rear, feeling like a fool
with the sword in his hand. He was an armorer, not a
fighter; armorers made swords, they did not wield them.
He was of divided mind about his present position.
Shouldn't he be helping to fight off the people who had
invaded Wenis's house? Yet here he was—

"Come *on!*" she said up ahead. "Don't lag behind!
They'll kill you!"

He bit his lip and followed her, thinking all the while:
*What am I doing? Why, I'm ruining my life! When Wenis
hears of this . . .*

But something impelled his feet forward as he jogged
lightly along, wearing only the white loincloth he'd been
wearing when she'd found him. Tuya had never lied to
him before—the house was, after all, on fire, just as she'd
said it would be. And that fight down the hall had looked
very much in earnest.

At the corner she disappeared. Lion paused for a
second to look back at him, as if to say, "Master! What are
you waiting for?" Ben-Hadad increased his pace, still unsure just what he was doing. . . .

But when he came around the corner into the main
hall, which ran the entire length of the house, he saw, to
his horror, Tuya struggling in the arms of two of Wenis's

servants. He recognized the man who ran the wine press—a fat giant, almost as wide as he was tall. He held one of the girl's arms as she struggled impotently. Her other arm was held by the other man, one of the field slaves. "Run!" the girl screamed, wriggling and kicking. "Don't let them get you too! Run!"

Ben-Hadad paused for no more than a blink, his heart sinking—and then his anger took over. "Let go of her!" he said. The wine maker merely grinned. He had been one of the servants who had resented him, a newcomer, from the first.

Ben-Hadad's hand gripped the sword tightly and he dashed forward. As he did, Lion went for the calf of the field slave, sinking his sharp little teeth deep into the flesh. The man screamed, releasing Tuya and cringing back against the wall as Lion skipped out of reach, then darted forward again, this time attacking an ankle.

With one of her arms free, Tuya pounded on her powerful captor with her tiny fist. She couldn't quite reach the knife on her other hip; the man's gross body had pinned her to the wall, jamming the knife in its leather scabbard behind her.

Ben-Hadad now lunged forward with his sword. It wounded the fat man in the side, but the blow did not go in deep enough to be lethal. Ben-Hadad prepared to strike again, but the fat man's hand was abnormally fast for a person of his bulk. It gripped Ben-Hadad's sword on the blade; Ben-Hadad pulled—and the blade emerged red from the man's hand. At almost the same instant, however, the fat man's other hand had darted to the knife in the girl's belt and wrenched it away from her. "All right!" he shouted, still pinning the girl to the wall with his massive body, while clutching his bleeding hand to his side. "Lay down the weapon, boy, or she's dead! I'll cut her throat right here and now!"

Ben-Hadad hesitated, his frightened gaze darting from one face to the other. Behind the fat man, the field slave had turned tail and was running down the hall as fast as his skinny legs would carry him.

"D-don't do it!" Tuya cried out. She was about to say something else when the fat man pressed the blade of the dagger against her neck, where the big artery showed against her fine skin. "R-run, Ben-Hadad. . . ."

The boy stepped back. The hilt of the sword pressed painfully into his hand, he held it so hard. "Tuya," he said, "I . . . I can't let him. . . ." His grip loosened on the sword. He held it in his two hands, lightly. He could feel the fat man's blood on the blade. . . .

Then, seemingly from nowhere, Lion sprang forward, straight for the wine maker's face in a mighty leap. When the little dog fell back to the floor, Ben-Hadad could see a terrible slash marring the fat man's face, opening his cheek to the bone.

Tuya, able to slip free at last, dived for the floor. At the same moment Ben-Hadad lunged forward. The fat man expertly parried the sword thrust with Tuya's knife and, recovering with amazing speed, sliced broadside at Ben-Hadad's naked belly. The force of the blow would have cut Ben-Hadad nearly in half, but the boy spun away and the knife's sharp blade only kissed his back lightly. Just above the red birthmark of his people a thin red line appeared.

The big man lunged, but Lion intercepted his knife arm. Sinking sharp fangs into the man's wrist, the dog hung from the meaty arm like some grisly appendage. Behind the wine maker, Tuya, scrambling off the floor, grabbed for a clay statuette in a nearby niche. She heaved it at him with all her might. It shattered harmlessly against his broad back, but the distraction was enough to get his eyes away for a split second—just as Lion's grip relaxed and the dog fell to the foor, got its legs under it, and prepared for another foray. . . .

. . . and Ben-Hadad, lunging with every bit of his young strength behind the blow, sprang forward, burying the sharp, broad blade in the man's midsection.

Ben-Hadad would never entirely forget the shock of that moment. The wine maker's eyes went wide, and his mouth opened to speak. He drew back with the knife, as if to strike—but the action was only a reflex. As the knife fell from his hand, life left his eyes forever. They were still wide open, unseeing, as his great, gross body collapsed to the floor.

Ben-Hadad left the sword in him. He stepped back slowly. "I . . . I didn't mean it," he said. "I . . ."

"Come on!" Tuya said in a tense voice. She had recovered quickly. "There's no time for—"

But then she saw, in the red glow from some distant fire, Wenis's daughter Tamshas. She was standing not ten feet away, her hand over her beautiful mouth, brown eyes wide. She was in her nightdress, hair disheveled, feet bare. Yet everything about her was exquisite, perfectly fashioned. She looked like one of the goddesses in a temple painting.

"Ben-Hadad?" the girl said, unbelieving. "What are you doing? Where's my father? Why—?"

"There's no time to explain," he said. "I . . ."

Tuya stepped forward. "Look, girl, we don't want to hurt you. Just get back into your room and lie low. I won't tell anyone I've seen—"

"Ben-Hadad! You killed him!" Tamshas said, her voice half hysterical. "Why—why, you're one of them! Father! *Father!*" Her words became a shrill scream.

They could hear footsteps pounding back down the hall, around the corner.

Ben-Hadad tried to approach her. "No!" he said. "Tamshas, it's all a mistake. . . ."

"You killed him!" she screamed. "Don't touch me! Don't hurt me!" She backed away down the hall and her screams rose in intensity. Just then two guards rounded the corner.

"You stupid little bitch!" Tuya said, and grabbed Ben-Hadad's arm, dragging him away. Ben-Hadad recovered almost immediately and set out after her as she scampered down the long hall. They could hear the guards' footfalls behind them, getting closer, closer. . . . Ben-Hadad paused just long enough to pull over one of the shoulder-high vases standing in the hall and roll it at the pursuers' legs. He saw it bowl the first man over, then took to his heels.

Once in the courtyard, they ducked a sudden rain of arrows from the darkness beyond the low bushes that lined the reflecting pool. "Don't shoot, you dummies!" the girl cried. "It's me! They're right behind me!" She led Ben-Hadad by the arm into the darkness, beyond the light that now shone from the burning villa. Safe behind a clump of ornamental shrubs, they crouched, Lion close beside them, to look back at the scene.

The villa burned out of control, with no one to fight the fire. Along one wing they could see flames leaping from open windows. One man—Ben-Hadad recognized Wenis's brutal overseer, Ankhu, a man widely hated among the slaves—leaped screaming out a window as they watched, his clothing on fire. The guards who had been chasing them down the hall now appeared at the front door, only to meet a volley of arrows. The unseen bowmen's fire was more accurate this time; one of the guards took four arrows in the chest, staggering with the shock of each. He stood for a moment, his body swaying. Then he fell on his face, rolling down the low staircase. The other man, badly wounded, retreated back into the burning house.

Now from the other side of the house came Anab, small and skinny, running as fast as his legs would carry him. In hot pursuit came two men, one armed with a spear. As Tuya and Ben-Hadad watched in horror, the spearman stopped, poised, the deadly javelin aimed at the fugitive's back.

"Anab!" Ben-Hadad yelled. "Hit the ground! Quick!"

Anab hesitated, his fear and confusion apparent. Then he dived to one side, just as the spear cut through the air right where he'd been. The spearman stood watching his cast—and caught an arrow in the throat. He clutched his neck, tearing at the shaft with his fingers.

"Anab! Over here!" Ben-Hadad dashed forward to grab his friend by the hand and haul him to safety behind the bush, just as bowmen from the house appeared and began launching their own arrows into the darkness from where the attackers' shafts had been coming. "Come on!" Ben-Hadad told the two of them, hauling them farther back into the courtyard's blackness, out of range.

His eyes blinked at the dark. "Let's see," he said. "The gate should be over there. Are your people holding it yet?" Anab and Tuya looked at each other for an answer, but neither spoke. "Well, we'll just have to find out. Tuya—where's Lion?"

"Don't worry, he's right here. Ben-Hadad! Over

there—I see the gate guard! He's on our side! Follow me. . . ."

The gate guard, a short, swarthy man, looked them over. "Hey," he said, eyeing Ben-Hadad, "I don't know this face. What's going on here?" He drew the sword from his belt, his eyes wary, distrustful.

"He's a pris—" Anab began.

Tuya cut him off. "He's one of us," she said. "As much as any of us is now. He killed his man tonight, saving my hide. And he risked his life to save Anab." She stood her ground, returning the guard's glare. "He's committed. He can't turn back now. They've seen him; they know his name. He can't even go back to Avaris. Wenis's daughter saw him kill one of her father's guards and then she got away. She can bear witness against him. If he shows his face among the Shepherds, he's a dead man. What better credentials do you want? Let us through!"

The guard was still looking suspiciously at Ben-Hadad. "Then where are you going to take him?" he said. "If he can't go back to Avaris—"

"Neither can I," said Tuya. "They've seen my face, too. As long as the daughter lives, I've no home left in the city." She shrugged. "Well, it wasn't much of a home, anyhow. There's only one place for us to go. To the encampment. Anab is going to take us there. Aren't you, Anab?"

"I—" Anab gulped, trying to get his voice to stop breaking. "Y-yes, Tuya."

"You heard him," the girl said, her manner still decisive. "If there's any question about the loyalty of any of us, it's for Benu himself to judge. Isn't that right?"

The guard made an unpleasant face. Behind his silence they could hear, in the long moment while he made up his mind, the sound of the roaring fire, the screams of the dying. "All right," he said. "Go. But don't tell who it was that let you through."

"It's a deal," the girl said. "We never saw you before." She turned to her friends. "Come on, you two. Let's get out of here."

*   *   *

Clouds had obscured the moon during the raid on
Wenis's villa. Now the clouds had passed, and light shone
down on the high road as they struck out across the fields,
following the raised track.

For a long time they did not speak. Even Lion, who
had scampered about in the first moments of their night
trek, had responded to the serious, pensive mood and now
trotted along easily beside his young master. From time to
time a wisp of cloud would drift across the moon, and
darkness would briefly descend, but for the most part the
road stayed quite visible, and they held a good pace.

Tuya, bringing up the rear, watched Ben-Hadad's
broad, naked back. The little cut had closed above the
lion's-paw birthmark; there was not another mark on his
body to show for their adventure. *Well*, she thought, *at
least I spared him that, if nothing else.*

But it was more than that. She had saved his life,
hadn't she? Even if it was at the expense of his good
name, his reputation, his home in Avaris. Surely that must
be worth something, even if it did mean the life she'd
saved was ruined, ruined beyond recall.

Suddenly the letdown began to hit her, and it got
worse with every passing moment. Suddenly it seemed to
her that virtually anything she could have done would
have been better than what she had in fact done. If she
hadn't come along, he still might well have survived the
attack. It was evident that there were going to be a few
survivors of the raid. And most likely, among them would
be the beautiful Tamshas, who would inform on Ben-
Hadad, making a wanted fugitive of him just on the brink
of the greatest success he'd ever dreamed of!

Tuya, half closing her eyes, conjured up once again
the image of Wenis's daughter: soft tresses hanging down
on both sides of a face so strikingly beautiful that it took
your breath away just to look at her. Wide-set eyes of
almond shape; a splendid, straight nose; heavy, soft lips
made for kissing; and the head set on a long, slender neck,
the neck of a goddess! Below, a body of enviable shapeliness:
high, exquisitely formed breasts visible through the transparent gown she had worn to bed; a narrow waist above
generous, rounded hips and long, tapering legs; delicately

formed hands and feet—soft, no doubt, soft for caressing, unlike her own utilitarian hands and feet, callused and, at the moment, lamentably dusty.

Even her voice, Tamshas's voice, had been sweet and beautifully modulated—until she had started yelling so. No wonder these rich men's daughters were so highly prized! What man could resist them, lovely and well kept as they were? Even without the rich dowries they brought to a marriage?

Compare it all with her—skinny, short Tuya, her uncoiffed hair cut off with a sharp knife every few weeks and left to grow wild; her small-breasted, meager body, with its narrow, unwomanly hips and short legs; her merely acceptable face—acceptable, perhaps, for the wife of a second-rate brewer, but nothing to capture the heart of a man used to the likes of Tamshas.

No. She was no prize catch, and certainly not for Ben-Hadad, who'd come to expect more of life. She'd have done better to let him alone. Besides, she'd ruined her own life as well, tonight. She'd taken part in a raid by wanted criminals, enemies of the Shepherd state. She'd been seen by someone who could identify her later. She could never go back to Avaris, either. No, there was no place left for any of them but the rebels' camp, wherever *that* was. The old life was gone. Ahead lay only whatever she could salvage from her moment of headstrong foolishness.

She held back the tears and, with great effort, got a grip on herself. Whatever the future held, she'd have to make the best of it. Even if—as she suspected and feared with every fiber of her being—Ben-Hadad came to hate her for her part in this evening's activities.

V

After perhaps two hours' walk they turned sharply westward, crossed a farmer's field, skirted a grove of olive trees, and entered a neglected stretch of semidesert. Tuya

wished she had worn sandals on the raid; the ground was
hard, dry, and uneven, and bruised her feet terribly.

Passing between two tall palms, she stopped abruptly,
almost bowling into Ben-Hadad and Anab. Before them
stood a semicircle of six men, bows strung and drawn. She
shrank back instinctively; in the dim light it seemed that
every arrow was pointing straight at her heart. "Wait," she
said. "W-we're friends."

"Let me handle it," Anab said. He glided forward
toward the bowmen. "Does anyone here recognize me?"
he said, turning his ruined face from side to side in the
light of the moon. The bows lowered and the bowmen
slackened the strings. "The password is 'Scourge of the
Herds.' Satisfied?"

The bowmen melted away into the shadows. Only
one of their number remained. "Anab I know," he said.
"But who are these two?"

"The girl is Tuya," Anab said. "She's blooded. At
least one Shepherd has felt her knife by now." Tuya
nodded in agreement with the adroit half-truth. Anab
hadn't said precisely *when* she'd killed her Shepherd, but
he hadn't lied about it either. "The other one is Ben-
Hadad. He came over to our side during the raid. He
killed a Shepherd guard and they saw him do it. He's
firmly committed to us. Even if he wanted to go back, he
couldn't."

The guard seemed satisfied with the explanation, but
as Anab turned to leave, he grabbed him by the elbow.
"Tell me about the raid," he said. "I'm still angry at not
being able to go along. My kin have felt the lash of
Wenis's overseer. I owe him a death, at least."

"Wenis is dead," Anab said. "I saw him fall. To his
credit he died with a sword in his hand, fighting like a
man. He—"

"Wenis? Dead?" Ben-Hadad said. For some reason it
hadn't occurred to him that Wenis might have died in the
raid. "B-but—"

"Later," Tuya said, shushing him hastily. She spoke
to the guard: "His daughter may have escaped. She's the
one who saw Ben-Hadad kill the wine steward."

"You killed that fat swine?" the guard said. "My

congratulations. He had a cousin of mine scourged until he couldn't stand. He was widely hated. A blow well struck."

Ben-Hadad was at a loss for words. "I—I'm still getting over the idea of having killed someone," he said at last in a toneless voice.

"You'll get used to it soon enough," the guard said. "Meanwhile, welcome to our number." He turned back to Anab. "The villa—you burned it?"

"One whole wing was in flames when we left," he said. "And that overseer you mentioned—I saw him fall from a window, his clothing in flames. If the fall didn't kill him, the burns probably will. If he lives he'll be a cripple, barely fit for a beggar's bowl in the street."

"Good," the guard said. "Benu will want to hear of this. Go to the tents and await him. I'll pass the word back to him by one of the men."

Anab seemed offended by the curtness of the order. "I suppose," he said, "that our noble leader must be too busy at this ungodly hour to hear news of the successful raid right away."

"Watch your tongue, half face!" the guard snapped. "There was a raid on one of the Shepherd outposts yesterday afternoon. A number of our men were hurt. Benu hasn't left their side since they were brought in. And I might remind you, my sharp-tongued friend, he would have done the same for you, if you'd been one of those who had come back with a grievous wound."

Anab looked genuinely contrite. "I apologize for my hasty words," he mumbled. "I find it hard getting used to the notion that you can trust anyone to be true and upright."

"Well, however few the number of people you can trust," the guard said, "Benu's name heads the list. If you've been loyal to him, you'll find no more staunch and steadfast friend. Now get going—and stop at the cook tent on your way, if you wish. There's food and drink, as always, for participants in a raid, successful or not. And you can brag about your exploits to the cooks. Everyone else does."

As the group passed, he clapped Anab on the shoulder reassuringly. "Good work. Every successful raid is a blow struck for freedom from the invader's hand!"

At the cook tent, as the guard had said, there was food waiting for them: sausages, figs, dates, and flat bread; and wine, too: a rough red wine, a far cry from the delicate vintages Ben-Hadad had been used to in Wenis's household, but plentiful and soothing.

Anab, finding that his hunger had returned, wolfed down two whole sausages before drinking, then packed a piece of flat bread with a third sausage and devoured part of it as well, all the while peering intently off into the bushes. Tuya wondered what he was looking at, but soon found the answer. Putting a warning finger to his lips and motioning her to keep silent, Anab waited until none of the workers at the cook tent was watching—then flipped the remnants of his sausage to the base of a clump of bushes at the edge of the firelight. As all three of them watched, a small gray snout darted out from the darkness and snatched the meat away.

"It's Lion," Anab whispered. "He's afraid of all these strange people. But better not let the cook catch you feeding him."

They all laughed, then Anab lay back on one elbow as Tuya made up a meal for Ben-Hadad before feeding herself.

"Anab," she said. "Benu looks after his people, then?"

"Yes," he said. "And not just by feeding them. Once one of his men was captured in a raid. Benu volunteered to replace him if they'd let him go. Of course the men wouldn't let him. In the end Benu led a rescue party and got the man out, at great risk to himself. And, Ben-Hadad, it's strange, but in a camp full of people all puffed up with pride, the one thing everyone agrees upon is that Benu is braver than anyone here. In a battle, he doesn't stay behind the lines and tell everyone what to do, the way a Shepherd general would. No—he *leads*." He bit off a piece of his remaining bread, chewed for a moment, his odd face working asymmetrically. "He's the first man into battle and the last man out. If one of us falls it'll be Benu, often as not, who carries the poor devil out on his back."

"No wonder they all seem to love him," Tuya said. "What is he like? Have you met him?"

Anab took a swig of wine. "No—not yet. But from what I've heard, he's cold and efficient. I guess you have to be, though, to fight the Shepherds and win."

"Does anybody know about his background?" Tuya asked.

"If they do they're keeping their own counsel. I would guess, though, that he was a soldier. He knows what he's doing. He plans everything, usually—but he also seems to know when someone else has a good idea, when it would be smarter to shut up and listen. If the idea's better than his, he'll go along with it—and if it succeeds, it'll be the other person, not him, who gets the credit. He's scrupulously fair about that, they tell me."

Tuya noticed that Ben-Hadad wasn't listening. She wondered what he felt like just now, having killed a man with his own hand for the first time. She remembered her own sick confusion, the night after she'd had to kill the Shepherd who'd tried to rape her. She hadn't been able to sleep; she'd been beyond comforting. . . .

She touched his arm lightly and spoke to him. "Ben-Hadad, are you all right? Is there anything we can do for you?"

He turned, and she could see the worry on his unlined young face.

"I . . . I was thinking of Tamshas," he said. "How she must be feeling just now, with her father dead, everything she knew destroyed. And what must she think of me, seeing me kill a man like that."

Tuya's heart sank into the abyss, and she looked at Anab, despair in her eyes. After a moment she had to blink away tears to see at all.

One of the guards interrupted them. "You," he said to Anab, "Benu wants to see you and your friends now."

Anab gulped down his wine and stood up; the other two followed his lead. They were led through the darkened camp, then into a tent lighted by a small fire in a low brazier. Behind the brazier, his lean face and leaner body grotesquely outlined by the small dancing flames, sat Benu.

Ben-Hadad could not help but notice how unlike Wenis he was. Benu was fine-drawn and fit, without an ounce of fat anywhere on his spare body. Deep-set eyes peered out from a skull-like face; his mouth was a thick, unsmiling line. His body was full of unresolved tension, as if prepared for anything: lies, betrayal, a physical attack by assassins.

Benu spoke suddenly, sharply. "I understand your mission was at least a qualified success. And you—" He stared Ben-Hadad piercingly in the eye. "You came over to our side. Why?"

Ben-Hadad started to speak, but his old childhood stammer, for some reason, came back. "B-b-b . . ."

Tuya sprang to his defense. "He killed one of Wenis's people who had caught me," she said. "He stabbed him with a sword. He was twice the size of either of us, the wine steward at the estate—"

"I know the man," Benu broke in, his voice still sharp and unyielding. "He had a reputation with the sword as well as the lash, and he was no coward. But that's not what I asked. What I asked was—why?"

"T-Tuya," Ben-Hadad said. "She was in trouble. She's my f-friend. And she came to s-s-"

Tuya once again stepped into the breach, braving Benu's fierce glare. "I warned him," she said. "He wasn't really one of them. He was just somebody Wenis had picked up off the streets. Wenis wanted to use his skills to ingratiate himself with the Shepherds."

Benu's face registered something at last. "Ah, this would be the senet player," he said. "I hear you're very good, boy, that the gods favor you. At least that's what they say in the marketplace. I, too, used to play senet, back when there was time for such things. I learned what you probably learned—that the gods tend to favor the man who works a little harder than his opponent at learning the secrets of the game. Isn't that right?"

Ben-Hadad gulped. "Yes," he said. "Not many people seem to understand that. W-were you a good player, sir?"

"As good as time allowed me to get." Benu's cold reserve seemed to crack for a moment. "I used to take a board along with me on campaign, and play with my officers the night before the morning's battle. It helped keep my mind off the waiting. The battles I never minded. It was the waiting."

"You were a s-soldier, then, sir?" Ben-Hadad said.

The question, unsolicited, put Benu back on his guard again. His words came out cold and distant. "We're all soldiers in the war against the Shepherds," he said. "And there's no time for senet here. Not when our people are wounded and dying. Do you have any other knacks? Surely you've learned more in your young life than playing a silly game?" Before Ben-Hadad could answer, Benu had risen to his feet and stepped around the brazier. "No, don't tell me," he said. "I can see for myself." He took Ben-Hadad's hands, held them palm up, inspected the palms, the pads of the fingers. Then, brows knit, he held Ben-Hadad's forearms out to the light, turning them this way and that to see.

"I should have known from the thickness of those forearms," he said. "You're no game player by profession, not with wrists like those. Not with all those burn scars, and calluses that would be hard to cut through with a sharp knife."

"No, sir," Ben-Hadad said. "I was trained as a metal-worker, far to the north. But the Shepherds w-wouldn't let me practice my trade. I was starving in the streets when I learned, just by accident, that I had a n-natural hand at senet. Anab, here, showed me how to make a living at the game, and I—"

"That's as it may be," Benu said. "Metalworker, eh? Well, maybe we can get some use out of you after all. A military camp can always use a good tinker. I suppose you can repair weapons?"

"I can *m-make* them, sir," Ben-Hadad said. "I could have shown you a sword I made . . . but I l-left it in a man's stomach." The gleam that had appeared in his eyes now vanished, and his gaze fell to the floor.

Benu scowled and, in a sudden gesture of rough compassion, clapped Ben-Hadad on the shoulder with a hand as hard, as callused, as any smith's. "You'll get over it, son. It'll bother you for a while. If it didn't, you'd be no

better than the Shepherds. Even now, after I've killed
many of the enemy, it sometimes bothers me."

"Y-yes, sir. I understand. It's just hard—"

"I know. But—you said you could *make* arms? Not
just repair them?"

"Yes, he can!" Tuya said proudly. "With the best of
them! You should see—"

Benu ignored her. "You can make them after any
pattern I suggest? If I can get you the proper materials,
supply you with assistants to fire your forge?"

"Yes, sir. I m-mean, I think I can copy any pattern."

"Any pattern? Because . . . well, I've fought the
Shepherds, and I know their weapons are better than
ours. Those damned swords they use—may the gods curse
the man who forged them! They have ours beat in every
way. That's why I always tell our people to look around
after a raid and take every Shepherd weapon they can
get their hands on. Even at that, there are never quite
enough to go around, not with our ranks swelling almost
daily. Here, have a look for yourself." He drew his captured Shepherd sword and handed it over, butt first.
"What do you think?"

Ben-Hadad hefted the weapon, lips pursed, brow
knit. "W-well, sir . . ."

"Forget that 'sir' nonsense," Benu said. "Speak freely."

Ben-Hadad glanced at his friends, saw the nervous-
ness on Anab's face, the pride on Tuya's. "Well, it's good.
But I've held better in my hands, up north. My great-
grandfather used to make swords. He had a pattern that
. . . well, the trick is in the balance."

"Balance! Yes, yes!" Benu's dark eyes gleamed with
enthusiasm. "Any soldier would agree in a moment. This
is a workmanlike job, perhaps, but you can tell a weapon
made by a *real* smith by the way it hefts in your hand.
And I know this isn't in that category, however much it
may excel the scrap our own people make." He took back
the sword. "You can better this, then? If I can get you the
materials?"

"Yes. And, frankly, I'll be happy just to get back to
work at a forge. Playing senet isn't exactly my idea of a
proper occupation for a man. I never would have learned

the game if the Shepherds hadn't taken away the profession I was trained to."

"Isn't that just like the stupid swine?" Benu said, sheathing his sword. For the first time he smiled at Ben-Hadad—a cold, hard smile splitting his lean face. "That's why we're going to win in the long run, my young friend, despite their superior numbers. If Salitis had any brains, he'd have put you to work making hardware to kill us with. Instead he puts you out of a job and eventually drives you into our arms. Well, we won't turn you away. Welcome to our camp—and to our cause. But, forgive me—I don't even know your name. Nor the names of your friends—though I gather they are already members of our growing band."

Ben-Hadad bowed his head politely. "This is my good friend Anab. He's bright and cunning and resourceful. And this is Tuya—I call her my luck. But she's more than that, I suppose. I owe her my life, tonight. And I am Ben-Hadad. We are all proud to meet the great Benu."

"Forget Benu," the warrior leader said. "That is a name I assumed for the benefit of our Shepherd friends. While in camp, you three may call me by my real name. Baka."

CHAPTER FIVE

MEMPHIS

I

"Interesting," Uni said, sitting back, his eyes fixed on the young man. "The baker, you say?"

Joseph, polite and self-effacing, inclined his head slightly in acknowledgment—a model of tact and protocol. He did not volunteer further information, but waited instead to be asked.

Uni, watching him, thought: *He learns fast. Almost too fast. He's much too smart for a slave. Manumit him and let him loose in the palace and he'd rise at a frightening speed.* As he thought how best to use the fact, he found himself thanking his lucky stars that his instincts had led him to treat the boy well when he was down. Loose, free, he'd be a formidable enemy. And heaven help those brothers of his who'd sold him into bondage!

Uni pursed his lips as he continued to scrutinize the young man. The better prison fare he'd been allotted had filled him out since their first conversation. "Go on, my young friend," he said. "I want to hear the whole story."

"There's not much to tell, sir," Joseph said. "Yusni is

a member of a conspiracy to assassinate the top level of the royal retainers. The poison was not intended for the king himself. The blame for that lies with His Majesty, for asking to share a dish prepared for Madir. It was Madir they intended to kill."

"You've proof of this?"

"No, sir. And I have no names. Nothing more than I've already told you. I'll have to leave the rest to you, sir. The guards told me you have experience at getting people to talk, once you've determined what it is that you want them to say."

Uni chuckled. His fine hand with the implements of torture was well known in court circles. "As ever, you've a delicate way of putting things," he said. "And the cupbearer? He bears no guilt in this?"

"None that I can determine, sir. He seems to be absolutely blameless. In fact, I'd say he was in many ways an admirable man, straightforward and honest. He's much abused in this jailing. I'd let him out, restore him to his former situation, and raise his salary. From the jailhouse gossip, I understand he was highly valued—an efficient and sober man."

"A very model of a royal cupbearer. Of course, Yusni was a fine baker as well. But the world is full of fine bakers. As a matter of fact, this is an excellent opportunity for me to find a fine baker in the marketplace and to have his name ready when Madir asks for a good replacement." He rubbed his hands together, as if washing them; the pleasure he felt was evident in his every movement. "And I'll make sure the man whose name I advance is my man, heart and soul."

"Yes, sir. And Yusni?"

"Leave him to me," Uni said. "He'll be meat on a skewer before the weekend's out. *After* I've extracted what I want from him."

When Joseph had left, the guard from the outer room came inside and saluted. "Sir," he said, "the noble Potiphar."

"Show him in, by all means." Uni sat up, assumed a more severe stance and demeanor, and, as the dumpy official approached, rose and bowed courteously from the waist. "My lord honors me," he said in an unctuous voice.

"Oh, don't bother with the fancy manners," Potiphar said. "The boy, Joseph . . . I've been thinking. . . ." He hesitated.

"He's a model prisoner, as prisoners go," Uni said.

"Look, Uni—my wife's been a bit distracted of late. Perhaps she was hasty. Perhaps she didn't mean . . ."

It took Uni great control to keep the smile off his face. *Didn't mean? She probably tried to rape the boy. When he struggled free, she panicked—and did the first thing she could to bury the evidence of her folly. She had him chucked into prison.* "My lord?" he said. "Are you thinking of changing the charges? Dropping them, perhaps? You realize, of course, the position this puts you in."

"Position? What do you mean?" There was sudden confusion in the man's eyes.

"Well, false accusations make you liable for the prisoner's room and board while he was in prison, for one. Not to mention making you, sir, with all due respect, look like the kind of person who makes frivolous charges and then drops them without explanation. Unless, of course, you're going to swear a statement that you don't believe what your wife told you. In which case people may think—"

"No, no!" Potiphar said. "No, we can't have that. Oh, what a terrible situation to be in! What can I do, Uni?"

That's better, Uni thought. *Come to me for help. I can use having you in my debt.* "Well, my lord, actually the young man's turned out to be of great help to me here. He more than half runs my prison now, if the truth were known. And there are other advantages to having him here. Thanks to his help, I'm about to break up a serious nest of subversion."

"Oh, that *is* different, isn't it? If there's a good reason for his being here, I mean. Isn't it?"

"Definitely. I'd say, sir, that you would do best right now by leaving things to me. Then, later, when the time's right, perhaps we can quietly slip him out of prison on some sort of technicality."

"Yes! That sounds much better. But—you said subversion? In the court? And he's helping you break it up?"

Uni nodded gravely, "But I'd keep it between us, if you don't mind, sir. I haven't told anyone but you, and I'd much appreciate it if it went no further just now, sir. Until the arrests have been made."

"By all means." Potiphar prepared to go. "Thank you, Uni. You've been of immense help. Your advice is always sound. I'll leave the whole matter in your hands."

As he mounted the stairs for the long climb back up to the light, Potiphar thought: Plot? Plot against the crown? But who? . . . And, for a fleeting moment, he remembered the day Joseph had been taken away, when he, Potiphar, had been approached by Hapu and Eben. They'd had some mysterious business in mind; there'd been a furtive, conspiratorial air about the two of them. What if they—?

No, that's foolish. They wouldn't.

He frowned, remembering Uni's astute disposition of the messy Joseph affair, and put that matter from his mind for now. This Memphis! So full of intrigues, plots, counterplots! People always scheming against one another! Why, they'd even begun bothering him with their stories! There was that young woman, Mereet, the wife of the blind armorer, and that crack-brained story of hers about overhearing high officials of the court talking treason—trying to get him, Potiphar, roped into her net. Even though she'd once been a friend of the family, he'd brushed her off as quickly as possible and left word to his retainers to tell her he was out every time she came to his door. And, like his present troubles, he'd put it from his mind. Even if there had been something to her story, even if there'd been something to his own suspicions, even if there were something to Uni's talk of plots and subversion, it made no sense for a man like himself to get involved. Better to close one's ears to all of it. . . .

Most of his day's duties done, Joseph sat in a patch of late afternoon sun that fell through a window high overhead, as he reviewed the prison accounts. The sun made him drowsy, and he caught himself nodding. Shaking himself awake, he sat up straight—and looked up to see Ameni, cupbearer to the Lord of Two Lands, standing before him, an earnest expression on his face. "Joseph," he said. "I don't mean to trouble you, but you did promise. . . ."

". . . to think about that dream of yours?" Joseph said, smiling. "So I did. And I think I know what it means. If I'm right, if the God of my fathers has not deserted me in my hour of need, I may have the answer."

"Then . . . it's a good omen?"

"Well, you said you saw a vine with three branches that began to bud and blossom as you watched. Is that right?"

"Yes! And soon there were clusters of ripe grapes. I was holding the Lord of Two Land's wine cup in my hand, and I took the grapes and squeezed them into his cup and made wine. Then I gave it to him to drink, and he accepted it."

Joseph heard him out—and noticed, as the man spoke, that Yusni, the baker, had edged closer to the two of them and was listening intently.

Joseph spoke clearly, so that Yusni, too, could hear: "I've thought hard about your dream. And what I think it means is—"

"Yes? Yes?"

"Calm yourself. If I'm right, it's good news. It means that in three days you'll be out of prison—"

"Oh, please! If only—"

"—and you'll have your old job back, a bonus for good and faithful service, and the everlasting goodwill of your master, the king." Joseph sat back, his face neutral. "What do you think of that?" he said.

"Oh, Joseph, if you're right . . . But thank you! I thank you from the bottom of my heart! How can I ever express . . . ?"

"I could make a suggestion," Joseph said quietly. "When you're back in your old position, cleared of charges of wrongdoing, you'll be a man of standing, of position, in the kingdom."

"Yes, yes. And?"

"You could do worse than to remember me. And, perhaps, put in a good word for me? I'm a stranger here, in a land far from the one I was born in, friendless and alone, without family. I've been thrown in prison for no good reason. Your word could help secure my release."

"Oh, yes! You can count on it!" the official said, and, bowing gratefully, went away.

Joseph glanced at Yusni. "He'll forget," he said a little sadly, with an edge of bitterness in his voice. "They all do."

"Not me, Joseph," Yusni said. "You told Ameni his dream; how about mine?"

"Your dream?" Joseph said. His eyes narrowed. "I don't remember. Refresh my memory, Yusni. My mind's been a thousand leagues away."

The baker squatted before Joseph. "I dreamed I had three baskets of pastries on my head. The top basket held all sorts of pastries, the kind the Lord of Two Lands likes best. But the birds came down and ate them."

Joseph sighed. "Yusni, don't make me do any divining today. I'm tired."

"Please," the baker said. "I heard the way you interpreted Ameni's dream. Joseph, if my dream came out the same way his did, I wouldn't forget you when I'd been restored to my old position. I'd remember you. I'd do more than put in a good word."

Joseph covered his face and wiped his tired eyes. "The light in here," he said. "I don't know how they expect a man to keep accounts. I can't even read my own writing."

"Joseph, please . . ."

Joseph took his hands away from his face and looked regretfully at the chief baker. His voice was flat and toneless as he spoke. "Yusni," he said, "are you sure you want to hear? I'm tired to death. I could be wrong. I could speak nonsense. If I do, you wouldn't hold it against me, would you?"

"No, of course not. But the dream . . ."

"Yusni," Joseph said, his voice showing his fatigue, "within three days you'll be taken out of prison—"

"Ah! Then it's just as—"

"—and you'll be led to the courtyard outside. . . ." He paused, peering at Yusni with eyes that were hardly more than slits now. His face, drawn with fatigue, seemed lined like an old man's. "Yusni, they're going to cut off your head."

"No!"

"And impale your body on a sharpened stake."

"No! No!"

"And the crows will eat your flesh. And everything you've ever owned will revert to the crown. Your wife and children will be sold into slavery. Army officers will be quartered in your house. They'll grow vines in your garden to make wine for their drunken brawls. The little space beneath the arbor where you used to grow herbs . . . pigs will root in it. Your youngest daughter will be sold to a whorehouse in Thebes. Your wife will die of a heart attack when they strip her and put her on the block to auction her off to the highest bidder. In their anger the traders will throw her body to the dogs. The memory of her name and yours won't survive the year. The waters of life will close around you, Yusni, and it'll be as though you'd never been born. Three days, Yusni. Three days."

From the terrace above, Uni, hidden by a screen, listened. The cold sweat ran down his temples. His hands trembled. He'd never heard anything like this before. Never.

How could he do it? How could he sit there, calm as you please, and speak such things? How could such words emerge from that baby face of his?

Why, he was a man fit to stand beside the prison torturers, the kind of men who'd taunt a victim even as they worked on him with their red-hot pincers and knives. . . .

Or was he? There hadn't been any joy in his voice, any gloating. The torturers—you could see it in them even before they spoke, and you could hear it in their voices when they taunted a man with the sweetness of the life he was about to lose.

This was different.

He hadn't been making this up. There was no air of improvisation about it. It had been more like a man reading from a scroll, his voice flat and tired, reading a list of things that had already happened.

That had already happened . . .

Uni's eyes widened and he stepped back, flattening himself against the wall, as the implications of this came home to him in one blinding blast.

The young man from Canaan—he really *was* a diviner. Everything they'd said about him was true.

He, Uni, had thought it no more than gossip, the tales people had brought to him. Tales of the future foretold, of lost things found, of . . .

He had attributed it all to the boy's amazing mind, his astuteness, his ability to disconcert and subsequently manipulate others, and then—like any master administrator—make the men he'd manipulated thankful to have been so used. Such skills were not uncommon, certainly, and, in some men, were honed and developed to an astonishing degree.

But this . . . this was *real* divination. The boy had looked into the future, and he had seen . . .

Or had he? Uni could feel his heart pounding in his chest, and he took a deep breath, composing himself. Any fool could see that the man would be beheaded and impaled, and that the crows would make short work of his remains. But the prophecies regarding his home, his wife, his child . . . He, Uni, would have to observe these matters carefully after Yusni's death. The predictions had been so specific, it would be easy to tell whether they had indeed been accurate.

But of this he was sure: Joseph would bear watching. For his, Uni's, safety, if for no other reason.

II

Eben, after visiting the palace a week later, ran into Hapu, the chief priest, in the street. "Well met, my friend," he said. "Have you a moment?"

Hapu glanced over his shoulder. The street was full of inconsequential people, on errands of no importance, paying the two of them no mind whatsoever. "Certainly. But let's

go somewhere more private than this. There's an inn not
far from here, with a grape arbor in the style of the Greek
Isles. It's something of a fad with the traveled and the
sophisticated, but not crowded at this time of day. We can
talk freely there."

The two conspirators fell into step. "You look troubled,"
Hapu said. "I trust it's nothing serious."

"I was upriver, in Thebes," Eben said. "I returned
only yesterday. I—I heard about Yusni."

"Oh," the priest said, keeping his eyes on the street
before them, stepping carefully to avoid the puddles and
the leavings of the stray dogs, a faint expression of distaste
on his lean face. "If you're curious about such things, his
remains are to be found where the city's garbage is dumped.
His head's on a pole somewhere, of course, as a reminder."
He stepped to one side to avoid a pile of slops. "Someone
pointed it out to me, but I forget which one it was. By
now he'll be quite unrecognizable, I suppose."

"Yes. But—before he died . . ."

"You want to know if he talked? Well, my informant
says no—although he also says that Yusni didn't live long
enough to feel it when they took the ax to him, that the
beheading was mainly gone through for the sake of form.
He says Yusni died in the torture chamber."

"He didn't talk? Tell me he didn't talk!"

"Hold your tongue! People can hear you. So far as I
know he didn't. I have no choice but to trust my informant.
He says they got from him only the fact that there was a
conspiracy, but that before he could tell any names, his
heart gave out." Hapu's mouth showed the trace of a
smile. "Uni was furious, from all I hear. He had the
torturer whipped until he couldn't stand."

They came out of the little street into a courtyard of
sorts, which at week's end was used as a market, but was
too poorly located, in this area of official buildings and
government warehouses, to support one in midweek. At a
corner stood the inn Hapu had mentioned. They had to
awaken the innkeeper to get a jar of wine and two bowls
brought to their table under the arbor—and then had to
bribe the man to leave, once he had been awakened and
had served them.

"You've eased my mind immensely," Eben said after they had spoken for a while. "I had visions of our whole ring being broken up, of the guards coming to our houses one by one in the dark of night—"

"Don't be foolish," Hapu said. "Nothing like that will happen." He sipped his wine and glanced at Eben. "Although it wouldn't hurt to keep our heads down until this business is forgotten. . . . Oh, there *was* one odd bit of information brought to me, though." His hairless brow wrinkled in thought. "Maybe two, now that I think about it. First, it seems Uni has himself some kind of soothsayer in prison. A young foreigner. Uni's feeding him well, keeping him in state. Reportedly the boy serves as both diviner *and* informant." He smiled frigidly. "A useful sort of prisoner to have around, I'd say."

"Diviner? You mean an astrologer? How can an astrologer read the stars from a prison underground?"

"No, no. Nothing like that. The lad's apparently a priest of some incomprehensible heathen deity somewhere up north. A boy priest—and he says his god tells him the future." He chuckled. "And here *I* have a whole pantheon to draw upon, and none of them ever shares his thoughts with me."

Eben permitted himself a covert smile. Hapu's cynicism about his own religion was one of the jokes of the palace, though it was seldom discussed aloud where the wrong ears could hear. He sipped his wine. "Uni is keeping this prophetic fellow under wraps, all for himself?"

"Yes—though I wonder how long he'll stay a secret from Madir. You know how superstitious Madir is."

"Well, Uni's ambitious. Obviously he has his own plans for the boy." Eben drained his bowl and licked his lips. "You said there were two things you were going to mention—"

"Yes. It seems some woman has been talking around, saying she'd overheard something about some sort of conspiracy."

Eben sat bolt upright, staring at him. "*Woman?* Who?"

"I don't know. You'll remember I wasn't as keen as you were on the idea of talking to Potiphar."

"No. It was my idea, but—"

"I don't trust the man. I didn't then, and I don't now. I think he's a weakling and not to be counted on. Anyone who'd let that vain, sluttish wife of his order him around like that . . ."

"I know. You were right. On sober reflection I came to that conclusion myself."

"Well, you were not of that opinion at first. So I took the liberty of suborning one of his servants. And it was the servant who overheard the woman trying to talk to Potiphar."

"I see. And the servant didn't get her name? What did she say?"

"Actually, she didn't get to say much. Potiphar wouldn't listen. He was still overwrought about that slave of his, the one his wife accused of—" He stopped. His face bore a surprised expression. "That's odd. That slave's in Uni's prison, too. *He* couldn't be the one who—?" But he dismissed the thought. "Pardon me. I was thinking out loud. No matter. Anyhow, he wouldn't hear her out. My informer says the woman gave up and went away."

"But what did she say before she left?"

"That is the ticklish part. She said she'd been in Madir's atrium, behind a palm or something, and had overheard two 'government officials,' she called them, discussing a plot to . . . well, she didn't get to elaborate. But it was obvious when the man told it to me that the two she was talking about were you and me, my friend." He watched Eben's expression, and waited for the shock of his words to subside. "She named the day, the time. It was the very day you tried to approach Potiphar and he shooed us away. She must have heard everything we said."

"Gods! But we talked about . . ."

"More than we should have talked about in such a place. And someone overheard us. Somewhere out there in the city there's a woman who knows enough to sit the two of us down on sharpened stakes, my friend, and we don't know who she is. The more I think of it, the more ominous it becomes." He frowned and drank again, quickly. "I definitely think we should both disappear for a while—leave the city for a month or two."

"But—can't we find her first? We have to keep her from telling someone else what she tried to tell Potiphar."

"I think not. There's not enough time. We should leave Memphis tonight. We'll just have to take our chances and hope that no one will believe her stories." He shrugged. "Potiphar didn't. After all, she *is* just a woman."

Eben still looked unconvinced.

"Trust me," Hapu said, gathering up his voluminous robes and rising from the table. "I know what's best for us. I am a priest, am I not?"

Eben did not return Hapu's smile. "I'll start packing," he said.

The subaltern Hori quickened his pace through the sprawling complex of forges several leagues north of Memphis, not far behind the Egyptian front lines. The heat, smoke, and noise did not make him want to linger on his errand.

"Shobai!" he shouted over the din of hammers and the wheeze of bellows. "There you are! You've complained of hearing nothing but bad news lately. Well, here's some good news: General Unas has come to see you."

Shobai's alert leonine head turned toward the speaker, like a great beast sniffing the breeze. "Unas!" he said, a smile breaking the somber cast of his features. He put down the forge tools in his hand. "Bring me water to wash myself, Hori. I'm all over soot and can't embrace my friend."

But before Hori could move, Unas had already grasped Shobai by the forearms. "Shobai," he said happily, "the day hasn't come when a field soldier minds a little honest dirt. How are you?" They embraced heartily. Then Unas stepped back, frowning. "But you don't feel good, my friend. You're off your feed. You've lost weight. Is something wrong?"

Shobai turned away for a moment, shouting orders to the line of smiths at their forges. Then he turned back to his friend. "It's nothing. Worry, I suppose. We're critically short of ore for our forges, and what we get isn't of anything like the quality that used to come across the desert from Timna. We've an exploratory party out look-

ing for a good overland route to the Red Sea, a track
negotiable by pack beasts laden with copper ore. If it can
be ferried across the sea, then brought overland . . ."

"Ah," Unas said. "So the new sources haven't come
through, then?"

"The upriver mines? It's a matter of time, I hope.
There's plenty of ore up that way—including tin ore,
which is essential to making the kind of bronze we need to
match the Shepherds' metals. But I hear they're having
the same troubles. Their lines of supply back to their
homeland and to the ṭin mines in the mountains north of
Assyria have been cut. As no doubt you've heard, there's a
new king in the Valley of the Two Rivers—a great leader,
if the reports are true, bent on unifying the whole area
under one rule and one law. He's made hash of the
Shepherd supply routes."

"Yes—Hammurabi, I believe he's called. But, Shobai,
our own sources . . ."

The big man frowned. "You'll have to excuse me, I've
been a bit distracted of late. Anyway, runners have come
back to us with news of Akhilleus's parley with the Nubian
chiefs at Kerma, where Ebana's people are from. They
report everything went well. We've already sent a delegation of engineers upriver to talk to them, to organize
mining operations on a large scale. But it'll take some
months to get anything set up and producing. People have
to be trained."

"Don't you worry," Unas said. "I can hold the line
until then—although it isn't easy when your own commander begrudges you every olive and fig he sends."

"Who, Harmin?" Shobai said.

Unas grunted, as if mere mention of the name upset
him. "I don't trust him, Shobai. Sometimes I fear him
more than I do General Vahan and all the Shepherd
troops."

Shobai nodded. "I've heard talk of Harmin, and I
understand you only too well. But still, if I were you, I
wouldn't underestimate Vahan."

"I keep forgetting—you worked for him once, long
ago, didn't you? Well, I promise I won't underestimate
him." He clapped Shobai affectionately on the shoulder; it

was a sign of the giant's towering stature that the soldier had to reach upward to do so. "Just attend to your end and we'll attend to ours. And don't worry—we'll still be here when your friend Akhilleus returns—even if we have to fight Harmin *and* Vahan."

"Good. That's the best news I've heard in quite a while," Shobai said, mopping his brow with a hand both sooty and sweaty, leaving a black streak across his face. "If—"

"Wait." The battle-hardened soldier reached down to the bucket of fresh water Hori had brought, filled a sponge, and, as if he had been a nurse, tenderly mopped the face and forearms of the blind man. "There, now. Come, Shobai. Take a break for a moment, won't you? Sit in the shade with me and have a glass of wine and some olives. I didn't come all this way just to talk business, but to see an old and valued friend. I get so little time off from the front lines, let's not waste it on war talk." He led the blind man away to a shaded area, sat him down in a chair his subalterns had brought along with his own favorite chair, and called for refreshments. "Tell me," he said at last, slipping into his seat, "how are Mereet and the twins?"

"Teti and Ketan are well and strong. I tell you, Unas, the girl's as strong as the boy. The birthmarks are a portent, my friend. I'm more than ever determined to break tradition and train the both of them in the family trade."

"What? The girl a smith?" Unas slapped his knee and chuckled.

"Go ahead and laugh now, my friend," Shobai said. "But don't be surprised if what I say turns out to be true. Remember, we're not just ordinary armorers. We're a separate caste, the Children of the Lion. We make our own traditions, our own rules. And if the gods want us to break the tradition and bring a woman-child into the craft, why, that's what we'll do, whatever anyone may think!"

The wine arrived. Unas shook off help and poured for the two of them. "Here," he said, guiding Shobai's hand to the cup. "To the health of *all* future smiths—*and* to victory over the Shepherds."

Shobai drank deeply, but now the troubled expression had returned to his face. "Ah, Unas, I wish that were all I had to worry about."

"Oh? There's more?"

"I hadn't meant to talk about it, but—you're a valued friend, the oldest I have here except for Musuri and Akhilleus, who are gone, and Tros, whom I rarely see these days. He's chief physician to the royal court now."

"I hadn't heard. Good fortune to him! But you were saying—"

"Unas, I think Baka's alive."

Unas's eyes went wide, and his tone became angry. "Shobai, that's impossible. I knew Baka, and I've spoken to men who served under him just before he was captured by the Shepherds. They said—"

"I don't care what they said. He's alive. And I've received a death threat from him."

The blind man's face was tense, drawn. Unas put a reassuring hand on his arm. "Look," he said, "there are always rumors. Any death threats you've received . . . forget them. I'm putting a double guard on you at the forge as of this moment. Your house will be watched day and night. Now . . . tell me about this person who calls himself Baka."

Tros of Ilios had been thinking for a long time, staring out of the narrow window of his small, cramped study. Everywhere behind him in the musty room, from floor to ceiling, on tables and shelves, were dust-covered rows and stacks of assorted vials, pouches, and jars, containing potions, distilled spirits, balms, and countless other powders, liquids, and creams.

In the center of all this clutter, Mereet stood patiently waiting. She wanted to sit down, but all the chairs were covered with boxes of medicines and half-unrolled scrolls.

Finally Tros turned back from the window. His trained physician's eye took in her unaccustomed tension. "Mereet," he said, "that's an amazing story. If it had come from anyone in the world but you—"

"I wish it had," she said. "I wandered around at first, trying to forget it . . . but I couldn't. I tried to think of whom I could tell. I couldn't tell Shobai. You, of all people, Tros, would know that. He has enough bad memories—something like this would only torment him. He would feel helpless."

The old physician pursed his lips and grunted. "And that, I suppose, is why you wouldn't say anything to Unas either—because your husband would find out from him?"

Mereet nodded. "I knew you'd understand," she said. "Shashank, who raised me after my father died, was close friends with the father of Potiphar, the chief cook at court. I went to Potiphar. I couldn't think of anyone else. I was reluctant to bother you—and at any rate, your calendar has been full for weeks now."

"I know. My apologies. From this time on, please tell my scribe that it's you. I'll leave instructions that I'm to be notified without fail, anytime you're here. If I'm with anyone besides the royal family or Madir, I'll break the appointment."

"Thank you. But . . . Potiphar, he wouldn't listen to me. He said he was occupied with problems of his own. He—"

"He was. That wife of his is driving him wild. She accuses every male around of trying to seduce her. Even me. Me, at my age! Fortunately Potiphar didn't believe her. But he's had at least one slave, a trusted young fellow who ran his entire household, thrown in prison on those silly charges of hers."

"In prison? But the penalty for a slave—"

"Quite. If the charges were taken seriously, he'd be dead by now. It's a measure of Potiphar's own disbelief in her stories that the boy's still alive. But back to *your* story. How much did you tell him?"

"Not too much. I didn't get a chance to. I didn't give any names, either, because as I told you, I wasn't sure of any—except for the general, Harmin, who, as I said, has plans to assassinate Unas."

"What a story!" The doctor shook his head. "Well, it's obvious this is serious. I'll give it some more thought, my dear, and see what I can come up with. We're treading on dangerous ground here, you know. If I told the wrong person . . ."

"I know. Truly, I didn't want to drag you into this. That was part of the reason I held back. Forgive me, please." She turned to go.

"No apology is necessary," he said, following her to the door. "Besides, it's my civic duty to do something about it, isn't it? This sort of business shakes the very foundations of the state, on whose bounty, after all, I depend. Actually, I should thank you for telling me, my dear."

Mereet smiled wanly.

"Meanwhile," he said, his tone warmly personal now, "how's my old friend Shobai?"

"In good health, though a little overworked these days. He worries too much about the war. And I'm no help."

"Ah. And the children?"

"They're fine. . . . Tros . . . ?"

"Now, don't worry. Put the matter from your mind. Let me see what I can do. I forbid you to worry about this anymore. It's in my hands now."

CHAPTER SIX

THE NILE DELTA

I

Tuya watched intently as the workers spread the night's winnings before them on the ground. Products of a raid on a Shepherd outpost the evening before, the weapons were being laid out in neat rows. There were bows and arrows, long thrusting swords, short ones, a few ornately fashioned scimitars with curved cutting edges, and several implements whose purpose was unclear. "Ben-Hadad," Tuya said, pointing to a grisly-looking hatchetlike weapon, "what's that? And the blade next to it?"

"That's a Shepherd battle-ax," the young smith said. "It's for close-up fighting by massed infantry. See the blood on the edge? Some devil took a terrible wound with it, I suspect."

"And the blade?"

"That's the blade of one of their larger broadaxes. It didn't make any sense for our men to bring back the handle. It's too long and bulky, and anyhow we can replace it easily—but it would take me a lot of time and trouble to make another head like that one. See the three

141

holes? They're for attaching a fresh handle. The handles often break because of the way you swing it . . . here, let me show you." He stepped back and spread his feet, holding an imaginary weapon at arm's length with both hands. Then, slowly, he began to whirl the invisible thing around his body in great sweeping circles. "The handle's about the length of a man's body. This would clear an area of about nine paces around me. Anything entering that circle would be sliced in half."

"Ugh." She watched him end the charade. "Blood-thirsty people, these Shepherds." She looked past him where the men were leading into camp two magnificent horses. Behind them, another man easily pulled a light two-wheeled war chariot. "Look at that!" she said. "Oh, how beautiful!"

"It certainly is," Baka said, coming up just then. "It's rare for us to capture one of those. The last one we got our hands on was in pieces, with a broken axle. We didn't have any smiths or wheelwrights among us then, and we couldn't repair or duplicate the axle. Perhaps we'll do better this time," he said, his words aimed at Ben-Hadad. "What do you think, smith? Could you make us one of those?"

Ben-Hadad, examining the chariot body with evident admiration, made a low whistling sound under his breath. "Duplicate the entire chariot, you mean? It wouldn't be easy. You'd have to steal the materials. That would be the hardest part. And we *would* need a good wheelwright. But what a beauty she is! Up in Canaan we never saw anything like this. Our chariots, what few there were, were heavy affairs, drawn by asses. Of course they couldn't approach this in speed or maneuverability. Why, with a responsive pair up front you could turn one of these in no space at all!"

"Yes. Very handy for killing Egyptians," Baka said, and there was such venom in his tone that both of them involuntarily shrank from him. "It's a fine design, all right. I know the man who developed it while in the employ of the Shepherds. An extremely clever man. Someday I'll meet him—and cut his damned throat for him!"

Ben-Hadad glanced at Tuya, her shocked expression

matching his own. Neither of them had yet seen Baka's composure shattered in this way, revealing the anger and malice underlying his icily controlled exterior. They looked back at him, but his expression had already changed: Now it was thoughtful, his mind was far away, and he seemed to be speaking more to himself than to the two of them. ". . . offering his services like that . . . beyond all comprehension. Selling out to the dregs of humanity . . ."

"Come," Tuya said, tugging at Ben-Hadad's sleeve, her words a low whisper. "Let's leave him alone—"

"No," Ben-Hadad said. There was an odd expression on his face as he watched Baka. "Excuse me, sir. This man—you say he went to work for the Shepherds?"

"Yes," Baka said. "It was up north, far beyond the land you came from. He was an armorer like yourself, a good one, with a fine name, or so I've been told. I've fought with captured swords he designed, and they're the best I've ever handled."

"Come on, Ben-Hadad," Tuya said again, pulling at his arm. The young man shook her off.

". . . fortunately, he'd first armed Carchemish for King Hagirum," Baka was saying. "If he hadn't, the city's armies would never have been able to hold out as long as they did. After he left the Shepherds, he helped arm Ebla, too—though little good it did them."

"But, sir," Ben-Hadad said, "if he did try to halt the Shepherd advance, was he really so bad?"

"Bad?" Baka said, the bitterness strong in his voice. "People asked that at the time, I'm sure. As he himself did, no doubt. After all, it must have been easy for him to learn the error of his ways; a blind man has plenty of time to think."

"Blind?" Ben-Hadad said in an odd, unsure voice. "Did you say blind? W-what was his name?"

"Name?" Baka said peevishly. He reached down and picked up one of the captured swords, his fingers unconsciously testing the sharp blade. "The name of the man I'm going to kill?" He thought it over, his eyes far away, and then muttered something unintelligible.

"Pardon me, sir?" Ben-Hadad said, fear evident in his voice. "I didn't hear the name. . . ."

"Name?" Baka said again. "Why, Shobai, of course. Shobai of Haran. Shobai, the traitor."

The farther they walked into the quarter of Avaris shared by the rich Egyptians and the Shepherd overlords, the less Anab liked it. It was broad daylight, and he glanced nervously from side to side. "Zosar," he said, "I don't like being here. I'm going back."

Zosar grabbed Anab's thin upper arm with a grip so hard it hurt. "No, you're not," he said. "We've come this far, and I'm not turning back—and neither are you. You agreed to come with me and talk to my friend, and I'm holding you to the agreement. Don't turn coward on me now."

They emerged from a street into the broad square where the new temple site stood, and Anab resignedly let himself be guided to the construction zone, where great blocks of stone were being carved and shaped into their final form by teams of artisans. Anab forgot his fear for a moment as he watched the men working the stones; he'd never been allowed this close to a construction project before.

The place was a beehive of activity. To his left, two workmen checked the trueness of the planes of a huge stone on its movable rocker, using long, straight rods for the horizontal areas and a wooden rule with a weighted plumb line for the vertical faces. As Anab watched, one worker found an imperfection in the horizontal face and dressed it expertly with a ball of harder, darker stone. Then, standing up, he summoned his supervisor, who double-checked the dress of the block with level and square.

Zosar approached one of the workmen. "We're looking for the priest Ashau," he said. "Have you seen him?"

The workman's expression registered nothing. "What business would you have with him?"

Zosar, as Anab had come to learn, was always at his boldest when bluffing. "If Ashau hears you've impeded my way to him, my friend, *you* won't have any business at all. Not at this holy site, anyhow. Now, I'll ask again, just once. Where is he?"

The workman's composure dissolved before their eyes. "Uh . . . he's at the south temple site. Sorry, sir. I had no idea—"

"Come on," Zosar said, steering Anab away without waiting for the man's apology. When they were out of earshot, he drew his companion aside. "Look, you've got to learn a bit of technique. These bureaucrat types are always afraid. All you have to do is make sure they're as frightened of you as they are of—" But then he looked at Anab's wrecked face and stopped. "On the other hand, perhaps you'd better leave it to me."

The two continued to pick their way through the disorderly pattern of rough blocks, each with its pair of workmen. Zosar spoke as they walked on: "The workmen are twice as frightened here as elsewhere. Other workers are at the mercy only of the businessmen and the Shepherds. These poor fish have the priestly caste to contend with as well. That's a fearful burden. You can bully them all you like, as a result."

Anab nodded timidly. "That may be. But I'm still not sure what we're doing here, this far into the enemy's territory. I don't feel safe—"

Zosar yanked his arm. "Shut up, will you? Look, you told me you didn't like the way things were at camp, that you were still unhappy about how Ben-Hadad sold you out. And you can't go back to your old life in the streets. You feel trapped. You look around you and see no opportunity to rise, to better yourself, to make a secure place for yourself in some little corner of the world."

"Yes, but—"

"Hear me out. I'm offering you a chance to make something of yourself. Sure, it involves some risk. Everything involves some risk, my friend. Sitting on your fundament and letting the world go by involves some risk, and has no rewards at all. At least with me you have the possibility of great rewards. *Great* rewards."

"Rewards? But—"

"Anab, my friend, who wants to be a mere follower when he can be a leader, eh? Answer me that, will you? Not me, let me tell you! I wasn't born to follow orders—I was born to give them. And you—you're smart. I can see that. Smarter than any of them, smarter than Onuris or anyone in camp except Baka. And Baka's blind mad. He's obsessed with the idea of killing the man who stole his wife. Really! He wears his horns like a penance. My feeling is, if the slut's untrue, let her go, and forget about her. Why waste your time sitting around, souring your stomach with vain ideas of revenge? After all, the blind fellow's many leagues away, on the other side of the battle lines. Meanwhile, there's plenty to occupy yourself with here. And women—women are cheap. The streets are full of them. Any fool can go out and nab one who'll be as good as anything you left behind when you left your happy home. . . ."

Anab closed his eyes in shame and bitterness, not hearing the rest of Zosar's words. They all talked this way. They all acted as though all you had to do to find love was go out and look for it. And for them it really was easy, perhaps. They didn't have to live with a face no woman would look at without a shudder! They didn't have to see the sick wince he saw every time a woman looked him full in the face. They didn't go around avoiding every polished stone surface for fear of seeing their own faces reflected back at them. They didn't close their eyes when they drank from the bucket in the well in the marketplace. They'd never understand! Nobody would!

In the end they found a man who'd been instructed to leave a message. They were to meet Ashau at moonrise in the middle of the circular masonry wall that stood in the center of the site where the new temple was to rise. Zosar applauded the choice. If any place would be safe for a dangerous conversation, this was the one. They had dinner and walked in the dusk hour to the meeting place. There they waited as the last rays of the sun faded in the west. As darkness fell, they sensed that they were not alone. "Zosar?" came a low voice behind them. They whirled, seeing the tall figure of the bald priest standing before them in his white robes, a notched pole in his hand. "I'm glad you came. But there's work to be done while we talk. Quick, one of you go stand by the wall, over there. I'll tell you what to do."

Anab did as he was told. The priest inserted the notched stick in a small hole at the exact center of the circle, then sighted through the notch. He motioned Anab to move a few paces to one side. "Now," he said, "take the chalk near your feet and make a mark about a handspan to the left of your shoulder. There . . . yes. Well done. Now come join us, young man." He stepped away from the stick and joined Zosar as Anab came up beside them.

"Well done," Ashau said—and winced, as the moonlight fell for the first time on Anab's half-face. "I . . . excuse me, Zosar. I don't know this gentleman. Would you introduce us?"

Zosar did so, his tone puzzled. "This business with the chalk," he said at last. "I don't-understand."

"You wouldn't," the priest said. "The alignment of the temple—the north-south alignment—has to be calculated precisely. There's a religious significance it would take me too long to explain just now. So I stand there, in the middle of the circle, and your friend here makes a mark for me at the precise point on the circular wall where the moon rises. We converse for a time, until the path of the moon approaches the point where it'll begin to disappear below the other part of the wall. I'll then ask your young friend to make a second chalk mark at the precise place where it disappears below my field of vision. In the morning the workmen will measure the distance between the two marks on the wall. The exact center will be computed. Then a line drawn from the stick here to the point midway between the two chalk marks will give us precise north and south. An amazingly simple formula, really. It's attributed to the great architect Imhotep, who built the step pyramid at Memphis for your illustrious namesake, the Third Dynasty monarch Zosar." He gave them a slightly superior smile, secure in his arcane knowledge, avoiding looking directly at Anab's face—a fact that was not lost on Anab.

"That's all very interesting," Zosar said. "But you called us here for some other reason than explaining the laws of the heavens."

"Ah, yes," Ashau said. He looked up, gauging the time it would take the moon to complete its visible arc through the sky. "You'll remember we talked about the possibility of our—of the priesthood's—joining your crusade against the Shepherds."

Anab stared, openmouthed. Zosar's fierce glare, however, warned him to keep silent. Zosar turned back to the priest. "As I recall," he said, "there was only one stumbling block to be removed."

"Exactly," the priest said. "I have found considerable support among my fellow priests for our enterprise, and there's only the one obstacle—the stumbling block, as you so aptly call it—in the way of our giving you our full, albeit covert, support. You realize, of course, that we can't support you openly. But situated as we are, with Salitis's court trusting us as they do, we can do your cause much good. Whereas if we were to show our true colors—"

"I understand," Zosar said. "And I'm sure you realize, in turn, how dangerous the removal of that stumbling block can be for us. We lose at one stroke the rallying point of the entire organization, as well as a number of key people in the movement who are there mainly because of their extreme loyalty—blind, emotional loyalty—to the very problem we seek to remove."

"That can't be avoided," the priest said blithely. "The people I've talked to here are adamant. They'll tolerate virtually any sort of aberrant behavior in a good cause, but they balk at flagrant and habitual blasphemy, at open and unashamed disrespect for their holy calling. I'm telling you right now, if you let us down on this one point, the whole deal's off. Worse than that: There are those among us who will almost certainly become your enemies, if your people continue to embrace what we consider a vile and insidious attitude toward all things sacred."

Zosar recoiled in horror. "You don't mean they'd sell *me* out to the Shepherds?" he said.

"I don't know if they'd go that far," the priest said calmly. "But think of it this way: Unless you can unify *all* the discontented, the subversives, the anti-Shepherd sentiment under one leader—which you might indeed be able to do, if you had our help—other such movements are bound to arise, in competition with you. They may well gain the ascendancy, particularly if my priestly brothers are behind them and are unhappy with your group. Who knows what mischief that might work, eh? Why, for one thing it would mean that you, Zosar, and your friend here would find yourselves on the losing side."

"Never!" Zosar said in a tight and angry voice. "We will do what must be done—whatever the consequences."

"Good," the priest said. "Now, if—"

"Pardon me," Anab said in a timid voice, the voice of a man afraid of the answer his question would bring. "I—I don't understand. You agree to what?"

"To what?" Zosar said irritably. "For the love of heaven, Anab, haven't you been paying attention? We're talking about Baka. Do you understand? Baka's in the way. He has to go." He made the universally understood throat-cutting motion. "Don't look at me like that! It was inevitable. Otherwise we'll get nowhere, nowhere at all."

II

Hot, sweaty, dirty, Ben-Hadad patted the last stone into place and stepped back to look at his creation. The little furnace he had built was not much to look at, perhaps, but it would smelt copper. Above ground you could see only the top layer of stones; below there was a hemispherical pit lined with clay and backed with more stones. A drain had been placed three quarters of the way down and blocked with a stone plug; it emptied into a circular trench with a mound of sand in the middle. On the side opposite the drain, a set of bellows fed air to the furnace through a pipe.

Tuya, her single garment now ragged, squatted down to examine Ben-Hadad's work. "It looks complicated," she said. "What does it do?"

Bebe the weaver, a querulous, persnickety man, well known as a lover of boys, stood peering over her shoulder. "It seems to be some sort of new outdoor toilet," he said, sniffing the air and wrinkling his nose.

"I wasn't talking to you, weaver," she said, and turned

her attention back to the small furnace. "Seriously," she said to Ben-Hadad, "how does it work?"

Ben-Hadad wiped his sweaty brow with a forearm. "Well," he began, "first we pile charcoal and ore into the pit here. The problem, of course, is to raise the temperature of the fire high enough to get the copper to separate from the malachite ore. That is the purpose of the bellows. You work them with your feet, pumping air in to raise the heat—"

"Could I be the one who does it?" Tuya interrupted. "I'd be glad to help."

"It's no job for a girl," Ben-Hadad said without giving it a second thought. "As I was saying, when the temperature reaches a certain level, the pure molten copper settles to the bottom, to a level below the drain hole. That's when I remove the plug and let the slag, the waste, drain off. What remains is copper. When it hardens, I lift it out of the bottom of the furnace with this rod. And I use this other hook to remove the slag after it drains off into the trough. It's really very simple. They've been using this method at Timna for centuries."

Bebe the weaver made a sour face. "An occupation for cretins, obviously. Might as well let her have the work." He quoted, with a learned air, the satirical work the scribe Dua-khety had written making fun of all other occupations, back in the days of the Sesostrises, only changing the masculine pronouns to feminine ones. " 'The furnace tender's fingers are foul and smell like corpses. Her eyes are inflamed from the heavy smoke. She can't wash off the dirt in the many hours she spends in the pond. Clothes are an abomination to her.' "

"You get out of here!" said Tuya, painfully aware of her rags. "You're going to get a rock bounced off your head in a moment if you don't learn to hold your tongue."

Ben-Hadad laughed. "Actually, it's a fairly accurate job description. I take it you've never seen smith and apprentice at work, Tuya. They usually work naked. It makes better sense than wearing clothes. After all, if a cinder pops out and stings the bare skin, all it does is leave a little blister that goes away in a day or so. But if it finds cloth, it sets it ablaze. And that leaves a serious burn, one that can incapacitate you for months, idling the forge in the meantime. That alone is a good argument against having a woman in the trade."

"Not at all," Tuya said hotly. "I've nothing against being naked. This dress hasn't much left of it anyhow." She looked down at her rags again with chagrin.

"You need a new one," Ben-Hadad said. "Weaver—what would you charge me to make her a good dress?"

The weaver's mouth twisted in obvious disdain.

"Oh, come now," Ben-Hadad said. "We're all in this fight together. Quote me a fair price."

"Say . . . one copper outnou."

"So much? Be reasonable, or I'll start quoting Dua-khety on weavers. It was almost the first thing I learned in Egyptian when I arrived here. I know it well."

"Not a jot less."

"You can't say I didn't warn you." Ben-Hadad grinned at Tuya. " 'The weaver is more wretched than a woman in labor, with his knees drawn up against his belly. He can't breathe the air inside the weaving house. If he loses a day's work, they give him fifty lashes. He has to bribe the doorkeeper with food to let him stick his head out of the door to see sunlight every so often. . . .' "

Bebe's eyes flashed petulantly. He quoted back: " 'I have seen the coppersmith at work at the door of his furnace. His fingers were black as the crocodile's claws, and his body stank worse than fish excrement.' " He made a wry face. "So there!" He stalked off with mincing steps, to the laughter of Ben-Hadad and Tuya.

"That should take care of him," Ben-Hadad said. "But seriously, Tuya, it's not work for a woman. You wouldn't really like it at all. Surely there's work in the cookhouse. . . ."

"I don't like cooking," she said. Actually that was a lie. But she had other reasons for rejecting this alternative—for, if the truth were told, she found herself unusually excited about the idea of working alongside him, their two naked bodies close together, perhaps even touching from time to time. . . .

"I'd rather work with you," she said stubbornly. "Besides, everybody has to pull his weight in camp. And if women can fight alongside men, and go along on raids as I did a while back . . ."

"All right; you win," Ben-Hadad said. "But don't say I didn't warn you. It's hard, dirty work. And the sting of a hot cinder on your bare skin may change your mind for you pretty quickly. Cinders don't care where they land."

"Don't worry about me," she said. "You just do your work and tell me what I have to do."

"Whatever you say." He smiled, submitting good-naturedly. "I've a cartful of stolen ore to unload first. While I'm doing that, perhaps you could fill the water jug. We'll get hot and dry once we start, and you'll find yourself drinking a lot of water. As a matter of fact, fill two jugs. By the time you've finished that, I should be done here."

"Two full jugs coming up!" she said happily, picking up the ceramic containers and scampering away. For the first time that day she didn't mind her rags, or her isolation from the busy street life of the city. In fact, all the deprivations she had suffered since coming to camp as a fugitive were now forgotten, and simply because he'd agreed to let her help him, to let her work alongside him!

Who cared how hard the work would be? Who cared that it would be long days of sweaty, grubby labor, of sweat and soot and burn scars? Beside these she could put the joy of working with him, being there with him, all day long. . . .

At the well, however, she ran into Bebe. The weaver gave her a superior smile. "Tuya, dear," he intoned, "are you still begging him to let you run errands? Or have you come to your senses and realized he doesn't know you're alive?"

She put the jugs down carefully—and suddenly her two strong little hands reached out and gripped his garment, pulling his face down to hers. "Listen, you!" she said in a voice that carried real menace in it. "I've had about as much as I'm going to take of your big mouth! Keep it up and I'll cut your spindle off for you! And don't you think for a moment that I wouldn't do it!"

"Hey, let go, Tuya!" he said, trying to shrink back. "I didn't mean it." She released him, but stood glaring at him as if his next word spoken out of line would be his last. "Look how you've rumpled the cloth! Besides, for heaven's sake, Tuya, haven't you any pride? Chasing him like that? When it's obvious to anyone with eyes to see that—"

"As if it were any of your business," she said. "What's it to you, Bebe? Did he spurn your own advances, perhaps? It may be true that he's not pursuing me like a lovesick swain, but *your* kind he isn't interested in at all."

"Say what you will, you're making a fool of yourself."

"Perhaps I am. But I'm not an aimless fool. I know what I want, and I'm not afraid to admit it. Why, look at your own life, Bebe. You've made your own choice, haven't you? Aren't there people around you who don't understand, who make fun of you for being what you are?"

"Why, yes, but . . . I had no idea that you'd be able to see it from my point of view this way, Tuya. I apologize, truly I do. I should have offered my sympathy, shouldn't I? Instead of sniping at you like a jealous bitch?" His eyes were wet now. He took her hand softly, gently, in compassion. "I'm sorry. I've been horrible. I *do* understand, really. There was that simply lovely young bowman I was so taken with, a month ago, the one who was killed in the raid just before you joined us. I simply *adored* him, and he couldn't see me at all. He treated me like a pair of cheap papyrus sandals you use once or twice and then throw away. How heartbroken I was!" He squeezed her hands, and the tears ran down his cheeks. "Tuya, I've been horrible. Can you forgive me?"

"Certainly," Tuya said. "But I've a hard row to hoe, too. Help me if you can. Don't make things worse for me."

"Of course! Oh, of course, darling! Anything! Just say the word."

"All right," she said, practical and down-to-earth again. "I'll be working naked with him, as he says, all grimy and covered with dirt. Goodness knows I'm no temple dancing girl, with my little bosom and narrow hips; as it is he'll hardly be able to tell me from a boy. I'll certainly be no vision of grace and beauty, sweating like a pig there at the forge. So on festival days I'd like to be able to dress up

and show him what I'm like when I'm all fixed up. You
know, put on a bit of style. Could you make me a . . .
could you make me something pretty to wear? Something
I could show off in? Surprise him? Something like that? I
could swap you; I'll cook you delicious dinners every night
for a week."

Bebe clapped his hands in delight.

"Oh, of course, darling! And, look—there's a way to
fix your hair. I can cut it just so, along here. It'll look
charming. And you can still work in it. I did manage to
bring my trunk with me when I came out from the city to
join Baka, here at the camp, to make clothing for this little
army of his. I can look in the bottom. There used to be the
most fetching wig . . . why, even *I* looked like a king's
daughter in it, if I do say so myself. I'll bet it would look
ravishing on you."

"Done!" she said. "Then we're friends? True friends?
No more sniping?"

"Oh, yes! Yes!"

As she filled the jugs she spotted Anab coming through
the line of tents under the date palms. "Anab!" she called
out. "Come over here and help me!"

He tried to look away but wasn't quick enough. Reluctantly he joined her.

"I can get only one full jug as far as my shoulder," she
said. "Carry the other one for me, will you?"

Anab shouldered the jug and walked beside her. He
found himself actually welcoming the hard work of toting
the water jug, and wished there were more such heavy,
punishing physical work awaiting him during the remain-
der of the day. Anything to keep his mind off what he'd
learned the previous night. Anything to distract him from
the walking nightmare his life had become since he'd first
talked to Zosar and agreed to go into Avaris with him.

Tuya was chattering happily beside him, and he let
his mind drink her words in, eager for the distraction.

". . . going to learn how to help him. I'm going to
make him need me, Anab. Just you watch. He'll wind up
noticing me. He can't help doing so. I'll make myself so
useful he'll wonder how he ever did without me. . . ."

"Please, Tuya!" Anab said after a few minutes of this cheerful babble. "You're giving me a headache. Go ahead and jump into bed with the poor fellow, but stop talking about it." As soon as he'd said it, he was sorry. He had wanted distraction, and here he was, voluntarily forgoing it. But hearing other people talk of love, people who, unlike himself, had at least some chance of finding it, that twisted in his guts like a sharp knife. "I—I'm sorry, Tuya," he said. "But I'm not feeling well."

"Oh," she said, teetering under the weight of the loaded jug. "I didn't know, or I wouldn't have asked you for help. Go ahead, put the jug down. I'll come back for it. It was kind of you to have brought it this far."

"No," he said, contrite. "I'll take it all the way. We're almost there, anyhow."

Somewhat perplexed at his behavior, she glanced over at him. "Anab . . . you said just now that I should go ahead and—and seduce him and get it over with. But can't you see—that's not the point. If I wanted to give up my virginity, I could find any number of men to sleep with. This is different. I want him to lo—"

"Please!" he said. "I don't mind the work, but the chatter's driving me crazy!" Putting on a new burst of speed, he lengthened his strides and passed her, carrying the jug to Ben-Hadad's side and dumping it down, miraculously without spilling a drop. "Here," he said, puffing. "Tuya asked me to help her. I'll be going now."

"But, Anab—" the young smith called after him.

Anab did not look back. His mind was in a terrible state. How could he have gone along with Zosar's suggestions? How could he have listened to him? Now he was committed to a terrible enterprise, a wretched and ugly piece of business. They'd proposed it, and he'd just stood there, not protesting. The only time he'd showed any courage at all was when he'd asked them not to kill Baka, just to capture him and put him somewhere where he couldn't get in the way of their plans. It had been extremely difficult for him, speaking up that way, and he'd been surprised when Zosar and Ashau had looked at each other and nodded gravely before agreeing with him. But he could take no pride in his performance, none at all. He had just stood there, passive and wordless, letting them get away with it. Why couldn't he have spoken up? Why couldn't he have objected?

But perhaps it's not too late, he thought suddenly. *I can still go to Baka and tell him. I can warn him. Maybe that way I can make up for everything.*

Yes—that was the way to handle it. He stopped dead in the middle of the path that ran between the rows of tents, thinking it over. If he could head off the trouble he had helped to cause, perhaps he could finally put an end to all this business of letting people push him around, bully him, force him to do what they wanted instead of what he wanted. Perhaps he could become master of his own destiny. . . .

Just like little Tuya! Of course she wasn't ugly the way he was—far from it, actually. She was rather pretty, or would be if she ever fixed herself up and started acting like a girl. She was in love with someone who had so far showed little if any sign of noticing her. But had she given up? Had she surrendered to her fate, let him go, given up? No, she'd made up her mind to go after him, to make him notice her! She decided to do whatever in the world she had to do—*whatever!*—in order to attract his attention and keep it. And, tenacious and tough-minded as she was, he almost began to believe that she'd succeed, that she'd make him start paying serious attention to her one of these days! Why, if—

Anab's heart almost stopped. Around the end tent came Baka himself! Heading straight for him!

He swallowed hard, tried to get his knees to stop shaking. If he could only . . . if he could get himself to . . . He ran the words over in his mind. *Baka, stop! Your life's in danger! They're going to kidnap you! Arm yourself! Surround yourself with guards! Quickly! There's no time to lose!* He stood, transfixed, his heart beating fast, too fast. Baka bore down on him—

"Hello, Anab," Baka said. Smiled. Passed by.

Anab just stood there. His mouth would not work. His hands shook as if palsied. He opened his mouth but the words would not come.

Baka was gone. And the self-loathing once again arose in Anab's heart, stronger than ever, blotting out all else. His one chance had slipped by, never to return.

III

Four days passed—four days of the most back-breaking work Tuya had ever done. She had never, never realized a smith's work was this hard. Yet difficult as her own tasks were, she could see with her own eyes that Ben-Hadad worked harder. When it came to carrying charcoal, ore, and clay molds, he was right there with her, effortlessly surpassing the work she did. And on the rare occasion when she could relax with the relatively untaxing donkey-work, pumping the bellows or blowing into a reed pipe to heat up the coals under a crucible, there was Ben-Hadad, pounding away as if he felt no fatigue at all.

Still she hung on grimly, tenaciously, telling herself that her stamina would increase as needed, that her muscles would toughen and grow. And, miraculously, after a few days she would sometimes experience a sudden renewal of strength, find a new wind. She thanked every god in the pantheon for this, and redoubled her efforts.

It was curious, she thought, how little their nakedness mattered to them most of the time. Working as hard as they did, neither of them tended to notice it. And it was true—it was much safer to work this way, for all that the occasional cinder would pop out and kiss her bare skin with a blinding flash of pain. She knew that the same cinder would have set any garment she wore on fire and caused a severe, incapacitating burn. She also knew that in this heat, virtually anything she could wear would seem unbearably hot. Besides, from time to time a slight breeze would sweep in from the trees, bringing cooler air, and the feel of it on her bare skin was, in these precious moments, absolutely delicious. She counted her few blessings and was thankful for them. And at the end of each day, true to her promise, she plodded down to the river, washed herself, put her rags back on again, and went to the cook tent to prepare the meal she'd promised Bebe the weaver.

So far Bebe hadn't given her a glimpse of the dress he was making for her. Still, she'd have a chance to inspect it, she knew, when it came time to try it on and adjust it to her wiry little body. She looked forward to this moment with eager anticipation, but for now it was best to put it from her mind. And after preparing his meal, she would catch a stray bite for herself, almost too tired to chew the food she had prepared, then would fall exhausted into her narrow bed and drift off into a night of untroubled dreams.

The first day or so she had had to endure the taunts of male passersby, who would comment satirically, often obscenely, on her thin body and narrow hips. But after a time Ben-Hadad, seeing her distress, had warned them off. They had looked at his own powerful body, bared by his work, at his broad shoulders and massive biceps, and had shrugged and gone away.

Now, as the afternoon wore on toward sundown, she stood, naked and smoke-blackened, atop the pair of hog-bladder bellows, and pumped them. Her arms were draped over the support post Ben-Hadad erected for her; her legs, half numb with fatigue, throbbed painfully from the too-close heat of the fire. As one foot tramped down, the other would let up, and at the same time she would tug at one of the two strings in her hands, letting air into the deflated bladder. Then, her bare toes curled into the bellows, she would rock to the other side and tramp down, simultaneously pulling the string in her other hand.

As she repeated this for perhaps the thousandth time, her attention began to wander. She watched Ben-Hadad as he hunched over the fire, watched the play of the rippling muscles in his back where it broadened out before tapering down to narrow, hard buttocks . . . and she yearned for him. As she continued to pump away, a gust of wind blew on her naked body and cooled it, sensitizing her bare skin all over. All of a sudden, for the first time that day, she *felt* naked. Her entire body seemed to prickle, and she shivered with the sensation.

Ben-Hadad turned just then, wiped his dripping brow,

and glanced up at her. He smiled, rocked back on his heels, and looked her up and down as her thin legs churned away on the bellows. Looked at her narrow body, bared for work, bared for him . . . and it seemed she saw, for a moment, something new in his eyes—

Her rocking motion on the paired bellows faltered. Suddenly she wanted to cover herself—but dared not let go of the strings that opened the two bellows.

"Oh, I'm sorry," she said, flustered. "I've lost the rhythm. Here, let me start again." But as her toes dug into the bags, another shiver went through her, so powerful this time that her body seemed to burn. There was the most amazing feeling in her loins, a feeling she'd never had before, almost as if . . .

"There, you've got it now," he said as her feet found the rhythm at last. "I—I was thinking, Tuya. These few days . . . you've lost weight. I've been working you too hard."

"No, you haven't," she said. "I can take it. Whatever work you give me." Her suddenly weak legs churned away doggedly.

"I'm sure you can," he said. "But I think you don't know how much energy you burn up here. You should be eating more, doing work like this. In fact, you'd better eat with me from now on; I'll see to it you get enough food. You'll feel a lot better, I promise."

His gaze—was it impersonal now? She couldn't tell, really—went slowly up from her feet to her face, pausing along the way. She felt her cheeks burn.

"Eat w-with you?" she said. "I—I have other duties for a couple of days, but after that . . . certainly! You tell me what I should be eating, what both of us should be eating, and I'll fix it for us."

"That's not necessary," he said. "I cook my own food. I'll just cook extra amounts of what I'm already eating, and you can have that."

"Oh, no!" she said, straightening her back, forcing new strength into her pumping legs. "I'll do it. Just tell me."

"Well, whatever you wish," he said, smiling at her, his eyes friendly and warm. He looked back at the forge.

"That's good: The coals are just right. Now, if you can keep that up for a few more minutes . . ."

She felt her legs quake. She gritted her teeth and forced her muscles to redouble their efforts. As he turned away, however, a smile crept onto her face. He had, in spite of himself, noticed her! In spite of his obvious resolve to keep their relationship on a friendly, impersonal basis, he had at last taken notice of her, no matter how involuntary his reponse had been. For, sitting on his heels there by the fire, he had been as naked as she, and her own eyes had wandered, as much as had his. Her smile broadened. She had seen the stirring of his flesh as he looked at her, and however brief his reaction had been, it had been real—and powerful. And that feeling his body had had, it was for her. *Her, Tuya!* Not for some namby-pamby rich man's daughter.

At day's end they had cleaned the forge, stacked their tools neatly, and bade each other good-bye. Ben-Hadad's parting smile had been warmer than usual, and Tuya carried the memory of it with her as she made her way to the bank of the river. Still naked and dusty, she had not bothered to put on her tattered garment, her sole remaining possession.

The place where she bathed was a little cove where the water eddied, calm and smooth, far in from the current. At water's edge she paused, dropped the garment at her feet, and knelt to lean far out over the still water, steadying herself with one hand gripping an overhanging tree branch.

What did she look like to a man, she wondered? The only naked women she'd ever seen to compare herself with were either dancing girls, spied through a window as they came off after their dance—still naked, they had sometimes paused to chat with her, to enjoy the evening breeze—or the matrons who bathed at the stream behind the inn back in Avaris. Yet their bodies had been nothing like hers. They had been ripe, womanly, large-breasted, wide-hipped, plump-thighed. She had thought: This was what men wanted. She had felt her own skinny body with her hands, hating her narrow, almost boyish hips and

small breasts, and she had marked herself down as one of
life's losers in this regard.

But now she leaned far over the water and saw her
little breasts hang out away from her body, and they didn't
look quite so insignificant, because a man—the man she
loved—had looked at them, and his body had stirred at
the sight.

She stood and, still holding on to the tree with one
hand, continued to stare at her reflection in the water.
Foreshortened this way, her body took on a different
aspect. Her hips did not seem so narrow, her bosom so
insignificant . . . and, at the middle of her body, there
was—almost unduly prominent now—the patch of curling
black hair, in the place where her body had felt so strange—
She shivered suddenly, recalling the sensation . . . and
turning, sought the dry land again. She looked down at
her dusty body and hugged herself, remembering . . .

. . . and suddenly sprang forward and dived into the
healing, chilling waters of the Nile. In a moment she came
up gasping and blowing, grinning, her ardor all but forgotten in the icy cold of the river's flood.

Fifty strides upstream, in another sheltered cove,
Ben-Hadad stood thigh-deep in the river, splashing water
on his tired and soot-streaked body, unaware of her prox-
imity but unable to get her out of his mind. And troubled,
profoundly troubled, by the disturbing fact.

What a fool I am! he thought. *Here I've been treating
her like a child, just because she looked like one.*

There was a certain amount of excuse for this. Tuya's
rags had hid as much as they revealed: Half again too
large, they had concealed the widening hips and the lovely,
delicate little breasts. All he had seen were the child's
short limbs and tiny hands and feet.

But she's a woman, he thought. *She's been one all
this time. And I haven't had the eyes to see.*

What an obtuse, unthinking ox I must appear. . . .

But today, somehow, what everyone else must have
noticed long ago had finally begun to get through to that
dim mind of his. And his body certainly had responded.
His body had known before his mind. And as quick as he'd

been to cover himself, it hadn't been quick enough. She'd noticed.

He closed his eyes, ashamed of himself. How ridiculous he must seem now, acting all this time as if she were an unsexed child. Ignoring her at the forge, ignoring what the men who passed by had seen, had noticed, had made insulting remarks about.

He thought about her now: thin, underfed, uncared for, she'd grown up in the streets of Sile, moving with so many others to Avaris when that city had begun to spring from the earth. Living from day to day, from hand to mouth, asking help from no one . . . and, more than anyone else he'd known since he came here, generous beyond reason to anyone who needed anything she had to give.

He had taken her for granted.

In his bitter shame he sank into the water, letting the chill waves lap around his neck as his body adjusted to the cool of the river. He splashed his face. Submerging, wetting his hair, he washed the dirt out of it . . .

. . . and wished he could wash the mud out of his stupid, uncomprehending mind. All this time she had followed him around, running errands for him, making herself always available for whatever needed to be done, even back in Avaris. She had shooed people away when he needed to concentrate, playing senet. She'd brought him food and drink when the game had gone on too long, when even Anab was too busy going from one person to another in the crowd, lining up bets, drumming up business.

She'd saved his life, too! At great risk to her own. And now she was doing the brutal, demanding work of an armorer's helper, never complaining, never shirking. Doing whatever he asked her to, out of the goodness of her heart, out of kindness, out of—

He blinked the water from his eyes, swallowing.

You fool, he told himself. *She's in love with you.*

He quickly got his feet under him and stood up, chest-high in the chilly water. As the cold gripped at his nakedness he could feel his body responding again, as it had before, responding powerfully, until his whole being ached, ached for—

He shook the water from his eyes, pushed his wet hair back, and walked out of the water. He was all goosebumps now, shivering, his body rigid where it responded. He wiped himself down with the tattered rags he'd brought along to dry himself with. By and by his passion subsided, in the shame of his self-knowledge.

Getting into his evening garment, he forced himself to reflect soberly on the day's events. *We can't go on as we have,* he thought. *She can't work at the forge anymore. Especially with nothing on. I'll have to talk to her, to tell her. . . .*

Tell her what? That she had to stay away from him? That she couldn't come to the forge anymore?

Ben-Hadad shook his head violently. The thought of not having her there—near him all the time, chattering away, responding when he said something, just *being* there—was so terrible that it fairly hurt to think of it. Simply discovering, at long last, that he cared, and this much, was profoundly disturbing. And suddenly he realized how much he wanted to see her again, to talk to her, just to be with her. He wanted—

"Tuya," he said in a strangled voice, and rushed off to find her.

"But—where's Bebe?" Tuya said. "I was supposed to—"

Baka smiled at her. "I know. He told me—or rather, I dragged it out of him. I mean, your little bargain. I told him he'd driven too hard a bargain. He agreed. He's let you off for the final three days of meal-preparing. Goodness knows, you work hard enough in the daytime as it is. He's working on your dress right now. Come, the dusk is lovely; walk with me."

Puzzled, she accompanied him. Baka had never paid her any mind before this, although he'd dropped by the forge several times and seen the two of them—soot-stained wretches, naked and sweaty—working away like demons from the pit. She shot a sidelong glance at him, fearing amorous advances and wondering how she'd handle them. His manner, however, allayed her fears, and she let herself be led to the edge of the grove, where they could watch the sun go down.

Baka did not speak for a long time. They watched the sun's brilliant flare pulse and die at the horizon. Then he said, "Ben-Hadad—I'm coming to think a lot of him."

She did not know what to say.

"You do, too," he said. "I can tell. You're in love with him, aren't you?" He turned and looked at her, and she couldn't lie to him, couldn't even equivocate. She nodded, her eyes full of the sadness in her heart. "I thought so. And he doesn't notice yet, does he? Well, he will sooner or later. He's as stupid as all of us men are in that regard, I suppose. I wasn't any better. I had the finest wife a man could—" He closed his eyes; his voice was tight, controlled when he spoke. "I neglected her. I drove her into another man's bed. But it wasn't her fault. It was mine." He smiled gravely at her. "Maybe I can help you. I think he might listen to me."

"Oh, yes. He thinks the world of you. But—there's something about you that he's afraid of, or concerned about. I'm not sure just what it is. I'll try to find out, if you want me to." She shook her head thoughtfully. "I was afraid of you myself, at first. I'm surprised now at how easy it is to talk to you."

"It's because we're friends," Baka said. "Give it no more thought. I feel to all of you like a father to his children. But you—you remind me of someone who mattered very much to me when I was younger. I'd like to save you some of the anguish I caused her, if I may. I'll do whatever I can for you with Ben-Hadad."

There was a sound in the brush behind them. Baka, his hand reaching for his sword, whirled—but the club caught him on the side of the head, felling him like a tree. He landed on his face and did not rise. Tuya shrank back, her hand searching her rags for the knife that was no longer there. From behind, strong hands closed on her, and held her despite all her struggling. She saw men, several men, reach for Baka, lift him. Her own feet cleared the ground; a man carried her as though she were a child's rag doll. And the moment when, the shock subsiding, she remembered to scream, they quickly silenced her, a hard hand clamping her mouth shut. She wriggled but could not shake herself free. Darkness was falling around her with terrible suddenness.

IV

Coming out of his tent, threaded needle in hand, Bebe was all but bowled over by the lot of them. The two carrying Baka's inert body shouldered him aside; he stumbled into a tree and dropped his needle. "H-here!" he said in his high voice. "You can't just . . . what are you doing? What are you doing with—? Guards! Help! *Help!*"

One of the others backhanded him to the ground, but Bebe, who had suffered abuse before, knew the way of such people, and gave to the blow. When he hit the ground he rolled. And as he rolled to safety, he caught a glimpse of little Tuya in the dim light, struggling in the arms of a big man he did not know. He ducked behind a tent and scrambled away . . . but not before he had spotted and, beyond doubt, identified one face he knew all too well.

There was no time for anything but escape just now, though. The light was dim, and there had been a lot of noise in the brush as they had come by. Who knew how many of them there were? Who knew whether, at any moment, one or two of them might come charging around the tent in search of him, Bebe? No: Quite definitely, the first thing to do was to find safety until they had passed. After that there'd be time to help his friends, if h could. . . .

He glanced longingly at the opening of his tent, th thought better of it. That would be the first place the look. He abandoned dignity and scrambled into a clum thick brush growing next to the row of tents.

From his new hiding place he could peek out, i gloom, and see activity down the way: men strug fighting . . . and now fire! Someone had lit a tor perhaps picked a faggot from the fire, and set the fir ablaze! As he watched, the man with the torch rai the row of tents, setting them all on fire.

When the man had passed his tent, mira sparing it for no apparent reason, Bebe decided th were entirely too close to the underbrush he w in. He scrambled back, into the trees beyon fringe of the encampment. Then he rose to hi

was about to take off like a frightened hare when he
suddenly felt strong hands gripping his arms.

"N-no—" he said, his heart in his mouth. "I—"

"It's all right," came a tense whisper. "It's me, Ben-
Hadad. I just got here. What's happening? It's a raid, isn't
it?"

"Yes! Yes!" Bebe said. "Please, you're hurting my
arm—"

"I'm sorry," Ben-Hadad said, releasing him. "How
many are there? What did you see?"

"I don't know how many. Over a dozen. They *would*
catch us napping like this, when most of the men are out
on a scouting party. But . . ."

"How did they get past the pickets?" Ben-Hadad
asked.

"Zosar must have got them in. He was with them. I
saw him. He probably lied to the guard—"

"Zosar? He's with them?"

"Yes. And, Ben-Hadad—they've got Baka. He may
be dead. They were carrying him by the heels. He was
out cold. And they've got Tuya, and—"

"They've got *Tuya*? Is she all right?"

"I think so. I mean, she was still struggling with them
as they dragged her off. She was still alive, anyway."

Ben-Hadad swore savagely under his breath. "If they've
harmed her, so help me, I'll—" He clapped Bebe on his
thin shoulder. "Look, Bebe, we've got to help them.
Come with me."

"Me? But I'm no good at fighting. I'm frightened."

"So am I. But we've friends out there, and they're in
terrible danger. Come on, now. Follow me."

"But . . ."

They skirted the long line of palms outside the encampment. The fires were everywhere, and in their glow they
could make out inert bodies lying on the ground—whose,
they could not say.

"Here!" someone shouted. "Bring the horses through!
It has to look like a troop of Shepherd light horse came
through here, destroying everything before them!" At this
order five horsemen cantered into the area, the horses'

hooves sending dry dust billowing around them in the weird glow of the fires. "Go ahead!" someone cried. "Kill the bastards! No survivors! You know what we agreed!"

" 'No survivors'!" Ben-Hadad said in a voice fraught with tension. "You hear that, Bebe? If they've killed Tuya and Baka—"

"No!" the tailor said in his high-pitched whisper, almost a child's. "I see them. Over there! They're loading the two of them on a cart. They're tying Tuya's hands."

Ben-Hadad breathed a silent prayer of thanks as he watched the scene. "All right. The cart's leaving, and the others don't seem to be following it, at least not yet. That's our chance. Here, come with me."

Bebe, helpless to disobey, followed. His heart was still in his throat, and his innards were all but paralyzed with fear. Yet somehow his limbs worked, and with great efficiency. He could hardly believe himself, running *toward* trouble!

Up ahead Ben-Hadad slowed, just where the track left the now unguarded front gate. Barely visible in the dim light, the smith gestured with his hands. Bebe understood his intent; they'd ambush the cart as it went past. Ben-Hadad signaled again: He, Bebe, was to grab the traces near the bit of the front horse. Well, that would be no problem, unless the horses bolted. He'd just have to trust Ben-Hadad to take care of the driver and the guard. Goodness knew, he was big and strong enough. Bebe firmed his narrow jaw and set himself for action.

"Now!" Ben-Hadad whispered, just as the cart drew opposite the bushes that hid them. Bebe, unthinking, his muscles acting of themselves, rushed forward, his hands groping in the dark for the leather traces. He grabbed them and held. To his left he could feel, rather than see, the action as Ben-Hadad rushed the guard, pulling him down from the cart's high seat and silencing him with a powerful punch in the face. The cart wobbled crazily as Ben-Hadad leaped into the guard's seat and grappled with the driver. The horses shied, tried to rear up. But Bebe clung to the lead horse's bit and hung there, in the air, heels dangling. The horse came back down to the groun' shaking its head, trying to dislodge him. He hung on for dear life—

Now, as the flames far to the rear caught the surrounding trees and roared heavenward, he looked back and could see the two of them fighting. Ben-Hadad's powerful hands closed about the driver's neck as the driver reached for the knife in his belt, finally freed it, and—

"No!" Bebe shouted. "Ben-Hadad! He's got a knife—"

He watched with horror as the driver's desperate hand drove the knife home . . . as Ben-Hadad's grasp loosened, and the driver drew back again—

"No!" he said, his voice almost a screech, close by the lead horse's ear, and at the same moment he let go of the traces. The horse reared, jerking the cart roughly to one side. The driver tumbled to the ground; the cart began moving forward at a slow pace, its great inertia battling the horses' panic. Ben-Hadad reeled atop the cart's high seat, about to fall.

"Hang on!" Bebe said, dashing for the cart. The driver got to one knee, blocking his way, but Bebe's mad rush spilled him over on his back. Bebe saw the cart roll over the man's body, heard his anguished cries rising to a shriek, then subsiding into low moans. He leaped for the cart's mounting step. His foot found the little platform, and he scrambled up.

Ben-Hadad slumped against the back of the seat, in obvious pain. "Bebe," he said, trying to sit up. "The horses . . ."

The little weaver sat him down again with gentle hands. "Get in the back," he said. "If you can untie Tuya, she can bind your wounds. We have to see if Baka's alive." As he talked, his thin hands picked up the reins and pulled back steadily. The cart, veering from side to side on the road until now, assumed a straighter course. "There," Bebe said, his firm hand on the reins gentling the animals. "Now if we can only get away before they notice who's in the driver's seat." Softly he shook the reins, guiding the animals forward, picking up the pace a bit.

Then, with terrible suddenness, something struck him in the back, driving him forward. It was as if someone had swung a club and pounded him there as hard as he could.

But when Bebe tried to turn to see what was behind him, there was a stabbing pain right in the middle of the place where he'd been hit. He wavered on the seat, feeling faint, feeling as though at any moment he was going to fall in a heap. . . .

"N-no!" he said suddenly. "I w-won't let it—" He gritted his teeth, firmed his jaw. He stiffened, trying to keep erect, to avoid doing anything that would lead to another such stab of pain. And he found to his surprise that his hands were still gripping the reins hard.

"Here! Stop them!" a voice to the rear said.

"I got one of them!" a man cried. And as his words died, Bebe felt a hiss of air pass his cheek and saw the dim light glint on the passing shaft of an arrow.

"Get up!" he said to the horses. Slow-moving, sturdy draft animals, they could not accelerate fast enough to suit him. "*Go!*" he cried, in a strange voice that somehow did not sound like himself speaking. "Faster! Faster!" Now he could hear footfalls in the road behind him, pounding, pounding. . . .

In the back Ben-Hadad struggled with Tuya's bonds, his fingers as clumsy as dry sticks, his mind reeling. The wound ached dully, but real pain hadn't set in yet. He didn't know what that meant. He struggled with the tangled knots—

"*Mmmmmff,*" said Tuya beside him in the dark, deep inside the high-walled cart. "*MMMMmmmmm!*"

"Oh," he said, "I'm sorry." Finding her face by feel more than anything, he pulled the gag from her mouth.

"Ben-Hadad," she said. "They've got Baka!"

"I know," he said. "He's right here. He's unconscious. I was so eager to get you loose I haven't had a chance to see if he's still alive—"

"No!" she said. "That's not Baka! They separated us back there!" He slipped the last knot and she rubbed her hands. "I don't know who *this* is. But Baka's still in their hands." She untied her ankles, her little hands clawing desperately at the ropes. "Who's driving?" she asked.

"Bebe," he said. "He came along with me. I—I think the driver stabbed me. Bebe took the reins over when I threw the driver to the ground."

"Bebe? You can't mean it," she said. She liberated her painfully chafed ankles and rubbed her feet, trying to get the circulation started up again. As she did the cart jounced hard against a rock, working itself to one side. They seemed to be moving much faster now. "Bebe!" she shouted. "Are we out of reach yet? Are we—?"

But there was no response. The cart wavered, swinging back and forth. "Something's wrong," she said. "Let me get up there and see what's happened."

She stood, her head high above the sides of the cart. She could see Bebe slumped forward, the long arrow protruding from his narrow back. "Bebe!" she said. "You're hurt!"

But Bebe was beyond hurt. As she touched his shoulder, the weight of her hand was just enough to upset the delicate balance that had held his body erect. "Oh, no!" she said, gasping. Her heart beating wildly, she sprang into the seat beside his now slumped-over body and took the reins from his nerveless hands.

After a time she managed to pull the cart onto a side road and, calming the animals, bring them slowly to a halt. Not until she had stopped the cart did she relax her tight grip on the leather reins. Then she reached down and felt Bebe's thin wrist. It was cold, and there was no pulse.

Feeling faint, she stood, turned around. Ben-Hadad, too, was trying to stand. One hand clutched his chest; the other clawed ineffectually at the slats of the wagon's sides. "No!" she said. "Lie down. Don't move, please. I—I'll get us to someplace safe. Just lie back. You're hurt . . . maybe pretty badly. I don't know. I'll do what I can for you, but first I have to get us to safety."

He looked at her, his face white with pain. "The dead man here—he's one of theirs, I think. One of Zosar's old friends. I got a glimpse of his face when the moon came out from behind the clouds a m-moment ago. Onuris, I think his name was."

"Don't pay any attention to him," she said in a firm voice that surprised her even more than it did him. "Just lie back and don't hurt yourself trying to move. I don't

know where we are, but I'm going to have to get us off the
track, somewhere where they won't think to look for us. I
can't do that if I have to worry about you back there trying
to get up and hurting yourself more."

"I—I'm sorry," he said in a weak voice. "You're right."
He let himself sink back onto the floor of the cart, into the
straw that was by now stained with his blood. But as she
turned back to the horses, he raised his head once more.
"You?" he said. "You're all right? You're not hurt?"

"I'm fine," she said in a voice strangely calm again.
"Don't worry about me. Just lie back and rest for a while."
She flicked the reins, chuck-chucking at the horses as she
had heard the drivers do back in Sile, in a time so seemingly remote that she could barely imagine it was within
her own memory. The horses moved forward, slowly, into
a grove of trees, and turned off the twisting track to a
path that skirted one of the many arms of the Great River.
Beside her the moon's pale reflection glinted on the black
waters.

A while later she pulled the animals up sharply under
a tree overlooking the river. The moon, two days short of
full, was out now, free from the drifting cloud cover; Tuya
could see all the way across the river. She strained her
eyes, then suddenly jumped down onto the ground and
dashed to the water's edge. Yes! She knew where she was!
This was only a little way downstream from where she had
bathed nightly for several days now. Across the river was
the little island she'd swum to, day before yesterday.
Nobody but her seemed to know of it. It had plenty of
natural cover and shelter of a sort—there were plenty of
shrubs and trees from which to make a lean-to, and papyrus reeds to cover it with. Tomorrow she could swim back
to the burned-out camp and see what she could salvage.
There might be some food, some dried beans or even
some meat that had survived the fire. Or perhaps she
could find a discarded weapon or two, for hunting and
fishing. Meanwhile, they'd be safe until his wounds had
healed. . . .

Come to think of it, there was even a reed boat
beached somewhere down the riverbank, not yet water-

logged, and probably capable of floating Ben-Hadad across the river if she could get him into it. If she could find it . . .

She bit her lip, thinking. She'd have to drive the animals away. She'd leave Bebe's body in the seat, with the reins in his hands. It would look as though he'd driven the cart away and at last died, with the other dead man in the back. Perhaps they'd forget that it had been this wagon that had had her in it. . . .

She paused, looking at poor Bebe's slumped body in the front seat. She knew how easily frightened he had been, how excitable. For him to come after her with Ben-Hadad, trying to save her and Baka, had been an amazing act of courage. What a pity to have to leave him like this, for the crows . . . but there was no other way. Not if she were to save Ben-Hadad and herself.

She sighed and climbed up to open the back of the cart, pulling the horizontal slats out one at a time and tossing them on top of the body in the far corner of the wagon.

"W-what—" Ben-Hadad said, trying to rise.

"Stay down!" she said in a loud whisper. "Save your strength; you'll need it. I'm going to try to find a boat. If I can get you in it, I'll try floating you across the river to the island. We'll be safe there. I can come back to pick through the camp for any supplies that may be left."

His hand waved to her, motioning her closer. "T-Tuya," he said.

"No time to talk now," she said. "You stay put. I'm going after the boat. I think I know where it is—"

But his hand, though weak now, closed on her wrist and held her there. "Tuya," he said again, his voice hoarse. His hand left her wrist, and his fingers brushed her cheek, softly, gently: a caress. An uncontrollable shiver went through her body, and the sound that escaped her lips was something like a sigh, something like a sob. She wanted to lean against his hand, but she forced herself to pull away. There was work, desperate work, to be done. . . .

A while later she eased him into the small, half-waterlogged boat she found beached in the reeds, and, swimming behind it, floated him across. In the shallows on the island she helped him out and walked him to shore, her eyes by now adjusted to the darkness. He stumbled once and cried out in pain, but she was there to steady him as they walked up the slippery riverbank. "Here, my darling," she said when they had reached the concealment of the underbrush. "Ease down here. . . ." Her bare soles groped on the sand and dry reeds for a soft spot, to which she guided him. Only when he was on his back and resting quietly did she slip away, looking for fresh boughs to lay over the two of them. Although his wound seemed to have stopped bleeding, he'd be in shock now, shivering. She'd have to keep him warm.

Finally she covered both of them with her own robe, then the boughs, and lay shivering beside him, feeling his slow and regular breathing; he'd passed out as much from exhaustion as from pain. She held him close and let his body warm hers, and gloried at the touch of his flesh against her own. She lay like this for quite some time, and was not aware when it was that she, too, passed over into sleep.

But in the night he moved, slowly at first, then more purposefully, pushing some of the boughs aside. They had been nested like shells, her little bosom and belly pressed to his back. Now he turned to face her. There was a little grunt of pain as his wound made its presence known, but ignoring this, he put one arm across her and pulled her close to him again.

He heard as well as felt her quick intake of breath. "You're awake," he said.

"Don't move," she said in a tremulous voice. "You'll hurt yourself—"

"No, I won't. Not enough to matter." His face came close. His lips touched her hair, her forehead. "Don't worry about me, Tuya. My rib stopped the knife, I think. The bleeding has stopped. I think I'm going to be all right." All the time his hand roved over her naked back, soft fingertips touching her skin. Her body seemed afire. His hand went to her bottom, and as he cupped one narrow buttock softly, she shuddered and held herself to him. She was afraid to speak, afraid to do anything for fear of doing the wrong thing.

"My dear one," he said, as his lips sought hers. The kiss was soft at first, then hard, demanding. She felt her body shake, out of control; her loins were ablaze with new, strange, different feelings. And she found herself returning his kiss, with an unfamiliar but undeniable passion. "Oh, Tuya," he said in a voice that was strong and sure. "I love you. I think that I've always loved you, even though I may not have known it before."

"Oh," was all she could manage to say. "Oh. B-but you'll hurt yourself. . . ."

She heard his low, satisfied sigh as he pulled her atop him gently, lifted her, and settled her slowly, tenderly into place. As the alien flesh entered her for the first time, in one alarming thrust, she gasped in pain—and then the new emotions and sensations shook her to the center of her being. Her heart was beating fast, her face burned, the skin all over her naked torso was alive, and the wind played softly upon her body. She shivered, then bent over to cover his face with her kisses. As if of its own accord, her body began to move, and a soft voice—could it be her own?—began to croon softly, then to moan. His hands caressed her breasts as the breeze sighed sweetly, musically, in the boughs above and around them. She was adrift on winds of flame; she was flying; she was . . .

Then the passion took her, once and for all, and tore through her like tornado winds, squeezing her dry and dropping her, exhausted and dripping with chill sweat, on his chest. His strong arms still held her and pressed her to him, and the soft voice whispered indecipherable things in her ear, things that needed no words to make them clear. She had never been so drained in her life. And her heart had never been so full.

CHAPTER SEVEN

MEMPHIS

I

At the sound of the commotion on the stairs, Joseph looked up from his accounts, the brush poised over the ink jar, the papyrus spread out on a board on his lap. He looked toward the heavy wooden door, with its barred opening, but no faces appeared. Curious, he carefully put down his writing materials and got up to walk to a place beside the door where he could hear what was happening.

". . . don't understand! I'm not a criminal! I'm a doctor! I'm personal physician to the lord Madir, vizier to the Lord of Two Lands himself! Surely," the despairing voice said, "surely you've heard the name! Unless there's been a revolution in the palace, he's your superior!"

Uni replied in an even voice. "So is the noble Harmin, general of the army, who ordered your arrest and immediate incarceration without a hearing. I'm sure the noble Harmin would not have done anything he didn't clear with Madir and his advisers."

"But that's what I'm trying to tell you!" the new prisoner said. "He cannot—I repeat, *cannot*—have done so in the present case. Madir has an appointment with me today to be bled. He has a disorder of the blood, and the operation has to be performed every moon. If I'm not there—"

"I'm sure your assistants will be able to handle it, sir," Uni's voice went on. "Or perhaps the lord Madir has acquired a new physician."

"New physician? Where's he going to find another physician of my standing, with the mouths of the Nile blockaded and all access to the Great Sea cut off these past two years? Is he going to import some witch doctor from Nubia?"

"I don't know, sir. All I know is that I have my orders. Whatever conspiracy you may have engaged in is considered very serious by—"

"*Conspiracy!* I'm not involved in any conspiracy! I merely passed on *information* about a conspiracy: information that, if anyone bothered to take it seriously, could save the king from . . ."

But the prisoner paused now, and when he spoke again it was in a different, shaken, chastened voice. "Ah," he said. "The people I talked to—they're part of it. Of course! What better way to silence me? What better way to make sure that—" But now something even more startling seemed to occur to him, for his voice took on yet another tone: one of fear. "Oh, good heavens. Somehow I've got to warn her. I've got to get word back to her—"

"Sorry," Uni said with finality, "but you won't be getting any messages out to anyone. Not for quite a while. Now, if you'll be so kind as to step this way—"

Joseph hurried quickly back to his pallet and was once again sitting cross-legged when the bolt was drawn and the door swung open, its hinges creaking.

He looked up as if his concentration had suddenly been disturbed. He watched the prisoner—an elderly Greek, from the cut of his hair—stumble inside, and the guards withdraw behind him to close the great door with a loud and ominous bang.

The prisoner blinked in the unaccustomed gloom, then turned his eyes to Joseph, who was sitting beside a work lamp. "Hello," he said. "You'd be the trustee here, right? The person in charge of—"

"Of everything behind these closed doors," Joseph said a little sadly, putting down his brush. "My name's Joseph—Joseph ben Jacob, back among my own people far to the north. We're something of a cosmopolitan community here behind bars, with people of many nationalities." Joseph scrutinized him: well dressed, hair well kept. "I take it you're from the Islands."

"No," the stranger said. "From Ilios, a colony on the mainland. My name's Tros. I'm a doctor. I was arrested for—" He sighed, not bothering to finish the sentence. "But I suppose you heard the rest from behind the door."

"Everyone's innocent here, sir," Joseph said tranquilly. "Rest assured that I believe you. Unfortunately, I can't do anything about your case. I'm just another prisoner, and what little authority I have ends at that barred door." He smiled and made a little gesture with the shoulders, universally understood in the East, implying that such was the will of whatever powers were in charge of things. "I'm innocent myself, for that matter," he said. "Falsely denounced, as you say you were."

Tros of Ilios slumped onto a bench against the wall. "I see. It's the way of the world. Well, it's not a phenomenon new to me. I've been in jail before, many years ago, on similarly trumped-up charges. I'll find my way out again, I suppose. But the very fact that I'm here puts a friend of mine, an old family friend, in the gravest danger. Her, and perhaps her husband and children as well."

"It is the will of the God," Joseph said. "If the God who knows all and sees all chooses to have this happen—"

"Eh?" the doctor said peevishly. "More of that one-God stuff, I see. I've run into people of your turn of mind before, up along the Canaanite coast. But—you said ben Jacob? You're not of the line of . . . oh, what was his name? Abra—?"

"Abraham," Joseph said, his eyes lighting up. "My great-grandfather. You've heard of him, then?"

"Oh, yes. I'm fairly well traveled. Doctors often are, if they've any curiosity about medical practices around the world. I've even been to Mesopotamian cities like the one your great-grandfather seems to have come from originally. Let me tell you, it's a difficult place for a doctor. If the patient dies, the doctor does, too. If an eye operation fails, the physician's hands are cut off. But you say you're of Abraham's line? What are you doing here, then?"

"That's a long story. I'll tell it to you one of these days. I'm afraid we'll have plenty of time to trade stories, if—"

The bolt of the great door was drawn once more, and the doctor sprang to his feet with surprising agility. The door swung wide, and one of the guards stepped in the lit opening, a short spear in hand. "A messenger from the lord Madir," he said. "He wants—"

The doctor clapped his hands in joy. "I was beginning to think I was lost forever in here. Well, young man, I wish you well, and—"

"He wants to speak to the slave Joseph," the guard said in a bored, matter-of-fact voice. "Immediately!" He gestured with his free hand. "Better get moving, slave, or he may change his mind."

Joseph put his writing materials down again and stood up. "I'm sorry, sir," he told Tros. "Perhaps he'll call for you soon."

"Please!" the doctor said, grasping his hand. "Tell him I'm here—perhaps he doesn't know. I have to talk to him, and quickly. An innocent person's life is in terrible danger!"

Joseph pulled his hand free, his face set in a kind of smile. "I don't know if I'll get a chance to say anything, sir," he said. "A slave speaks when he's spoken to and isn't supposed to volunteer anything. Especially in the presence of one as highly placed as Madir. But I'll see what I can do."

Harmin, general of the army to the Lord of Two Lands, didn't look much like a soldier just now. His hair was arranged in the elaborate coif of a courtier, and his robes were those of a man of leisure, carefully draped for the proper effect. Unas, angry-eyed, looked him up and down and saw that the general had recently had a mani-cure and pedicure. Pedicure! For a field general! Well,

Harmin hadn't spent much time in the field lately, that was for sure.

"Good to see you, Unas," the general said, in cultured tones. "What can we do for you today? I presume everything is going well at the front?"

"Going *well*? What in the name of fifty demons do you mean, going well? My troops are nearly starving! They don't have enough weapons to defend themselves with! They have to steal swords, spears from the dead! I even have an assassin running around camp, trying to kill me!"

Harmin's eyes widened imperceptibly at the mention of an assassin. Then he dismissed the matter airily with one hand. "These things happen. Even Madir himself is not immune to such dangers." He smiled innocently. "I take it there's been some sort of failure of communications, then?"

"Is that what you call it?" Unas said, stupefied. "When your damned crooked sutlers steal better than half the supplies intended for the army and sell them to the villages behind the lines? When the food that does get to us is rancid, the meat crawling with maggots, the flour full of weevils, the—"

"These are serious charges," Harmin said. "Serious indeed. I presume you have some sort of proof to back up such strong words?"

"You know damned well I don't. I sent the proof back by armed messenger, all the way to Memphis. I've traced the messenger's steps right to this office. The evidence disappeared from sight, apparently forever, right here." Unas began to forget himself, his rank, his subordinate status. His voice rose. His tone dropped all semblance of military courtesy. "How can you do this to us? When we're all that's keeping the Shepherds out of your lap?"

"How can *I* do it? Do you realize what you're saying?" A cold glint appeared in Harmin's eye.

Unas ignored the warning. "My men captured a runner behind the Shepherd lines, a man bound for the front with an official message from Vahan. He's ordered reinforcements from as far back as Sile, draining the Shepherd garrisons all over the delta to give himself the strongest force he's ever been able to deploy along our line. He has every intention, it appears, of being in Memphis by the solstice."

Harmin smiled superciliously and daintily offered Unas figs from a bowl. Unas shook his head angrily. "Delicious," Harmin said, biting into the fruit. "Fresh from the Fayum. I'm going to take a holiday there shortly. Would you like me to bring you back a sackful of these? My groves are the best in—"

"Holiday? What do you mean, holiday? You can't take a holiday now! I'm telling you Vahan will be in Memphis when he says he will, if we don't do something, and fast!"

"Oh, come now. The Shepherds aren't that strong. Surely you can whip them once again. You have before. See what trust I have in you?"

Unas's fist came down with a crash on the table between them. "Trust! Oh, how flattered I am! Well, you can take your trust and—" His two fists clenched and unclenched. "Keep the trust. Send weapons. Send clothing. Send food. If you can't spare the food"—he shot a sharp glance, full of enraged contempt, at the bowl of figs— "then for heaven's sake send the weapons. I know they exist somewhere—I visited Shobai's forges. He says he's got the men working day and night, turning out a veritable arsenal. He says he's made enough weapons in the last four months to outfit an army twice the size of mine, despite a shortage of ore that he says is getting more critical every day. But none of the weapons ever gets to me. Where are they going, Harmin? Tell me that, will you?"

The general smiled unpleasantly. "They've gone to arm the palace guard," he said. "There have been rumors of a conspiracy. We've doubled the size of the city militia, levied a draft on the young men of the outlying districts—"

"So *that's* where the new drafts have been going!" Unas fairly screamed the words. "When my own lines are spread thinner than they've been in the entire war! When the Shepherds have two men for our every one!"

"The sacred person of the king our god must be

protected, Unas. Even if it means cutting back the fresh drafts to the front lines."

"You fool! You epicene, posturing fool! By the solstice, the Lord of Two Lands will either have been driven, along with the court, along with the rest of you, upriver to Thebes—or he'll be picking his way through the snares and pitfalls of the netherworld along with the departed spirits of the rest of us! Either way, Egypt, including the ground you're standing on, will be in the hands of the Shepherds!"

"You're losing your temper, Unas," the general said, spitting the fig skin into his hand. "An officer who loses his temper loses the respect of his men. I'll leave you with that thought. However, you'll start getting your reinforcements, and, yes, your weapons too, when the arming of the Memphis garrison is complete. But not a day sooner. I'd advise you to relax. Things probably aren't as bad as you think they are."

Unas, beyond anger, just stared. He wasn't going to get fresh troops, new weapons, or even adequate rations, not until Harmin had finished feathering his own nest here at the capital. He was stuck with what he had. Meanwhile the Shepherd armies opposite his lines grew stronger, their ranks deeper, their men better armed, fresher, better trained. And all because of this obscene, unspeakable toad. "If you think—" he began, his voice tight and strangled.

"The interview is over," Harmin said, turning his back. "You may leave now."

The setting that the vizier Madir had chosen to receive visitors was carefully calculated to disarm. Instead of using the customary state reception rooms, which were always thronged with pompous and noisy retainers, he met his guests in a quiet, shady atrium, amid a miniature forest of rare and imported flowers and dwarf trees, all lovingly tended and artfully arranged. Surrounded by this peaceful, quiet splendor, Madir, himself dressed simply, would sit on a platform, making a show of pruning priceless flowers.

Now, as if annoyed at being distracted from his labors,

he glared down at the guards as they brought in the prisoner and stood at attention, waiting. A thin, birdlike hand emerged from his white robes and waved them away.

"So you're Uni's pet seer," he said, hardly glancing at Joseph. "Don't try to deny it. I've spies in prison as well as everywhere else. I can tell you what you ate for breakfast yesterday—and what you left on your plate uneaten." Madir sounded bored, as though he had made this speech many times before.

"My lord knows everything," Joseph said. "What more could I tell him?" He bowed deferentially.

"That's more like it," Madir said, finally turning away from his pruning. "See here—I'm not superstitious, as men go. But I'm also no fool. If some soothsayer has news for me, I'll at least listen to him. If he's wrong, dead wrong, a word from me will put an end to his prophesying. Forever. But if he's right—" He shrugged. "You're on trial right now, young man. What does the future hold? For me and for Memphis? Make it for Memphis. That's general enough—and easy to check on a week or two from now." He observed Joseph's reaction to his words. "Now *that's* interesting," he said. "Already you entertain me."

"I do, my lord? How?"

"You're not afraid of me. Perhaps you're ignorant of what power I wield here. Perhaps you're stupid. Or perhaps you really can look into the future." He snorted and turned back to his flowers. Then, after a long pause, he glared coldly at Joseph. "What are you waiting for?" he said. "Memphis—its immediate future. Quickly, now. No cheap theatrics, and no stalling."

Joseph's expression remained calm and cool. "Very well, sir. As you wish." He closed his eyes and thought. Madir started to interrupt, but was struck by something in the young man's manner, and held his tongue.

"Vahan arms, hires mercenaries. Your own army is weakened by treason." Madir's eyebrow went up sharply, but he kept silent. Joseph continued. "The Shepherds attack. Memphis falls. You yourself are safe, sir, along with the court. You have retired to a prepared line of defense upriver . . . at . . ."

"At Thebes?" Madir said, leaning eagerly forward to catch every word.

Joseph's eyes did not open. His voice had a strange quality to it now, like that of a man dreaming aloud. "Not so far upstream," he said. "Above Lisht, where the Twelfth Dynasty kings reigned. There the retreating army turns and makes a stand. The Shepherds, confident of victory, attack in force. There is a great battle. I . . ." His voice faded. He shook his head, opened his eyes. "I—I'm sorry," he said. "My vision failed me. The God of my fathers would speak no more."

Madir clapped his hands. The guards reappeared and stood flanking Joseph, awaiting further orders. "That's enough for now, young man. I can make use of what you've told me so far."

"Then I can go, sir?"

"Yes," Madir said. But the icy glint was still in his eye. "Return him to prison, for now," he said. "But keep an eye on him. See that nothing untoward happens to him. And send Uni to me, immediately."

II

A short time later, Uni appeared. Madir, a smile playing on his thin, aristocratic features, watched the jailer's ritually correct bow, listened to his honeyed words, and thought: *Ah, ambition* . . .

It was a good sign. Nothing could so bind an underling to you as his ambition—provided it was channeled in the proper direction. Otherwise it could be dangerous—especially in Uni's case. Madir glanced down at his visitor. "I've talked to your young man Joseph ben Jacob," he said. "He's every bit as impressive as you report."

"I thought it best to bring him to your attention, sir," Uni said. Their eyes met and registered their mutual recognition that Uni, at first, had meant to do nothing of the kind, that the only reason Joseph had come to Madir's attention was that Madir's spy—whoever he was—had reported to his master and forced Uni to reveal his secret. Nevertheless, Madir was now making it easy for Uni to save face, and both of them knew that, too.

"And well you might," Madir said. "Because if I had uncovered this—this *wonder* by myself, instead of having him brought to my attention by you, my most loyal subordinate, my anger would have been great indeed."

Uni gulped and cursed himself for being unable to conceal his discomfiture.

"As it is," Madir continued, "you have promptly reported to me. I applaud your initiative, which, if course, shall not go unrewarded." He waved a hand, and one of the two armed guardsmen at the door stepped forward to hand Uni a small purse.

"My lord is generous," Uni said.

"Your lord is realistic," Madir said. "If it were known here at court that I was listening to the trumpery of a foreign soothsayer—and one who looks like an unfledged cherub, at that—people would soon start referring to me behind my back as Madir the Credulous. But you and I know the boy is genuine enough. No matter what heretical means he may use to achieve these divinations of his, they tend to work, don't they?" He didn't wait for an answer. "Take that business about the chief baker and the cupbearer. Any intelligent fellow in his position, authorized by you to spy on his fellow prisoners, could have found out who was guilty. But those other predictions, all that about his wife and child—quite another matter indeed. As you know, it turned out just as predicted, in the smallest detail, and without help from you or me. No, what we have here is the real thing."

"Yes, my lord," Uni said, swallowing, and thinking, *How in the name of fifty demons could he have known all that? Who stood nearby while we talked?* And there came, in a blinding and fearful flash, the chilling realization: *He has a spy in my prison. And he's had him there for quite some time, monitoring my every move, my every word.* Briefly he wondered who the spy was—but there wasn't a thing he could do about it, was there? Not if the spy, somehow, was reporting everything he heard and saw to Madir. Catch the spy and attend to him by the usual means, and Madir would know of it in a moment. He felt like a fly caught in a trap.

"I tested this Joseph fellow," Madir continued. "I asked for predictions of what would happen to Memphis, to the court, in the immediate future. This was something I could easily check him on, since the plans of the present government for the disposition of the court are a matter I have confided in no one as yet. In fact, you will be the first person I tell, Uni." Madir fixed his gimlet gaze on Uni's suddenly sweaty face. They both knew what would happen if anyone heard about those plans before Madir wanted them to be released; Uni would be the first to fall.

"I'm grateful my lord reposes such, uh, confidence in me," Uni said, feeling intensely uncomfortable.

"A fitting reward for your loyalty," Madir said, smiling. "Anyway, what Joseph told me I knew already. He said that my army is riddled with traitors, and that at this precise moment, Vahan, the cleverest of the Shepherd generals, is preparing an attack against our weakened defenses. They will crush our front line, and drive them back to positions we've prepared—on the southern side of Memphis." He paused, letting his words sink in.

"*Southern* side, sir?" Uni said. "You mean we'll have to abandon Memphis to the Shepherds? We'll lose the city?"

"Yes. It is not yet possible for me to crush the traitors. They have friends within the royal family . . . and at the moment I have reason to believe they have left the city. In any case, I have to prove treason. When I can do this, I can wreck them. But first the treason has to bear some fruit. The only way I can convince the Lord of Two Lands that the conspiracy is indeed real is for something drastic to happen, something that strikes at the very heart of the kingdom." His lips twitched into a momentary half-smile. "The answer? We have to lose Memphis, but without really losing anything."

"Lose Memphis?" Uni was still thunderstruck. "But . . ."

"Memphis is a difficult city to defend. I've already prepared virtually invulnerable positions upriver near Lisht. If we fall back to there, we'll be able, at worst, to prolong the war a year or two. And we'll still have the Fayum—without which we fall in a fortnight."

"But the court, sir? The people? Their possessions?"

"As Joseph correctly predicted, I'm moving the court to Lisht immediately. As for the people . . . well, they'll have to fend for themselves. I'm sorry, but those are the realities. When they see that our first line of defense is beginning to fall, they'll understand, won't they? They'll evacuate themselves. We'll post guards, reducing the necessary disorder of a mass flight from a beleaguered city. Don't worry about the people, Uni. They don't worry about you. And I wouldn't be reposing such confidence in you if I thought you were the sort to be swayed by such . . . such *common* concerns."

"Oh, no, sir," Uni said. "I just thought—"

"That's good."

Madir descended from his platform and began strolling about the room, stopping every so often to caress or smell the rare flowers. He spoke without looking at Uni. "By the time the court's at Lisht, the army can fall back in an orderly fashion to our prepared positions. If I know the Shepherds, even Vahan won't be able to keep them from losing valuable time looting, raping, and killing—time better spent pursuing us."

Uni's heart was in his mouth as he followed Madir around the room. He really meant it! He *wasn't* going to warn the people! He was going to let them fend for themselves, knowing a sizable percentage of them wouldn't leave the city, or in some cases *couldn't* leave the city. He'd leave the sick, the elderly, the lame . . . and the slaughter of these would occupy the Shepherds long enough to allow the Egyptian army to retreat and await the Shepherd advance from stronger positions. Memphis would be an undefended city, its residents sacrificed to the invaders' ferocity. . . . He shuddered. Thinking of it was enough to line his forehead with dots of cold sweat.

Madir was still pacing. "Then, when the Lord of Two Lands realizes that Memphis, where his fathers were born, is in the hands of the enemy, it'll be easier to pursue my charges of treason against those who weakened our defenses in the first place. Mind you—treason's merely a

charge. I happen to disagree with some people at court as
to where the new court would best be set up. Some idiots
favor Thebes, which, you know, would mean giving up the
Fayum. It would also mean having to share power with
the Nubians at Kerma, and that would dilute my own
strength intolerably. I'm not too happy as it is with sending that fellow Akhilleus off to raise a mercenary army of
blacks, probably more loyal to him than to me . . . but I'll
have to deal with that when the time comes. For now, the
most pressing problem is to make sure the Thebes faction
doesn't win out. And the best way to do that is to bring—
and prove—charges of treason."

Madir stopped pacing and looked straight at Uni. "I'll
need help for that. Loyal and steadfast help. That's why I
called for you, Uni."

"M-my lord is too kind."

"I'm never too kind, Uni. That's the secret of my
success. But I am generous to my loyal friends—very
generous. I assume I have your loyalty, Uni. Am I correct
in this?"

"Y-yes, sir. Of course, sir."

"Splendid. Now, this Joseph."

"Yes, sir?"

"He's in jail because of some trumped-up charges
brought by Potiphar's idiotic wife, right?"

"Yes, sir."

"You and I know the woman's a whore, and that the
young man would as soon lay hands on a crocodile. But
the fact remains, the lad's in jail. And you, seeing his
situation and appreciating his potential usefulness both to
yourself and to me, treat him right. But it wouldn't occur
to you to let him go just now, eh?"

"No, sir. Not unless you desire it."

"Good. Very soon I'll be giving the order to move the
court, the government, and the families of all the officials
concerned to Lisht. I suggest you use the time between
now and then to sell your house and other properties to
some poor fool who doesn't have the benefit of your advance knowledge. Sell for cash, I mean, or comparable
properties in a safer area—safer and, once Memphis has
fallen, more valuable. I'd recommend a piece of land in

the Fayum, if you can manage it. Food is going to become expensive in a few months, Uni. A man in a good position to *sell* food—"

"I see your point, sir."

"Good. Now, when we move, there's no need to take the entire population of the jails with us, is there? I mean, why move a collection of convicted felons at the state's expense? Right?"

"You're absolutely r-right, sir."

"I'm glad you agree. But this Joseph fellow, now, he's different. He's not just another prisoner, is he? I'd figure out some way to see that he's moved to Lisht. To someplace where he can be watched, of course. Take good care of this young man, Uni. He's going to be worth his weight in gold coins to us. Not just to me, but to you as well, Uni. Because if I have judged your ability and loyalty rightly—and I think I have . . ."

"Of course, sir. Count on me."

"I will. As I say, you'll rise with me. As my power is consolidated by the steps I'll be taking, I'll need a strong and sympathetic ally in court. One who, like yourself, knows how to keep his eyes open and his mouth shut— shut to everyone but me, of course."

Uni nodded.

"There'll be a place for this slave Joseph as time goes by. He's too useful to remain a slave for long. As you've learned yourself, he's an able administrator. Imagine, before his first master's death, when he had barely mastered our language, he was already in charge of a household of—let's see, how did he put it exactly? 'Of thirty slaves and sixteen bond servants, with full power to assign work and render an accurate accounting of my stewardship.' That's quite impressive."

"Yes, sir." Uni's legs felt weak. Gods! How did Madir quote with such accuracy the *exact* words the boy had used? It was not without reason that the court gossips called him Madir of the Thousand Ears.

"Not only am I eventually going to make him a freedman, Uni—one intensely loyal to me and grateful to me"—he smiled craftily—"I'm going to raise him to a position right beside me in the new capital. I'm going to make him my chief administrator."

His gaze bored into Uni. Uni writhed, intensely uncomfortable under such scrutiny.

"Even if it means cutting off a few heads to make room for him."

"Chief administrator, sir?" Uni said. "That's a lot of heads to fall, sir."

Madir shrugged. "Of course I'll need another man close to me—*very* close to me, Uni—to lop off those heads. To remove all opposition, silence all dissent. Someone skilled in intrigue. Someone who's used to . . . well, murder."

"M-me, sir?" Uni said, his voice hoarse, a croak.

"Precisely. You, on the same level with Joseph, both of you answerable only to me. *Loyal* only to me." The smile, the eyes, were those of a cobra ready to strike, hypnotizing its victim. "Keeping that in mind, I think you will find it advisable to work out, right now, an altered relationship with the young man. Oh, I realize you treat him well. But look ahead to the future. Think of him as raised to a status equal with yourself, Uni. Think of how much easier it'll be working with him then, if in the meantime he's come to look upon you as a friend."

"I see, sir. Then . . . he doesn't know what you've planned for him?"

"Nothing. As I say, you're my first confidant. Well, Uni . . ." he said, changing his tone—a sign, Uni knew, that the interview was over—"I suppose—oh, there is one more thing."

"Yes, sir?"

"There's an old Greek in your prison just now. He's a friend of mine—my private physician, as a matter of fact."

"Yours, sir? But . . . I'm sure there's been some mistake. . . ."

"No mistake. The man was making some noise about a conspiracy . . . actually, the very conspiracy that I'm going to impale a few people for. However, I don't want anything done about it just yet. I want to gather evidence I can use when I eliminate my enemies. But if there's some way of letting the doctor go while telling him, very quietly, to shut up or be silenced permanently—"

"It's as good as done, sir."

"Excellent. But his information's secondhand. He got it from a woman. I don't know who she is. Get to work immediately and find out. I don't want her shooting off her mouth."

"Yes, sir. I'll have her silenced . . . permanently."

Madir frowned. "Nothing drastic, please. Be subtle. I don't want to offend my friend."

"Subtle?"

"Have her arrested quietly. Efface all trace of her name. I want her to disappear and be forgotten. Dump her in a cell many levels down, where the light never penetrates the darkness. And . . ."

"Yes, sir?"

"Leave her behind with the other scum, for the Shepherds to find. They can have whatever the rats leave."

III

Hori, sunning himself on a flat boulder while waiting for Shobai to finish at the forge, stirred lazily and opened his eyes. General Unas, flanked by five or six attendants, was blocking his sun. "Sir!" Hori jumped up and snapped to attention, pulling his belly in.

There was a terrible pause, and Hori's knees felt weak with fear, but he forced himself to maintain the stiff brace as Unas scowled at him. His own eyes straight ahead, taking in nothing except the spotless, almost blinding white of the general's kilt, Hori waited for the inevitable reprimand. But none came.

"At ease," Unas said sarcastically. "You wouldn't happen to know, by any chance, where Shobai is?"

"At Forge Number Three, sir," Hori replied crisply. "I'll go after him if you like, sir." His "at ease" stance was only slightly less stiff than his "at attention" stance had been.

"Don't bother," the general said. "I'll send one of my
aides. I want to talk to you while we're waiting." One of
the attendants came forward without waiting to be called.
Unas sent him running off. "And don't cater to him," he
shouted after the man. "He's blind, but he's not helpless."
He turned back to Hori. "I've a bit of bad news for the
both of you."

"Sir?"

"Oh, don't act stupid. You know what the gossip's
been for the past week. The urchins in the streets of
Memphis know it already. I handpicked you as Shobai's
personal dogrobber because I knew you were a good one
for keeping an ear to the ground."

"Then—it's true? Vahan's preparing a major offensive?"

Unas grunted. "He's going to hit us with everything
he has, and believe me, my young friend, that's a lot. He's
drained his outposts to the north. And he's hired mercenaries." He shook his head in disgust. "Including some
of our own people who've gone over to his side."

"It's a disgrace, sir. An embarrassment to—"

Unas ignored him. He seemed to be addressing no
one in particular. "Of course we're at the weakest we've
been in years. Years! And do you know why? Because
we're out of weapons up front!"

"Out of—? But Shobai has been—"

"Harmin has been siphoning them off for the royal
guards. They haven't been getting to us." He shrugged
impotently. "The only consolation is that the royal guards
will wind up having to use those bright, shiny new swords
just like the rest of us. Our line won't hold. We'll be
driven back to Memphis by the second assault, I estimate.
Then I can draft the royal guards to save the palace—"

"But, sir—you . . . you can't."

Unas's attention snapped back to the present. "Can't?
What do you mean? In imminent danger I'm allowed to
press anyone into service—anyone not of noble rank."

"Uh—not if they're not here, sir."

"Not here? Of course they'll be— What are you talking about?"

"The word went out late this morning, sir. Madir—

he's ordered a withdrawal, sir. For the sake of the safety of the Lord of Two Lands, and the court."

"Withdrawal? But—" Unas's mouth hung open.

"Yes, sir. The court's abandoning the city. *And* taking the royal guards with them. To Lisht, I think, or someplace near it."

"I—I know the place," Unas said, recovering a bit, but still obviously nonplussed. "I . . . I helped oversee the construction. Yes, it's a fine place to withdraw to. A strong second line of defense. But, damn it—it was supposed to have been a place to fall back to after an attack, not before."

"But, sir—*we're* not falling back. The army's to stay here and defend Memphis. And the people of the city, sir, they're not going. Just the court. That's what I heard. The messenger from court is probably still trying to find you."

"You're telling me the truth, Hori? Because if you're lying—"

"I swear it, sir, on my oath as an officer."

"Gods!" Unas said. "When they break through . . . why, the city will be undefended. It'll be a slaughter! And we won't be able to avert it. We'll be too busy trying to re-form, trying to—"

"Look, sir," Hori said. "Here comes Shobai."

The blind giant was being led forward by Unas's attendant. "Shobai!" Hori said. "The general Unas is here."

"I know," the blind man said. He let Unas walk into his open arms, smiling as they embraced. When they broke they continued for a moment to hold each other by the forearms. "Then you've heard," Shobai said.

"Yes," the general replied. He nodded to his attendants, dismissing them. Hori stood off to one side. "And I can't believe it. Although I suppose I'll have to in the end. That's the sort of thing Harmin *would* do. For the love of all that's holy, Shobai, get your wife and children out of here—and fast. You've the rank to merit special consideration. I'll dictate the order myself and sign it with my own seal. Send them to Lisht. Better yet, send them to the Fayum. I think that if I can get the men re-formed and redeployed after the first mad rush southward, we ought to be able to hold the Shepherds at the second line of defense."

"All right. I'll take your advice. But I'm staying, of course."

"Don't be a fool. You won't be able to do any good here. Harmin's been stealing all those weapons of yours anyhow and giving them to the palace guards."

"I know. *I* learned just yesterday. I made those swords to bite into the necks of Shepherd soldiers, not for some fattened courtier to cut his own throat, out of fright. But . . . then the situation on our front lines is as bad as they say it is?"

Unas grasped the giant's burly forearm. "You're a friend, and I'll tell you straight: It's worse. We're weak, underarmed, undermanned . . . and Vahan grows stronger daily. He's hiring mercenaries from up north, as well as deserters from our own side." He spat disgustedly into the dirt. "Sometimes, Shobai, I wonder what my duty is. What am I doing ordering soldiers into battle, when they're going to be sold out by their own people?"

"As they say Baka was sold out? Or is that just another rumor?" Shobai patted his friend's hand. "Oh, don't get angry—I've not enough time these days to worry about rumors of Baka. But as for your duty—*our* duty— you know the answer to that as well as I do. You told me yourself, once: A man does his job. Without regard to what the coward on his left does, or the traitor or slacker on his right." He sighed. "It seems simple enough, but I had to learn it the hard way, and from a cripple hardly half my size, a man who'd never struck a blow in anger in his whole life. He gave his life for me, for his city, for his neighbors." Shobai's voice broke off, and he turned away for a moment, as if to prevent the others from seeing his face.

"Shobai?" Unas said.

The giant turned back. "His name was Hadad—Hadad of Haran. He was my brother. You may have heard of him."

Unas's callused hand fell softly on the blind man's shoulder. "I'm sorry," he said. "I know you wouldn't willingly desert us up here at the front. But, Shobai—

when we've fallen back we'll still need you, perhaps more than ever. And we'll need you unhurt and healthy. If I have to, Shobai, I'll give you the orders myself, sending you upriver."

"You're right—I'll go," the blind man said, his voice hoarse with emotion. "Besides, I'd only slow down the retreat if I stayed. It's just that—well, as long as there's something left that I can do here . . ."

"There isn't. But I wish to heaven everyone on our side had a tenth of your steadfastness. As it is, I'm going to have to start preparing our own retreat."

"Retreat? You're not going to cover their—?"

"I'll cover them—though I know good and well that I'll lose a lot of good men doing so. But I'll be damned if I'm going to sit idly by and let them sign the death warrant for my whole army. No, by heaven, I'm going to make sure we can fall back in an orderly fashion, when we're forced to—losing as few men as we can. We won't hand them the city without a struggle. We'll make them pay for every street, every bazaar." He bowed his head in thought, and his next words were barely audible. "Those poor bastards left in the streets. The sick, the old, the women, the slaves . . ."

"Like Melid," Shobai said.

"What?"

"Melid," Shobai repeated. "I once saw the Shepherds sack Melid. It was a peaceful city. Of course I had my sight then—though it would have been better if I were blind. Anyway, after Melid I was no longer neutral. I was against the Shepherds, regardless of whoever was fighting them. I went south and helped my father arm Ebla. Ebla fell, then Arvad, and the cities of the sea. I barely escaped with my life."

"Then you've been fighting—how long? Ebla fell many years ago."

"It seems as if I've been fighting the Shepherds all my life. Perhaps it's no more than half. And for a time, after Ebla fell and the Shepherds marched down through Canaan and across the Sinai into Egypt, I fought no more. I learned the harp, memorized a hundred songs in a dozen or more languages, went from city to city, following the trade winds. Then fortune, as much as Akhilleus's ships, brought me to Egypt—and I met Mereet. And suddenly the war was on for me again."

"Yet—surely you can leave when you like. An armorer—"

"Perhaps my children will have the luxury of an armorer's free life, not bound to any one lord, any one cause. It won't be the case for me, I'm afraid. It's my destiny to arm all who fight against the Shepherds, whoever, wherever they may be. As long as I'm alive . . ." A shadow passed over his expressive face. "Well, that may not be forever," he said resignedly. "But so long as I've breath . . ."

"I understand. I could go abroad myself. My contract with the Lord of Two Lands ran out long ago. But you're right. It's a matter of destiny, isn't it?" He clapped Shobai on his gigantic bicep. "After all, we're not licked yet. We may prevail in the end. There's always Akhilleus. A few troops of Nubian mercenaries could make all the difference."

"Yes," Shobai said. He moved to sit down, and Hori hurried forward, guiding him to the flat rock. He seemed suddenly weary. "I think of Akhilleus a lot these days," he said. He felt the space beside him on the rock and made a place for the general. "Here, join me." Unas did so, his head half turned, his eyes on the giant's profile. "Only . . . Unas, it isn't quite the same Akhilleus. It isn't the big jolly clown and braggart. When I imagine him now, it's as if, well . . . he's grown *taller*." He smiled sadly. "I've never seen him with these eyes, of course. Nikos described him for me once or twice. But now, in my mind's eye, he's grown great and dignified and powerful. I don't know—maybe my memory is playing tricks on me."

"It's possible," Unas said. "Or perhaps what you imagine . . . perhaps it's a good omen."

Shobai shook his head doubtfully. "I hope so," he said. "Because I fear for him, Unas. I fear that he will never return. He's been gone far too long."

"I wouldn't worry," Unas said, patting Shobai's knee reassuringly. "He'll come back safe and sound. I know him. And he'll be his old self again, just as we remember. He'll boast of his adventures, of his victories, of—"

"No," Shobai said, "he won't be the same. That's something I'm sure of." He shook his head. "We'll all be changed—those of us left alive. Don't ask me how I know it—I just do. Nothing will ever be the same again."

Mereet, dressed in her finest linen robe, could have been preparing for a royal audience. Her face betrayed little emotion as she applied the last touches of eye makeup from the obsidian jar before her using a slender ebony stick. Only the dark eyes themselves, now outlined carefully with the jet-black kohl, betrayed her air of sad resignation. She held up the golden mirror Shobai had given her, turning it this way and that. Finally, after smoothing and straightening her black hair, which fell evenly just to her naked brown shoulders, she let out a great dejected breath and turned to Heket, putting the mirror down carefully on the low table beside her.

"You know what to do, now?" she asked the servant. "You're sure you'll remember?"

"Yes, ma'am," the servant said. "I'm to take the babies to the Fayum, to your country property there—"

"And when you get there, you're to send a message to my husband. Address it to Hori, the young officer who walks him home here every day. They're inseparable; Hori will always know how to find him. But—if anything's happened to Hori, I want you to contact Unas."

"Unas? The g-general, ma'am? But I'd be too frightened to—"

"No, you won't. You'll find the courage to go ahead and do what I say. You're a good girl. You've more spunk about you than you let on. That's why I'm entrusting the children to you. I know that you will stay with them and take care of them, no matter what happens." She let her voice break for a moment, and choked down a sob. "No m-matter what happens."

"Yes, ma'am. But, ma'am—what *is* going to happen?"

"I—I may have to go away for a while. Perhaps . . . perhaps for a very long while. I'm to be . . ." Her voice became almost inaudible. "I'm to be arrested. Please don't ask me why. I learned only this morning. There was a messenger from the vizier. The guards have been watching the house all day. I . . ."

"Oh, ma'am . . ."

Mereet's eyes had filled with tears. She looked down at the children, playing happily at her feet. "My—my darlings. How can I leave them? How can I—?" She reached down and ruffled Ketan's hair with her hand, in a gesture infinitely tender, infinitely motherly. "But . . . sometimes one can't have things as one wants."

"I'll take care of them. As if they were my own."

"I know you will. And, Heket—please take care of Shobai."

"Ma'am?"

"I know you love him. I know you desire him. When I'm gone he'll be desolate, in a way even the children won't be. Go to him. Love him. Sleep with him. Comfort him. Don't let him lie there alone in sorrow. He's been hurt so much in life. He's known such suffering."

"Ma'am! I couldn't—"

"Please. Whatever you may think of me for saying this—whatever I may think myself—I can't bear the thought of his being alone. Please—"

There was a knock on the door. Loud, imperious, commanding.

"J-just a moment," Mereet said in a broken voice. The two women, looking each other in the eye for the first time, embraced. Mereet hugged each child in turn and put them down again. "Oh, my darlings," she said. "Try to remember me. Try. Perhaps someday . . ."

The knock sounded again. Louder.

A shudder ran through Mereet. Then, with a supreme effort of will, she clenched her fists and straightened her back. And, head held high with regal pride, she opened the door.

Six royal guards, fearfully armed, stood in the street. Their leader stepped forward. "Ma'am, we're looking for—"

"I'm the person you're looking for, Captain," she said. "If you're ready, we can go now."

CHAPTER EIGHT

THE NILE DELTA

I

It was dusk of the second night since the raid on Baka's camp. Tuya had returned to poke through the ashes and what remained of the tents, but the raiders, followed by the voracious jackals, had left nothing of use. Now, slipping from tree to tree in the quickly fading light, she worked her way through the grove to the back door of the house of Akaba the olive merchant. Picking up a fist-sized, sun-baked clod, she threw it hard against the planks of the back door. It shattered to bits when it hit, but made a satisfyingly sharp noise.

Akaba's face appeared at a rear window. "Who did that? Eh? Go away, whoever it is! I'll tell your father—"

"*Psst!*" Tuya said, showing herself. "Quiet, Akaba! It's me, Tuya!"

"You! What do you mean throwing things at my house? What are you doing here? The guards—"

"Oh, be quiet and come here," Tuya said, not frightened at all. Her only fear had been in slipping past the two men who guarded the grove, outside. "I need some food, Akaba. Olives. And bread and cheese, too."

"Food?" the woman said, stepping out into the dim light. "You have the nerve to ask me for anything, after the way you stole so many olives—"

"Oh, don't give me that," Tuya said. "They were overripe in the first place, and you'd have cheated anyone who offered to buy them. But I don't have time to argue. I need bread, cheese, olives—"

"You need a good thrashing! If my husband—"

"I know your husband, Akaba. If he were to be miraculously transported here this moment, just as he is, you'd find him bleary-eyed, stark naked, and blind drunk, wondering what in heaven's name had dragged him suddenly away from the flea-infested bed of his favorite whore. Let's talk sense, Akaba. Let me have the food. There are two of us to feed, and I can't go into town."

"You certainly can't! You're wanted by the guards! If I were to have you arrested—"

"If you did that you'd find that you'd bought more than you bargained for. I'd be forced to tell them about the unpaid tax, the bribe paid to the scribe, all the rest of the cover-up. A lot more heads than just mine would fall, Akaba. You know how the Shepherd overlords view bribery, particularly when it isn't them that the bribe is paid to."

"The gods save me!" the woman said, sighing heavily. "If I'd never met you I'd be a lot happier. And I suppose a little richer. But—"

"I knew you'd come around," Tuya said. "Do you have a sack of some kind? Something I could carry the olives in?"

"A sack? Next you'll be asking me for a slave to help you carry it all away!"

"A good idea," Tuya said. "And ordinarily I'd take you up on your generous offer." She grinned insolently at Akaba's outraged expression. "But right now I'm not too keen on letting anyone know where I'm staying. The bread, please? The cheese?"

Akaba's head disappeared around the corner. When she reappeared she was carrying a quarter-circle of goat cheese and half a dozen pieces of flat bread. "Will this do, Your Majesty?" she said acidly.

Tuya had already helped herself to a basket of olives she had spied on a table just inside the door. Now she popped one into her mouth, chewed, and spat out the seed. "Very nice," she said. "A sack, perhaps?"

"I don't have any," Akaba said sourly. "You'll have to improvise something of your own. As it is, if anyone finds out you've been here and I haven't reported you—"

"Oh, stop worrying," Tuya said. She pulled her single raggedy garment over her head and, naked, began stuffing it full of olives. "I'll be out of here in two shakes."

"Shameless little slut," Akaba said in an offended voice. "Going around like that, as if—"

"I'm not ashamed of my body," Tuya snapped. "Not like some ladies I know who haven't taken care of themselves, who have to wait until all the other women are gone before they feel free to bathe in the river."

Akaba watched her pack up the cheese and bread and lift her bundle to one shoulder. "You should talk," she said spitefully. "You've no hips or breasts to speak of. One could hardly tell you for a girl except for—"

"Your words can't hurt me anymore," Tuya said. "I've got a man, Akaba, a real man—one who desires me just as I am. Big breasts aren't the only commodity a girl has to offer, Akaba."

"You? A man? Don't hand me that—"

"A better one than yours, that's for sure. He's big and handsome and strong and smart. *And* brave and loving and tender. I wouldn't trade places with the likes of you for—" Suddenly she stopped, and her expression softened. "But here we are bickering like a couple of foul-tongued old fishwives, and over nothing. Thank you for the food, Akaba. If the occasion ever arises when I can return the favor . . ."

Akaba's eyes flashed. Suddenly she looked a lot older, more vulnerable. "Just get out of here!" she said. "And take the side path. The guards we hired don't look over there, usually."

"Thank you," Tuya said, and, her naked little body

bent nearly double by her burden, she disappeared behind a row of shrubs.

It was dark by the time she reached the road. The moon had risen, and by its pale light she walked unhindered all the way to the fork, where she paused to put her burden down. She could feel the light breeze drying the sweat on her bare body, and the sensation was ever so pleasant. She shivered and hugged herself. Then, taking a deep breath, she started to pick up her burden again—and stopped, savoring the moment, the way she felt. . . .

She closed her eyes and stood absolutely still. The night blossoms had opened, and their soft scent was heavy in the air. She could hear the buzz of the midges down by the river and the soft lap of the current against the shore. She could hear, too, the light wind, the gentle breeze that bathed her nakedness in its delicately sensuous touch. The night was alive, and she was in love.

Was this what happiness was? Not merely to have a man loving you, but the best man you'd ever met in your whole life, a man fifty times finer than you'd ever dared to dream of all those years?

And . . . yes. Yes. He loved *her*. Her, Tuya! He'd more than just said it—he'd proved it. And her first time with a man, ever, had been a joyous adventure, a peeling away of layers of artifice between them until there had been nothing left to hide for either of them, ever.

She looked up at the moon and smiled. The breeze stirred again, flooding her senses with the soft, sweet air of evening. . . .

"*Hey! Tuya!*"

She whirled, instantly on the defensive. She crouched low, reaching in the dirt at her bare feet for a rock to throw. "Who's there?" she said warily, her fingers closing about a sharp-edged rock.

"Over here," the voice said in the same loud whisper. "It's me—Anab."

She straightened up, but kept her grip on the sharp rock. "Come out where I can see you," she said. "You're alone?" There was a hostile edge to her tone that she did not bother to disguise.

"Y-yes," Anab said. He crept out from behind a bush beside the road, looking frightened, ready to dive for cover at an instant. "Tuya, put that down. Please. I mean no harm. I'm on your side. Really. Even if . . ."

He hesitated, but she had caught something in his tone. "Even if what?" she said, keeping a firm grip on the stone. "Something's wrong, Anab. I thought Ben-Hadad and I were the only ones left alive after the raid. Where were you when it was going on? Where—?"

Then it hit her. "Anab! You *knew* about it! And you weren't there! Were you?" She raised the rock, prepared to dash out his brains with it, if need be. "Anab! You betrayed us, didn't you? You betrayed Baka! You—"

"No! It was all a mistake! Zosar—he made me! I—I didn't know what I was getting into. Then, when I knew, it was too late to get out. He swore me to silence. He told me he'd kill me if I didn't—"

"He *should* have killed you! You cowardly, lying, back-stabbing little—" She searched for a word rotten enough, but could not find one. "And to think that I used to stick up for you when people would call you names! To think Baka trusted you—yes, and Ben-Hadad trusted you, too! Like a brother!"

"No, Tuya! I didn't mean—"

"I ought to kill you myself, right here and now, and rid the world of a sneaking, rotten little traitor who—"

"Please, Tuya! I—I know where Baka is. We've got to save him."

His words stopped her, just as she was about to raise her hand over his head, to slash away at him with the sharp rock. "You know where he is?" she repeated after him in a changed voice. "Then he *hasn't* been delivered to the Shepherds yet, has he? Because I know that when they get hold of him, he's a dead man."

"You're right. Z-Zosar thinks that if he can hold on to Baka long enough—torturing him, if he has to—he can find out who Baka's spies are inside the Shepherd camp."

"Spies?" she said. "I never heard of any spies."

"Neither had I, until . . . well, people don't talk about that sort of thing, for obvious reasons. But Zosar's been with Baka from the first, from the day Baka was let out of prison, when Avedis declared himself Salitis, king of kings, and emptied the jails to show his clemency. Zosar knew about the spies, but he didn't know who they were. Now he thinks that if he knows who they are, he'll be in a better position to bargain."

"Bargain?" She fairly spat the words out. "Bargain with the Shepherds?"

"Shepherds? No, no! With the priests! He's making a deal with the priesthood. I met one of them. They have plans—"

"*Ahhh*," she let out in disgust. "I should have known. They're always at the root of our problems. They and their eternal politicking and intrigue. So Zosar sold him to the priests, and they in turn—"

"No! Zosar still has him. And he will keep him, at least until he can get the information he wants. He's afraid otherwise that the priests will no longer need him, after he hands over Baka. But if *he* has the information, then they have to deal with him."

"I see . . . I think," she said. "How well guarded is Baka?"

"I don't think you and I could get him out, all by ourselves. But if we had help—"

"Ben-Hadad's with me."

"Alive? He's alive? I was so afraid—"

"As well you might have been. He's hurt. He took a shallow knife wound and lost a lot of blood. But I took care of him, and I think in a day or two he'll be ready to move. He can join us. He's worth two other men, even hurt as he is." She smiled at the thought, thinking of the night before. He hadn't been hurt all *that* badly.

"Well, we'll have to hurry. Tuya—I feel terrible about this. I got in over my head, as usual. And then I couldn't figure out how to get back out again."

"A lot of people are dead because of you."

"I know. I know. You can't imagine how terrible I feel."

"Remember Bebe the weaver?"

"Yes. He was always kind to me. He never made fun of me, the way the others did. Is he? . . ."

"He's dead. He died helping us escape."

Anab looked at her, and she could see tears in his eyes. "I'm sorry," he said. "But, Tuya . . . I didn't know! Honestly, I didn't know this would happen. I guess I just didn't think that anyone would be . . . be killed. In the world I grew up in, nobody ever thought about anyone else, not for so much as a moment. Everyone was out for himself, and that's all there was to it. I'm *trying* to see things as you see them, as Ben-Hadad and Baka see them. But—it's not easy. It's not natural to me."

"I understand," she said, laying a hand for a moment on his thin arm. "Let's forget about it. What's important now is to get this food to Ben-Hadad and tell him about Baka. Then we'll see what we can do."

"Thank you," he said. "And, Tuya, I'm not trying to make excuses for my behavior. I was wrong from the first. I know because it *felt* wrong, every step of the way. It's just that—"

"If that's the case, Anab, there's hope for you. Because I think if you were a bad person, a really bad person, you wouldn't have felt guilty at all."

"I . . . I think I know what you mean. Here, you can't carry all that. Let me help you."

He quickly stripped to his loincloth. Looking skinny and defenseless in the moonlight, he started transferring half the load to the garment he had taken off.

They found the reed boat and loaded the food inside. Mindful of its half-waterlogged condition, they both stayed in the water, swimming it across, each with a hand on the boat's low-riding gunwales. At the far side they beached the boat in the reeds and carried their parcels inland to the dense underbrush, and through that to a small clearing in the center of the islet.

The coals still glowed. Tuya threw dry wood atop them and felt the rising heat on her bare body as the water dried on her skin. Beside her, Anab, also naked now, wrung out his wet loincloth, shivering in the evening chill. She glanced behind the bush that hid Ben-Hadad. "He's sleeping, I think," she said, her voice hardly more than a whisper. "You'd do well to sleep yourself. You look haggard." She noted his protruding ribs. "You haven't been eating properly."

"I can't keep anything down," he said. "Not since Zosar . . ."

"I see. Do you think you could eat any of the food we brought along? You ought to."

"No—nothing. I'll just try to get off to sleep."

"Not some cheese? Some bread?"

"No. Perhaps my appetite will come back when I've— when we rescue Baka."

"Suit yourself. But go around starving yourself and you won't *live* long enough to save Baka. Don't punish yourself, Anab. It won't help anything."

She patted him on the shoulder and said good night, then crawled into the brush and lay down beside Ben-Hadad on the pallet she'd made for them. She was preparing to turn over and try to sleep when she felt him stir, felt his warm hand touch her naked flesh.

"Tuya," he said in a husky voice.

"I brought food," she said. "And I found Anab. He knows where Baka is. We're going to find Baka and rescue him. Now, my darling, try to get some sleep. . . ."

"Sleep?" he said. "Forget sleep. Come here." And, wound or no, he pulled her to him in an embrace at once powerful and gentle. With no desire to resist, she melted into his arms.

II

Dawn broke chill and damp, and a low fog lay on the bottoms. Anab, sitting with his knees drawn up before the sluggish fire, poked at the coals with a charred stick. A chill went through him, and he shivered and edged closer to the coals. He threw on another couple of dry twigs.

What am I going to do with myself? he thought.

Of course he knew the first thing he must do. He must free Baka. However he managed it, it absolutely must be done. He had to undo at least some of the damage his own folly had caused. As to the rest . . . well, it was too late now. Imagine, Bebe dead—Bebe, who had harmed no one, who'd always been kind to him. And all the others. Ben-Hadad hurt, and—

He pressed his eyes shut and bit his lip. He had to put the others from his mind. He couldn't do anything about them now. He *could* do something about Baka. That was what he had to concentrate on. If he could just rescue Baka—

But the other thoughts refused to be put aside. *All the innocent dead—they're your fault. Yours! All because you were afraid to say no to Zosar, afraid to back out when it was still possible to back out. And even then you could have turned around and warned Baka, exposed the conspiracy. . . .*

Instead, by failing to betray his enemies—Zosar and his hateful conspiracy—he had betrayed his friends.

He stirred the coals again with the stick, jabbing at them disconsolately.

I wonder, he thought. *Am I a bad person? All around me I see people who I think are bad. People who hurt others and seem to enjoy it. Am I one of them, perhaps?*

Or was he simply weak? Easily pushed around, easily steered and manipulated? A born stooge for others?

He sighed. Either way, he certainly didn't seem to amount to much. He was, if you came right down to it, not worth anything. Not to anyone. Certainly not to his friends, the ones he'd betrayed.

Certainly not to himself.

He jabbed the coals fiercely. But as the black thoughts crowded their way into his mind, there came with them, oddly out of place, the fragile wisp of a hope long preserved, never quite abandoned. Anab clenched his teeth and shook his head violently, as if to drive the thought away. *But what if, somewhere in the world, there was someone who might love me?*

But how could this be so? He hadn't been loved even by his own flesh-and-blood mother, who had abandoned him on a doorstep—and that was before he'd been hurt, before he'd been left forever with this ugly face.

His other "family"—the people who'd raised him,

sent him into the streets, taught him the ins and outs of thievery, who'd shaped him—even they hadn't cared for him much, not from the first memories he could dredge up from the black depths of his mind. And after the accident . . . well, it was better not to think of it. It was a memory that cut like a knife, even now. He'd watched their faces turn aside, and he'd not known why at first. Wasn't he the same Anab? Why did they treat him differently?

Then, bending over the well one day to drink, he'd caught sight of his face at last, and learned what it was that he looked like. And why everyone treated him the way they did. And why not? If he saw such a face, would he have acted differently? It was the face of a monster. Something not quite human.

But the days of weeping had, over time, come to an end. They'd been replaced, long ago, by days and nights of rage, anger, and resentment, and of cold, aimless hate. . . ,

But no. That wasn't quite correct. He knew all too well what he hated. He hated himself.

Well, perhaps that stage would soon be over, too.

Perhaps, once he'd done his duty by Baka, rescued him from the predicament his, Anab's, own foolishness and cowardice had landed him in, it would be time to put an end to all the stages: the pain, the crying, the anger, the self-hate—and all the silent and hopeless longing.

Perhaps it would be time to seek peace in death, peace he had never known in life. . . .

He closed his eyes and tried to wipe the thought from his mind. Kill himself? No! The thought was repugnant. . . .

And, his mind told him, *infinitely desirable! An end! An end to all of it!*

He dropped his charred stick in the dying coals and covered his face with both hands, trying to drive the thought from his mind. But he could not. The more he tried to drive it away, the more insistent it grew, until it blotted out everything else.

An end to feeling. An end to pain. An end . . .

*   *   *

He was still sitting thus, legs pulled up, neck bowed, face in hands, his thin body shaking helplessly, when Ben-Hadad and Tuya emerged from the clump of bushes. After a moment's pause, Tuya started toward Anab, but Ben-Hadad put a restraining hand on her shoulder. He winced at the pain the movement caused him—the knife had broken a rib but had penetrated no farther—and separated himself from her, walking slowly over to where his friend crouched and wept.

As he put one large, comforting hand on Anab's shoulder, Anab's body jerked violently away and a hand shot up, as if to fend off a blow. "No—" he began.

Ben-Hadad gently but firmly grasped his friend's arm, stood him up, and, gritting his teeth against the pain, embraced him. Now the sobs came in earnest, the tears, the racking convulsions that shook the young man's skinny body. Ben-Hadad hugged him closely, patting him on the back, ignoring the burning pain in his own chest.

"Anab, it's all right," he said. "We're here, and we're still your friends. Tuya's told me all about it. You're not to blame, really. It's—"

But Anab pulled away from him and, his back to the both of them, rubbed his eyes. "I—I thank you for your solicitude," he said, "b-but my mistakes are my own. I have to do something about them."

"I know," Ben-Hadad said. "But we can help you—first of all, to save Baka. Then I'll need your help for a project of my own."

Anab's back stiffened and he turned, slowly, to look at them. "You . . . you need me?" he said. "For what?"

"That's more like it," Ben-Hadad said. "Sit down here with me by the fire and I'll explain." He sat himself, grimacing at the sharp ache in his chest.

"There," he said, as Tuya and Anab sat next to him. "I was going to tell you both eventually, but I guess now is as good a time as any." He smiled at the curious expressions on both their faces. "Do you know—either of you—why I came to Egypt in the first place?"

Anab and Tuya looked at each other quizzically, and shook their heads.

"I thought as much. Well, as you know, I came here

from up north, in Canaan, where I lived with my mother. She had met my father in Haran, back before the time of the Shepherds. One of my father's friends there was a man named Jacob, who, it turned out later, was a sort of exiled king from down in Canaan. Jacob became a second father to my family and promised to take care of my mother if anything should happen to my father.

"Then—mind you, this was all before I was born— then my uncle, a famous armorer named Shobai, took a job far to the north, working for the Shepherd Kings. It's not unusual, you must understand, for an armorer to hire out to whoever is willing to pay for the work. Anyway, maybe Shobai didn't know what the Shepherds were like. But after a time, seeing their true nature, he rebelled and tried to leave. They wouldn't let him, however. They beat him senseless and even chained him to a metal stake driven into the ground. Still he defied them." He smiled. "Apparently we're a stubborn lot in my family."

"You're not," Tuya said.

"Maybe I am," he said. "My father certainly was. He eventually learned that his brother was being held captive by the Shepherds. This was just about the time that it was becoming apparent the Shepherds were heading for Haran. Father decided, all on his own, that he had to save Shobai— yes, and Haran too. In spite of the fact that he was badly crippled and no fighter." He looked at Anab. "He was smaller than I am. Maybe about your size, Anab."

Anab's eyes were wide. There was a curious expression on the mobile half of his face, but he did not speak.

Ben-Hadad continued. "When Mother found out he'd gone north to try to save my uncle, she was crushed. She was alone and pregnant with me. And at the time it looked as though the Shepherd armies were going to break through our lines and destroy Haran. She was frightened half to death."

"As well she might be," Tuya said.

"Yes. But my father had made provision for her. His friend Jacob, around this time, left Haran for his home country to the south, and he took Mother with him. He treated her as if she were his own daughter. And shortly after his caravan had crossed into Canaan, both Mother and Jacob's wife Rachel came to term—and Jacob's favorite son, Joseph, and I were born on the same day."

"What a story!" Tuya said. "But what happened to your father?"

"Well," Ben-Hadad said, "he seems to have slipped into the Shepherd camp, disguised as a crazy, hunchbacked clown. When they caught him, trying to save my uncle, he tricked them into thinking he had the plague. It was believable enough. Plague wasn't unusual in Haran, and he'd cleverly faked symptoms of the disease. The Shepherds broke camp and scattered.

"But when my father went to the cage where they'd imprisoned my uncle, he found him blind. And the man who'd blinded him, a traitor from Haran named Reshef—"

"I know that name!" Anab said. "They called him the Snake."

"Yes, that's the man. This Reshef had blinded my uncle. They'd had an earlier disagreement, and this was his way of paying my uncle back. Father tried to free Shobai and succeeded in holding off Reshef for a while—Reshef was a master swordsman, and my father had never fought in his whole life. Anyway, he fought Reshef until Shobai could find his way to safety. But then Reshef killed my father, in cold blood."

"How horrible!" Tuya said. "The poor man."

Ben-Hadad sighed. "I wish I'd known him. I've been told he was a warmhearted and generous man.

"In any case," he went on, "Jacob pieced all this together years later. Mother and I had moved away from him for a time when my mother remarried badly. But before my stepfather died, we went to live with Jacob again. And Joseph became my best and closest friend, my blood brother. He was a remarkable boy, brilliant, a seer—and his brothers resented this. So one day—as a cruel joke, it seems—they sold him to traders heading for Egypt."

"What a terrible thing to do!" Anab said.

"That's why I left," Ben-Hadad said. "I felt I had to find Joseph and bring him back." He shook his head in self-deprecation. "It was a foolish thing to do, perhaps—but we owed Jacob everything, you understand, and . . .

well, I suppose I'm my father's son. I had notions about becoming another Hadad."

Tuya reached out to put a comforting hand on his knee.

Ben-Hadad put his large hand atop her small one. "As you can see, I've not found him. But now I think I'm on the wrong side of the battle line to find him. When I first got to Egypt, I checked with all the incoming caravans. None of the ones that came through Sile in the proper period had any slave answering Joseph's description. I think he's down south, on the other side of the Shepherd lines. He's probably a slave in Memphis, if he's still alive."

"Ah," Anab said, rapt, his troubles all but forgotten. "You want to continue your search."

"Yes," Ben-Hadad said. "And there's another reason. My uncle, Shobai—he's alive. He's apparently working for the Egyptians in Memphis, working again as an armorer, despite his blindness."

"But—" Anab and Tuya spoke almost simultaneously.

He waved away their objections. "I know it seems impossible. But I can imagine how one might, although blind, remember enough to be very useful in the training of apprentices and journeymen.

"The tricky part comes next, though. Shobai first entered Egypt at Saïs, west of here. While he was there he met a woman, the wife of an Egyptian general reported missing and presumed dead. They fell in love. They married and were part of the great migration south to Memphis when the Egyptian armies abandoned the delta."

"I think I see," Anab said. "This general . . . did he later emerge from prison?"

"Yes," Ben-Hadad said. "And now he swears revenge. Not only on the Shepherds, but on the blind man who stole his wife away while he was in the Shepherd prison. He swears he's going to kill Shobai. He's already sent a messenger across the lines with a death threat. I know because I've talked to the general. And"—he glanced at Anab—"I'm frightened at the intensity of his hatred for my uncle."

"Baka!" Tuya said. "You're talking about Baka!"

"Yes. It was from him that I learned the latter part of

my uncle's story." He frowned. "Of course, the easiest way to save Shobai is to leave Baka to his enemies, and let them kill him. But I can't do that. Baka's our friend. We have to rescue him—and I have to turn his anger aside somehow. I haven't any idea how."

He shook his head despairingly. "And that's just the beginning," he said. "Somehow I have to find Shobai—it is what my father would have wanted. To show Shobai that somehow everything turned out all right, after all these years."

He looked at them in turn. "I've set myself quite a task. Do you see now why I need both of you? I can't do it all myself. I need friends, the best I can find."

There were tears in Anab's eyes. Tuya, after a long while, broke the silence. "You're a true son of Hadad," she said in a voice full of love.

III

Ben-Hadad set the pace on the dusty road, striding along lustily on strong young legs. For a time Tuya walked beside him. Then, seeing Anab lagging behind, she fell back to talk with him.

"Anab," she said, "are you still brooding over your problems? Because—"

"No, no," he said hastily. "Actually, I was watching the two of you. I was remembering how you used to grieve over the fact that he took no notice of you. Back in the bazaars, I mean, when we all first met."

"Was it that obvious?" she said. "I must have seemed like a silly, single-minded little fool."

"No," Anab said. "Just ornery. I could understand that, though. Growing up in the streets the way you did, you have to be always on guard."

"True," she agreed. "But . . . you mean I'm not that way now?"

"No. You've changed. I can tell it right off. Tuya—what's it like?"

"What's what like?"

"Being in love. And being loved back. If . . ." He had begun to say something else, but seemed to think better of it, and held back. "You—you know what I mean."

Tuya blushed, and her gaze fastened on the road as they walked. "I—I think what I like most is that I can love him as much as I want and not be afraid anymore. Not be afraid that he'll ignore me, refuse me, hurt me in any way. It's a wonderful feeling. It's—" She caught herself, embarrassed. "You have to realize, this is a new experience for me. If I were a jaded woman of the world, with a dozen lovers behind me, I might have the words to express it more easily."

But when she glanced at Anab, at the half of his face that worked, she saw the pain in it, the longing. Impulsively she reached out and grasped his hand, with a quick smile. "What a fool I am. Talking away like this, rattling on about how full my heart is, how happy and secure I feel—and telling it all to someone who's lonely." He tried to pull his hand away, but she held it. "You are, aren't you? And you think that you're the loneliest person on earth. Isn't that right?"

He jerked his hand away and did not answer. He looked angry, and suddenly increased his pace.

Tuya, quickening her own steps to keep up with him, thought the matter over for some time. Ahead, the sun sank behind a row of date palms. The sky was full of incredible colors. There was a soft evening balm in the air, and an idle breeze stirred the palm fronds.

"Anab," she said at last, "I think that if you could find some way to meet people halfway, perhaps they'd do the same for you. Maybe not the first time you try it. Maybe not even the fortieth or fiftieth. But, after all, we're your friends. If you were as vile, as unlovable, as you think yourself, would you even have friends? Friends who'd pick you up when you fell? Who'd overlook it when you went astray now and then, so long as your heart remained good?"

He tried to speak, cleared his throat, and tried again. "Why?" he said. "I wouldn't have forgiven you if you'd betrayed me. At least I don't think I would have."

"Sure you would," she said. "As long as we showed you any regard and didn't treat you with contempt. It's yourself you never forgive. And for what? For being human? For being fallible?" She lowered her voice a bit and said soberly, almost timidly, "For not being handsome? Rich? Of good family?" She waited for an answer, her eyes on the road at her feet, dark in the long shadow Ben-Hadad's moving body cast before them. When she spoke again, it was in a calm, slow voice.

"Look at me, Anab. I'm no prize. I'm neither ugly nor pretty. I don't turn any heads as I walk by. You've seen me naked; you know I'm no palace dancing girl. What have I got to offer a man . . . except a heart that's true? In the end, what have any of us got to offer except that? A loving heart, one that's constant despite all temptations and setbacks. Anab I'm still walking around in a rosy haze at my good fortune. I don't think I've ever been really happy before. If this is what happy is, then I'm sure I've never known anything even remotely like it. But I sometimes think it's not all good fortune—and I think you know that, too, Anab."

Now it was his turn to look at her. And when he did, it was with no expression at all on his strange face. He tried to speak but failed, then turned away to stare into the distance. As he did, the sun faded and died in the west, and she could not make out his expression at all. Perhaps there was none there to look for.

Zosar's crony Tumbos, an out-of-work butcher who had recently murdered a Shepherd officer in order to even an unpaid debt, shook his grizzled head and tugged at his thick lower lip. He was perspiring freely, and he looked worried.

"He's never going to tell you," he said. "Be sensible, Zosar. You've kept him here three days. You've tried everything short of killing him outright, and you've learned nothing you didn't know before. Why don't you just—"

"Get out of my way," Zosar said roughly. His own patience was all too obviously at an end. "Do you think I care a hang for the pittance those priests will give me for turning him over, dead or alive? I didn't risk my neck for only money. What kind of fool do you think I am, anyway? The money's quickly spent, and afterward you have nothing. But, power—that's different. Power can earn you all the money you need. If I can only find out the names of his spies before the priests get their hands on him—" He spat into the fire.

Tumbos glanced again at Baka, naked, bruised, bleeding, spread-eagled on his back on the long table, like a piece of meat. Ropes leading up from the underside of the table were bound tightly about his ankles and wrists; his hands were dark red, almost immobile. His eyes were closed. "I went along with you," Tumbos said, "because I hate Shepherds, and you paid me well. But *this* business, Zosar"—he nodded toward the prisoner—"it's sick stuff." He shook his head, clearly disgusted. Zosar pushed him aside.

"Bah! Weak stomachs!" he said. "I'm surrounded by cowards!"

Tumbos, still staring at Baka, didn't seem to notice the shove. "I don't like this, Zosar," he said. "Torture is for scum like the Shepherds. I say either we release him—"

"*Release* him! You're a dead man the moment you do that! Do you know how many friends he has up and down the countryside? Why, first off, there's the raiding party that wasn't at the camp when we attacked it. They'll be coming after us if they ever suspect the truth. As it is, we're damned lucky Baka's the only one who can identify us."

"I don't think that's true," Tumbos said nervously. "There are two of them who might have escaped. Maybe three. I just found out today. I think one may have been the smith, the boy who used to play senet in the bazaars."

Zosar frowned. "Damn!" he said. "I thought we had killed them all."

"Well, he was badly wounded. He might be dead by now. But there's also a girl, someone who was helping him at the forge."

"Tuya! I should have stuck a knife in her myself. She was the one who saved the smith, back in the raid on Wenis's house. Are you sure she's missing, too?"

"That's what I heard. And what about your little friend, the one with the face?"

Zosar scowled. "That's my fault," he said. "I was stupid to trust him. Where's he got himself to? Could he have gone over to the Shepherds? The priests? If the priests find out I've detained Baka—"

"That's all we need," Tumbos groaned. "But I'm more worried about the smith. I heard he was close as thieves with Baka. If he's alive . . ." He swore under his breath. "Even the girl—she's got a reputation in the bazaars as a quick hand with a knife. There's a burglar in the Thieves Quarter, I've been told, who has one arm hanging loose, as useless as a dead stick of wood. He tried to grab her with it when she didn't want him to. Out came that little dirk of hers, *swish!* right through the tendons."

"I know, confound it." Zosar's red face and sweaty brow betrayed his own anxiety. "That's all the more reason that I should hurry and get what I want out of Baka, whether he wants to give it or not. If you don't like it, you can leave, but don't meddle—"

"All right. You can call me a weak stomach if you want, but I don't like to watch a man butchered like a side of beef on a slab. I'll wait outside until you're done."

"Do that." Zosar, his face still ruddy with anger, watched him go. Then, picking up a blackened poker from the windowsill beside him, he crossed the room to the long table and the inert and bleeding body tied to it.

He looked down at Baka for a moment, watching the closed eyes, the drawn face, seeing the prisoner's chest rise and fall with the regular breathing of an unconscious man. Then, suddenly, his hand whipped out and slapped the captive in the face, hard. "Wake up, Baka!" he said in a harsh and impatient voice. "Wake up, you pig!"

The bound man opened his eyes and tried to raise himself. His head lifted off the table, then sank back against the hard wood. "Oh," he said. "I dreamed I was in paradise, surrounded by unearthly beauty, being waited on hand and foot by naked dancing girls lovelier than the full moon. And here I wake up and there's nothing to look at but your ugly mug, Zosar."

"Keep it up," Zosar said. "You'll talk another way in a

moment or two." He was silent as he stirred the fire with the poker, then set the implement down with the tip close to the hot coals, watching it as it began to glow.

The captive spoke without raising his head. "I haven't so far," he said. "And you've run through your little bag of tricks twice. No, Zosar, you're never going to get me to talk. The Shepherds couldn't do it. Why should you think you can succeed where they failed?"

"Watch your tongue!"

"That's odd. One of the Shepherds said the same thing to me two years ago. I told him to cut it out for me and lay it on the table so I *could* watch it. He was so stupid he almost took me up on it. Then he realized that if he did it, I couldn't talk if I wanted to."

"You'll talk," Zosar said. "But this time I think I'll need someone to hold your head while I work. Damn it . . . Tumbos!"

There was no answer. Zosar thrust the poker deep into the white-hot bed of coals and went out of the room. "Tumbos, where are—?"

One of the guards lay in the doorway, his neck sticking out at a crazy angle. Tumbos's body was in the middle of the floor. There was a horrible splash of red at his throat. "What—?" Zosar, fear rising in him, reached for the knife at his belt.

But another hand, far quicker and nimbler than his, had already removed the knife from its scabbard. He whirled, backing away. "Anab!" he said. "Give that back, you little—"

Anab rushed him. As he did, a forearm as thick as a strong man's thigh went around Zosar's neck, choking the life out of him. His hands clawed at the mighty arm—and Anab's knife struck him just below the rib cage, ripping upward with force sufficient to jerk him off his feet. He did not have the chance to feel the pain as life rushed out of him in one blinding moment.

Gently they cut Baka loose. Before they could assist him he sat up, with stoic disdain for his wounds, and rubbed his wrists. In the meantime, Anab had stripped the robe from Zosar's inert body, and now he brought it to

Baka. "Here," he said. "It's stained—but not as badly as the others. I'm sorry I did such a sloppy job." He gently helped Baka into the garment, trying to avoid the more recent wounds.

Baka grinned at him. "And I thought you didn't have what it takes, Anab," he said through clenched teeth. "Well, I've been wrong before, and I'll be wrong again. But not about the lot of you."

"Hush, now," Tuya said in a low semiwhisper. "We've got to get away before the others get back. How many are there?"

"Maybe five or six," Baka said. "They're in town, dickering with the priests."

"The more reason for us to get on the move," Ben-Hadad said. "Anab, there's a wagon outside and a couple of tethered asses. Do you know how to hitch them up? There's a harness against the wall. I saw it on the way in."

"Coming right up," Anab said, and he disappeared through the open door at a run.

Baka let the others help him carefully to his feet. The first time he tried to stand, his knees buckled. Then he got himself under control, with some difficulty. "That Anab—" he said. "I had my doubts about him . . . but it seems he was true. Truer than some of the ones I trusted. I—I thank you, my friends."

He did not see the glance that passed between Ben-Hadad and Tuya behind his back, or hear the words Ben-Hadad mouthed at her silently: *Don't tell him.* . . .

Using the slow-moving cart, they eventually got him to the river. There they loaded him onto the little boat they had left hidden in the reeds, as Anab drove the cart into the brush and abandoned the animals. Baka did not speak as they swam the boat across the river to the island, and the only sounds he made as they helped him out of the boat were those of a man in pain quietly cursing rather than submitting to his hurts.

Anab joined them around the fire. Above, the half-moon drifted in and out of the wandering clouds. They fed Baka with soup Tuya made from stolen ingredients. After

they had dined, no one spoke for some time. Baka was the
first to break the silence.

"I've done all that I can here," he said. "As soon as I
can travel I'm going across the lines to fight with the
Egyptians against the Shepherds."

"What?" Tuya said, astonished. "Abandon the fight
here?"

"The Shepherds are planning a big push before
Memphis," Baka said. "This time Vahan will break through.
He'll drive our army back—perhaps as far as Memphis.
He may even take Memphis. The Egyptian lines are weak,
exhausted. They can use every body they can get, and all
the better if it's someone who's had a little experience of
war." He smiled weakly at the two men. "How about the
two of you? Will you join me?"

"Join you?" Anab said. "But—how? How do we get
through the Shepherd lines to the other side?"

"Let our beards grow. Disguise ourselves. Join Vahan's
mercenary army. Then, at the right moment, go over to
the other side." His face seemed to regain color as he
spoke, his enthusiasm animating him. "I'm tired of this
sniping. I long to hold a sword in my hand again and feel
it bite into Shepherd necks. Besides"—his tone changed,
darkened ominously—"there's something I have to do before I die, and it can be done only on the other side . . . to
someone I've been waiting to meet for a long time." There
was a mad glint in his eye as he stared into the fire.

That night Ben-Hadad lay awake, thinking, while beside him, Tuya slept peacefully.

After a time, tucking their few rags about her, he
slipped out of their bed of rushes and, restless, paced the
shore of the little island.

The more he thought about it, the fewer choices he
saw. He'd *have* to go along with Baka; that much was
certain. There was no other way he could keep him from
reaching Memphis and killing Shobai. Not without killing
Baka himself. And that was unthinkable.

He'd already tried to talk to Baka—indeed, he'd tried
before the raid—timidly venturing to steer him off his
ruinous course. Mere mention of the subject, however,

had brought nothing but a violent and immediate reaction. Baka's mind was set.

He had no choice but to tag along with him and see what sort of diversion he could improvise. But what would become of Tuya in the meantime? How could he provide for her and keep her safe until his return? Who would watch over her?

His gaze wandered out over the river . . . and, in the corner of his vision, he detected a light-colored shape detaching itself from the shadowed brush at water's edge on the opposite bank. He peered through the semidarkness, waiting for the moon to come completely out from behind a cloud. A small animal of some kind, probably come to the water to drink.

No. Whatever it was, it did not drink. It stood, front legs firmly planted, head held high, alertly looking at him. . . .

"Lion!" he said, recognizing the stance, recognizing the wagging tail. In the warm night Ben-Hadad had come from their bed naked. Now, elated by the sight of Lion, he dived into the water and swam with powerful strokes to the other shore. In a moment he was embracing the little dog, holding him to him, his heart racing with joy.

"Lion," he said, "I wonder if you have any idea how happy I am to see you." He ran his fingers over the coarse hair on the little animal's head, scratching him behind the ears. "You never desert me, do you, boy? I can always count on you. I always have, and I always will. You'll watch out for her, won't you? You and Anab? You won't let any harm come to her while I'm away. I'll leave her with you—that's what I'll do. And when I come back, with all my chores done, we'll find us a part of the delta where no one will bother us, and we'll settle down. Then you and I can grow old together in peace, eh, boy?"

He grinned happily as the dog licked his face. All the troubling thoughts that had bedeviled him all night now gone from his mind, he splashed back into the water. "Come on," he said. "I'll race you to the island."

CHAPTER NINE

THE NILE HEADWATERS

I

All day long they had followed a smooth, beaten track along the slopes that rose above the raging river, with low hills rising before them and, far to the southwest, the foothills of a towering range of mountains easily visible in the clear hill-country air. The air was cool, but the sun was warm on the naked bodies of Akhilleus's party as they marched. Only with evening would the chill force them to wear the animal skins the hunters had brought back from a foraging party several days before: skins of leopards and zebras and antelopes. Now they marched bare, the sunlight gleaming on their swords and on the bronze points of their spears.

By now even Musuri had abandoned his loincloth, and his burly, scarred body was burned dark by the sun, so that it looked like weathered old leather, hardly lighter in shade than his sword belt. A month before he had been puffy, short-winded. But now, as the party worked its way ever upward into the mountainous sources of the Great River, his old legs found new strength flowing into them, and, grinning proudly with broken teeth, he picked up his pace, passing the long line of bearers to catch up with Akhilleus at the head of the column.

As he caught sight of the expedition's leader, he marveled once again at how the long trip had pared away the extra flesh on Akhilleus's giant frame. Now he was neither long and lean, like the native bearers they had hired back in the Sudd, nor yet the obese monster he had been when the journey had begun. Broad-backed, with the mighty shoulders of a galley oarsman, he looked like nothing so much as a strapping, heavily muscled Mediterranean warrior—except half again that warrior's size. At his side marched Ebana—who herself stood taller than Musuri—and the two naked black bodies gleamed like polished ebony statues. *I was right. They're a pair of gods come to earth,* Musuri thought.

Akhilleus turned and looked back at him. "Ah, Musuri," he said, smiling. "Come join us." He slowed to let the soldier catch up, taking the occasion to examine the old warrior with some approval. "You know, I think this mountain country agrees with you. You haven't looked this fit since we first met, back in Tyre, all those many years ago."

"Perhaps it's all the climbing," Musuri said, "for the mountains do seem to put strength into one. I tend to forget, having lived and fought in flat country most of my life, but I was born in the mountains of Moab. In a sense I'm coming home, too." He remembered his errand, though, and changed the subject. "I was going to ask—I talked to Lule, the guide we hired yesterday. He wanted to know why you took the left fork a while back. This one goes nowhere, he says. Just into the rocks. He recommends that we backtrack and take the other fork for easier passage."

"Tell him not to worry," Akhilleus said. "As it turns out, my bones, more than my head, remember this track. And we're going this way for a purpose, even if it means some backtracking later. It's in the nature of a pilgrimage for me, and I wanted to share it with all of you." He turned his concentration back to the trail as the path steepened. They were picking their way through a boulder-strewn defile. Ahead, in the rocky hills above, there was a low rumble, almost a roar, steady and pervasive.

Musuri looked perplexed. "Whatever you say; you're in charge . . . but what's that sound up ahead? Some sort of cataract?"

"The river is flexing its muscles," Akhilleus said. "I think it's going to show off for us in a moment or two. I wanted you to see it. This many months' march from the delta, the Nile remains as powerful and majestic as it is when it floods and buries the delta islands. It is the source of all life, of all strength, in all these southern lands."

"I'll take your word for it," Musuri said. He pulled even with Akhilleus and, his curiosity getting the better of him, forged ahead of the big man to break trail himself. "You've already shown me more strange sights than I've ever—"

His mouth hung open; he had stepped out from behind a fallen boulder into the light spray, and now caught his first glimpse of the "cataract" Akhilleus had wished to show them.

High, high above them, the Nile's mighty waters roiled through a narrow trough, hardly wider than the length of three men's bodies, and roared, in two incredibly powerful surges, down through a ragged cleft in the black rocks. At midpoint in their fall, the crashing waters hit a hard place and changed course, bouncing off the steep walls of the narrow canyon, sending waves of mist rushing high into the air. The next fall pounded its way to the main bed of the river and also sent up airy clouds of spray—and a bright rainbow, many-hued, light, and delicate in the middle of this awesome display of crushing, unbelievable power.

Akhilleus silently moved to his side. Musuri, looking up at him, saw the goose bumps on the giant's black flesh. Beneath their feet the earth trembled. "The Nile," Akhilleus said, his booming voice barely audible above the roar of the crashing waters. "It is our father and our mother. From it we were born, and to it we will return."

Musuri was struck dumb by the sight and sound and feel of it. It was as the black man had said—as though they were in the presence of a god, the great god of gods who fathered all. Before such power nothing could stand. "Akhilleus," he said, his words inaudible to anyone else but him, "where are you bringing us to? What sort of place is this?"

Akhilleus's giant hand, callused still from his many years on the oar, fell gently on his shoulder, and the black man leaned down to speak into his ear. "Don't be afraid, Musuri," he said. "It's not the portals of death you're looking at. It's the gateway to life itself. I'm home, Musuri—or almost so. Beyond the falls lies the land I was born in. I know it. I've been here before. My father brought me here. My father, Ma—" He straightened, and as Musuri looked up at his face, his lips moved, searching for syllables, for a word, for a name. "Magi—"

For a moment the spray rose, thicker than before, and almost blotted out the giant's face, two heads above Musuri's own. When it faded, Akhilleus's face could be seen, dripping with water, the black brow knit, the lips still moving but, for now, making no sound.

Akhilleus closed his eyes. "I almost remembered it," he said. "It almost came to me. After all these years of wandering, of exile . . . I think I'm on the verge of knowing who I am."

They turned and retraced their steps along the track and took the other fork. It led away from the river, along a more gradual path, steadily upward but at a gentler angle. When at last the trail stopped climbing, they could see that they had reached a vast tableland whose rolling hills never again dipped so low. Ahead, where the river branched, they could see the neck of a great lake. "Is this the body of water you were telling me about, Akhilleus?" Ebana said. "It doesn't look so big, after all. You told me you couldn't see across it."

"Then this can't be it, can it?" Akhilleus said. He smiled gravely. "No. We've entered a land of lakes. We'll pass others besides this before we come to the one I told you of. It will make all of these—yes, everything but the Great Sea—look small and puny. *Everything* here is larger than what you're used to. To the southwest there are Mountains of Fire—mountains that belch forth flame and smoke, and cast boulders the size of twenty houses into the sky, and spew molten metal and rock down the side of the hills to bury whole towns, whole jungles. I speak of mountains that, sleeping and silent, would take weeks to climb across."

"That must be what lies behind the bank of clouds over there," Musuri said. "The hill country would be chill and damp, I suspect, and in this climate, fog would lie on the slopes most of the year."

"Correct," Akhilleus said. "And, Musuri—high on those chill slopes live apes larger by far than men, weighing twice what I weigh. They're gentle and eat only vegetable matter. But if you blunder upon their nests, they'll fight like demons. And they can crush a man with one blow."

"Gods!" Musuri said. "It's as if we'd entered another world altogether."

"You have," Akhilleus said. "It's *my* world. Look before you and you will see why I've always felt myself a stranger, a fish out of water, for all these many years. I think that with the new eyes I've grown in the last few days I'll always look on the world we left behind us as an odd and foreign place. That world—*it's* the strange one. This is the real one."

They started down the path again, but as they did, two dozen hard black bodies silently, suddenly, stepped out from behind the dense brush to surround them. The newcomers brandished stone-tipped spears; their faces were taut, tense, ready for action.

Musuri reached for his sword, but Akhilleus stayed his hand and himself stepped out in front of the caravan. He spoke, loudly but haltingly, in a tongue that none of the others, save their most recently hired bearer, could understand. The bearer, Lule, jogged up to the head of the column, eyes wide, and joined Akhilleus.

A tall, powerful-looking warrior detached himself from the group and stepped forward to within a few paces of Akhilleus. He shook his spear menacingly, then spoke, spitting the syllables out arrogantly.

Musuri edged closer to Ebana. "What are they saying?" he asked. "Can you make out any of it?"

"Not a word," she said. "But I do know Akhilleus was

mumbling some gibberish in his sleep last night. At least it was gibberish to me. When he awoke, though, he said that in his dream he'd found out who he was—but waking he couldn't remember."

"Whoever he is," Musuri said, "I hope he can persuade these fellows here to stop pointing their spears at—"

"Musuri," Akhilleus called back, "could you step up here, please?"

The old soldier hurried to his side. "What's happening?" he said.

"Give me your sword," Akhilleus said.

Musuri did so. Akhilleus handed it to the young warrior, who examined it carefully—even biting the blade.

"Now call up one of the bearers," Akhilleus said. "Have him bring a sample of copper ore." Musuri barked out an order, and in a moment the bearer was at his side with a bag of samples. Akhilleus took this and offered it to the warrior, who was vigorously swinging the sword to and fro. Now he tucked the sword under one rock-hard arm and opened the bag. He took out a green-tinged rock and looked at it. Then he held up both rock and sword and said something, obviously a question. Akhilleus answered with a single syllable, then in turn asked an incomprehensible question. The warrior went away and conferred with his companions.

Akhilleus took the opportunity to explain. "His name's Kimala," he said. "He's captain of some sort to Ramogi, leader of all the armies of the region and son to the great emperor Bukango.

"Kimala here is interested in our metal weapons. He's never seen any before, of course, and he's quite impressed. Think of all the necks he could hew with these! I asked him if there were any men, brave men, in the region who liked to fight, who would like to get rich. Maybe even learn to make weapons like these, to use against their enemies."

"Make them? But—"

"Why not? Shobai can train anyone who wants to learn. And one can't have too many armorers, or warriors, either. Besides, if I guess right, in a moment young Kimala here is going to turn back to me and, fortified with information from his friends, is going to tell me what I already know."

"Which is?"

"That the Mountains of Fire I told you about are full to bursting with ore like this. That you can pick up rocks bearing copper ore right in the middle of the path. That this may well be one of the richest copper-bearing lands anywhere."

Musuri's eyes widened in amazement. "When you set about finding help, you don't fool around, do you?"

Akhilleus shook his grizzled head, apparently amused. "Do you realize, Musuri, that I can make out better than half of what he says? I think we're going to have an interesting time of it here, my friend. Not safe, perhaps— but interesting."

"Not safe? You mean these people are dangerous?" Musuri put a hand on his empty scabbard. "Suddenly I want my sword back."

"You may need it soon enough," Akhilleus said in a low and thoughtful voice. "This Bukango—he's apparently very old and ill. His son, no doubt, is getting ready to take over the moment the old man dies."

"So? How does that put us in danger?"

"There is always danger during a transfer of power. Even more so now—and for us, of all people. You see, I just remembered my father's name—and my own." He shook his head slowly. "The ways of the gods are mysterious, Musuri. That we should be here, just now."

"What do you mean?" Musuri said.

"My name is Mtebi," Akhilleus whispered, leaning close. "Don't use that name aloud, though—nor my father's. His was Magimbi. And this great and mighty king, Bukango—he's my uncle. He's my father's younger brother." Musuri stared openmouthed. "Don't repeat this to anyone other than Ebana, whatever you do. Apparently, my father must have died after I was taken away. Whether Bukango had a hand in my kidnapping I don't know yet. But he succeeded my father, and he wouldn't have if I'd been here. Now he's about to die, and here I am, with a stronger claim to the succession than either he or his son has."

"And his son?"

"His son, Ramogi, controls an army that commands all the lands from the Mufumbiro—the Mountains of Fire—to the high peaks of the Karamojong in the east. An army that surrounds us, my friend, even as we speak."

II

But when Kimala returned to where he had conversed with Akhilleus earlier, there was no mention of ore. Instead, he handed back Musuri's sword and looked Akhilleus squarely in the eye, sizing him up.

Akhilleus smiled and, half turning, tossed the weapon to Musuri. "Splendid," he said. "This is a warrior worthy of generalship himself. He's telling me nothing. He's quite sensibly stalling, as I'd do in his place." He spoke haltingly to Kimala in the language they shared, his deep voice booming out even here in the hills, where the vastness around them tended to swallow words.

Ebana moved nearer to Musuri. "What's happening now?" she asked. "Are these people going to stand in our way?" Behind her, others who had been with the party since early on moved within earshot, drawn by curiosity. Musuri saw among them Obwano and Uranga—the latter at last naked like all the rest, his fine athlete's body glistening with sweat from their climb.

"We may have a problem," Musuri said, sheathing his sword. "Possibly nothing that Akhilleus can't talk his way out of. He's remembering the language quite well, apparently. These warriors around us—I gather you've figured out that they're his own people, and they don't recognize him."

"I wondered," she said. "I notice they don't scar themselves the way the earlier tribes did. That accounts for his own lack of ritual cicatrices."

"That or the fact that he left when he was too young,"

Musuri said. "But—he asked me to keep it quiet—he remembers who he is. And if they find out, we're in a great deal of trouble."

"Indeed?" Ebana said. "Who is he? And why should they care?"

Musuri started to speak—and then saw Obwano and Uranga leaning forward, their faces betraying their curiosity. For an instant he again felt the sense of foreboding that had troubled him throughout the journey. "You two!" he said. "Pass the word back: Nobody's to do anything at all without direct orders from Akhilleus or me. Particularly anything that could be interpreted as menacing or warlike. Now, get on with it. Run the message back yourselves, to the whole caravan. Hop to!"

As they took off, Akhilleus turned to speak to Ebana and Musuri. "We're to make camp in the valley ahead, under their supervision. We're to do nothing until Kimala has heard from Ramogi. His runners are on the road already. Ramogi's camp is far to the south, in the foothill country my father's people came from, and the runners will reach him in a day or two. They'll find relays along the way. It seems this Ramogi has his army well prepared and highly organized. Lokosa would have approved."

Musuri was scrutinizing Kimala, watching him issue orders to his fellow warriors. "So far I'm impressed myself," he said. "But who's this Lokosa you speak of?"

"My grandfather," Akhilleus said in a low voice. "The old king of my childhood, the man who first unified all the tribes under one rule. Now *there's* a name to conjure with around here. He's achieved the status of something like a god. It's a shame I have to act as though I never heard his name before, or Bukango's."

"Lokosa? Bukango?" Ebana said. "Don't talk over my head, Akhilleus. I'm not one of your backcountry brides, content to sit silently in the *hareem* and leave it all to the men. Who are these people? What are these names?"

Akhilleus grinned. "Now, there's a queen for you," he said. "Under other circumstances she might have become one. And I'd have been king of . . . all this." He cast a longing glance at the green, rolling hills around them. "It would have been a good destiny, too—it's rich, fertile, splendid country. Gods! How the sight of it brings memories back, memories I'd thought I'd lost forever." He sighed, and closed his eyes for a moment.

"Lokosa had two sons," he said. "The younger was Bukango, who now rules, who has ruled fifty years and more. The elder—the *elder*, mind you—was my father."

"Then *you* were the rightful heir?" Ebana said.

"Yes. Apparently when my father died—I don't know just how—he, having no son, was succeeded by his brother. I'd disappeared earlier, of course. And yes, I do wonder whether *that* was arranged in order to ensure the subsequent succession. In any event, it might all come out sooner or later—if we can contrive to live that long. So far I've told them only that I'm a traveler from afar. But this Kimala is no ordinary soldier. He's sharp-eyed as a hawk. I have a feeling that he's onto me already. Don't be fooled by the stone weapons. Just because these people haven't learned to work metal, don't make the mistake of thinking they're stupid or unsophisticated. They haven't *had* to learn to work metal. Those stone blades are sharp enough to shave off your beard with, Musuri. In fact, the one Kimala's carrying has been used to kill a lion, so he's told me. And forget the tame lions at court, back in Egypt— they capture only the sick, lame, and indolent ones. The lion Kimala had to kill to make himself a man was full grown, fit, and hungry."

Musuri again glanced at Kimala. "And you say he's onto you?"

"Quite possibly. He knows something's wrong. If I'm a traveler from a far land, why do I speak his language? Why do I bear no ritual scars, when his people alone among all the known tribes have none? Why am I his height, when few others are so tall? What is there in my face—I'm guessing, now—that vaguely reminds him of someone?"

Ebana frowned. "Here he comes again," she said.

Kimala approached. He almost seemed to be smiling, Akhilleus noticed. His eyes bore—what? Was it a slight touch of humor?

"You will camp by the river below," he said. His nod of the head indicated the others: Musuri, Ebana, the

bearers, the guardsmen. "You, *Akillu*, will dine with me."
He did what he could to approximate the proper pronuncia-
tion of the unfamiliar name. "You will tell me about the
lands of the Great River, beyond the lakes: whether the
tribes are prepared and well defended. You will tell me
also of your own land."

Akhilleus could not help but smile. "You're thinking
of invading? Of spreading your ruler's domain past the
ridge of hills?"

"I speak of no such things," the young warrior said.
"The more I know, the better soldier I am." His gaze
moved up and down the black giant's powerful body,
pausing at the sword belt at his side. "You will also,
perhaps, tell me how it is possible to make such weapons
from the stones of the Mufumbiro—"

Kimala had slipped. He immediately recognized his
mistake, however, and scowled.

Akhilleus tried to conceal his amusement. "So there
is ore in the hills to the southwest?" he said.

Kimala's eyes narrowed. "You know the name of the
mountain country to the southwest?" he said, recovering
and thrusting in turn, like a master swordsman. "I think
indeed we shall have much to talk about."

They made camp under the eyes of more than fifty
watchful and fearsomely armed warriors. The site chosen
had been selected for an obvious purpose—it was the least
easily defended spot in the valley. Surrounded by warriors
more than five times their own number, Akhilleus's party
would be totally vulnerable in case of a sudden shift to
hostility on the part of their hosts. Musuri took note of the
fact and didn't like it at all. Securing his flanks as best he
could, he went to Akhilleus. "Look," he said, "I think our
lives are in your hands. Don't say anything to make anyone angry, eh?"

"I'll try not to," Akhilleus said, smiling. "Actually, I
think Kimala would attack us only under direct orders. He
has too much to gain from keeping us alive. We represent
knowledge to him, knowledge he may be able to use
sometime. He's smart—and perhaps ambitious. How much
so I can't say. I'll know more after I've talked with him."

"Ambitious? Why do you think that?"

"A feeling. I wouldn't put anything past him—or put anything beyond his reach, either. He's very able. He'd most likely make a good king."

"But he's not of the blood—is he?"

"No. But my grandfather, the great Lokosa, came to power as a usurper, casting down a corrupt king. It's happened many times before, and . . . I don't know. I may be wrong, but to me his tone seems stiff and formal when he mentions my cousin Ramogi. I have a feeling there's no love lost between them."

"Then you think that when the time comes, he might tell Ramogi only what he thinks Ramogi ought to know about us—and reserve the most useful information for himself?"

"That's my guess. I'd say that a sticky time is ahead for all of us—not least for Kimala. During a transfer of power, as you know, people spend a lot of time looking over their shoulders. Anything can happen. A tribe—like an army command—may simply decide that its loyalty does not extend to the old king's successor. Whoever takes over from Bukango, when he dies, will have a hard time of it. And this Ramogi—I suspect that he has enemies. Kimala, for one, if I'm any judge of people."

"*Hmm,*" Musuri said, frowning. "A fine time for us to be here. I feel like a duck waiting in the marsh while the beaters come closer. Waiting to become someone's supper."

"All the more reason," Akhilleus said softly, "to be quiet and careful." He clapped the old soldier affectionately on one shoulder and strode briskly away.

Musuri, watching him go, shook his grizzled head at the spectacle of old Akhilleus, with his gray beard, seemingly grown young again. *A king?* Musuri thought. *A king returned from many years' exile in foreign lands, preparing to . . . to do what?*

The hunters had been out all day and had returned with four fat gazelles. These the warriors roasted over a blazing fire, carving off the choicest bits for Kimala's guest. Akhilleus regally accepted these as his due, and thanked the servers as if from on high. Kimala observed him silently and with interest. Finally he spoke. "Then . . . you are a great man in your own land? This land of far away, which you tell me about?"

"My land?" Akhilleus laughed heartily. "I've lived so many years and journeyed to so many places, that truly I do not know what to call 'my land.' For many years I was a slave, and my only home was a plank on a galley—a great warship rowed by many men, on a great sea. When I was freed, I became a pirate captain, preying on the ships of powerful merchant-princes. Then I became a merchant-prince myself, a very rich man." Again he laughed. "Perhaps I still am rich, if my stewards have managed my affairs properly in my absence."

"But you do not know? You cannot learn of this? Yet you can mount an expedition, at great expense, to come this far?"

"The land to which I last journeyed, the land of the Great River, was invaded by nomads, fierce warriors whose numbers were too many to count. They rode on animals as swift as the gazelle and fought with terrible metal weapons, like the one I showed you. I could no longer find my way to the sea, to my ships, without passing through the ranks of the invaders. And I had come to love the people among whom I lived in the land of the Great River, the land called Egypt. So—I joined them, and after a time I came south, looking for new ore to make weapons, and for new warriors to help us in our fight."

"And you expect to find these here?"

"I hope to." Akhilleus smiled as he picked up his beer bowl. "Join me," he said. "I could use an able captain like you."

Kimala seemed to be caught off guard. "You—you speak of new weapons, of new ways of fighting . . . and your words are tempting to a warrior who wishes to learn of these things. But I think that I am not done with what I must do here, in the land in which I was born."

Akhilleus peered over the beer bowl and put it back down untasted. "You have plans?" he said. "And they tempt you as the thought of fighting in strange new lands does not? As the thought of learning to make swords of metal does not?"

Kimala put down his own bowl, and it was quite some time before he spoke. "I would know with whom I am asked to fight," he said calmly. "There are many questions you do not answer. And—you appear just now, when Bukango is about to die, and the tribes do not rest easy in their villages."

Akhilleus's brow rose. "Then Bukango's succession is in doubt? Is he not the rightful emperor? Or is it Ramogi, your commander, whom the people fear?"

"Your curiosity knows no bounds," Kimala said.

"As you yourself said, the more one knows . . ."

Kimala looked long and hard at Akhilleus, as if trying to read something in his features. At length he seemed to reach a decision. "Bukango was a second son," he said. "His older brother, Magimbi, had a son—but the boy disappeared one day and was never found. Magimbi reigned five years, and his reign, the old people say, was humane and just. I cannot say myself: It was before I was born. But shortly after his son disappeared, he died of a sudden illness. Sudden and, some said, mysterious. Bukango was named successor, and the chiefs of the eastern tribes rebelled—the tribes who live in the hills you saw this morning."

"The Karamojong."

"Yes. How did you know their name? I have not spoken it. But let it pass; I'll finish my story. Bukango, with aid from the enemies of Magimbi, put down the rebellion. Many warriors—and their wives and children— were killed. There is still bad blood, and there have been small uprisings since. Ramogi, at the head of his father's armies, has crushed these with no mercy. Many died. Many."

"Then this Ramogi is a man of mature years? If Bukango has reigned fifty years and more—"

"Bukango has had many wives. The *hareem* is extensive. Most of them bore not at all. Some bore daughters. Some bore sons who died young. Of them all, only Ramogi's mother, who became wife of wives when Bukango was growing old, produced a son who lived to adulthood. Bukango named him his heir only a few years ago. Ramogi is not yet thirty. He is young, and the young tend to be . . . impatient."

Akhilleus thought he noticed an angry glint in his host's eyes, in the light of the fire's dancing flames. "And Bukango—he dies slowly, of old age?"

Kimala nodded, once.

"Perhaps too slowly for some?"

Kimala frowned. "It has been you, not I, who said this. But no matter. Ramogi sees gray hairs in his beard. And still the king lives."

"And still his son, and the tribes, perhaps, remember how Bukango himself came to power?" It was a question, not a statement of fact.

Kimala looked at Akhilleus once again for a long time without speaking. "Let us drink," he said at last, lifting his beer bowl. "Your visit here"—he did not smile—"may it be fruitful . . . and safe."

CHAPTER TEN

THE NILE DELTA

I

For months, the great army of the Shepherd Kings had steadily been augmented as mercenaries recruited in all the regions of the Fertile Crescent continued to stream in, lured by the promise of good pay, a one-sided fight, and the chance of helping to loot what had once been the greatest kingdom on the face of the earth.

Young and old men from the Shepherds' satellite city-states along the Canaanite coast came first to join the plunder. Soon after them came Hittite adventurers, then seafarers from Crete and the Greek islands and Anatolia, then others with strange faces, bearing unpronounceable names and hailing from places not even the traders regularly sailed to. From even more inaccessible areas came Elamites, Assyrians, Luvians, Phrygians, Scythians—some of them old soldiers, some of them farmers or tradesmen who had to be taught how to hold a sword properly.

The Shepherd recruiters, asking no questions, accepted anyone who seemed able-bodied. The same applied in the case of the native-born, who, braving the contempt and hatred of their neighbors, enlisted in the Shepherd cause to fight against their own countrymen. Vahan's orders were strict and unbreakable: All healthy comers were to be accepted, bar none. He was counting on the sheer weight of numbers to overwhelm Unas's defenses and to assure the final and fatal breakthrough. From his headquarters at Athribis, where once the Egyptian general Baka had held sway, Vahan oversaw the operation, dispersing the newcomers to head off the possibility of a "Thracian unit" or a "Hittite unit" that might in time demand special treatment or autonomy.

Along the broad battle line raiding parties went out nightly, their purpose to harass the defenders. The lines had been stabilized for more than six months now, and Vahan's commanders had not een able to advance. Their problems were exacerbated by the fact that the Great River itself cut the battle lines into several pieces. For the sake of convenience, Vahan's troops had been arbitrarily divided into units representing, and occupying the southernmost parts of, the old Second, Tenth, and Thirteenth Nomes. These communicated with one another via light oar-powered skiffs that crossed the river's channels just after dark or before dawn each day. During the daylight hours, crossings were made farther downriver, well out of range of the accurate shooting of the Egyptian bowmen.

Vahan's troops were arrayed thick and deep along the lines, and far to the rear, new units—drafts uniting men of twenty or more nationalities but with a single common goal of plunder—now marched into place behind them. When all of the newly arrived units were in place, Vahan would call the attack, and by now, hardly anyone on either side of the lines had any doubt about what the outcome would be. Only the most hardened old warriors could contemplate that end with anything but trepidation—the more so as the news had already leaked out across the border that the court had deserted Memphis, leaving in the ungarrisoned city none but the poorest of the poor, who could not afford to join the caravans in which the well-to-do were already streaming south, taking with them whatever possessions could be salvaged. When the end came, the slaughter of the innocents and the rape of the

city would be fearful things, and even those charged with
the execution of these terrible acts shuddered to think of
what they would shortly be doing in the name of conquest.

Athribis had once been no more than a military
encampment, fortified and walled like a city, with a shallow moat around it. Now the Shepherd engineers, working
with slave labor—prisoners captured in the war and put to
work naked, chained, and starving—had erected on the
site of the old camp a city three times its size, fearfully
armed, its near-impregnable walls slanting outward after
the distinctive Shepherd pattern.

Bearded and long-haired, their skins burned to a dark
brown by the strong delta sun, clad only in white loincloths,
Baka and Ben-Hadad looked up at the sloping walls. Baka
shook his head with disgust. "It's all theirs now," he said
scornfully. "Vahan sleeps in my old quarters, I suppose.
Well, let him have it—for now. It's hard duty out here. In
the old Egyptian army, service at Athribis was accounted
no more than a step or two above service at Sile, on the
edge of the Great Desert." He spat and turned away.
"Come on, let's go."

"But—aren't we going to enlist here?" Ben-Hadad
said.

"No. For one, there might be someone this close to
headquarters who would recognize me. I've changed a lot,
but I still look like myself, even with the beard. No, what
we're going to do is swim the river again and enlist over in
the Second Nome, near Khem."

"You know best," Ben-Hadad said. "But why the
western front?"

"Oh, come on, my young friend," Baka said with a
humorless grin. "Where's your sense of adventure? Of
curiosity? If we go that way, we go through the Valley of
the Kings. Haven't you ever wanted to see the pyramids?
The tombs of the great kings of long ago? They're reck-
oned among the wonders of the world."

"Yes . . . I suppose, but . . ."

"I've another purpose as well," Baka said in a harder
tone, his grin turning icy. "When we change sides it'll be
easier for us if we go into the desert and around their

flanks. Besides, my spies tell me the camp of the armorers is on that side of the river. Perhaps I can pay a visit to Shobai."

Ben-Hadad started to speak, then bit his lip in frustration. He knew it would do no good to try to talk Baka out of this line of thinking. All he could do was tag along and try to divert him somehow or warn Shobai when the time came. "Lead on," he said, concealing a resigned sigh. "You're the one who knows his way around here."

"Spoken like a man," Baka said. "Come—we've a couple of long swims ahead of us, and a lot of walking in between. We can't go upriver from this side. There are guards along the roads. We'll have to swim to the island over there—the army post on it has been deserted since Vahan began raiding the smaller garrisons for troops—then we'll swim the other branch of the river. That means traversing the tip of the Tenth Nome."

Fighting the fear in his heart, Ben-Hadad nodded gamely, and they set off toward the river.

The first swim across, to the great island that divided the two main channels of the Nile, turned out not to be necessary. The ferryman was an old friend of Baka's before the Shepherd invasion, and he took them aboard without asking for a fare. As they crossed, Baka and the boatman chatted about bygone days, leaving Ben-Hadad to himself.

He sat down in the bow of the boat and let his hand trail over the side, the cool water rippling between his fingers. Soon the warm sun made him so drowsy that he closed his eyes, enjoying the gentle breeze on his half-bare body, feeling it caress him . . . as Tuya's hands had caressed him. He shuddered pleasantly and, forgetting Shobai for the moment, abandoned himself to thoughts of her. His belated discovery of the love that lay between them had happened so swiftly! He had hardly had time to consider it, to make some sense of his jumbled feelings. The nights in her arms had been so magically beautiful . . . how had he ever managed to force himself to take his leave of her? How had he talked himself into coming along with Baka, into certain danger—perhaps even his own death? What a fool he must be, to leave the sweet to pursue the bitter!

And now, for some reason, it finally occurred to him: She must have loved him all the while, from back when he'd first come to Avaris. Yes—now that he thought of it, she used to haunt the bazaars where he played, never missing a match . . . no, not even once, as far as he could recall!

What a stupid, insensitive fool he must have been! Imagine having someone that loving and devoted so close by, yet hardly noticing! How had he managed to do without her, when it was clear that, now he had tasted such delights, a day spent without her was a day bearing in it more pain, more anguish, than he had known even in the terrible days when he had been an unwanted stepchild, mistreated, beaten. . . .

Tuya!

He closed his eyes and saw her in his imagination, tiny, frail-looking, but with a steady, courageous gaze and bright smile. He felt the arms that pressed her small body to his, felt the warm mouth pressed to his. . . .

Gods! What was he doing here, on this foolish, wild chase? He had already wasted years on a futile search to find his friend Joseph . . . now who had appointed him Shobai's savior, made him follow Baka into bloody battle? Why couldn't he have stayed with Tuya and left such onerous duties to others—to Anab, perhaps, who would eagerly have volunteered to accompany Baka?

Instead, what had he done? He'd left her in the care of Anab and Lion, trusting them to remain true to her and to him, trusting them to keep her safe until his return. And off he'd gone, deserting her and hating himself for it. . . .

But he intercepted his own negative thoughts. *Come, now,* he told himself. *What does all this self-recrimination accomplish? You've vowed to accept a duty and to carry it through to a proper completion, and having done so, the only honorable path you can follow is to complete the job and come back safely to her.*

Why, this was no ephemeral love affair, easily begun, easily ended! Quite the contrary—it was the sort of thing

that lasted all your life, until you were old and gray . . .
and if what the priests and others said was true, it could
even unite the two of you for all eternity, in the lands of
the dead.

But what would he come back to? And where would
they go then? If there were still a peaceful place to live
anywhere in these war-torn lands, he would, with any
luck, find a town or city where he could practice his
profession, settle down, father a child—perhaps many
children—and grow old with them, with Tuya, gracefully
and lovingly.

He sighed. How could an armorer settle down and
grow old in one place?

Yet surely not all armorers wandered from country to
country. Mother and Jacob had told him of his ancestors,
the great line of smiths his father had descended from.
Not all of them could have lived lives of constant wandering—they *had* raised families, hadn't they?

Why, his own father, until he was forced to venture
into the Shepherd camp, had never even left Haran,
and . . . Ben-Hadad shook his head. His father hadn't
really been an armorer. He would have been, perhaps,
had not his own father, Kirta, gone off to Crete, abandoning his wife and sons to spend so many years in pursuit of
the secret of smelting iron. He could have stayed and
worked in Haran, as his son Shobai had done after him. . . .

Now, however, Ben-Hadad tried to recall what he
had been told about Kirta's quest. Was it really true, what
Jacob had said—that Kirta, in his years abroad, had actually learned the secret of the smelting of the black metal?
Jacob had said that Kirta had taught the secret to Shobai
during the Shepherds' seige of Ebla, before the Shepherds
had broken through, forcing the two of them to flee for
their lives.

Kirta had become desperately ill, had actually lost his
reason to the point that he could not remember who he
was. He had been separated from Shobai, yet somehow
had found his way south over the years, working as a
tinker, with dexterous hands that remembered what his
mind could not. Eventually he had turned up in Jacob's

land, providentially just in time to give his life in order to save the life of his grandson, Ben-Hadad.

But he had taken the secret of the black metal with him to his grave. That is, unless he had taught it to Shobai, as Jacob said he had.

But no—that was impossible. He would have heard of it by now, surely, if anyone on the Egyptian side had learned the secret of the making of iron weapons. Iron swords cut through bronze ones the way a wire, stretched taut, cut through a wheel of cheese. If iron weapons had turned up on the Shepherds' front, there would have been Egyptian victories to talk about.

But no such breakthroughs had occurred. Was this therefore proof that Shobai had not mastered the art his father had taught him?

Or was there another explanation?

Of course! Perhaps it had been a matter of securing the proper ore! Perhaps Shobai had not made iron swords because there was no iron ore available to the Egyptian side now that the delta, Egypt's only path to the sea, was sealed off and in Shepherd hands.

But . . . if iron ore *was* available, could Shobai, a blind man, make use of it? Cuuld he train the workers to smelt it into the black metal? Ben-Hadad's brow wrinkled as he considered the problem. As far as he could see, there was no reason why a blind man couldn't supervise such an operation, if he had able and willing apprentices to execute his commands.

Apprentices like me.

He found his heart suddenly racing. What if he could persuade Shobai to supervise the completion of his own unfinished apprenticeship, help teach him the proper working of copper, of bronze—*and* of iron?

The objections abruptly rose in his mind but were just as quickly swept away by the sudden rush of enthusiasm. Yes, he'd do it! He'd not only save Shobai from Baka, he'd apprentice himself to him! He'd learn the secret Kirta had brought back from Crete! He'd *make* Shobai teach it to him!

And then—somehow—he'd find a way to send for Tuya.

II

They enlisted at Khem, along with a long line of oddly assorted ragtag mercenaries. When the scribe in charge of swearing them in came to their assumed names, he did not bother to look up, but handed each man his single copper outnou and, gesturing not only at Baka and Ben-Hadad, but at approximately twenty of their associates as well, barked out, "Thirtieth Company—infantry."

They lined up again to receive rations and weapons. Baka, behind Ben-Hadad, took note of the fact that the Shepherds were not issuing the shields or body armor that most of their own warriors possessed. "Look to your own hide, my friend," Baka said, "because it's obvious the Shepherds won't be looking out for it. We're expendable. Try facing an Egyptian spear or sword in your bare skin and you'll be hacked to pieces before you've had a chance to touch your enemy."

Ben-Hadad took his new weapons—a curiously shaped battle-ax and a decently made dagger—and moved away from the line to await Baka. "It could have been worse," he said when Baka rejoined him. "These aren't half bad."

Baka was absorbed with his own weapons, hefting his ax and turning it over in his hands. "No Shepherd armorer made these," he said matter-of-factly. "These are captured Egyptian weapons, taken from the bodies of our own dead. At least I'd prefer to think of it that way; I hope they weren't dropped on the field of battle by some coward running for his life."

"Not mine," Ben-Hadad said. "Look—it has bloodstains on the handle."

"So it has. And the blade of mine's blunted at the corner. I assume it bounced off some Shepherd's body armor." He shrugged. "Well, in the old army we always said it wasn't the weapon, but the stout heart behind it."

Ben-Hadad took a few practice swings with his battle-ax. "It's splendid arms making," he said. "That much I can say. I've never seen this design before. The blade's longer and thinner than usual, which would give it much more penetrating power. And what superb balance! Any armorer would be proud of—"

He stopped in midsentence and looked at Baka. "But—if this was Egyptian . . ."

Baka's expression did not change. "Yes, the blind bastard does know his job, doesn't he? Though these were probably done by a journeyman working under his supervision. I give the devil his due, not that it's going to save him, when his time comes. And that shouldn't be long. I was talking to an officer of irregulars over by the mess wagon, an hour or so ago, and he said that Shepherd soldiers have overrun the Egyptian positions on the far bank of the Nile and driven the defending troops all the way back to a position only a league downriver from the capital. Reinforcements are coming up, and when they arrive, the Shepherds will start ferrying men across the river and hit the enemy from the flanks. That means we'll be hurried into action too, if I've figured correctly. Vahan will wait for us to attack the Egyptian front, in depth, and then he'll throw a flank attack at the city. And that will be all."

"You mean—?"

"Oh, don't worry. The king and his court will have fled south. There won't be anyone left in the streets of Memphis for our victorious Shepherd troops to rape and kill but the poor." He spat onto his ax blade and polished it to a high sheen. "Well, this will have to do, nicks in the blade or not. Come on, someone's calling for formations. We're obedient Shepherd soldiers now."

In the field, under the hot sun, the troops stretched farther than a man could see. They were organized into two-hundred-fifty-man units each led by a single officer and identified by its own standard-bearer. The officer in charge of Baka's and Ben-Hadad's unit shouted his men to silence, stood them at attention, and wheeled smartly to face away from them.

"What's going on?" whispered Ben-Hadad.

"Some bigwig's coming to inspect us—or, more likely, to make a speech," Baka whispered back. "Then we'll—"

But he cut his sentence off sharply as he caught sight of the personage who was to confront them. "Gods!" he said. "It's Vahan himself! The old fox!"

Ben-Hadad, keeping his head facing forward, swiveled his eyes and at last caught a dim sight of the tall figure, broad of shoulder and gray of beard, who marched impatiently before the massed troops, favoring one leg and trailing a small army of retainers and subordinates.

"That bad leg," Baka whispered, "a bowman of mine gave it to him the time he was fool enough to lead a raid on Athribis personally." He chuckled sourly. "I'm glad he has something to remember my unit by—"

"Silence in the ranks back there!" the officer said in a threatening undertone.

Vahan strode forward, limping, and stopped before their unit. "Is this the Thirtieth?" he said.

"Yes, my lord!" the commander said proudly. "All present, my lord."

"Good," Vahan said. "You should tell them about the unit, Commander. It has a distinguished history. It was a spearman of the Thirtieth—a mercenary from Kizzuwatna, as I remember—who killed the great warrior Oshiyahu before the walls of Carchemish, after Oshiyahu had bested in single combat Karakin of the Hai, a soldier many had thought invincible. Most mercenary units have spotty records at best, but this one is an exception. Make sure it stays an exception, Commander."

"Yes, my lord."

Vahan shifted his attention to the unit itself. His sharp eye went from man to man—pausing, it seemed, at Baka, for longer than Baka found comfortable. The pair locked eyes, and Baka could feel the sweat pouring down his temples in the hot sun. But then the terrible eyes moved on, and at last Vahan spoke again, this time in a more informal tone.

"Men!" he said. "The enemy's dug in on a line stretching from the northernmost of the Fourth Dynasty tombs to the river. They're strong, but they're not deep. What we're going to do is beat them back by sheer weight of numbers. First the chariots will hit their line from the flanks, their bows putting the enemy off guard. Then we'll hit them head-on with two waves of infantry—regulars and shock troops. Before they've had time to catch their breath, we'll repeat the entire action. I expect either a break-through or a retreat by the third wave."

He turned and paced toward the next unit, still talking in a powerful, rasping voice. "Now, I know their general won't have failed to anticipate this. He'll have several prepared positions to retreat to. But if our pursuit is quick enough, and keeps him harried enough, it won't be an orderly retreat. In short, we ought to be in Memphis by tomorrow."

"Did you hear that, men?" the next unit's commander said. "Memphis! Women! Plunder!"

Ben-Hadad half expected Vahan to turn angrily on the officer. Instead he smiled. "That's right, men. A Memphis undefended except by troops on the run. The court has already abandoned the city, taking with it the fearless palace guards." He smiled and continued striding down the line. His words began to fade in the vastness of the semidesert.

"He's got it all figured out," Baka said in a whisper. "And when the fighting gets to Memphis, the flank attack will strike from across the river. He's quite a soldier." He watched as a line of chariots, light, thin-wheeled, and maneuverable, appeared on the horizon and raced after Vahan. They paused at one point, and the old commander took his place in one of them. Then the group sped away. "Prepare for a long, dull, dusty march," Baka said. "This is the kind of soldiering nobody likes, not even the commanders. But there's no other way to get us there." He spat into the dirt beside them. "Did you see those chariots? That design was developed by my friend Shobai—when he was working for the *Shepherds*."

His last words were hissed out with an icy venom. Ben-Hadad, standing beside him in the hot sun, silently shuddered at the hatred in his friend's heart.

Clattering, jouncing, the chariots sped across the rocky and uneven ground. Vahan, standing beside his driver in the slightly outsized chariot reserved for his use, held on to the siderail for dear life as the driver, his feet seemingly glued to the small platform, whipped the horses forward.

They passed the third line of massed troops; the

second. And now, from a low ridge, he could see on his right the unmistakable triangular outlines of the three greatest of the royal tombs on their high plateau. For perhaps the fiftieth time he wondered at the ingenuity, the engineering skills, the sheer ability to organize labor on such a large scale, of the half-forgotten rulers who had erected these monstrous monuments so many centuries before—and thanked the heavens above that it was the weak, decadent descendants of these people he was charged with defeating, and not the giants who had built these pyramidal tombs.

Now, from the ridge, he could see the enemy's order of battle, and silently he cursed Unas's brilliance in picking out a strongpoint to defend. Unas's men—what there were of them—were arrayed on the slopes of the high ground opposite his own men. Between the armies lay a low wadi. His men would have to cross this in full sight of the bowmen above and would be vulnerable the whole time. Then they would have to fight their way up the slopes, at a grave disadvantage, under a rain of arrows. Once at the top, his warriors would meet fresh troops coming up from the rear as Unas redoubled his efforts to cast the attackers down.

He strained his eyes toward the mighty pyramid of Khufu and saw—as he had expected to see, indeed—Unas's scouts surveying the battlefield from their commanding height. They were scattered at precise intervals down the side of the great edifice, close enough to hear one another. This would allow questions to be relayed to the topmost lookout and answers to be relayed back.

The chariot slowed as they approached the slope descending to the wadi, and Vahan could see, beyond the Great Pyramid and a little to the west, the almost equally huge pyramid of Khufu's son Khephren. Behind both of these was a third pyramid of less than half the height of the two great ones, but still of imposing size. Clustered about all of these were lesser pyramids—the tombs of wives, viziers, and other long-forgotten notables—as well as temples and, barely visible from this vantage point, the head of a great bearded statue of some now-obscure king the builders had given the body of a lion recumbent.

The chariot came to a stop, and the driver jumped down and offered his hand. Yet Vahan stayed atop the chariot's narrow platform. He gazed down at the wadi, and then again up at the positions his men would have to storm. For a moment, he toyed with the idea of sending against the deadly heights opposite him two or three waves of untrained mercenaries, the better to tire the defenders and deplete their stock of arrows before his own rested elite troops could make the final assault. After all, it would be only irregulars, mercenaries, whose lives he would waste in that first wave or two, and they didn't amount to much, since he'd invested next to nothing in their training. If a large number of them died in the assault, what would it matter? There were many more where they had come from, in reserve back at Athribis and at various encampments in the Fourth Nome. And every mercenary who died now would be one fewer mouth to feed tomorrow.

But then the soldierly pride in him took over, and he steeled himself. Better to stick with the plan, even if it did make things rougher on his own troops. The only modification he'd need to order concerned the chariots. Closely viewing the assault terrain for the first time, he could see that the chariots' usual run past the flank of the enemy lines would be quite impossible here. The storming of the heights would have to be strictly an infantry attack, backed by foot bowmen below.

But what could he do with the chariots? His choices were few. They could be kept in reserve, to be used after a breakthrough . . . or perhaps they could be moved into the desert west of the tombs, along with a few units of mercenaries. Then, as his frontal attack drew the attention of Unas's men, other units could move into place for a flanking attack from the far side of the Great Pyramid. They would be invisible to the scouts ranged along the eastern flank of the pyramid, and could be secretly moved into place in the shadow of the sprawling field of slope-sided tombs—what did they call them? Mastabas? Then, after the first wave of attackers had withdrawn, he, Vahan, could order a second wave into position—early, seemingly too early, but taking advantage of Unas's own withdrawal and his bringing up of fresh troops from the rear. While

Unas coped with the confusion that the hasty second attack occasioned, the chariots and a unit or two of infantry could strike from the flank, from the corridor between the tombs of Khufu and Khephren. And there would still be the obstruction of the smaller, eastern, mastaba field to hide the flankers from view. To avoid being detected early, the drivers could walk their horses and chariots until they were in range, then remount for a lightning attack on Unas's unprotected flank. Actually, the place of attack was a little to the rear of Unas's front line; all the better, then. With any luck Unas would be caught by surprise.

And then what? Once he'd beaten Unas's threadbare army back into Memphis, once he'd taken the city, what? What would be his life once this war was won, once the last Egyptian resistance had been crushed and the whole of the Nile Valley had been made safe for the Hai, his people, safe for Avedis (*pardon me, I mean Salitis*, he thought, making a wry face) and his heirs, for the no longer nomadic Shepherd Kings? What lay ahead for a man like himself, who had known no other life but one wholeheartedly devoted to war?

It was a vexing question, and had begun to bother him more and more as the end of the war approached, as it became apparent that the Egyptian resistance could not hold on much longer. When the Valley of the Nile became, once and for all, subservient to the victorious Hai, what place would there be for him, Vahan, in this new world Salitis had created, had decreed?

There was always retirement, of course, but . . . He frowned at the very thought. Somehow he could not see himself as the retired general, ending his days in a villa, ordering surly Egyptian servants about, growing flowers, going to the capital once a month to meet with other old soldiers and refight old battles like a doddering fool, looking ever more ridiculous and out-of-touch with every passing year. No, this was no destiny for him, Vahan.

But what alternatives were there, if he dismissed the thought of retirement? Could he go to Avedis—no, *Salitis;* he'd have to start remembering that—and ask him for a place at court, an advisory position? Some sort of sinecure to keep him well fed and keep his idle mind busy?

Contemptuously he dismissed this thought. What a fool he'd look, holding down a position all too obviously created for him! In his imagination he could hear the younger men talking, their words edged with condescension: *"I suppose we'll have to pretend to consult old Vahan, just as a matter of form. What a waste of time, though. What a pity some old fossils don't take the hint Nature gives them in the way of failing sight, hearing, and kidneys and quit while they're still halfway presentable. . . ."*

No. Far better to take the warrior's way out: to put himself deliberately in the thick of the battle, during the final assault, say, and go down fighting like a respectable soldier. Far better to arrange his own death in the moment of a great victory, so that when future generations came to talk about this last great battle that smashed the Egyptian army, they'd always associate it with his own death, as people associated the fall of Carchemish with the deaths of Oshiyahu and Karakin.

But suddenly a stray thought entered his mind and held it: *Somewhere out there, somewhere not too far behind the lines, is Shobai.*

Yes—blind Shobai, who now armed the Egyptians against him, but whom he'd known well and had called friend back in the days before the Snake, Reshef, had taken the giant's eyes. Shobai had come north from Haran to the Hai's great encampment, offering his services as armorer, paying no mind to the consequences of his work, as armorers tended to do. He'd reacted with stunned horror when he, Vahan, had taken him to observe the fall of peaceful Melid, which Karakin's troops had sacked with their accustomed brutality—and from that moment had refused to work for the Hai, refused even at sword's point, with the newly scarred flesh of the slave brand on his arm and shouted threats of certain death echoing in his ears. . . .

Vahan pursed his lips and thought. Shobai had made a choice, a hard one, and stuck to it despite all threats, despite even the loss of his sight and the murder, in his very presence, of his brother. He had found a principle in life and had held to it with great bravery, first in the siege of Ebla, and now here, many years later.

Vahan suddenly wanted to stand before Shobai, see him once more, and speak with him as friends, as old comrades. Wanted, above all, to confront him with the one question that now plagued his heart: *"Shobai—which of the two of us is the fool? Which the wise man?"*

He reached up to wipe the sweat from his face. "Call the commanders," he said suddenly, with brusque authority. And when he had assembled them and announced the revised battle plan—taking particular pains to place the Thirtieth Infantry in the flanking group that would attack through the mastaba field *(Who was the soldier with the burning eyes? Where do I know him from? But no matter. Send him to a quick and violent death in the first wave of the assault, along with the others.)* —he dismissed both Shobai and the future from his mind. "Prepare the troops," he said. "We attack at dawn."

CHAPTER ELEVEN

THE VALLEY OF THE PYRAMIDS

I

In the shadow of the great pyramids, Unas paced up and down impatiently. "You're sure you told him?" he said exasperatedly. "Told him that it was a direct order, from one officer of the line to another?"

"Yes, sir," Hori said. "But he said that as long as one of his men was manning a forge, he, Shobai, would remain at his side."

"Oh, for the love of heaven," Unas said. "The stubborn ox! He agreed to head upriver weeks ago. He was lying then—but now he's disobeying a direct order! Well, tell him again. And tell him that the order goes for all of his journeymen as well. They must all fall back. It's too late to make new arms now—we'll have to get them from dead Shepherds. Tell him to get out while he can; I can't guarantee his safety any longer. Soon this place is going to look like a whirlwind hit it. Tell him to—" He clenched his jaw angrily, knowing the order would go the way of his earlier one. "Come with me," he said. "I'll tell him myself." He barked orders to his adjutant, walking briskly away as he did. "Captain! Take over—according to plan! You know what to do?"

"Yes, sir. Retire in waves, sir. We'll make them pay for every step they take."

"Good!" Unas said, over his shoulder. "Come on, Hori—no time to lose!" The two climbed into Unas's chariot, sharing a platform barely wide enough for one, and Unas whipped the yoked pair forward, steering the light carriage around a pothole as the superbly trained horses accelerated quickly to a gallop.

Standing by his forge, not three leagues away, Shobai took the newly made sword from his assistant, ran his huge hand over the blade, then grasped the hilt as a soldier would. "Step back, please," he said. He waited a moment as the assistant moved back, then he held the weapon out and cut right, left, stabbed, parried an imaginary thrust, stabbed again, and recovered to slash backhanded in a mighty arc. "Not bad," he said. "Not bad at all, my friend. And I say this having held in my hand a sword made by Belsunu of Babylon. Not bad! Reward the man who made this—but wait until we've retired to do so."

"Yes, sir," the assistant said. "But"—his eyes were anxious—"when will that be? The order to evacuate came yesterday."

Shobai stood holding the weapon in his two hands, his face fixed in the inscrutable expression of the blind. "Did it?" he said. "Then I should have obeyed. Unas will be furious with me. But I can't pull back when I'm needed here."

"Sir," the assistant said, "here comes Unas now—unescorted, with only Hori beside him. And, as you said, he's angry."

Shobai listened as the chariot pulled up and Unas, hardly waiting for the vehicle to come to a halt, leaped down.

"Shobai!" Unas shouted. "For the love of all that's holy, man, why haven't you closed up shop here? Didn't you get my order to fall back?"

"Yes," Shobai said. "But—"

"Don't give me any buts," Unas said. "Hori, get them all loaded up in the wagons. I'm entrusting this matter to you. Put them on a boat and take them upriver to our position south of the city." He turned to Shobai. "Set up your forges there. That's the permanent line, the one we'll eventually retire to once we've made them waste their strength here."

Shobai nodded. "All right," he said. "I assume the terrain's more easily defended there."

"Yes," Unas said. "But first we'll make them waste their best troops taking the slopes before the pyramids. Then we'll fall back to secondary positions. As soon as they've regrouped, we'll fall back again, making them chase us and redeploy. The idea is to do this three times, tiring them and getting them more annoyed. When they're at their worst, whenever their organization falters, we counterattack."

"Good," Shobai said, picturing the strategy in his mind. "A fine plan. But here I am, keeping you from your duty. My apologies, my friend. I'm a fool. I only thought—"

"I know," Unas said, clapping him on the shoulder. "And even misdirected valor is worthy of commendation in an age of cowardice and folly. But it's already past time to go." Now, however, he noted the troubled expression on the blind man's face. "What's the matter?" he said in a softer voice. "Have you heard any word of her whereabouts?"

"No," Shobai said. "Heket said the men who took her away wore Egyptian army uniforms. And here I am helping to—"

"Those were no fighting troops," Unas interrupted. "They had to be troops of the palace guard—Harmin's people. I've asked around in my own command." He put one hand on each of the blind giant's shoulders and spoke earnestly. "I know—I think I know, anyway—what you must be going through. But we haven't time to find out anything more until we've dealt with the Shepherds. Shobai, if I live through all this . . . I promise you Harmin's going to be brought to judgment. And your wife will be restored to you."

"I—I just can't understand why they'd want Mereet. She's harmed no one!"

"These are dark times at the court," Unas said. "Times that may require bloodshed, a general cleansing. But the cleansing can only be done after the Shepherds have been dealt with. If *they* win, there'll be no cleansing other than what they do themselves. I wish I could help you more directly—and I promise to do so, on my word of honor as a soldier, the moment the front has stabilized and the army's entrenched in new positions at Lisht. But right now . . ."

His voice trailed off. "Listen!" he said. "That sound . . . Hori, did you hear that?"

"The horns, sir? Yes. If—"

"Right! Shepherd horns! Shobai, I've got to get back to the lines. I have a feeling. They'll hit us at dawn—I'm almost sure of it. But . . . what if they've crossed us up? What if they've decided to strike this afternoon?" He turned to Hori. "I leave him in your hands. Get him to safety. And heaven help you if anything happens to him."

"Yes, sir, I'll—" Hori began, but it was to his general's retreating back that he spoke.

On the heights opposite them, it was obvious that Vahan was staying his hand, bringing up fresh troops for the second and third waves of his planned dawn attack. Unas's men watched the growing Shepherd ranks with trepidation. There seemed to be no end to them, and even beyond the countless units opposite them they could see the plains black with Shepherd reinforcements. They counted their own meager numbers and shuddered. Taking a fresh grip on their swords, they waited for night—a tense and sleepless night—and for a pale and hateful dawn that each of them knew might be his last in this world.

Those in the rear ranks could look back to the second line Unas had prepared, could see the troops dug in there, ready to receive them when they fell back in what everyone hoped would be the orderly retreat Unas had planned. The second line was deployed in an even less easily assailable position, and the ground across which the attackers would have to fight their way under a heavy rain of arrows was low, rocky, and uneven. The attackers would have to have their eyes on their feet most of the way, and would not be able to look up to dodge the arrows of Unas's bowmen.

If everything went according to plan, the defenders would manage to hold the first line for a day, then would retreat by night, under a moon nearly full, to the second line, out of view of the Shepherd lines. When Vahan prepared a full-scale attack for the second day, he would find nothing across the gully from him but abandoned positions. He would then lose a day marching and redeploying. And his every step forward would be on unfamiliar ground, under a rain of arrows. He would, of course, attack on the following morning. Whether he would meet then a concerted and vigorous defense or the abandoned evidence of yet another prepared retreat would depend on Unas's assessment of the situation. In either case, Vahan's troops would be the more fatigued, and if their time could be occupied marching, deploying, and then marching again, so much the better. The more time Vahan's men spent marching, setting up camp, and then breaking camp again without getting a chance to fight, the worse their morale would be. Conceivably, the chase could go on for days, until the Shepherds were disorganized, impatient, and at one another's throats. Then the defenders would turn on their attackers and scatter their forces.

But anyone who believed this would be the outcome was, everyone knew, living in a dreamworld. The likelihood of everything going according to plan depended, of course, on Vahan's acting more or less as Unas wanted him to—and no one believed the wily old Shepherd general would do so. In point of fact, Vahan was, if anything, the better general, and certainly an older and more experienced one. He would quickly see through Unas's plan, as he had previously seen through the plans of the defenders of Melid, of Carchemish, of Ebla—of all the hapless cities the Shepherd armies in their might had battered down and destroyed on their long march from the bleak mountain country far to the north of the Assyrian empire, across Mesopotamia and Canaan, to the borders of the Egyptian lands.

Vahan would strike when *he* wanted to, not when Unas expected him to. . . .

*   *   *

"Where are we?" Shobai said. "I hear voices."

Feet braced on the floorboards, the blind giant held tight to the high seat of the wagon underneath him as the oxen drew him and his apprentices slowly across the no-man's-land between Unas's lines of defense.

"We're passing the third line," Hori said. "I can see the city ahead. Memphis."

"Well, the sooner the be—"

The sudden sideways lurch of the wagon nearly jarred Shobai from his seat. One of the apprentices in the back actually fell to the ground and had to scramble back onto the platform, brushing himself off.

"Hold on, now," Hori said to Shobai. "We're crossing a dry streambed. This is where the Nile splits in two at floodtide and the wadi cuts Memphis off from the Valley of the Kings. It's very rocky down here."

"All the better," Shobai said, bracing himself as the wagon wobbled ponderously beneath him. "In a day or so the Shepherds will be fighting their way across this. Beside that fact, any discomfort we feel now is negligible."

"Right," Hori said. "Now—one more bump and we're on the high road. Careful, now—" The wagon lurched precariously again, and then they could feel the hard road under them once more. "Good. I—" He stopped for a moment, and when he spoke again it was in a weak, altered voice. "I had almost forgotten," he said, "that they'd abandoned Memphis. For a moment I couldn't figure out what it was that looked wrong."

"You mean there are no guards at the city gate?" Shobai said.

Hori grunted in reply.

"I would have been surprised if there were," Shobai said. "Just watch, too—when we get through the gates you'll find no one but the court and the very rich has left. Everyone else will be going about his business as usual—trusting that poor, threadbare army of ours to keep the Shepherds away."

"Worse than that," one of the apprentices said from the rear. "Some of them, poor fools, are actually looking forward to the Shepherds' arrival. There are some in the city who think business will be better under the Shepherds than it's been under Harmin and Madir."

"I've seen it all before," Shobai said, his voice resigned. "I've no wish to see it again."

"You mean the Shepherds didn't come in peace?" the apprentice said sarcastically, "waving flowers? Laying down their arms, the way the appeasers tell us they will?"

"What they waved were swords and spears. And before the day was over the spears were red with the blood of women and children and the aged. I saw them pick up babies and toss them in the air, to catch them on their spear-points. It was all the same to them—a joke."

"Gods!" whispered one of the journeymen in the rear.

"When I lost my eyes," Shobai said, "I tried to comfort myself with the thought that at least I would never again have to behold such a sight. I hope none of you ever has to, either. I can still see it, sometimes, in my mind's eye. And nothing can close *that* eye. Nothing but death."

II

Uni came to a halt in the middle of the street, taking in the scene before him. He couldn't quite believe what he was seeing.

The brickmakers stood barefoot in a sluggish mix of clay, sand, water, and chopped straw, treading the mucklike stuff down and flattening it out. Off to one side, other workers used their hands to dig out portions of the mix and pound it into rectangular molds. These, when finished, were carefully emptied onto the ground and left to dry in the sun.

Beside them, the ultimate destination of the bricks stood half finished: a circular granary, as yet no more than waist-high. Uni looked at this and then looked back at the workers with exasperation. "What in the name of . . . just what do you think you're doing?"

The foreman looked up and saluted humbly. "We're building a place to put the grain, sir."

"Building? When the town's about to come down around your ears? When the Shepherds are less than a day's march from the undefended city walls? Don't be an idiot, man!"

The foreman bowed again. "I have my orders, sir. And if death shall chance to take me, sir, it will take me working as I have always worked, sir, since I was a lad half your size, sir. And, by your leave, sir, what rules the master, meaning myself, sir, rules the bondmen. I and mine, we'll do as we've been told, sir."

Uni could only shake his head in wonderment. "Amazing," he said in a tone of profoundest disgust, and walked away, saying no more. Imagine! Building a silo!

He picked up his pace and rounded a blind corner, knocking a frail ancient to the ground. In other times he might have taken hasty note of the man's rank and, if it proved expedient or politic to do so, helped him to his feet with apologies. Now he didn't bother to look back at all as he strode onward, hardly missing a step. All the people of rank and power had left the city some time before, and anyone whose feelings were worth considering would, in the half-deserted Memphis of today, wear a uniform or a sword.

Bah! Honor, duty, propriety! Stale abstractions at best, fit only to trot out for show's sake in fat times, when life was easy and one could afford such nonsense.

No. He'd look out for himself first and save his own neck, and feather his nest, too, if he could. (Madir's tips had come in very handy, indeed, as he'd concluded some timely land transactions in the Fayum on the basis of his advance knowledge.) The time to think of your neighbor was after your own oxen were safe in their pens.

Now? Now it was time to be on the road south, to abandon what little he had left in the city and save himself. He'd go back to the prison, commandeer the one remaining guard, and take him along on the trip south to insure his own safety. He'd also take the slave Joseph, of course, and leave the rest to starve to death and fight the rats—or to be found by the Shepherds when they slashed their way into the city over the dead bodies of Unas's ragtag army. . . .

A brilliant thought struck him, however, and to consider it he stopped again in the middle of the empty street.

The woman. The woman Mereet.

Madir's orders had been clear. He wanted her left to die, left for the Shepherds to find, if they bothered at all to make their way down to the lowest levels of the dungeons before putting the whole stinking building to the torch. If possible, it was to look as though she had been forgotten, by some misfortune. She was not to be killed by him, Uni—that was clear. If anyone with access to the court, down to the most lowly guardsman, chanced to kill the woman, there was a bare outside chance that word of it would, in time, get back to her kin, who were said to have connections at court. But if she died by other means, all of it—her arrest, her incarceration, even her death— could be made to seem no more than an unfortunate series of ill-starred coincidences, and Madir and all his underlings—Uni among them—could be shown afterward to have been blameless officials merely carrying out their duties, trapped in the web of circumstance.

But die she must, in order to cover up something.

What exactly did she know? What did the woman know about Madir, that he would have her silenced by such elaborate means?

Uni's broad face took on a slow, cunning smile.

When he retired to Lisht, bringing with him Joseph, and presumably having abandoned all the other prisoners to a terrible death, he'd have committed a criminal act— one which put him in horrible peril. Even the fact that he had operated under orders from Madir wouldn't excuse it—and besides, Madir could always deny having given the orders.

Yes. Madir would have a weapon he could use, with sudden and deadly effect, any time he tired of his no longer useful underling.

I must protect myself, he thought. *I must have something on Madir in my turn. Something that can put him in equal peril.*

And what could possibly frighten Madir? He didn't know just yet. But it had something to do with the woman Mereet. She knew something that could be used against Madir and his circle. Something that meant danger for Madir.

The woman mustn't die. I mustn't lose track of her.

A noise in the street behind him broke into his thoughts. He turned and looked. At the end of the long thoroughfare, where it emptied into a little square, he could see the rioters. They had overflowed from the Thieves Quarter already! He watched them attacking the market stalls, tearing down canopies, smashing open cabinets. . . .

He ducked hastily into a side street. He'd have to move swiftly; they'd be in his area before long. And with only a lone guardsman to protect him.

He set out at a dog trot, puffing at the unaccustomed exercise. He turned a corner, slipped up an alley, and found the side entrance to the jail complex. Once inside, he barred the door behind him and strode to the stairs. Down he went: one floor, another. . . .

"Halt!" cried a familiar voice. "Halt and be recognized!"

"It's me, Uni," he said, moving into the man's line of view. "Come on, we have to get two of the prisoners out. Then we're heading south, you and I."

"Only two, sir?" the guardsman said. "But—"

"Just Joseph . . ." Uni hesitated. Then, taking a deep breath, he took the plunge. "And the woman. The one on the bottom level. Tell you what, my friend—you get Joseph and I'll go after the woman."

"Yes, sir. But . . . what'll I tell the others?"

"Tell them Joseph's being taken up to answer questions about his accounting. Tell Joseph himself no more than that, as a matter of fact. The less anyone knows, the better. And be quick about it!" He spoke the last words on the run, hurrying down the stairs to the lower levels.

At the bottom level he snatched the keys from their peg on the wall. "You! Mereet!" he called out. "Come along! It's Uni, the chief steward! I've orders for your release!"

As he fumbled with the lock he could see her through

the bars, naked, filthy, shivering. "Oh, thank heaven!" she said. "I knew they couldn't keep me, when I'd done no—"

Uni threw the door open and took her by the hand, hauling her along up the winding stairs. "Explanations later. We're getting out—leaving for Lisht, and safety. The Shepherd armies are on the verge of a breakthrough, and we're retiring to land easier to defend."

She fell once, opening a cut on her knee. Assisting her to her feet, he could not help but notice her still-young body, the graceful limbs, the fine breasts. When they reached the landing he said, "Here, sponge yourself down. You don't want to attract attention outside. There's a cloak over there. No time for anything fancier, I'm afraid. We're in great danger."

"But—my husband. My children . . ."

"They've been taken to safety," Uni said. "They'll meet us where we're going. No time to explain now." He looked up to see the guardsman leading Joseph forward. "Good work," he said. "We'll go out the back way. The looters will be at the front door by now."

Joseph glanced over at Mereet as she struggled into the oversized cloak Uni had given her. Then he looked back at Uni, his expression only mildly curious. "Your pardon, sir . . . but where are we going?"

"Going?" Uni said. "Why, I'm saving your hide, my boy. We're going south, where the court is. The Shepherds are about to attack, and it's my feeling that the army won't be able to hold them out of the city for long."

"Yes, sir. But the others . . ."

"Look, my young friend, don't question your good fortune. I can perhaps ensure your safety, and this good woman's here, but that's all. Don't you understand? The guards—they're gone. Gone south with the court. There's a mob outside, out of control. It'll be all I can do to get the two of you to the river without incident."

"But if you left the doors unlocked, perhaps the others—"

"The others would probably try to kill us," Uni said, a trifle peevishly. "Now, follow me, all of you." He led the way up another staircase, this one leading to an underground hallway. "It should be the middle door, if I remem-

ber properly." He opened the door and led them up a
narrow stairway. When he unbarred and opened another
heavy door that stood at the top of the steps, blinding
sunlight made him hesitate for a moment. "This should
have let us out at the rear of the . . . ah, yes. There's the
alley. Come quickly, now!"

Running down the long back street they could hear
the noise of the crowd on the other side of the high wall to
their left: loud, angry voices, the sounds of violence, inter-
spersed with the ominous quiet of death. As they hurried
forward a head appeared at the top of the wall, and a shrill
voice rang out. "Here! There's people over here! And a
guardsman! You! Stop! Where are you going?"

"Don't look back!" Uni cried, picking up speed. "This
way!" He led them around a corner into a transverse alley,
under a low arch, and into a cul-de-sac. At the end of the
passage he stopped and pulled at a door handle. "C-come
on, now, confound you . . . *there!*" The door swung free
suddenly, almost knocking him down. He held it open for
them. Then, as the last of them passed through, he followed and pulled it shut behind.

They found themselves outside the city wall, overlooking a broad esplanade that fronted a wide canal. Long ago
some forgotten king had ordered this canal cut to bring
the waters of the Nile to the very edge of the city. Beyond
the canal was the island thus formed, and beyond it, the
Nile itself.

At canal's edge a small but serviceable-looking boat
lay pulled up onto the quay. To Uni's surprised delight it
was not the standard papyrus-stalk raft, but a real wooden
boat, made by meticulously combining small pieces of
wood, mortised together and glued. It sat hull-down on its
keelless bottom.

Uni reached the boat first and pushed hard on it,
trying to move it forward into the water. The others joined
him and shoved. Slowly the vessel moved across the sloping stone quay. "Easy," Uni said. "We want it in one
piece when it gets into the water."

Behind them there were sounds of commotion again.
They looked back. The people from the other side of the
wall had spotted them and were coming after them!

"Push!" Uni said. "If they catch us—"

But just then the boat stopped. Uni looked down with a curse; the vessel was hung up on a small curbing in the quay. "Quick! Up and over!" he said, hearing the sound of the pounding feet getting closer, the shouts of angry voices. The four of them heaved mightily; the boat jerked free and, reaching quay's edge, slid into the water. Uni grabbed for it, holding it firm in the sluggish current. "Now, in you go! Mind your step, there!" He ducked as a thrown rock whizzed by his head.

Mereet stepped in first and scrambled to the stern, taking the tiller. "You, boy," she said to Joseph, "pick up that pole and get us moving downstream, and quickly!"

"Downstream?" said the guardsman, taking a seat and looking back anxiously at the approaching crowd. "But—"

"Do as she says!" Uni said, pulling himself over the side. He slid awkwardly into a seat and his arm shot up, deflecting another thrown missile. The boat wobbled but stayed upright. Joseph poled the boat free of the shore, and the current caught it, pulling it downstream. Mereet expertly steered it to the far side of the canal, out of range of their pursuers.

Uni looked back. The crowd was at water's edge, screaming and cursing. "A narrow escape," he said. "Now, my dear—keep us on this side of the canal, please. When we reach the river, we'll cross about a league or so downstream, where the channel narrows."

"Cross the Nile on this?" the guardsman said. "But— the current . . ."

"No, no. We change vessels. I've ordered a larger boat moored at the narrows, a galley with a dozen rowers. We'll need them, too, making our way upriver against the current."

They passed the tip of the island, where the canal rejoined the river, and now they could see the boat waiting for them, its high rudderpost and furled sail standing above its empty decks. "Confound it!" Uni said. "Where are they? I don't see anyone. There must be . . ."

"I saw one of the oars move," Joseph said in the bow. "I think I see someone aboard."

Mereet steered them closer to the shore. "Uni, are

you absolutely sure this is right? Because I won't pull in unless you—"

"It's all right," Uni said, a little nervously. "What else have we got? If you don't land us, the current will take us north into Shepherd territory. Pull in here. They have to be aboard."

Mereet obeyed. Joseph laid down his pole and stepped ashore to pull the vessel to land. Uni got out, followed by the guard. Only then did Mereet relinquish the tiller and jump ashore.

"The fellow who's supposed to be waiting for us here is named Narmer," Uni said as they walked toward the larger boat. "I paid him a good sum to be on hand to take us upstream, with the promise of an equal sum on our safe arrival. In times like these you can't be too sure. From the moment I heard the city would be abandoned I set up not one, but two escape routes. One was by land. I suppose *that* fellow's still waiting for me, south of the city, with his caravan. Frankly, all else considered, I'd prefer to go by water. It's hellishly rocky ground between here and Lisht, and even traveling by wagon—"

He paused as they drew near the boat, whose high sides towered above them. "This is odd," he said. "They should have been here. You said you saw one of the oars move?"

Joseph nodded.

The guardsman nervously fingered the sword at his side.

"It could have been your imagination," he said. "No one on board, as far as I can see."

"It doesn't matter," Mereet said. "We don't need the oarsmen. I can sail her upstream if you three will crew for me. I've been sailing since I was a little girl." Uni looked at her, surprised. "Come on," she said, "let's board her." Without giving it another thought, she walked up the notched plank to stand on the vessel's broad deck. "What are you waiting for?"

Uni shook his head and followed her. "Any port in a blow," he said. "I never heard of four people manning a vessel this size, but it appears we have no choice."

Mereet waited until Joseph, the last of the four, came

on board, then, with his help, pulled the gangplank onto the deck. "Now cast off, guardsman. You two take those lines there—the ones that lead to the yard up above. Get ready to unlash them when I say to. . . ."

The boat had drifted away from the shore, and the current was beginning to tug at it. Mereet manned the tiller, putting her shoulder into its long shaft. "Now, unlash the lines and play them out slowly." As she gave the order, she looked over the bow and saw another boat, under sail, working its way upstream against the steady pull of the current. Standing on its deck was a tall, commanding figure, his head held high, his eyes covered by a narrow white cloth band that encircled his head.

She almost let go of the tiller in her shock and surprise. Then she got an even firmer grip upon it and, turning the boat sharply out into the current, called out once: "*Shobai!*"

But as she did, the sound of feet could be heard, pounding up the wooden ladder from below. And suddenly from the deckhouse came soldiers! They were heavily armed, wearing uniforms that did not belong to Egyptian troops. . . .

Shepherd warriors! And archers, whose powerful bows were bent into triangular shapes, the feathered shafts trained on her and the rest!

A Shepherd officer emerged from the deckhouse, his polished body armor glinting in the bright sunlight. He smiled up at Mereet high in the stern, then motioned to two of his men.

"Take her below," he said.

III

The moment he heard the single cry, Shobai cocked his ears for further sounds. But there was nothing, only the wind in the rigging and the lapping of waves against the hull. "Hori!" he shouted. "I heard a voice call my name! Hori! Where are you?"

The officer rushed to his side. "Where, Shobai? What

did you hear?" He peered across the water. "That boat up ahead . . . there are Shepherd warriors on it! They're not supposed to be this far upriver! Captain! *Captain!*"

The vessel's master rushed forward. "Yes," he said, "I see them. And a squad of bowmen, at least. Confound it! What a time to be heading upstream without a single archer on board! *Steersman!* Hard to larboard!"

"Someone called my name—a woman's voice!" Shobai said, gripping Hori's forearm. "I . . . I think it may have been my wife!" His grip tightened; Hori winced at the pressure. "Hori—is she there? Can you see . . . ?"

"No, I don't—" Hori began. "Wait—I do see a woman; she's at the tiller! But the soldiers have got her! They're taking her away. I can't see her face . . . she keeps moving . . ." He pulled himself free of Shobai's hand and moved closer to the rail for a better view. "They've taken her below. She was struggling. Shobai, I'm not sure; I couldn't see. . . ."

"It is!" the blind giant cried. "It has to be. Mereet's a fine sailor. Who else—*Mereet!*" he screamed. "*Mereet!*"

Hori turned; tears flowed down the blind man's face as he continued to call out his wife's name.

"Get him back from the rail," the boat's captain said. "Quick—get back, all of you. Behind cover! The bowmen are taking aim!"

"Come on, Shobai!" Hori said, pulling at the blind giant's arm. "You can't help her now—whoever she is! You'll only get yourself killed if you stay here!"

"*Mereet!*" the giant cried. The first wave of arrows flew, three of the shafts embedding themselves in the deck at their feet. "*Mereet!*"

But by now the helmsman had turned the vessel's stern to the enemy ship, and, temporarily out of danger, Hori and the captain managed to drag Shobai from the rail.

The sentry came to wake Unas just as the first rays of red began to peep over the horizon in the east. He found the general sitting up, polishing his sword's blade to a fine sheen. "General?" he said quietly. "You asked me to call you at dawn."

Unas put the weapon back in its battered scabbard, stood up, and stretched mightily. "Thank you, my friend," he said, yawning. "Just cleaning up a bit. We may all face death today, I think. When I do, I want to meet it looking my best."

The under-officer seemed only slightly perturbed. "You think the situation looks bad, sir?"

"No worse than many times before, I suppose," Unas said. "I've faced bad odds more than once and lived to tell about it." He yawned again, cavernously. "Yes, and even won a few underdog battles, for that matter. Yet . . . I have an odd feeling about today. I think this will be a very special day in my life. It may be my finest. It may be my worst. It may even be the day I die. I have no idea which. All I know is that something very special will happen to me before the sun sets."

"Let's hope it means victory, sir."

"Oh, I doubt that," Unas said calmly. "In the sense of driving the Shepherds away, that is, or even driving them back temporarily. I'm not even set up to pursue Vahan if he does turn tail and run. I don't know what we'd do if he did. But we could surprise ourselves and hold the line. Or we could fall back to the next positions, in good order, and make our stand there, and still keep Vahan out of the city."

"Then let's hope it's one of those, sir," his subordinate said. "Will you go out now, sir?" And, ever the attentive servant, he had Unas's helmet ready for him to put on before the general reached the door of the tent.

On the heights opposite, Vahan looked across at the Egyptian lines. His adjutant hovered close at hand. "Ready, my lord?" he said.

"No," Vahan said. "Make them wait. Make them think. It'll put them on edge. Besides, I haven't seen Unas yet. I want to see Unas. I want to see him personally."

"Yes, my lord," the Shepherd officer said. "Do you think he'll actually take part in the fighting?" His voice had a skeptical tone to it.

"He will if I do," Vahan said. "And . . . I think I will. He's not like Harmin. I think it's my day to earn my salt for a change. I've sat back in the rear and directed others for too long. I'm losing my self-respect." He loosened his sword in its scabbard. "Maybe I'll prove fortunate. Maybe I'll find my way to Unas himself. If I do, the devil help the soldier of the Hai who fails to spare Unas for my sword!"

The adjutant cleared his throat. "But, my lord . . . if you were to get hurt, my lord; or worse, if—"

"If I get myself killed, someone else will take over. No man's indispensable. Karakin wasn't. Manouk wasn't. Neither is Avedis, who calls himself Salitis now and makes absurd claims to godhood after the Egyptian manner. And neither is Vahan."

"But then, my lord, command would pass to . . ."

"To Sahag. He's next in line. Although often I wish it were not so." He scowled. "Sahag . . . he's an able warrior, and a fine tactical leader. But he thinks of today only, as Karakin did. I'd remind you that we'd never have come as far as this, no matter how great our numbers, if Karakin had ruled alone, without the superior mind of Manouk to draw upon."

"Yes, my lord. But of course Sahag would have ample advice as well, would he not, my lord?"

"Certainly," Vahan said, his eyes scanning the enemy lines still. "But, being Sahag, it's unlikely that he'd listen." He shrugged. "It's all moot anyhow, isn't it? For me, I mean. After all, the only way any of this could take place would be if I were dead."

"The gods forbid such an eventuality," the adjutant said. Hastily he made the sign against evil.

"Still, there's another reason I might prefer to see another in Sahag's place," Vahan said thoughtfully. "A good leader controls his passions. Can you keep a secret, Commander?"

"My lord?"

"Of course you can." Vahan smiled knowingly. "Sahag—he's an animal. A wild beast. A commander who has such an animal under him need only point to trouble and say, 'Remove it!' and the animal attacks with fang and claw. In such a case, the more savage, the more unforgiving, the better. Sahag was a fearsome sight to see at Carchemish, at Shechem, at the siege of Sile, when all we had to do was grind an enemy to powder and then march heedless over his ashes."

"And now, my lord?"

"Now we are no longer called on merely to kill. We are called on to conquer. And afterward we must rule over the people we have conquered. You perceive the difference, I take it?"

"Yes, my lord." His brow furrowed. "A conqueror must understand the uses of mercy, justice. And Sahag . . ."

"Sahag doesn't," Vahan said. "When one rules a conquered enemy firmly, but with mercy and fairness, memories are short. In a generation there is peace again. But the hard and unforgiving hand is in its turn hard to forgive. After a generation of rule by the likes of Sahag, our children's children will have our battles to fight all over again. And the armies that will rise up against them will not be the rejects Unas has to throw against us today for want of better. They'll be tough, tempered, and full of hatred for us and all we stand for in their eyes."

His adjutant was plainly skeptical. "Is it possible, my lord, for the sons of slaves to defeat the sons of conquerors?"

Vahan's thin smile was distant and dispassionate. "You think," he said, "that only a weak nation, one born to be ruled, is ever conquered. Well, the ancestors of these Egyptians once thought that way. And they ruled an empire greater than that we now control. But they grew weak—as we of the Hai will grow weak." His lip curled at the expression on the adjutant's face. "You think I jest with you. We have *already* grown weak—fat and soft and weak. Ever since we landed in this green and fertile land. In a generation we will be vulnerable, and the Egyptians will already have begun to grow strong again. Their hatred of us will have fed their growing strength. Your sons, my friend, will have their hands full." He glanced at the adjutant and saw skepticism still in his eyes. "Well, that's not my affair," he said. "You will have to weather *that* storm without the benefit of my, uh, wise counsel." His gaze returned to the enemy positions. "I think we have waited long enough," he said.

Almost wearily, he raised his arm high, with the sword in it. A thousand eyes were on him as he did. Then the sword struck downward, sharply, swiftly. And from a thousand throats in the front lines the low roar rose, slowly, building in strength as the hordes swept down the hillside, until the vast wave of sound from the many throats filled the hollow between the armies like water in a well.

To the watchers on the far hill it all seemed odd and dreamlike at first. A few chariots came past broadside, their occupants lofting arrows into the Egyptian ranks, hoping to draw return fire in order to gauge the range of the enemy bows. But the Egyptians held their fire, and except on the rare occasion when one of the Shepherd shafts found its mark, it all had the look of a parade-ground maneuver. Twenty paces down the line from Unas's headquarters, a soldier fell, an arrow in his shoulder. He was quickly replaced on the line by a man from the next rank.

Then, as the foot troops reached midpoint in the hollow and began working their way up the gradual slope, Unas's own bowmen went to work, with deadly effect. Perhaps one Shepherd in six was struck. Of these, half were hit in the body armor and the metal-tipped shafts glanced off harmlessly. But the other half fell back—or fell in their tracks. The infantrymen took a firmer grip on sword and spear, feeling their own tension rise. The advancing line grew closer and closer; the bowmen once again went to work, with even deadlier results.

But behind the first line of advancing Shepherd infantry were others. Wave after wave of Shepherds moved down into the hollow. The Egyptian bowmen began shooting at random, their volleys uncoordinated. Unas swore at them, but in the deafening din of the Shepherds' battle cries, his curses could not be heard.

And now the first ranks of the Shepherds reached the Egyptian lines and engaged the defenders with sword and spear. The Egyptians fought with desperate bravery and repelled the first wave of attackers, leaving a front line dotted with Shepherd dead.

Then the second rank hit them. The second rank had not been thinned as efficiently by Egyptian bow-and-arrow fire, and was at any rate made up of Vahan's toughest, most seasoned troops. They were not so easily driven back. When they met with Unas's front-liners the battle was even odds, at best. Unas's men hacked away at them valiently, but the Shepherd swordsmen were older, more experienced, and Unas lost a full third of his defenders on the front row before the second Shepherd wave finally fell back.

Unas quickly rushed new troops into the gaps. His own sword was already bloody from the two Shepherds he himself had killed; he had a light line of blood running down his naked arm from a flesh wound on his shoulder. "Good work, men!" he bellowed above the Shepherds' din, striding down the line behind the front positions. "Now here comes another wave! Let's show them what Egyptians are made of!"

But as he called out his encouragement to them, his own heart sank as he looked out across the little valley and saw the Shepherds coming, always coming. *Gods!* he thought despairingly. *How many men has Vahan got on this front, anyway?* He grabbed his passing second-in-command by the body harness and hauled him to one side even as his men prepared for the next assault. "Notify your lieutenants," he said in as soft a voice as he considered practical, "to prepare to fall back. We can hold off the next two assaults, but they've got the reserves to break through."

"But, sir—"

"No buts. Better that we fall back in time to prepared positions, just when they've the hope of smashing our lines, and make them chase us a bit—better that than have them score a break in our lines."

"Yes, sir."

Unas looked down again at the next wave, storming its way up the hill. "Bring up the second rank, right after this attack. Have them assume the positions vacated by the first rank when they fall back." He glanced up to his left, where his lookouts dotted the side of the Great Pyramid. "Any word from them?"

"No, sir. The messenger came in a few minutes ago. He confirms your assessment of the Shepherd order of battle."

"Good. If there's one thing I don't want it's surprises just now." He scowled at a suddenly opened hole in his own front line. "You! Get someone in there! On the double!" As he spoke an arrow sang its way past his face, narrowly missing him, and spent itself in the bare ground a dozen steps behind him. He spoke to his assistant again. "Now, prepare the change of personnel. Do it as unobtrusively as possible."

Vahan shaded his eyes, squinting across the disputed terrain before him. "Wait," he said to no one in particular, "they're changing men on the front line. The first-liners are falling back and being replaced by fresh troops. What the devil's he doing now?"

"I'm not certain, my lord," his adjutant said, "but . . . I'd guess he's preparing to retreat. Although why he should do that just now—"

"Damnation, man, you're right!" Vahan said. "Brilliant. I'd have done the same myself, in his place. He knows how deep we are in every position. He knows damn well that if he stays immobile, we'll grind him down by sheer weight of numbers. No. He's too smart for that by half."

"I don't understand, my lord—"

"Bah!" Vahan didn't bother to take his eyes off the battle in progress. "If you weren't my sister's son—"

"My lord," the adjutant said, in a tone of injured dignity. "What do you want me to do?"

"Do?" Vahan said in a rage. "Get my horse up here, damn you! And bring me a messenger—a mounted one! Where's that flanking attack? Where's the Thirtieth, anyway? They should have hit Unas's left flank long before this! Damn incompetent cowards! Fools! Can't any of you do anything right? If he falls back and catches us at just the right moment, gets us chasing him . . . and then turns and fights from a favorable position and with fresh troops . . ." He closed his eyes, trying to remember his mental picture of the terrain beside the mastaba fields. "Yes. I know just where he'll stand and fight. Damn him! He's a warrior after my own heart. No doubt about it—this is one I have to kill myself. I'll flay the man who touches him. *Horse!* Where's that horse of mine?"

IV

Under a supporting barrage of arrows from their massed archers, the Shepherd troops stormed their way up the incline, catching Unas's reinforcements slightly off balance. To one side, Vahan held his cavalry back until the foot soldiers had gained the top of the ridge and had engaged the defenders in bloody hand-to-hand combat. Then, with a fierce bellow that belied his age, he ordered a charge against Unas's right flank. The horsemen surged up the hill, spears at the ready. Vahan, with sword and buckler, led the way, hacking mightily at the heads of the Egyptian fighters who faced him, ignoring a leg wound received in the first moments of the attack.

Unas's line held in the middle—but gave on the right, before the ferocious assault by Vahan's horsemen. Vahan penetrated the lines and wheeled, his horse rearing beneath him. "*Unas!*" he bellowed. "*Unas! Vahan calls you to stand and fight!*"

But the Egyptian commander was occupied at the moment on his own left flank, holding off with sword and shield two powerful Shepherd fighters. Parrying a thrust by the first of the two, he finished the motion with a mighty backhand slash that tore the leather helmet off the attacker's head and left his whole face bloody on one side. As he did, the second soldier thrust at Unas's unprotected belly. Unas spun away adroitly, the thrust slipping harmlessly between his arm and chest. He stiff-armed the Shepherd soldier in the face and followed with a thrust of his own, catching the second soldier just below the rib cage. As the blade sunk in, Unas could see the expression of stunned shock on the man's face and could see his eyes suddenly roll back in his head. Unas stepped away, yanking hard on the bloody sword in his hand, just in time to recover and fend off a second thrust by the other soldier.

"Damn you, you're persistent!" Unas said. He feinted at the man's face, but instead thrust at his neck. The sharp blade just caught the side of the soldier's uncovered neck and sliced clean through the artery. Blood spurted and the soldier fell back. Unas quickly lost sight of him.

He looked around him. "Stand fast, men!" he yelled. "Hold the line! Hold them back!"

But then he chanced to look up—up and to his left, to the side of the Great Pyramid, where his lookouts were waving their arms, signaling frantically. He wheeled around; his adjutant was nowhere to be found. What were they waving about up there? He cursed under his breath at the distance between them and at the din of battle. Obviously they were screaming at the pitch of their lungs up there— but not a word of it could he hear.

Then he noticed some of them were pointing—pointing toward the rear of his own lines! To the left flank of his second line of defense, where the retiring troops must by now be taking up their new positions . . .

Suddenly another Shepherd lunged at him. His instincts were as good as ever, however; his arm moved almost without his bidding, and his sword found the man's shoulder and bit deep. The attacker fell back. Unas, seeing an opening in the fighting mass of men, dashed to the top of the knoll behind his own front lines.

"Gods!" he said. "A flank attack! They're hitting our second line on the flank!" He cursed his own stupidity for not foreseeing this; he should have known! He should have—

A spent arrow whizzed by his head, and he turned to face more immediately pressing problems. A Shepherd attacker, having broken through the front lines, made at him with a spear. He stepped to one side, grabbed the spear, and yanked. Off balance, the man stumbled toward him, only to take Unas's ready blade square in the face. His attention immediately turned back to the flanking attack, and his heart sank. He had recognized the guidon of the Shepherds' Thirtieth Infantry. The Thirtieth, he knew, was under the command of Sahag, Vahan's most vicious general.

Where were his officers now? Where—?

His eyes swept his front lines, and he saw with pride that his men were standing their ground. He clenched his jaw and took a fresh grip on his sword. *Good lads!*

But then his gaze moved past them, to his right flank, where the Shepherd horsemen had broken through.

"Damn!" he said, and rushed forward. As he did, he could
see a tall, heavily built warrior atop a sturdy charger hack
powerfully, backhand, at a defender and batter the man's
buckler backward, slicing through the heavy leather. The
horseman turned, raising his weapon once more. . . .

Vahan! Unas's hand convulsively gripped the hilt of
his sword, and he felt the rush of blood to his limbs, the
odd exhilaration of the moment. Vahan! At last! Now, if
only no one else managed to strike him down first . . .

Even as Unas thought this, Vahan's horse backed into
the path of a Shepherd arrow, and it caught the animal in
the hindquarter, sinking deep. The horse faltered and
stumbled. Vahan, his own reflexes still fast and sure, got
his feet out of the stirrups and slipped easily to the ground
just as the great horse went down with an anguished
whinny.

But when Vahan's feet touched ground it was evident
that there was something wrong with one of his legs.
Unas, sprinting forward, could see the wound in the Shepherd commander's thigh, could almost hear Vahan's grunt
of annoyance as he limped forward, favoring the leg.

"Vahan!" Unas shouted. "Vahan! Come fight me—
Unas!"

The Shepherd commander stopped and turned, frantically seeking the source of the cry. When he spied Unas,
his rugged old face contorted in a mad and terrifying
smile. "Unas." He seemed to speak the name to himself,
and swinging his great sword two-handed, he hacked a
path through the defenders toward his quarry.

In small groups of twos and threes they had crept
through the mastaba field, a sprawling complex of oblong,
sloping-sided tombs. Now, however, they had been sighted
by the enemy lookouts, and there was nothing for it but to
dash forward across the intervening ground and fall upon
the second line of Egyptian defenders in a headlong,
whirlwind attack, fighting like madmen. Thus they poised
at the edge of the open ground, awaiting the signal from
Sahag.

Baka's sharp eye secretly scrutinized the Shepherd
commander; he did not like what he saw. "I've come this

far with the bastard," he said to Ben-Hadad in a sarcastic whisper, "but I'm damned if I'll strike the first blow for him."

Ben-Hadad, crouched in the shadows against a tomb wall, was staring out across the open field at the Egyptian lines. "Of course," he said, looking up. "We can't fight our own people, can we?"

"No," Baka said. "This is the time to change sides. If there's any way we can disrupt the charge, all the better." He glanced again at Sahag, who was not more than thirty paces away, sharply issuing orders to his aides. "I think he's decided not to wait for the chariots," Baka said. "That means he'll be on foot. I could kill him easily." He shrugged. "It's tempting. But it's best not to take chances. Although I must say my sword hand itches at the thought." He spat at his feet. "Look, he's about to signal. There goes his hand up. Now . . . go!"

As Sahag's arm swept downward the entire unit rushed forward, making the strange low-pitched cry the Shepherds always made during a charge: an unearthly, echoing ululation that rose in pitch and swelled as they ran. Across the plain they could see the Egyptian archers snap to on inaudible orders from their commander, fit arrows to their bowstrings, aim, fire. A thick volley of wooden shafts flew through the air, fell short. In hardly more than a heartbeat the bowmen had their bows strung again and were taking aim.

Baka slowed and dropped back even with Ben-Hadad. "I can't pass up the chance," he said. "I'm going to hit him. If you're with me, get the man to his left."

"Who?" Ben-Hadad yelled, on the run. But Baka was off ahead of him, on swift feet, his sword held close by his chest. He flew across the uneven ground after Sahag, gaining steadily, heedless of the arrows that fell thick and fast around them.

Now, putting on an extra burst of speed, Baka reached the Shepherd leader. With lightning quickness, his sword rose high and struck down, cleaving through the bare, unprotected spot on Sahag's back where the body armor did not cover him. Sahag stumbled and fell on his face.

At the same moment, Ben-Hadad himself tripped and

almost fell. Recovering, he took out after Sahag's second-in-command, a Lydian mercenary. The Lydian turned to aid Sahag, in the process breaking stride and losing ground. Unable to stop himself, Ben-Hadad ran into him and knocked him down, tumbling headfirst past him. He had managed only to get to one knee when the Lydian rose, snarling, sword in hand, and lunged at him.

Ben-Hadad jumped aside and down, hit the ground again, and rolled. When he righted himself he saw the Lydian standing in a crouch above him, his sword gone, his hands clawing at the polished shaft of an arrow embedded deep in his chest. Ben-Hadad did not wait for the man to fall. He ducked a second, spent arrow and turned to see Baka finish off Sahag with a powerful roundhouse slice of his sword that nearly decapitated the Shepherd captain.

By now their former companions had reached the Egyptian lines and were battling with the defenders. Baka screamed at him across the space that separated them: "Help them!" he said. "Help the Egyptians!"

Ben-Hadad's mind froze, but somehow his body had begun to obey Baka's words. He found himself rushing forward, sword in hand, toward the back of a Shepherd soldier who had just stabbed an Egyptian soldier and who was trying to disengage his blade. The man turned at Ben-Hadad's approach, but did not free his sword quickly enough. Ben-Hadad's sword arm, seemingly of its own will, stretched out in front of him, and the weight of his body propelled the weapon forward as he hit the soldier, driving the blade deep into the man's midsection. The Shepherd staggered and fell forward onto the waiting and eager sword of a defender, who, the kill completed, stared, puzzled, at Ben-Hadad.

"I'm on your side!" the boy said—and ducked aside as one of the attackers came at him from his left. He pivoted, extending his sword arm to keep his balance, and when his turn was complete, the blade, coming around and rising, again seemingly of its own accord, sliced through the shoulder of the Shepherd as neatly as if the cut had been intentional.

"Look out!" Baka called out behind him. He turned to see Baka parrying an attack on his, Ben-Hadad's, unpro-

tected back. Baka drove his man back in a flurry of expert
thrusts and cuts, but an Egyptian spearsman lunged forward and took the kill away from Baka. The spearsman
stood, trying to free his spear-point, and looked sharply at
his unexpected ally.

"You!" he said. "But . . . you're dead!"

"Not yet, I'm not!" Baka said, and jumped back into
the fray, hacking wildly with his bloody sword at a gigantic
Moabite mercenary.

The spearsman stood as if struck dumb, his comrades
now beginning to carry the fight away from him. He
stared at Ben-Hadad. "You two . . . you came from the
other side! And that's Baka! But Baka's dead!"

"Not—not dead!" Ben-Hadad said, catching his breath
in great gasps. "Baka's alive! He's back!"

His words must have carried during a slight lull in the
sounds of fighting, for the word quickly spread from soldier to soldier: *Baka! It's Baka!* And suddenly the sneak
flank attack faltered, the attackers lost their momentum,
and one, two, then many, began falling back. As the
retreat became a rout, the Egyptian bowmen methodically
went to work, their accurate arrows finding target after
target. Soon the dozen or two dozen stragglers had become a handful, and the handful one or two. Then, of all
the attackers, only one man remained in the field, sprinting desperately across the uneven ground toward the mastaba field, now beyond range of even the Egyptian bows.

The cheer that all at once went up from the Egyptian
lines was full-throated and hearty—the victory cry of men
who had been tested under pressure and found true, and,
at the same time, the joyous cry of recognition, as they
welcomed an old leader and comrade to their ranks again.
"Baka! Baka!"

Slowly, warily, the two fighters circled each other in
the broad space they had cleared behind the Egyptian
lines. Vahan's men had fallen back; the Shepherd commander was now trapped inside the lines of his enemy.
Yet no man wearing the colors of Egypt dared interfere
with the personal battle that had developed between Unas
and the Shepherd general. Over the proceedings there

hung a curious quiet, in which one could hear the heavy breathing of the two combatants, their weary grunts of effort.

In the first passage of arms between them Vahan had appeared the stronger of the two, Unas the quicker of hand. After they had been fighting for some time, however, and with little decisive result, both had begun to tire. Vahan's cuts and thrusts were no longer so powerful; Unas's ripostes were not so swift, so sure. Unas's arm bore a gaping wound from a sword cut; Vahan was limping badly.

It was past time for taunts and insults. By now, for that matter, neither warrior felt moved to either form of comment, for each had won the other's respect, and both men knew that whichever man won the contest, he would not dishonor the body of his fallen foe.

Now, however, Unas began to tire of the fight itself. The problem was that there was only one way to end it, and that was to kill Vahan. He had come to sense that the Shepherd general would never surrender, would only be taken dead or dying. And in the back of his mind a nagging thought tugged steadily at him: *What a pity. What a waste!* If only the two of them could sit down under truce flags and talk man to man: What wisdom would Vahan impart? What stories would he have to tell, after having brought his nomad armies all the way from the mountain fastnesses above Lake Van, having marched them farther than any army had ever marched in all the annals of war! What delightful soldier talk might the two of them have, over cups of mulled wine, as the campfire coals guttered and died. . . .

But now Vahan attacked once again. From some hidden source the nomad general found the strength to bull forward, hacking, cutting, thrusting, driving Unas back. Unas parried, gave ground, counterthrust—only to have his sword almost torn from his hand by a powerful forte-against-forte parry. He recovered, gave ground, feinted . . .

. . . and somehow (afterward he was never able to reconstruct the sequence of events, so fast did it all come to pass) he found himself standing his ground as Vahan lunged, ducking a wicked thrust at his face, and, counter-thrusting, finding the free spot in Vahan's body armor. His blade sank in, going deep, the great weight of Vahan's huge body impaling itself on Unas's sword until the blade went all the way through and emerged from his back.

Vahan's sword fell to the ground. For a moment he stood leaning on Unas, his hands on Unas's shoulders. He looked around him with eyes suddenly grown dim; then he looked down at Unas, just as his legs began to fail. For a heartbeat Unas thought the giant was going to say something. A smile played uncertainly on Vahan's mouth, only to be replaced by a gout of blood. Then Vahan— Vahan the conqueror, greatest of the fighting generals of the army of the Shepherd Kings—slowly sank to the ground, despite all Unas's efforts to hold him up.

Unas stood, weaving, looking down at the man he had killed. After a moment, he wearily bent down to retrieve his sword, pulling it gently from the dead man's body. He wiped his brow with the back of his hand and was conscious that there was blood on his face—but whether from his hand or from a cut on his head he could not say. He looked around him, at the awe-struck faces. "W-what are you doing, standing there?" he said, his voice sounding far away in his own ears. "Get back on the line! They're going to counterattack before—"

He never got the chance to finish the sentence. From the vale below came the shrill howl of a thousand throats, as the Shepherd infantry charged again. On the Egyptian right flank the Shepherd horsemen once more stormed the defenders' ranks, and in the center wave after wave of Shepherd attackers was thrown against the Egyptian lines. Unas, recovering his presence of mind, cursed his ill fortune and the resilience of the Shepherd force—and its damnable depth. Now there'd be no chance of an orderly fallback, as he'd planned. Vahan had won! He'd delayed the retreat by fighting Unas, by prolonging the duel until his own men could recover and once more storm the Egyptian lines!

Unas fell, a bronze-tipped Shepherd spear piercing his body just below the joining of the ribs. His ragtag first line saw his death and panicked, turned tail and fled amid a hail of arrows, throwing their weapons to the ground. The attack had become a rout. And now the Shepherds advanced on the Egyptians' second line with nothing else separating them from the undefended walls of Memphis.

CHAPTER
TWELVE

BEHIND THE SHEPHERD LINES

I

The great strength and depth of the Shepherd force began to reveal itself at last as the subsidiary garrisons poured forth in seemingly unending streams of soldiers. Every village along the Nile found its boats commandeered to ferry troops across the river to their new positions. Granaries and storehouses in every town were raided to provide food for the newly arrived soldiery, and landowners arriving to collect rents on their groves found the olive trees and date palms picked clean. They cursed and called down the wrath of the entire Egyptian pantheon—but softly, under their breath, lest a Shepherd overseer hear them. Yesterday's riches had become today's poverty for many born to affluence in the rich and fertile Black Lands.

Below these, the poorest of the poor, dispossessed even of the little they had had before, found themselves homeless, without hope of shelter or provender. And, in desperation, a great migration began—a migration in search of food and shelter—a migration without form or leadership. Some sought refuge in the thinly settled western nomes, where the Shepherd hand had touched only lightly since the Egyptian forces abandoned the area two years before. Others, those with skills, built reed boats of marsh papyrus and put them out in the current with their families aboard, in the hope that better conditions could be found downstream, near the mouth of the Great River.

Still another group, larger, perhaps, than either of these, set out as scavengers in the wake of the advancing Shepherd armies, picking through the rubble of abandoned Shepherd encampments and Egyptian outposts alike, living off what they could find.

These last were a raggedy, ill-assorted, desperate crowd: widows, cripples, beggars, petty criminals, street urchins. They were the ones without friends or families, the ones who traveled alone. There was little communication among them. They were people reduced to a single thought: to find, by whatever means, the wherewithal to get through yet another weary and perilous day.

And there were the scavengers who preyed on the scavengers, moving among them armed with blade and staff, stealing at knife's point whatever they found, as coldly and impersonally as jackals feeding upon the dead and the dying. . . .

"There's one over there," Nub said. "Over there, Sakar! See? He seems to have found something." A full head shorter than his hulking partner, Nub had to look up to speak to him. He spoke in an obsequious whine, tinged with fear; the larger man had in the past proved quick with a cuff. One hand hung poised, ready to shield his face, to ward off a blow.

The bigger man's mind was elsewhere. "What?" he said in a guttural croak. "Where? Oh! Over there by the palm, eh? Well, go and find out what he's got. Don't just sit there like a toad on a rock."

"Yes!" Nub said. "Yes!" He took off after the huddled figure he had pointed out. Only when he was within a bound or two of his prey did he stop, slip his stolen Shepherd short-sword into his hand, and call out: "You! You, there! What have you got? Turn, damn you!"

The man addressed turned slowly and looked at him.

He was old and white-haired. He held up his hands to show they were empty. "Please, sir," he said in a quavery voice, "I've found nothing. I thought I'd seen something here, where somebody's tent had been pitched. See?" He pointed out the irregular circle on the ground, the crushed grass where a squad of soldiers had slept perhaps no more than a day before. "But it turned out to be nothing."

But Nub had spotted the purse hanging at the old man's waist. "Nothing?" he said, waving the sword menacingly at the man's face. "What's that? What's in the bag? Hand it over, you old fool! Quickly, or I'll—"

"No, please!" the old man said. "It's just . . . just worthless trinkets . . . some memories of my family. It would be worthless to you."

"Hand it over!" Nub said, the old man's weakness and subservience making him feel suddenly strong, dominant, as he so seldom felt in Sakar's company. "Pass it over, you old bag of bones, or I'll cut out your tripes!"

"No, please! Don't make me. . . ."

The old man's hand stretched out to him in entreaty. Nub ginned at him—and the sword flashed. The old man pulled his hand back; it was covered with blood. "Give it over, you!" Nub said, stepping forward quickly, holding his hand out toward the old man.

Nub had expected to feel his fingers close over the purse: Instead, he clutched air. In a rage he lunged with the sword and buried it in the old man's belly. The old man grunted, slowly bent double, and fell to the ground. Nub, breathing hard now, kicked the prostrate body, turned it over, and winced at the open wound his sword had made. "I'll just relieve you of that," he said, and cut the purse loose, just as Sakar came up alongside him.

"What's in it?" Sakar said. "Anything valuable?"

Nub squatted, opened the drawstring, and poured the contents of the little bag onto the ground. To his disgust, there was, as the old man had said, nothing but the trinkets left behind by the few people who had for a time shared the old man's life. A worthless string of beads some forgotten woman had worn. A pocket image of some god, its surface so worn by someone's fingers that the name and nature of the god could hardly be guessed at. A tiny, broken toy abandoned by some long-ago child . . . "Bah!" Nub said. "What a waste!"

"Hardly worth the bother of killing him," Sakar growled in that cold, gruff bass of his. "Follow me. There's a few up the way who look like better pickings. See?" His finger pointed. Nub squinted and tried to make out the figures. "One of them may be a woman, from the look of her."

"Woman?" Nub said, suddenly interested. "Well, now, that's something else." He grinned, showing broken yellow teeth, and instinctively turned to check behind him. It wouldn't do to get too distracted by the novelty of finding a woman in the field. There were other bullyboys abroad who had ideas of their own as to whom the spoils of war were due, and some of them were as good with a blade as he and Sakar were. It would be stupid to forget, as they had two days ago, down by the river. They'd barely got away with their skins intact, battling off those three soldiers. If Sakar hadn't been so damned big and strong . . .

But as he scanned the landscape behind them he could see, in the distance, only a lone scavenger, small and skinny-looking, hooded against the bright sunlight. No trouble there.

He turned back to the business at hand and set out after the three figures up ahead, trotting to catch up with the hulking Sakar.

Tuya saw them first. Streetwise and wary, she sensed trouble the moment the two men took notice of them. "Hey!" she said to her nameless companions as they bent over a pile of Shepherd rubble, picking through the soldiers' leavings. "There's a couple of men heading our way. I don't think they mean us any good."

The crippled man turned, his withered arm hanging loose at his side. He pulled at his friend's garment with his good hand. "Look there!" he said. "Where the girl's pointing! Trouble! We'd better get out of here!"

When the second man looked up from the cluttered campsite the Shepherds had abandoned only a day before, it was obvious to Tuya that he had only the dimmest idea what his friend had said. He had some odd ailment that left him unable to stand erect, or to hold a coherent thought in his mind, for that matter. "Eh?" he said, his mouth working uncontrollably, his eyes rolling of their own accord, like an idiot's.

"Come on!" the man with the withered arm said. He pulled at the spastic's garment again, almost dragging him away. "Danger! Bad men! They want to hurt you! Hurt, do you hear? *Hurt!*"

Dim recognition dawned on the man's face. "Hurt? Danger?" he said, and let himself be pulled forward.

Tuya glanced back. The pair were gaining on them. She had seen their like before: the hulking bully with his fawning satellite, the smaller man always taking the larger one's leavings. Fishermen who worked salt water, at the mouth of the Nile, would sometimes come into a river port and talk of the large predatory fish that lived in the Great Sea. All teeth and appetite, they would devour anything that swam their way. You could see them clearly as they swam past, the fishermen said, together with the parasitic small fish that accompanied them everywhere, swimming barely a handspan from the great jaws, living off what the great predator's rapacious saw-teeth missed. There had been a quick moment of recognition as Tuya had listened to the sailors' accounts. There were men like that—men like the large fish, all cold, brainless appetite, taking what they wanted, without thought; and men like the little parasite fish, who served the bigger fish and took their leavings.

She shuddered at the thought—and picked up her pace. But as she did, the two men caught up with the cripples. There were quick, harsh words; blades flashed. She averted her eyes and, picking up her raggedy skirts, hurried forward.

"*You! Girl!*" a harsh voice bellowed behind her. She half turned, her eyes on her pursuers—and as she did, her bare foot came down on a loose rock. Her ankle turned painfully under her and she fell heavily to the ground, the pain shooting up her leg.

She was on her knees in hardly more than the blink of an eye, but as she struggled to her feet she found that the ankle would not bear her weight. She tried it, and fell heavily, crying out at the sudden pain. An icy wave of panic swept through her. She got up again, swaying on one leg, trying to hop forward . . .

. . . and the smaller man quickly caught up with her. His hand grasped the long, enveloping garment she'd stolen the day before from an abandoned pile of rags. She dived to the ground, and the raggedy garment tore across. She pulled her knife free of the robe just as it gave again, leaving her connected to it only by the belt she'd improvised from a piece of reed rope. As the man pulled at the garment, she cut through the rope and rolled free, her spare brown body naked once more under the bright Egyptian sun.

The small man's mouth opened in an ugly, broken-toothed smile. "Better put the knife down, girl!" he said in a high-pitched whine. "Put it down, now. I won't hurt you. . . ." He edged closer, his gaze darting from her bare body to the knife in her hand as she got to one knee, attempting to get at least her good leg under her.

She took a firmer hold on the knife, preparing in her desperation to sell her life dearly if she had to . . . and then sudden panic rushed through her. *The other one! The big one! Where was he?*

Just then the big hand fell on her head and seized her by the hair, yanking her erect as if she weighed no more than a newborn child. And as she swung the knife around in blind, unreasoning fright, she felt the big man's other hand—a great hairy paw four times the size of her own little brown fist—close on her wrist, squeezing it so hard that for a moment she could feel nothing, not even pain. Her fingers opened and the knife fell to the ground with a dull clank. The great hand, grasping her by the hair now, held her in the air, her feet kicking in vain, her other tiny fist battering without effect at the stone wrist that held her tight. Behind her she could hear the behemoth's hateful laughter, low, foul, and demeaning. She had never felt so helpless, so defenseless, so naked. . . .

Nub watched the girl struggle, her tiny feet kicking like those of a baby held up by its mother, and felt his pulse quicken, his throat go dry. *Helpless*, he thought.

But still full of spirit. Well, Sakar would break *that* soon
enough. He'd have her begging him to stop in a moment
or two, begging him to let her go. But he wouldn't do it,
of course. Sakar was as single-minded as an animal that
way. He'd go about the business of satisfying his own
hungers as impersonally as if the girl had readily acquiesced,
ignoring any fight she put up or any noise she made. And
if she grew too bothersome, he'd knock her cold and
continue until he was finished. It was, he thought, exciting to watch. It always made his hunger all the greater, to
see Sakar break the spirit of a woman. He would find his
own passion growing as he watched the great buffalo of a
man having his way, debasing his victim. . . .

He heard the footfalls behind him too late. He turned—
and saw the demon face. His heart almost stopped. Then
the sword took him high on the neck, with all the aveng-
ing demon's weight behind the silent swing. He staggered
to one side and fell heavily. His eyes blurred; strength,
sense, life left him all at once, in a great sick rush.

Trembling with rage, fear, and a host of other emotions he could not name, Anab moved on before Nub's
body even hit the ground. His hands shook on the sword
hilt as he drew up behind the hulking brute who had just
pinned Tuya naked to the ground beneath his ape's body.
"*You*—" he began in a shrill, tight voice; but words,
coherent thoughts, failed him. The blood rushed to his
hands as he gripped the sword hard, lifted it high, and
with all his weight swung down. The blade cut into the big
man's back. Anab did not pause, but drew back the sword
again, momentarily losing his balance as he did. The big
man tried to straighten up, rolling off the girl's body.
Tuya, seeing her chance, scuttled to safety as Sakar, clench-
ing and unclenching his mighty fists, struggled to his feet.

Anab's heart sank. *If he gets up* . . . he thought in a
blind panic. And, two-handed, he hacked down and to one
side, like a woodsman chopping at a tree trunk. The blade
bit into the leviathan's shoulder, driving him to his knees
once more. The man roared, at the same time rising to his
feet and charging forward . . .

. . . just as Anab lunged at him with the bronze

weapon's sharp point. The blade caught the hulking Sakar in the mouth, breaking his front teeth with a sickening shatter, then slid down his throat until it hit bone. The big man's weight ripped the sword from Anab's hands as Anab dodged to one side.

The helpless giant tore at the weapon by its blade, trying to pull it from his mouth; but it would not budge. Anab saw the red blood spurt from the mouth, then from the big man's ruined palms, sliced through by the blade he clutched with ever weaker hands. He barely had time to jump aside again as the big man fell toward him, his weight driving the sword-blade all the deeper.

Anab turned away, retching, sobbing, falling to his own knees, trying to wipe from his mind the thing he'd just done, the sight he'd just seen. Only gradually did he come to feel Tuya's warm body pressed against him, her arms around him, hugging him. Only little by little did he become aware of the soft comforting words she was murmuring soothingly into his ear as he wept, shaking, beside himself with a mixture of mad, uncontrolled emotions.

Afterward, Anab could not bring himself to look at the dead men, much less touch them. Tuya had to search the bodies herself, and she cried out in triumph as she held Sakar's bulging purse high. "Look, Anab!" she said. "Money! And food, too! Cheese! Olives!"

The thought of food made him ill again. "P-please," he said weakly, his back to her. "Don't mention anything to eat."

"It's all right," she said brightly. "Don't think of it now. What a haul!" She grunted with the effort as she rolled Nub out of his clothing, leaving him naked except for his soiled loincloth. "Well, it's a little big," she said, holding up his bloodstained tunic. "But it'll have to do." She slipped into the garment and fastened it around her with her newly acquired sword belt. She held up Nub's short-sword. "This ought to stand me in good stead," she said, swinging it around twice before replacing it in its scabbard.

"How glad I am that you came!" she said. "I'll never be able to thank you enough. Two of them! Anab—you're a new man. I hardly recognize you. You're as brave as a lion!"

Anab turned slowly to look at her, his face still ghostly white from the ordeal. "I . . . I had time to think, a while back," he said. "After Ben-Hadad and Baka left, I mean. I knew you'd go after them, even though you promised you wouldn't. I knew you'd follow Ben-Hadad wherever he went. I was planning to go with you, whether you wanted me to or not. But then you stole away from me, before I awoke."

She looked at him meekly. "But you don't have to come with me, Anab," she said. "I'm grateful, of course. You know that. Dear Anab! You didn't have to follow—"

"But I did," he said. "You see . . . I did you all an ill turn. You should have k-killed me."

"Anab!" she said. "You know we wouldn't—"

"Please," he said. "He forgave me. Ben-Hadad *forgave* me. I—I think I hadn't understood what . . . what it was to have a friend before. You see, I'd never had one. I'd never had anyone accept me, with all my faults, and—" He hesitated. "Tuya," he said, "I was ready to kill myself. I had nothing to live for, you see. . . ."

"Anab," Tuya said in the softest of voices. "I—"

"Let me talk," Anab said. "I . . . then I thought of something to live for. If there was nothing else to live for, at least I could—I could b-bring you back safe to Ben-Hadad. If I could do that, if I could keep you safe until you found him, well, maybe I'd be worth something. So I came after you, with Lion, too. But he disappeared yesterday."

Tuya stood watching him as he tried to speak again and failed, his voice breaking. He would not look up at her.

"I see," she said at last. "Poor Anab. *Dear* Anab. Well, don't worry about Lion. He can take care of himself. Meanwhile, you take care of me . . . and I'll try to take care of you. Ben-Hadad would be crushed to lose his friend, to lose you, Anab. So would I."

At last he looked up at her, wide-eyed, hardly comprehending.

"How about it, Anab? We'll look out for each other

from now on. You've more friends than you know. Besides, we both have another duty, one you don't know about. We both have someone else to deliver safely to Ben-Hadad." She smiled at him and would say no more for a moment.

"I . . . I don't understand," he said, his face blank.

"I didn't think you possibly could," she said. "Anab—I missed my curse this month. I think I am carrying his child."

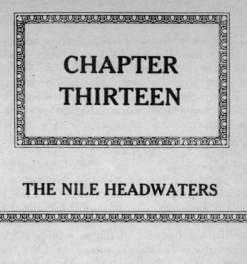

CHAPTER THIRTEEN

THE NILE HEADWATERS

I

The center of Bukango's realm was mostly bare, rolling country, punctuated with steep hills that rose sharply and suddenly from the unforested landscape: land given over, where it was occupied, to cultivated fields of millet, broken here and there by the startling green of a banana grove. Akhilleus—who had once roamed these rolling foothills as a boy named Mtebi, heir to a great throne—journeyed through it largely silent, asking only an occasional question of Kimala. Yet the giant's eyes remained observant and his expression was thoughtful. Neither Kimala nor Akhilleus's companions failed to notice his air of alert watchfulness.

Orders had come from Ramogi, by runner, stipulating that the strangers were not to be allowed access to the ailing Bukango in Ramogi's absence. Ramogi, it appeared, was occupied at the moment with the settlement of a border dispute, a business that might require a number of days to complete.

In the meantime, Akhilleus had suggested a side trip

to the Kigezi uplands, in the shadow of the mighty Mufumbiro, the Mountains of Fire, where, as Kimala had let slip, they might find deposits of copper. Akhilleus had expected an argument from Kimala, but had got none. Indeed, the warrior seemed to welcome the excursion, the more so as it increased his opportunities to speak with the foreign visitors.

Thus the party, provisioning in the piedmont villages, had struck out to the southwest, through country Akhilleus recognized immediately from his half-forgotten youth. The track, a narrow path worn down by the feet of countless travelers over thousands of years, wound its way slowly up the valleys, over and around rounded knolls dotted with dark patches of volcanic rock, patches that seemed to be more and more frequent as the expedition made its way ever upward into the high country.

"See all this?" Akhilleus said to Ebana, stooping without breaking stride and picking up a pitted piece of dark rock. "This was once liquid fire, raining down on these hills from the mountains above—mountains so far away that you can't see them from here through the clouds that obscure them."

Ebana took the rock, inspected it, and shook her head. "Mountains of Fire?" she said. "Mountains that spit hot rocks up into the sky, to fall on lands many days' march away? Akhilleus, if I didn't know better, I'd swear you'd gone back to being your old jesting self. I'd swear you were making a fool of me with your tall stories."

"Trust me," he said. "It's no tall story. We've serious business to transact here, perhaps more serious than you think. Besides"—his big hand closed over hers affectionately as he helped her over a washout in the trail—"my days of joking are over, Ebana."

She squeezed his hand in reply, smiling up at him as she climbed back onto the path. "I know," she said. "And I prefer you this way."

"Good," he said. "Because this is the way it's got to be. Back in Egypt, among our friends, we could afford to jest. But here—we're in danger, and every eye is on us. Decorum and dignity are called for." He touched her arm, drawing her attention to the terraced hills opposite them.

"Look," he said. "See how thickly the crops grow here. The rain of fire hurts at first. Then it heals the land on which it has fallen. This is rich land. Yams, millet, beans, peas. Everything grows well here."

"It certainly is green," she said. "And there's a strange quality to the light. The colors are all muted."

He looked around him at the soft, green hills. "Yes," he said. "I loved this country so when I was a boy. My father had business here every so often, and twice he took me. I looked forward to subsequent trips, but then I was taken away. I'd forgotten all of it until now. But now it seems as though I'd never left."

He caught her as she stumbled, and she could feel the immense strength in his hands, guiding her once again to the irregular path underfoot. "It's a land of many wonders," he said. "The second time my father took me up here, he showed me a sight I'll never forget entirely. The highest of the Mountains of Fire is called Muhavura. Muhavura does not explode or rain fire, like the others. Instead, at the top is a great hole in the ground, with a lake inside it, hidden from below, and fed by the rains."

"It must be very beautiful," Ebana said appreciatively. "You'll have to show it to me sometime."

"I will," he said. "But, there's more. Sometimes it rains and rains up here, and the lake, with no natural outlets, fills to the top. Then it overflows, and the waters run down the sides of the mountain. When this happens, the villages below say that the mountain is weeping. And in fact, that's what it looks like: tears rolling down the face of Muhavura, the Mountain That Weeps." His voice was full of wonder as he spoke. "This is a land of magic."

Something in his tone made her fall back to look at him as she walked beside him. "Akhilleus," she said, "has it entered your mind to stay here? To contest the kingdom's succession with Ramogi when your uncle dies?"

"*Shhh*," he said, touching her hand again in mild reproof. "The time to talk of such things is when we know ourselves to be truly alone. You never know which of your words will carry, up here. But"—he turned to her, smiled, and whispered—"yes, it has entered my mind."

*   *   *

The caravan came to a halt at a place where the earth had shaken underfoot, many generations before, and a great slab of mountainside had broken loose and fallen into the valley below. Kimala climbed out on the broken rock face, filled his food-purse with loose rocks, and clambered back to safety. "Here," he said to Akhilleus. "What do you think?"

The giant turned the specimens over in his hand. "Musuri! Where are you?"

The old Moabite moved to his side. Kimala had not failed to notice the many scars of battle crisscrossing his chest and limbs. "Let me see," Musuri said. He took two of the rocks from Akhilleus's huge palm, hefting them. He spat on one and rubbed it.

"Well?" Ebana said.

"Oh, it's copper all right. Good quality, too, I'd say. But how much is there here? And how much trouble is it going to be to get to it?"

Akhilleus shot Kimala a few fast questions and listened attentively to the answers. Then he turned to Musuri. "As much as one could possibly want, according to our friend here," he said. "Less than a day's march away."

Musuri's brow rose. "But there's the problem of mining it, isn't there? And transporting it safely once it's been mined."

Akhilleus seemed lost in thought. He dismissed Musuri, then looked at Kimala, trying to decipher the gleam in the young soldier's clear eyes. Suddenly Kimala smiled, ever so slightly, and Akhilleus saw in the smile a certain understanding, almost a look of complicity. Or—had he misread what he saw? Could it be, on the other hand, that Kimala was just one step ahead of him?

The presence of copper in the Kigezi confirmed, they turned back, retracing their steps down the mountainside. Seen from above, the rolling foothills were even more enchantingly beautiful than they had appeared before. Ebana commented upon this more than once, but

Akhilleus's mind was on other things. The giant was strangely silent through most of their slow descent.

As the path grew less steep, they could see ahead to where a troop of soldiers awaited them. "What's all this about?" Akhilleus said to Kimala.

"I don't know," the young soldier said. He barked an order to an associate, who scampered down the trail to confront the troop's towering leader. In a moment the messenger turned and trotted back up to where they stood. He spoke in a low voice to Kimala, who nodded, dismissed him, and turned to Akhilleus.

"Akillu," he said, "you will get your audience with Bukango, if he lives long enough to receive you. Ramogi has said it. He is with Bukango now, awaiting our arrival."

Akhilleus frowned. "I had hoped for a less formal meeting, but we will see them on whatever terms they prefer." Kimala nodded and signaled for the group to continue down the hillside.

The moment Kimala was out of earshot, Akhilleus called Musuri to his side.

"It appears we're to be allowed to see Bukango," he said, "but only under Ramogi's supervision. I don't like it; it's a little too easy."

"The more reason to be on our guard," Musuri said. "I'm going to make sure everyone's armed and alert all the way in to the village." He chewed his lower lip for a moment and then said, "I've been meaning to talk to you, Akhilleus. There's something . . . well, not quite right here. Ever since we've been in your home country, I've sensed trouble. As if someone was constantly watching us."

"I know what you mean," Akhilleus said. "I don't think it has anything to do with Kimala, either. I've been too busy trying to sort out my thoughts the last few days to worry about it, but . . . keep your eyes and ears open, both of you, and I'll do the same. There's no doubt we're all in danger—perhaps in more ways than one—and I've a feeling it will take all the wits we can muster to come out of this with whole skins."

*   *   *

At nightfall they made camp and feasted on boiled millet, beans, and—to Musuri's intense disgust—termites fried in oil, a local delicacy. Akhilleus made sport of the Moabite's squeamishness. "Look at it this way, Musuri," he said. "Bugs have been feasting on your flesh all day; here's a chance to get back at them." Musuri made a wry face and turned away.

Ebana found herself enjoying the new and strange customs of her husband's homeland. She had learned that while the men of the region went naked in virtually all weather, the women preferred to adorn themselves to some extent. After dinner she wandered about in the camp and noticed that the native soldiers had been joined by a number of men and women from a nearby village. The women clustered around her, giggling, and she let herself be dressed by them in the local fashion: a small goatskin apron covered her sex, while a wire necklace acknowledged her status as a married woman. Finally they pressed upon her a short, cloaklike garment, which, she gathered, would prove useful as they approached the great body of water her husband had told her about: a lake the size of a sea, so large that you could not see across it, even from the highest of the surrounding hills. Akhilleus had said the morning fogs around the lake would test her ability to live as the locals did. Very well, she'd dress as they dressed—and it appeared that the local women, at least, weren't above covering themselves against the morning chill.

Back at the campfire she showed off her newfound finery, to Akhilleus's amused delight. She was pleased to see that Akhilleus cut short Musuri's attempts to tease her. He was, from the look of him, actually proud of her appearance and of her accommodation to local custom. And that night, in the shelter the local people provided for them, his embrace was that of a man half his age, vigorous and proud.

In the night the assassin, restless, sat at the edge of the moonlit clearing, trying to make sense of the startling information he had come by that afternoon. *Akhilleus, son of a king!* he thought. *Can it be true? And Bukango his uncle? And we'll be here when the king dies and Ramogi has to establish his claim to supremacy. But what will happen when Ramogi finds out that Akhilleus's name is mentioned with that of his own?*

That's simple enough. When the truth comes out, Ramogi will want Akhilleus killed. Perhaps he'll try to do the killing himself. And what's to stop him, then, from killing the lot of us as well?

The assassin frowned, staring across at the improvised hut that housed Akhilleus and Ebana.

But what if Akhilleus were struck down by one of his own party—after Ramogi had learned of Akhilleus's real identity? And a message were then sent to Ramogi explaining that the killing of Akhilleus, the usurper, had been done as a token of fealty to the new, legitimate, king, Ramogi? Perhaps to spare Ramogi the task of soiling his own hands with a kinsman's blood?

Yes . . . it might work. But first Ramogi had to learn who Akhilleus really was. Then, with the motive for the assassination known, and, with it, the advantage to Ramogi of having the work done by a loyal volunteer, so that his own name need never be linked to the murder . . .

The assassin smiled, as his fingers played idly with the knife at his side.

II

Bukango, like his father, Lokosa, had been born in the same Kigezi foothills Akhilleus had roamed as a boy. Yet when he came to rule he had moved his capital to a site midway between the two great mountain ranges, in territory that was home to none of the contending, warlike tribes Lokosa had unified to form the great nation Bukango now ruled.

Akhilleus, marching through the approaches to the king's territory, saw the logic of it: Effective management of the unified nation must depend on striking a balance between the opposing tribes, favoring none and accommodating all. If this neutrality was strictly observed, Bukango could rule with a lighter hand than Lokosa had employed in subduing the intertribal antagonisms of half a century ago.

The very fact that Bukango had allowed the unified tribes to remain intact—each with its own ruler subordinate to only himself, Bukango—meant, however, that the old king's successor would not find automatic approval by the tribes, but would have to establish his sovereignty to the satisfaction of all if he were to rule without overt dissention or even civil war.

Akhilleus saw evidence of this on all sides as his party drew closer to the capital. A general migration was in progress. Each of the tribes, it appeared, was sending a large, heavily armed delegation to the capital to assure that its own interests would be adequately represented in the coming transfer of power. Ramogi, Akhilleus felt sure, would have his hands full in the next few days, and no doubt would have to earn any power he assumed.

But that was as it should be, Akhilleus thought. The alliance Lokosa had forged, so many years ago, had to be confirmed by the will of the people, first by Magimbi and then by Bukango. It was proper that the people should have some voice in the choosing of a successor, who through all of his reign would have to adjudicate border disputes between the tribes. And, from what little Akhilleus could glean from Kimala, it was apparent that there was still bad blood between the hill tribesmen of the Kigezi and the Karamojong.

Indeed, considering the two tribes' long-standing bitterness, it had been a miracle that Lokosa, a man raised among the Kigezi tribes, should have been accepted by the Karamojong, as well as by the tribesmen who dwelt in the plains between the high mountains. But accepted he had been, and both of his sons had learned from his example, forgetting their own tribal prejudices in the service of unification, and ruling with justice over all the tribes. For nearly two generations, this impartial policy had kept intact a kingdom larger and more complex than any ever seen on the shores of the Great Lake.

Still, the miracle Lokosa had wrought and his sons

had preserved remained, many years later, a fragile and delicate construction, capable of splitting apart on the smallest pretext. It would, Akhilleus knew, take a man of the stature of these three to keep the confederation together on Bukango's death. Yet . . . what was there in the tone of voice of Kimala and his men that suggested Ramogi might not be viewed in this light by the tribes?

It was, he realized, something he could not, at least not yet, discuss openly and directly with Kimala. So far Kimala had been friendly and respectful—but detached, circumspect, keeping his own counsel. From the others in Kimala's party he had learned that Kimala himself was a prince of one of the lake tribes, but had disobeyed his father's wishes in order to seek employ in Ramogi's armies. Kimala had given as his reason a desire to learn the arts of war and the skills required to lead men, but his father had not understood or forgiven him. A virtual exile in his own lands, he was now, for all purposes, a man without a homeland, his only responsibilities being to Ramogi, who paid his wages, and to the loyal troops who served under him.

This much Akhilleus had managed to piece together. But there was more to Kimala than met the eye. He was, Akhilleus had decided, a most unusual young man, one with intelligence and maturity beyond his apparent years.

Now, however, Akhilleus's thoughts began to turn toward Ramogi, the more so as, approaching the capital, the expedition found itself stopped time after time by armed elements of Ramogi's guard, men who scrutinized every visitor wishing to penetrate the virtual wall of defense Ramogi had thrown around Bukango's capital.

After one particularly formal challenge-and-answer, Akhilleus drew alongside Kimala as they passed the massed troops whose armed might had enforced the challenge. "We're getting close, aren't we?" he said. "They had the look of an elite guard, if I'm any judge."

Kimala chuckled at this. "Elite, indeed," he said. "They were members of Bukango's personal bodyguard. We are now inside Bukango's realm, where, in time of unrest, nobody but the townspeople and the tribal chieftains are allowed. I remain astonished, Akillu, that you are

welcomed at such a time. As you well know, we may be
present at a transfer of power; Bukango, from what I hear,
is only days, perhaps hours, from the time when he must
join his fathers. It is not the custom to welcome outsiders
at such a time. The choice of the successor to the dead
king"—he used the word *kabaka*, which brought a sudden
twinge of recognition to Akhilleus, who had often heard
the word in his forgotten youth—"is seldom done publicly,
before those not of our tribes." His voice lingered on the
words "not of our tribes," and his gaze seemed to bore
into Akhilleus.

"I am, of course, honored beyond my poor deserts,"
Akhilleus said.

Kimala did not miss the irony in the black giant's
words. "I had thought of suggesting that I attend you as
translator when you had your audience with Bukango," he
said, "but I see now that my services in that regard would
be unnecessary. Although my wish still is to attend you
when you meet with our *kabaka* for the first time, Akillu,
I think I will keep silent, unless I am asked to speak. I
think I shall learn more that way."

"One should, of course, study the world about him as
though he were going to live forever," Akhilleus said,
appreciatively. "Look, here comes yet another guard to
bar our way. This one seems to have quite a welcoming
committee with him."

Kimala halted their progress and, waving Akhilleus
back, advanced to converse in low, terse words with the
guard. They were at the outskirts of a village, and a press
of curious onlookers soon surrounded Akhilleus and his
companions.

When Kimala returned to Akhilleus's side, he said,
"The guard would know whom to announce when we
approach Bukango, Akillu. How would you prefer that I
describe you?"

Akhilleus had not anticipated this moment. His heart
beating wildly all of a sudden, he turned and looked back
at Musuri and Ebana, at the spreading crowd that had
begun to surround them on three sides. He turned his
back to Kimala, and taking a deep breath and throwing
back his great shoulders, he spoke in a steady, clear voice.

"Tell the great *kabaka* Bukango," he said, "that there attends upon his pleasure his loyal and respectful kinsman Mtebi, son of Magimbi, grandson to Lokosa, beloved by all and greatest of kings in the Land Between the Mountains."

The crowd hesitated a moment, then began to back uneasily away, as if this stranger's words had the power to harm them. Even Kimala was visibly shaken.

Akhilleus knew he could not turn back. "Tell him, Kimala," he said, "tell him Mtebi, son of Magimbi, has returned from a long and arduous journey in foreign lands, and now asks to be allowed to pay his humble and affectionate respects to his father's brother."

Memory, which had come back to Akhilleus slowly at first, returned to him now in a flood of unassimilable sights and smells and impressions as he neared the kraal of the great king. At first the assault on his senses was so total that there was no room for thought or analysis in his overcrowded mind. But then the answer to his unspoken question came to him in a flash of insight. *Of course! The land changes, and the landmarks. Many years have come and gone. But the home kraal of the great kabaka would have been purposely maintained without change, each straw-thatched hut replaced as it began to show signs of age, so that all would remain new and fresh, betraying no hint of impermanence. And, yes, I would know it better than the rest of the land. After all, I'd spent most of my childhood in this compound, as the only son of a great king.*

They had taken away his personal weapon at the entrance to the compound. Now, alone and naked and feeling totally vulnerable, he was at last ushered into the darkened hut of the *kabaka* Bukango. To his back and sides stood lean, long-muscled young warriors, fearfully armed and almost as tall as he. And to his left—it could only be Ramogi, son of Bukango. In the center of the hut, however, the throne stood empty.

Akhilleus turned to the heir apparent with a questioning glance, taking in the downward slant of the cruel lips, the watchful eyes with their wide-open glare.

Scowling, Ramogi stepped aside, and there behind him, against the wall on a fur-cushioned pallet, lay Bukango.

Akhilleus, his movements slow and deliberate, bowed low, and, when he rose, caught his first clear look at his uncle.

The greatest shock was the man's apparent age. He was shrunken, wizened, as ancient as the hills. The wrinkles in his face were so clustered together as to erase all expression from his countenance. The aged hands rested immobile in his lap. Only the eyes moved, to examine Akhilleus, to look him up and down . . . and to return their gaze once again to his face. The wrinkled lips quivered; the counselor at his head bent and put his ear to the old man's mouth. Then the counselor stood again. He said, "The great *kabaka* would have all leave him. All but the stranger who calls himself Mtebi."

His words provoked a commotion. Ramogi at first refused to leave. Only a reiteration of the dying man's words could get him to comply. And when he finally left, trailing a string of heavily armed retainers, it was with a hot glance of rage at Akhilleus—who nonetheless bowed respectfully, to usher him out.

The counselor departed, and Akhilleus was left alone with the aged king. Bukango's fingers moved, beckoning him closer with movements of such economy that Akhilleus could barely recognize their meaning. He knelt by the side of his father's brother, their two faces hardly more than a handspan apart.

Bukango spoke. The effort involved in making coherent sentences was evident, but the quavery old voice was clear, however weak it might sound. "At last," he said, "the son of my brother returns." Akhilleus nodded. "Yes. Yes, I can see Magimbi's features in your face. He never lived to your age, you know." The parched lips pursed and spoke again. "I have dreamed of this day. For a long time, many years, I lived in fear of the day Mtebi might return." But there was no tremor in the old voice as he spoke. "Now . . . now I do not fear you. What can you bring me, son of my brother, whom I wronged so—what can you bring me but the death I now await with more than a trace of impatience?"

Akhilleus smiled. "I bring nothing but friendship, kinsman. And—forgiveness, if that is what you want."

"Forgiveness?" The old lips seemed almost to smile for a moment. "Yes, forgiveness. There has been much to forgive. But . . . it is good for kinsmen to make up quarrels before death parts them, I think. Yes. I accept your forgiveness—and give you the blessing of the king."

Akhilleus's mind raced. Blessing? But—that meant Bukango was leaving the kingdom to him, Akhilleus, didn't it? "My uncle," he said, "there is your son. He knows the tribes, knows their mind. I have spent my life in foreign climes. I do not know the ways of my own people, much less the other tribes Lokosa brought together under one rule so many years ago."

"My son," the old man said. "Yes, my son knows. But the peoples of the Land Between the Mountains also know my son. The kingdom built by Lokosa, and maintained by Magimbi and me—it would come apart in twenty pieces under Ramogi, undoing all we have done. No. I see you before me. And I see what it is I have to do before I die."

"But, Bukango—" Akhilleus began.

The withered fingers, feather-light, touched his arm. "Mtebi—I did not kill your father. He died of a fever. But . . . as he lay sick, dying, as I am now . . . I looked into my own mind, and I saw that if I did not do what I could to remove you, to put you as far as possible from Magimbi's side, the tribes would hail you king, for all your tender age—so powerful was his hold on them, so great was the love they bore him."

The aged throat grew dry; he waved the skeleton's hand at the water jug nearby. Gently, almost tenderly, Akhilleus helped the old man drink.

Then Bukango spoke again. "It is strange, Mtebi," he said. "If I had succeeded Magimbi naturally, I think I would have been a bad king. I was young and heedless. But . . . almost as soon as the slavers had abducted you at my bidding, I tried to get you back. I sent messengers after you. I scoured all the lands south of the dry Sudd—to no avail. You were gone, perhaps dead."

Akhilleus started to speak, but the dry old fingers waved him to silence. "Do not interrupt," Bukango said in a hoarse half-whisper. "I do not have long to speak with you. The hour of death is close—very close. Attend me, Mtebi."

Akhilleus nodded and leaned forward, hanging on every word. The old man continued:

"My sorrow at what I had done haunted me day and night. It did not leave me in peace until I made a pact with myself. I had, you see, removed from my people the son of my wise brother, who—for all I knew—would have reigned long and well over our people. All I could do to make up for my crime would be to try to reign as a wise and just man, as my brother had reigned—and as his son would have reigned. . . ." He smiled now, showing toothless gums. "As the man I can now see you became, in spite of all the sorrow I must have caused you." A tear glistened at the corner of the old man's eye and hung there. The weak hand touched Akhilleus's hand again, and the giant's big fingers closed gently around it. "Oh," the old man said, his voice breaking, "how fine you became. I'm so proud of you. . . ."

Akhilleus began a gruff denial, but thought better of it. He gave the bony old hand a squeeze.

Bukango tried twice to speak, and succeeded on a third attempt. "Perhaps . . ." he said, "perhaps there is some justice in our destinies, Mtebi. I did you ill, but the ill I did made me a better man than I began."

"Yes," Akhilleus said. "And if there is merit in me now, if I make you proud, it is the result of the life I have lived. I . . . I think I am a good man now, my uncle, a just man. I was not always so. I have often been a blackguard and a fool on the way to these gray hairs. Who knows? If I had lived the privileged life Magimbi planned for me, I might have remained a fool and a knave. And the people might have suffered much at my hands. It is past time for sorrow at our folly, my uncle. I think that both of us, you and I, served the will of whatever gods there may be—yes, and served the people as well; you by your presence, I by my absence."

Bukango's eyes focused on his and drew him close. His voice was almost inaudible as he spoke. "The people," he said. "First, last, always, the people. . . ."

The words trailed off. And the aged hand in Akhilleus's went suddenly limp. When the finality of the king's last words had sunk in, Akhilleus reached over with a gesture of great tenderness and closed the old man's eyes.

They found the two of them there, the old man's inert hand still in Akhilleus's large one. Akhilleus's eyes were full of tears and his face was blank. He did not notice even the white-hot anger on Ramogi's twisted face as the counselors gently motioned him away and laid out the body of the old monarch. In a daze, Akhilleus let himself be led away, back to his party at the kraal's entrance. One thought alone drove all others from his stunned mind: He had a decision to make—perhaps the hardest he'd ever had to make in his long and adventurous life. And it had to be made now.

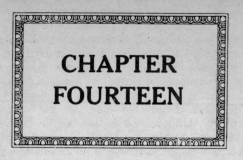

CHAPTER FOURTEEN

OUTSIDE MEMPHIS

I

The dust from the returning chariots of the Egyptian rearguard had obscured the view to the west for some time, but at last the choking cloud of grit had swirled past, whipped up and dispersed by the prevailing river wind.

"Is that the last of them?" Baka bellowed up the line. There was no answer for a moment; impatient, he raised his voice again. "Curse you, answer me when I ask a question!"

One of the under-officers, covered from head to foot with the reddish-brown dust of the desert, came forward. "Sorry, sir. We were just checking the—"

"No excuses!" Baka said. "Don't make me give an order twice. The next person who does will find himself two steps lower in rank when pay time comes around. Now, are they all in? Is that the last of them?"

"Yes, sir!" cried another officer up the line. "All in and accounted for!"

"Good," Baka said. "Close ranks, then. From now on nobody makes it through the line!" His voice, strong and authoritative, carried well in the open air. "Here we stand. We've given them more than I wanted to give them, but when the front line broke it did away with all chance of our holding Memphis."

He climbed atop a rock so that all the troops nearby could see him. "I mean no disrespect to Unas," he said sharply. "He was a gallant soldier and died a fine death. The name of the man who slew Vahan will be long remembered. And the orderly retreat we have just completed was masterfully planned—no one knows it better than I, who have had to execute it. All honor to Unas's name. *But*—" The suppressed anger was evident in Baka's voice, and the soldiers, looking up at him, could see the tension in his wiry body as he spoke. "But let us not forget that we gave ground here. That we left our home city undefended, for barbarians to pillage!"

He wiped the sweat and grit from his brow, and, pausing, took note of the downcast faces of the men massed before him. "Egypt has been shamed!" he shouted at the pitch of his lungs. "Shamed by barbarians!"

He paused to regain his breath. Then, with an angry shake of his head, he mastered himself and went on. "Hear me," he said. "I had to abandon a city once, in the delta, in order to preserve a command broken in half by a Shepherd attack. From behind new lines, I could hear the voices of the injured, the dying. I heard the voices of women raped and then put to the sword. I heard the cries of children murdered by the Shepherds—for sport. It was all I could do to keep myself, and my men, from breaking ranks and going into the city to save them. But if I had weakened then, or if my men had disobeyed my order to hold fast, the Shepherds would have had the whole delta a year sooner—and I would not be here leading you now."

Again he paused, as a gust of wind carried his last words away into the desert silence. "I tell you this because I know, because I understand, what you'll be thinking when you look down the river toward Memphis. That is why I am issuing the order for a squad of bowmen to be on the line during the night. Any soldier who breaks ranks and tries to make it into the city after dark will be shot on the spot. There will be no exceptions. I don't care if it's relatives or friends you think you'll be saving. All you'd be doing would be adding one more death to the total—your own."

An angry soldier shouted from the rear ranks. "But what can we do? When we know what the bastards will—"

"Do?" Baka said, a cold, sharp edge in his voice. "Harden yourself, my friend. Tell yourself that when revenge comes, you'll be there. Remind yourself that this is a debt that will be repaid, and with interest. For I tell you, as sure as I stand here: For every civilian who dies tonight in Memphis, two Shepherd heads will fall, and before the next flood of the Nile. Because—and remember this, every one of you—the only reason for retreating is to fight again on the morrow, on terms advantageous to yourself. That's why we're where we are."

"On the morrow?" someone said, and there was a low murmur among the men. "You mean we attack tomorrow?"

Baka's eyes narrowed. "No," he said, his voice lower. "Tomorrow the Shepherds will be finishing the ugly job they have begun tonight. Most likely the next week and the day after they'll be idle, too. Then they'll come straggling back into camp still half drunk, their minds addled by the sport they'll have had. They'll deploy opposite our lines, confident in the knowledge that we're a bunch of cowards who won't hold fast to save our city, knowing we won't have the guts to attack them." He paused, and as he did, understanding began to dawn on the many faces arrayed before him.

"Yes," he said. "Only by this time we 'cowards' will be half again our present strength—I will see to that myself, when I have a chat with the dignitaries at court. *And* we'll be rested and lean and angry—and eager to feel our swords and axes bite into Shepherd necks!"

He let his words sink in, and saw the smiles spread across the upturned faces. The cheer that rose spontaneously from a hundred throats quickly spread down the lines. He waved his hand in an acknowledging salute, then jumped down from the rock. His eyes swept the small group of officers before him. "Menes!" he said in a voice meant for their ears alone. "Where's Menes, captain of the Sixth Infantry?"

"Here, sir," a tall young officer said, stepping forward.

"Good," Baka said. "Look, I've some work to do—back *there*." He jerked a thumb at the area behind his own lines. Menes understood this to mean the court, now safely installed at Lisht. "I need a reliable man, someone I can trust. I've heard good reports of you."

"Thank you, sir."

Baka took him by the arm and steered him away from the group. "Put your command in the hands of your assistant for now. Don't worry—it's highly unlikely that you'll miss any action as a result of this. The other side will be occupied pretty much as I described it to the men. I've been fighting the Shepherds for a long time now, and I know them."

"Yes, sir. But what are you—?"

Baka reached inside his garment and withdrew a rolled papyrus. "Here," he said. "Have a look at this. This is an order for the First and Third Regiments of the royal guard to join us on the lines."

Menes stared at his superior, making no move to open the scroll and read it. "B-but . . . sir! Harmin will never release—"

"Yes, he will," Baka said with a coldly confident smile. "There's more here than an order. There's a message, intended for Harmin's eyes alone. You can read it, but you won't understand it. Nobody but Harmin will. You see, it's something of a secret between us."

Menes looked perplexed. "Something, perhaps, that would upset the king?"

"Exactly. This is merely a reminder. And as you have guessed, it's information that would be extremely embarrassing to our great general. If he refuses me what I ask, he'll have only three alternatives: kill himself, have me assassinated—or face ruin."

"Ruin?"

"Beheading. Impalement. Whatever. And I'm not that easily assassinated, mind you. You see, after Harmin's cabal betrayed me to the Shepherds, I spent quite some time in a Shepherd dungeon. I think you don't want to know what *that's* like, my friend, yet—here I am. I may not be immortal, but I'm the next best thing. I take a great deal of killing."

"That fact will reassure me when I ride at your side, sir," the young officer said.

"Good," Baka said. "Now let me tell you what you've got to do. . . ."

By the time Anab and Tuya, still in the wake of the Shepherd army, reached the edge of Memphis at nightfall, the conquerors had been in the newly fallen city some four hours. With no armed resistance confronting them, the Shepherd soldiers had simply been let loose in the city to do as they pleased. Evidence of their passing was to be found even on the northern outskirts of the city: Bodies of the slain remained where they had fallen, and the normally timid jackals of the desert's edge had crept to the city's walls to feed on the fallen. As darkness came on apace, the glow in the southern sky indicated that fires had either broken out spontaneously from untended hearths or had been set by the boisterous, half-intoxicated marauders roaming the city.

Anab paused, looking up at the unguarded city walls and at the open, untended gate—a gate that had never, until now, been found ajar after dusk. "Tuya," he said, "I think we'd do well not to enter the city at all."

"I agree," the girl said. "I think it'll be a rare Egyptian who comes out of Memphis alive." She shuddered as someone screamed in the distance, and her eyes nervously scanned the top of the deserted wall. "As a matter of fact, the farther we stay away from the city, the better. What's out that way, I wonder?"

"I'm not sure. There's supposed to be some sort of temple complex—a temple to Ptah, I think. Memphis is sacred to Ptah—although, right now, it looks more like it's sacred to the jackal." He gnawed at his lip and unconsciously let his hand go to the sword at his side. "I bet it would be a good way to get past the city. We can keep the temples between us and the city walls." He looked up. "I don't know whether to thank the gods or curse them for giving us this much moon, though. We could easily be seen." He made a sour face. "I think we'd better find cover right away, before someone staggers to the top of the wall and spots us."

As they moved off toward the dark shadows of the temple complex, the screaming started again. This time they could make out some of the words. The voice was a woman's. *"No . . . please . . . please don't. No! No! No—"* The words were cut off suddenly. Then echoes of the same words—fainter but almost as clear—could be heard from two sides.

Tuya held her hands over her ears as she and Anab approached the tall, imposing outline of a massive building. Perhaps this was the temple to Ptah that Anab had spoken of. Its two visible faces were crowned with tall pylons and covered all over with intricate carvings. Beyond the temple's walls, a bulky, irregular shape loomed against the night sky. "Anab," she whispered, "what's that? It looks like a huge stone lion."

"It's a sphinx," he said. "On the plateau of the great pyramids, there's one just like it, but much, much bigger. Someone told me about it back in Avaris. The beard alone is supposed to be the height of a man standing on another man's shoulders. Back then, I wasn't sure whether to believe the man's story . . . but these people up in the Red Lands, they build things large." He took her hand, helping her over a gutter in the pathway for water runoff during the rainy season. "Someday, if the war ever ends, I'd like to come back and see all this, in broad daylight. I bet—"

He never finished the sentence. The bandits were upon them before they knew it, and only his quick reaction averted disaster. He sprang straight toward the three attackers, unsheathing his short-sword, swinging it wildly, and screaming like a demon from the netherworld. The three assailants, who were armed only with daggers, skidded to a halt and took to their heels.

Anab watched them disappear. Then he turned back to Tuya and, smiling, sheathed his sword with a flourish. But at that very moment, at least a dozen more desperate-looking men, drawn like vultures to Anab's screams, appeared from behind the sphinx.

"Anab—let's get out of here!" Tuya grabbed the sleeve

of his cloak, and one look back over his shoulder was all the urging Anab needed. They were both swift on their feet, and the ground around the temple complex, though mostly sand, was level and ideal for running. After putting on a sustained burst of speed and vaulting a low wall, they found themselves in a field of slope-sided mastabas. When they looked back, their ragged pursuers were far behind— though, for some reason, they had not given up the chase.

"Come on," Anab said, "let's see what's on the other side of this graveyard."

They trotted silently past row after orderly row of doorless, windowless tombs, each the same as the next. The cemetery seemed to stretch on forever—a veritable city of the dead, Tuya thought, as she followed Anab down the moonlit passageway. Finally, when they were nearly exhausted, their legs ready to give out, they emerged on the other side and stumbled to a halt.

Anab cursed. Straight ahead in the distance, and stretching left and right as far as the eye could see, was a line of torches. Within the circle of light cast by each of the widely spaced torches was an armed Shepherd sentry.

Anab and Tuya stared a long while at the disheartening sight. "It must be the main road from the river to the city," Anab said. "We'll never get past it. We'll have to head for the river—it's our only chance."

"But you're not a very good swimmer, Anab. What if we can't find a boat?"

"Do you have a better idea?"

"No. But we'd better do something—and fast." She didn't have to explain. Both of them could hear the shouts of their pursuers—drunken, from the sound of it—echoing faintly down the tomb-lined passageways.

"Follow me," Anab said. They reentered the mastaba field, jogging silently toward the last row of tombs on their right, on the side away from the city and nearest the river.

"Anab . . . wait." Tuya had stopped. She stood panting, facing one of the sloping tomb walls. She was crouched over, hands on knees, as though trying to gather her strength.

"What's the matter with—?" Anab began to say, but just then Tuya sprang at the wall, jumping up and clutching for a handhold in the smooth masonry surface. But there was none, and she slid back to the ground and collapsed on her backside with a silent curse.

Before Anab could say a word she was up again, ready for a second assault on the wall.

He stepped in front of her. "Here—let's try something else." He took her by the shoulders and spun her around, backing her gently but firmly against the wall.

"Anab—"

"Now, stay there and I'll climb up over you; then I'll pull you up."

The drunken shouts were getting closer, and Tuya knew they didn't have much time. Obediently she cupped her hands together, and Anab boosted himself up. In a moment he was standing unsteadily on her shoulders. The top of the wall, however, was still three feet beyond his reach.

"Help me up with your arms," he said.

Tuya did as he said, and, one foot at a time—the other foot using her head for support—he scrambled up. His short-sword clanked loudly—too loudly—against the stone. She could feel the callused soles of his feet in her palms. She had never realized Anab was so heavy. Her elbows began to shake, then buckle—but suddenly his feet were gone, and she heard a thump as he dropped over the wall and landed on the flat roof of the tomb.

"Tuya."

When she looked up, she saw his head pop back over the top of the wall. His naked shoulder and arm, dangling his robe down to her, quickly followed.

"Grab it," he said.

She jumped up, but could not reach the robe.

"It won't work," he said. "Toss yours up—quickly."

They could clearly hear the drunken curses now—and footsteps as well. Tuya slipped out of her garment in a flash and heaved it up to Anab, whispering a silent prayer for him to hurry. She didn't dare speak aloud.

After what seemed like the longest prayer she had ever said, the robes, now tied together, came back down. Instantly she grabbed them with both hands, and Anab pulled as she scrambled up the wall with her bare feet.

Her legs, exhausted from the long run, slipped and gave way once, but her hands held on . . . and finally she grabbed the top of the wall, Anab holding her by the shoulders. Her legs still dangled precariously over the edge.

The voices were nearly below them now.

Instead of falling to the roof, Tuya silently swiveled her body sideways on her stomach so that she lay along the top of the wall. She held her breath.

The voices and footsteps lingered for a moment, then passed on.

"That was close," she whispered to Anab, lowering herself the short distance to the roof. Anab, with his robe off, looked pale as a corpse. He lay back on the roof, still trying to catch his breath.

Tuya lay down beside him—and not until then was she conscious of her nakedness. But she was too relieved and too exhausted to care, or to do anything but lie there, gazing up at the stars.

A long time later, after their breathing slowed, they sat up and looked at each other, as if for the first time—their pale, skinny bodies could have been those of twins—and both began to laugh. Anab, with some difficulty, undid the knot he had tied in their garments, and they put them back on.

Only then did they hear the scratching.

Anab touched Tuya's arm and motioned her to keep silent. Crouching, he moved to the side of the roof where the noise was coming from. They both could hear it clearly now—a scraping, scratching sound, as if someone was trying to scale the wall, as Tuya had done earlier.

Anab slid his sword from its scabbard and cautiously peered over the edge of the wall. There was a long silence. Tuya moved closer.

"I don't believe it," she heard him whisper. He turned to her. "Tuya, you're never going to believe this."

"Anab—for the love of all the gods, what is it?"

"It's the dog. It's Lion."

II

By the steady light of the white-hot coals in the low fire before him, Ben-Hadad held up the sword he had just repaired, sighted along the blade, then reversed it to test its balance. He handed the weapon back to its owner.

"That ought to do," he said. "But next time you're in a fight with the Shepherds and you happen to see one of their weapons abandoned on the ground, grab it if you can. This sword is from an old lot and doesn't measure up to what your friends have been fighting with."

"No, sir," the soldier said. "I got this when my mess-mate died. It's from back before Shobai joined us."

"I suspected as much," Ben-Hadad said. "That would be . . . at least three years ago, wouldn't it?"

The soldier holstered his weapon. "Yes, sir. Not that we've seen a great deal of his work since. Unas—may his spirit find rest—said the palace guard was stealing most of the arms Shobai and his workers were making for us. Well, thank you, sir. I'll be getting back to my unit now." He saluted—more in tribute to Ben-Hadad's expertise than anything else—and disappeared into the row of tents.

Ben-Hadad shook his head as he watched him go. *What a sad, pitiful army!* he thought. Undercut on all sides by the court, their weapons stolen to outfit pampered royal bodyguards, betrayed again and again by their own supreme commander, Harmin—yet somehow managing to hold the line against the vastly superior Shepherd force despite all obstacles, drawing on their own individual courage and stamina and on the native shrewdness of their line officers. Pitiful? he thought, chiding himself. Why, they're heroes, every one of them—for all that they haven't the slightest notion that that's what they are.

Shaking his head to himself, Ben-Hadad picked up one of the many sword-blanks stacked against the forge and buried its blade-end in the coals. Then, not bothering to search for his assistant, he applied himself to the hand bellows, pumping with the steady rhythm of long practice.

Perhaps Baka, he thought, having returned to the army, could make some changes. Perhaps he could get the court off the army's back and ensure a steadier flow of weapons and rations—and maybe even pressure the court into levying a draft on the spoiled sons of the upper classes. In fact, he had talked of going to Lisht personally for just this purpose. And for all Ben-Hadad could see, there was no better source of reinforcements. Certainly there was no doubt that every able-bodied man was needed on the painfully thin front lines these days.

He had heard talk of an expedition led by a black man—a former galley slave, at that—which was supposed to seek out new troops—mercenaries—and perhaps even new sources of ore and other supplies. But it would reportedly be quite a while before they returned. From all the soldiers had told him, it would appear that this Nubian, Akhilleus, had been a friend of Unas's and was an exceptionally able sort.

Ben-Hadad paused in his labor, wiped his sweaty brow, and glanced over at the coals. He resumed pumping the bellows.

It was strange, but he, Ben-Hadad, also seemed to have a tenuous link to the black man. According to talk around the camp, during his years on the galleys Akhilleus had become close friends with Ben-Hadad's grandfather, Kirta of Haran—and had for many years since been a staunch friend and protector of the blind Shobai. It had been on Akhilleus's own boat that Shobai had confronted the evil Reshef—the man who had blinded him and murdered Ben-Hadad's father, Shobai's brother, Hadad. And the arrow that had killed Reshef, it was said, had come from a bow wielded by Mereet. And *she* had been trained to shoot years before, by Baka!

Thoughts that paired Shobai and Baka abruptly sobered and saddened Ben-Hadad. He let go of the bellows, snatched up his tongs and hammer, and quickly pulled the glowing bronze sword-blank from the coals. He gripped his hammer . . . but did not strike. *Baka has a sword like this*, he thought. His expression darkened and he lowered the hammer, no longer able to concentrate on his work.

Now that the Shepherds showed no immediate sign of pressing farther south, and Baka planned to leave for Lisht on official business, he might be tempted to seek out Shobai. Ben-Hadad frowned. If only he could somehow head off a deadly confrontation between the two of them! If only he could in some way soothe Baka's vengeful and unforgiving spirit!

He pushed the sword-blank back into the coals and put down the tongs.

Having talked with the soldiers, Ben-Hadad could see in what respect both men were held by the army: Baka the austere, totally dedicated soldier, who'd almost single-handedly held together the threadbare, fading delta forces, right up to the moment when, betrayed by traitors on his own side, he'd been captured and imprisoned by the enemy; and Shobai, the gentle giant who towered a whole head above the Egyptian troops he had never seen but whom he'd helped to arm: unsparing of himself, totally committed to the war against the invader, always ready to turn out at any hour to help the defenders' cause. Why did these two men have to find themselves on a deadly collision course, one that could have only one tragic result?

He thought of Shobai. How wonderful it would be to meet his uncle! Only Baka's own name elicited more admiration among the army forces. You could hardly find another soul—Baka always excepted—to speak an unkind word about the blind armorer. Many, so very many, of them turned out to owe the blind man a favor . . . and all had good words to say about Shobai's courage. On one occasion, for instance, Shobai's visit to the lines had coincided with a sneak Shepherd attack. The officers, caught in a rain of Shepherd arrows, had ordered Shobai to the rear, but he had refused. The soldiers said he had gone about his work as calmly as if nothing at all were happening, with Shepherd arrows whizzing about him. Most important, he had done so—deliberately, some said—in the presence of green, unfledged soldiers ready to break and run. His quiet valor had put new heart into them, and they had rallied to throw back the Shepherd advance, inflicting heavy enemy losses.

How fine it will be, meeting him! he thought. Half unconsciously, he let his hand stray to the spot on his lower back where he, like all Children of the Lion, bore the wine-red birthmark shaped like the paw print of a lion. He'd only once in his young life met anyone else who bore the strange and magical mark: his grandfather Kirta, whom he'd only come to know in the last moments of the older man's life. Before then, Hashum, his brutal stepfather, had kept him ignorant of the true nature of his family traditions, until Jacob had at last told him just who he was, what line he had come from. Even now he knew only a little more than what Jacob had told him. When he met Shobai, however, all that would change.

If he met Shobai.

His hands balled into fists. He'd have to do something, and now, before Baka acted precipitately. Baka's wrath *had* to be turned aside. And he, Ben-Hadad, was the only one who could do it.

He stood erect, his back stiff and straight, his mind made up. Yes—he'd go to Baka right now, and say what he had to say. He'd do whatever it took to turn Baka back from his deadly course of action.

Grimly, but full of a fierce resolve, he laid down his hammer and set out for the long line of tents and campfires, his steps unwavering and his heart beating fast.

On his way to Baka's tent, Ben-Hadad ran into one of the headquarters aides and learned, to his dismay, that Baka was apparently preparing to leave camp, since he had ordered a horse to be readied for him after the evening muster.

Now, coming down the long line of campfires at a rapid pace, Ben-Hadad nodded at a sentry on lookout duty and received a deferential salute in return; the smith's status had not yet been decided upon, but he was known to have the ear of Baka, the new commander. Not to be delayed, Ben-Hadad was about to hurry past the man when the sentry's partner, posted on an archer's fire step, called out in a loud whisper: "Hey! There's somebody out there!"

Ben-Hadad paused and shot the sentry's partner a worried glance. He said nothing, but quickly realized he was expected to respond in some way. He approached the fire step. "How many?" he whispered.

"Two, it looks like. They're coming up the slope." He

reached back into his quiver for an arrow. "Strange. They don't look like Shepherds."

Ben-Hadad turned to go for help, then hesitated. He could not have said why, but something—some sense he could not identify—seemed to want him to pause. "Wait," he said. "Let me have a look."

I'm probably being a fool, he thought, *meddling like this.* But the instinct was strong, and he obeyed it. He mounted the fire step, and looked over the earthen rampart . . .

. . . to find himself suddenly staring at the crouching but unmistakable silhouette of Anab! He blinked, straining his eyes in the dark, and his gaze went to the second person crawling up the slope. *"Tuya!"* he said.

The two stood—and as they did, a pair of low, lithe shapes struck from the darkness: jackals, male and mate, skinny, bright-eyed, sharp-toothed. One nipped Anab in the arm. He kicked it away, the animal emitting a yelp of pain, and Ben-Hadad could see, in the dim moonlight, the bright blood on Anab's forearm. "Quick!" Ben-Hadad said, holding out his hand to Anab.

But as he did, he could see past his friend to where Tuya, waving a knife, was holding off the jackal's mate. And in the darkness beside her another pair of eyes glowed.

As soon as Anab slid over the bank to safety, Ben-Hadad scrambled to the top of the rampart, his own sword out. He let out a bellow, intending to distract the jackal, but the animal, ignoring him, crouched, preparing to dive at Tuya again. Ben-Hadad rushed toward her, cursing his sluggard legs for moving so slowly—

—and now the other creature, the third one, launched itself out of the darkness—but at the jackal's throat! It caught the predator by the neck and bowled it over sideways, then hung on tenaciously as the two of them rolled. The first jackal had circled back, though, and suddenly it sprang at the intruder.

"Lion!" Ben-Hadad said. He made for the tussling animals, but it was Tuya who reached them first. Her knife flashed in the moonlight, once, twice, and came up bloody the second time. The jackal's mate dashed off with a whimper of pain. Again the knife flashed, and this time struck home in the belly of the other animal. The jackal grunted and fell asprawl, taking with him Lion, whose teeth were still sunk in the scavenger's throat.

Ben-Hadad grabbed her by the arm. "Tuya," he said, "get back to the trench!" And with his own blade he dispatched the jackal. Only then did Lion's grip relax, and the little dog stepped back, sniffing the air cautiously. "Come on, Lion!" Ben-Hadad said. His own eyes, adjusted to the darkness by now, scanned the area for further trouble. Finding none, he dashed back up the incline, Lion at his heels, to jump over the rampart into the welcoming arms of his friends.

Reunion was sweet—as sweet as anything Ben-Hadad had ever experienced. He heard out their adventures, and recounted his own, sitting at the fireside opposite Anab, one hand holding Tuya's while his other stroked the short hair on Lion's shaggy head. "I can't believe my good fortune," he said. "I'd have beggared myself for the mere sight of any of you, and here I find all three of you. And Baka was asking about you, too. Just the other day I was telling him that—"

He stopped in midsentence, and a crestfallen expression appeared on his face. "Good heavens, I was just on my way to find Baka. I have to stop him from going back to the Fayum to kill my uncle!"

"Your uncle?" Tuya said. "You mean Shobai? But you said Baka had taken the command here when Unas died."

"He did. But, Tuya, you don't know how obsessed he is with Shobai. He said that the only thing that kept him alive back in the Shepherd prison was the thought of killing Shobai. Tuya, I *have* to stop him, and not just for Shobai's sake, but for his own. You don't know Baka the way I've come to know him. If he murders a just and blameless man in cold blood, it'll weigh on his heart forever after. It will break him, sooner or later.

"Anab, brave comrade and staunch friend, I can't thank you enough for protecting Tuya for me. If you could take care of her for only another few moments, I have to go talk to Baka." He bent down to kiss Tuya's hand; then he saluted them all affectionately and set out down the line again, Lion at his heels.

But when he reached Baka's headquarters he found a subordinate in command. "Baka," he said, mounting terror clutching at his heart. "Where's Baka?"

"Why, he left for Lisht hours ago," the officer said. "Soon after sunset."

"Just Lisht?" Ben-Hadad said. "Did he speak of going anywhere else?"

"Yes. And it's odd that you mention it now, because I was wondering about it myself. He said that . . ."

At the soldier's brief pause, Ben-Hadad held his breath, waiting for the fateful words. And sure enough, they came.

". . . that first he had urgent business in the Fayum."

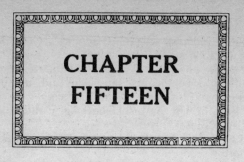

CHAPTER FIFTEEN

CENTRAL AFRICA

I

Standing atop a promontory bare of all but the green grass underfoot and occasional patches of tall brown grass that rustled in the breeze, Ebana looked out over the hazy blue of the Great Lake below, with its green islands and distant shorelines. "What are those black spots down near the shore?" she said. "They seem to be moving."

"They are," Musuri said. "A herd of hippopotamus. Apparently they're a bit of a pest here, as they are back in the delta. They tear up the nets of the fishing tribes who work the shoreline of the lake."

Ebana squinted down at them through the mist that hung over the water, despite the bright sunshine and gentle breeze above. "Back in the delta . . ." she said, echoing Musuri's words. "I wonder if we'll ever see it again." She turned to look at the old soldier. "I wish I knew what was happening. Can't you ask?"

"I could," Musuri said. "And I could come back with the same answer they've given me the last three times running." He yawned—but she was not fooled; she saw the wary glint in the Moabite's eye. "I'm as much in the dark as you are. Of us all, the only one who knows both their language and ours—*and* can be trusted—is Akhilleus. And he's still jabbering with Kimala and the chiefs of the Banyankole, Batoro, and Basoga tribes, among others. I'd wager that Ramogi would like to know what they are discussing with Akhilleus." He made a grim face. "They are not the ones I'm worried about, however. Last time I had a chance to talk to Akhilleus, he said Ramogi had the full support of the Karamojong and the Acholi—two of the largest tribes in the entire kingdom."

"Then there's a good chance Ramogi will indeed succeed his father," Ebana said. "I gather that's trouble for us. Ramogi isn't going to want a pretender around, watching him go about his work, is he?"

Musuri gazed down at the lake. "No. If he wins, I'd just as soon be far away from here. But . . . the swing vote appears to be the largest of the lake tribes—and they're Kimala's people. Unfortunately, Kimala's father threw him out a long time ago, when he went to work for Ramogi."

Ebana looked at him, sighed, and tried to quell the panic growing in her heart. "Why did we ever come south?" she said. "I mean, we could have turned back after enlisting my own people, at Kerma. Now we are heaven knows how many days' march from anything I'd recognize as civilized, totally at the mercy of our enemies, and—"

"Now, stop that," Musuri said. "You're sounding like a fishwife, not like the widow of a great soldier or the consort of the wisest and ablest man I ever worked for. Where's the Ebana I used to know?"

"I don't know," she said. "I used to think I could handle any predicament I found myself in, but now I'm not so sure." Her brows lowered in puzzlement. "Strangely enough, the more confused *I* get, the more confident Akhilleus seems to be."

"The obvious answer is that he knows something we don't," Musuri said. "I'm inclined to trust his instincts, Ebana—more now than ever before. I've never seen him so completely in his own element, and I've been with him for many years, ever since our first meeting in Tyre. I think he knows what he's doing." His voice, however, took on a more wistful tone as he added, "I only wish I knew what that was."

Obote, chieftain of Basoga, easternmost of the lake tribes, had remained silent while the others spoke. Now he raised his voice for the first time. "You have spoken of the right to reign. It would appear that both sides have their adherents, both among us and among the other tribes. It is time to speak of the probable results. What kind of king would Mtebi make? What kind of king would we have in Ramogi?"

A buzz of comment went around the circle of men. Chief Mutesa, of the Banyankole, angrily snapped, "You know what kind of king we would have in Ramogi! His foot already lies heavy on the necks of the tribes. Remember what happened to your own cousin's son! The fine levied on him took half his herds! And for what? For disputing hunting rights with the Bagwere . . . who, I might remind you, always win in such a dispute when Ramogi is arbiter. Small surprise, when his wife of wives is of the Bagwere!"

"Calm yourself," Obote said. "I remember with great clarity all you refer to. This is what we would have with Ramogi at the head of all the tribes between the mountains. What we do not know is what the alternative would be." He stared cold-eyed at Akhilleus, his face expressionless. "Of the man who claims to have returned to the tribe, who calls himself Mtebi, we know nothing."

Mutesa spoke again. "We know he speaks as one who once knew the land and the people of our fathers."

"He could have been taught to speak thus," said Ngo, called the Leopard, chieftain of the Bunyoro. "Anyone can repeat what someone has told him to say."

At this there were shouts of agreement from the chieftains at the far end of the group. "Yes! Yes!" But these gave way suddenly as Kimala stood and, eyes blazing, glared around the circle of much older faces.

"You all know me," he said. "Kimala, son of Kavuma, chieftain of the Baganda who dwell by the shores of the Great Lake. I speak as a prince of the Baganda, for all that my father and I parted our ways some years ago. I have lived for many years with the army of Ramogi, learned what a man can learn only by being of no tribe. And this I have come to know: that the confederation the great Lokosa put together in the days of our grandfathers is a great house made of strong ingredients—but held together with mud and spittle. It could come apart in a moment, and we could be at one another's throats, killing, burning, destroying, as we were for so many generations before Lokosa brought us together. Now we are peaceful and prosperous and live along one another's borders as neighbors. But how much longer will this last?"

Kintu of the Batoro broke in angrily. "Tell the puppy to sit down and stop haranguing his elders!" he said, only to be shouted down by the others. Kimala looked around him and saw curiosity and, in many cases, approval.

"I make no claim to wisdom," he continued, "but neither will I deny what I have learned. I tell you only what experience has told me. The man who holds this confederation together will not be a hotheaded youth, full of passions. He will be a mature man who has passed beyond these tempers—or who has never been a slave to them in the first place. And think of this: I alone among you have traveled with both Mtebi—whom you see here— and Ramogi, whom I have served for two bond terms. My last bond term ended a year ago, yet I have continued to travel with Ramogi, of my own accord and without obligation. I have seen his cruelty grow, fed by his ambition—and by the fact that of all the tribes, there was none to say no to him."

This prompted an outpouring of dissent and denial. Kimala tried to continue, but could not make himself heard above the others. Finally, Obote's strong old voice cut through the din. "He speaks correctly!" he shouted. "The young prince of the Baganda speaks the truth! We have all let Ramogi's power grow out of hand! All of us—even I myself! So have you, Kintu—and you, Mutesa! We have let him grow in his cruelty, just for the sake of maintaining order! We have become prosperous, as the young prince says—but we have also become fat and lazy. We have left the judging of border disputes to Ramogi— and he has dealt harshly with the people we ourselves were born to govern. Too harshly! He grows too strong, too arrogant!" Obote's eyes flashed angrily as he spoke; his words bit like the pincers of fire ants, and his listeners hung their heads in silent recognition.

"And what happens when we make this arrogant young hothead the great *kabaka* of all the lands between the mountains?" he said. "Whose hand will then prevail against him, rein in his cruelty?" He let his eyes go from face to face, and not one would gainsay him. "Very well. Let us now speak of another choice—this man who calls himself Mtebi, son of Magimbi. Should we believe him, and if so, on the strength of what? His own word? Or a tall tale told us by one of Bukango's retainers, who eavesdropped on the conversation between the foreigner and our *kabaka*? How are we to know that the retainer was not bribed by the stranger to say what he said?" There was sudden and angry rejoinder from several of the chieftains at once, each trying to speak.

Obote held up his hand. "Peace! I say this because more than one of you has said it to me beforehand. But this retainer I, Obote, happen to know well. The one who told the tale is the man call Nkima, and it was he whom my father gave to Bukango as a gift on the day of his accession. Nkima was Bukango's shadow for five times ten years, waiting on the old man hand and foot. I would myself stake my life on his word. If he says he heard something, he heard it."

Another clamor of voices arose. "Attend," said Obote, holding up his hand. "I anticipate your objections: Even if Nkima told the truth about what he heard, what if Bukango was not of sound mind at the time? This is what you are thinking, is it not?" He looked around and saw agreement on the faces of those who had spoken. "Look, my friends," the old man said. "I myself—I, Obote—spoke with Bukango the morning before his death. I had never seen him more clear, more acute. He gave me advice on how to settle a dispute between the sons of my brother, and without acrimony. I will unhesitatingly put his advice into practice the moment I am back in the land of the Basoga."

Kintu of the Batoro raised his hand for recognition. "Do I then understand that the lord of the Basoga suggests we abandon our personal claims to the throne of Bukango? That we should abandon our search for a just and able man to lead us, and instead hand over leadership of the tribes to a stranger?" A chorus of voices broke in; he waited for them to cease. "I'll grant you the stranger may be of the blood of Lokosa. And he may be an able man. But—"

This precipitated a veritable babel, as every one of the chieftains began to speak at once. Obote tried to silence them, but their shouts were too loud and too insistent. "Please, my friends!" he said, raising his voice. "This is no time for—"

But then, to everyone's surprise, the one person around the circle who had been silent from the first rose and bowed with dignity to them all. The voices trailed off, became silent.

Akhilleus inclined his head in respectful deference to the assembled chiefs—and, some noticed, to Kimala as well—and spoke in a low voice with little trace of accent, halting occasionally on a word he had to reach for. Every eye was on him.

"Obote of the Basoga, lord of the eastern lake tribes. Kintu of the Batoro, in whose mountainous realm I spent some of the happiest days of my childhood. Ngo, fierce leopard of the Bunyoro, whose tribe's valor was legendary in my father's time. Kimala, wise and judicious young prince of the great Baganda. And, perhaps last, but in no man's heart least, great Mutesa of the Banyankole, blood brother of my father, famous for the hospitality of your ancient house. Hear me, lords of the Land Between the Mountains. To each man is my house beholden. I, Mtebi, son of Magimbi, honor you all, and bring to you the greetings of the mighty pharaoh of Egypt, a great king whose emissary I am."

There was a low murmur of interest. It was obvious that some of the fiercest among them, at least, were mollified by Akhilleus's unassuming and respectful tone. Obote's eyebrows raised and lowered, and he exchanged glances with Ngo as he sat down, prepared to listen for a change.

"Thank you, my great and noble lords," Akhilleus said. "You have all spoken, wisely and eloquently, on either side of the question regarding my lineage, my possible claim to the throne."

He put his hands together, and looked over their heads, trying to find the proper words. "When I was a child, I used to dream of returning here," he said softly. "Then there came a time—as often happens to a stranger captive in a strange land—when the dream faded, when I had to realize that I would probably never again see the blue lake, or the green mountains rising above it. Never again see the softly rolling hills of the Kigezi or the towering Mufumbiro. With much tears and suffering, I put these dear things from my heart—or at least I thought I had done so. For one never loses the longing in his heart for the land in which he was born."

He looked around him, his sharp eye missing nothing, his ear catching the low murmurs of assent and recognition.

"Shall I tell of my wandering, in the many years before I once again placed my foot on the sacred soil of the land of my fathers? Of the wonders I saw in places strange and terrible? Of the many peoples through whose realms I passed?"

Every eye was on him, agleam with interest. "Very well," he said. "In the end, the decision as to the succession of the throne of Bukango is yours. But for myself, I have already made my decision, based on all that I learned in my years of wandering. When I am done telling my tale, you will understand why I say what I say."

He caught several nods of agreement. Taking a deep breath, he went on, in the low, spellbinder's voice he had learned from Shobai during the armorer's years as an itinerant bard, after he had been blinded. "Very well. Attend, my lords. Far, far to the north we traveled, day after day, across mountain and plain, across desert and marsh, until even the stars in the skies above no longer fell into the same patterns I had known in my childhood. We passed through many strange and wondrous lands, until at last we reached the shores of a great sea. . . ."

In a dark, secluded hut far outside the walls of Bukango's city, three men stood silently, also listening to the tale of a stranger.

Ramogi, flanked by two armed men, stared unblinkingly. His face was as hard, as cold, as a carved ebony mask.

"Are you finished?" he said at last to the speaker, his voice rasping and toneless.

One of the armed men beside him, acting as a translator, relayed the question. The other armed man, Ramogi's adjutant, barked, "A likely story! I say that we kill—"

Ramogi's abrupt wave of the hand silenced him. "No," he said. "I think he is telling the truth. The stranger . . . he is indeed Mtebi, returned from the dead. I know it. I have felt it in my bones from the first moment a description of his party reached me. Besides, there is Nkima, who overheard Mtebi's conversation with my father. He would not lie. I know him well—he is too stupid to lie."

The stranger looked questioningly at Ramogi, waiting in vain for a translation.

"No," Ramogi said thoughtfully, "this man is telling the truth. I think he really was sent here to kill Mtebi. And will do so, too, if I let him."

The adjutant looked at the assassin with contempt in his eyes. "Then let him—and have done with it."

Ramogi smiled, but it was the cold smile of a predator. "I will," he said. "But it must be done with the greatest care. I must not look like the man who hired him. In fact, it must be done in such a way that I will appear the bravest and noblest of men. And this assassin must not outlive the moment, to speak of what has passed between us here."

"I don't understand," the adjutant said.

"You will," Ramogi said. He beckoned to the translator. "Attend now," he said, "to what I wish you to tell him."

II

A crowd of curious onlookers had been milling outside the kraal all morning. Musuri had to stand on his tiptoes and crane his neck to make out the source of the sudden commotion. "Look, Ebana," he said. "Ramogi's coming back. And he has the two chiefs of the big northern tribes with him. They're heading for the hut where Akhilleus and the others are." His hand clawed the air by his right flank, naked not only of clothing, but also of the sword belt he had had to surrender before entering the kraal. "Confound it, I feel so helpless. No weapons, not even a knife."

"You couldn't do much, anyway," Ebana said phlegmatically. "We're surrounded by armed men. Even if you had a sword, it wouldn't do any good. Try to relax, Musuri." She put one reassuring hand on his scarred old arm.

"It's not just Ramogi," he said, watching the small party make its way through the parted crowd to the great thatched hut, where Ramogi stopped to exchange a few words with the guards outside. "It's something—something more. I don't know just what." He spotted one of his runners going past and hailed him. "Lule! Come here!" The runner saluted him deferentially. "Look, I want all of our party gathered here, immediately. Obwano, Uranga, the porters, everyone." Lule nodded and sped off. Musuri's eyes had never quite left the trio who stood before the big hut's open door.

"Do you see them, Ebana?" he said quietly. "The heavy one, I've been told, is Nankyama, chief of the Karamojong. His people have a long-standing feud with the Baganda, the biggest of the lake tribes. And the other— that's Gwasaze, of the Acholi. We marched through their land back where the great waterfall came down through the mountains. Akhilleus says these two are powerful, the greatest of the chiefs. But neither of them can put a man of his own tribe on the throne. There are too many blood enemies of the Acholi and Karamojong among the other tribes. Yet no one can rule who doesn't have their support. For one, they control the most important trade routes leaving the country, to the north and east."

Ebana looked troubled. "And Ramogi seems to have their support. That's not good."

"No, it's not," the old soldier said. Once again his

hand went to his side, searching for a weapon that was not there. "Curse the luck! I wish I knew what was going on in there."

". . . but as I sailed into Egyptian waters," Akhilleus said, his grave eyes searching their faces one by one, "I saw disorder where there had been order, famine where there had been riches, bloody and brutal war where there had been a peaceful land for a hundred generations and more. I saw how heavy the hand of the barbarian invader lay upon the land—"

He stopped, his eyes on the doorway. In stunned silence, all the other heads turned to where he gazed.

Ramogi, Bukango's son, stood in the open doorway, flanked by the two chiefs. Akhilleus's hurried conversation with Kimala, an hour before, had identified them for him: Gwasaze of the Acholi, a robust figure of a man in his late forties; and broad-shouldered, stockily built Nankyama of the Karamojong, a man whose legs looked like carved oak from his years of patrolling the mountain passes far to the east.

Ramogi, with the two powerful chieftains on either side of him, was a formidable sight in his own right. It was Akhilleus's first good look at him. He stood stiffly erect, his eyes cold, a basilisk's, his ebony face seemingly without muscular structure, the cruel bones accentuating the starkly inhuman cast of his immobile features.

He's young, too, thought Akhilleus, *perhaps half my age, and in the peak of condition.* He noted the arrogant carriage of the man, the strength and endurance evident in his nakedness. A *magnificent adversary,* he thought; and for a moment only, his mind toyed with the idea: *What an ally he would make.* . . . But when he looked into Ramogi's eyes again, he could not suppress a shudder.

Suddenly, Ramogi broke the silence. "I seek the impostor," he said in a soft, almost unassuming voice, but with a chilling edge to it. "The one who befouls the name of my father's brother Magimbi by calling himself his son."

The announcement took the group by surprise not so much for its content as for its timing. This was not the normal tribal protocol in the Land Between the Mountains.

Three of the chiefs sprang to their feet indignantly. "How is it that one not invited to this gathering," old Obote said in a voice tremulous with rage, "disgraces it not only by entering our presence without permission, but by insulting our guest?"

Burly Nankyama laughed aloud, derisively. "This is Obote," he said, "disrupting dinner again by arguing over who gets the first fish to eat." He raised his voice to shout down the hubbub that ensued. "Silence!" he said. "Ramogi will speak. He, the son of Bukango, has suggested a way of making our decision a simple one."

Again the clamor rose, and again Nankyama bellowed it to silence, this time aided by Gwasaze. When the chiefs, all of them standing now, were quiet again, Nankyama spoke. "On the death of Lokosa," he said, "your fathers and mine confirmed Magimbi as king, as there was no man present with a more legitimate claim. Then, when Magimbi died, leaving no male heir"—he paused, and glanced icily at Akhilleus—"we confirmed his brother Bukango as successor."

"We are aware of the circumstances of previous successions," Obote said impatiently. "If you would do us the favor of getting to the point—"

"As I say," Nankyama continued, "Bukango is dead. And now for the first time since we, the chiefs of all the tribes in the Land Between the Mountains, first accepted Lokosa to reign over us, there are two pretenders, not one. Therefore—"

Ramogi impatiently broke in. "Therefore we must choose. And there is only one way." He glared around the circle of faces. "No king can reign while a pretender lives. Where there are two, there must be one." He paused again. "My suggestion is a simple one," he said. "I claim the right of reversion to the old blood rites of our ancestors, who settled disputes of this nature by only one means."

His final words were awaited with a deathly silence, for everyone knew what they would be.

"The claimants must fight. One must die."

This provoked the worst clamor yet. "No! No!" Obote said, indignant. "Are we savages? Are we beasts who walk on all fours? Was it for this that Lokosa showed us the ways of civilized—?"

But now it was Akhilleus, standing half a head taller than any of them, who motioned silence, "My friends," he said. "Please! I would answer the statement of my cousin Ramogi."

They made room for him, and all eyes were on his leonine head, with its gray-patched beard, balding pate, and deep-set, wise, and gentle eyes. When he spoke, his voice was so soft that some had to strain to hear him.

"I honor the customs of my people, so long forgotten by me in my unfortunate wanderings," he said. "I honor the wisdom of my noble cousin in suggesting a return to them. What he says is correct. A king may not reign peacefully, not in this land or in any land, with the knowledge that another claimant to his throne lives. In this, as in so many ways, the old customs remain the wisest and best. With your gracious leave, my friends, my brothers—I accept the challenge of my cousin Ramogi."

"No, Mtebi!" Obote said. "We cannot return to the barbarism of the old days. We must—"

But Obote was shouted down, and again Akhilleus held up his hand to ask for their attention. "My friends," he said, waiting patiently. The voices stilled one by one. Only when there again was silence did he speak.

"I claim one right," he said. "Ramogi is young and strong, and I am old and not what I was. I claim the right to even up this disadvantage in the only way I can. Among the peoples of the lands around the Great Sea, there is a custom—one which I would like to invoke here." He looked Ramogi in the eye. "Subject to the approval of the chieftains present, I, being the person challenged, claim the right to choose the weapons with which we shall contend."

He bowed politely to the chiefs in attendance, who, puzzled, looked at one another for counsel. Weapons? How could this change the advantage Ramogi had over a man twice his age? Ramogi was equally proficient with sword and knife, with the long throwing spear and the short stabbing spear, with the bow. In none of these did he have a master in his entire army, unless it was Kimala.

As if by spoken agreement, the chiefs looked at Ramogi, to see his reaction, and his reaction was a coldly superior smile.

"Certainly," Ramogi said, his deep voice thick with disdain. "Let the man who calls himself my cousin pick the weapon by which he must die. I have no objections. I am the master of any barbarian with any weapon known among us." He spoke directly to Akhilleus: "Very well, barbarian. Choose the weapon by which I shall kill you."

Akhilleus looked around at the faces of the chieftains once more. He held up his great hands, as if to invoke some god, then slowly lowered them to chest height, to stare at them thoughtfully. "I choose—these," he said. "Bare hands. To the death."

Perhaps the guards at the door had heard, and had passed the word on to friends standing nearby. Perhaps someone had been lurking behind the rear wall of the big hut. However it had come to pass, by the time the chieftains and the combatants-to-be emerged from the hut's open doorway, the news was halfway around the great encampment. Thus there was little surprise when Kimala, as deputy commander of the contingent of Ramogi's army that was in garrison at the time, began shouting orders. The army would gather near the sporting field when the sun was high, an hour from now; only an elite cadre would be armed, in the event of a riot; all other activities of the garrison would cease until the event had taken place. The kraal, of course, would remain under the usual heavy guard, both inside and outside the walls.

Ebana and Musuri, still ignorant of the latest news, had wandered back to their vantage point, to await the gathering of the small force under Musuri's command. The last to arrive was Uranga, who brought the news. "Musuri!" he said. "One of the guards told me—Akhilleus and Ramogi. They're going to fight."

Musuri scowled. "I was afraid of that. Confound it! And we're without a weapon among us! What I wouldn't give for just my short-sword now." He bit his lip, turning to Ebana. "How could he let himself get roped into something like this? I *told* him no good would come of his playing politics here, where he doesn't even know the rules!"

Strangely, Ebana seemed the least disturbed of the lot of them. "Patience, Musuri," she said. "He's been waiting for this, believe me. Don't you worry."

"Don't worry?" he said. "When your life and mine, and that of every man here, hangs on whether Akhilleus bests a man every bit as strong as he is, and decades younger?"

Her lips bore the ghost of a smile. "I never worry about Akhilleus when he's fighting," she said. "The only time I ever have doubts about him is when he's using his brains, not his hands. When he starts scheming, that's when I get nervous. But . . . even in that, I don't know. As you observed before, he's been undergoing a change in the last six months. He's been forsaking his clowning seaman's ways, and now, well . . . I'm not sure just how well I really know him. And if *I* don't know him, Musuri, how can you?"

Kimala, having assembled the troops in a vast circle around the sporting field, went to Akhilleus and greeted him respectfully. "Ramogi does not waste time, does he, Akillu?" he said, looking the older man over with concern as two tribesmen covered the old giant's body with white ash that would allow the fighters to get better purchase when gripping each other's bodies.

Akhilleus merely grunted in reply, and Kimala's heart sank. Could such a man, at this advanced an age, stand for long against so perfect a physical specimen as Ramogi— particularly without weapons to redeem the advantages of age and condition?

"So it's back to 'Akillu,' eh, Kimala?" Akhilleus said a little sadly. "It's true, then, that my claim to be the vanished Mtebi has not found a lodging in your heart, my young friend?"

"I did not mean to say this, Mtebi," Kimala said. "My lips did not obey my mind."

"On the contrary, my friend," Akhilleus said. "I have found that the lips' mistake is often what the mind really meant to say. But no matter. Come, take my hand, Kimala;

it may be for the last time. I think—I know—that I have
your heart. If I have this, what if your mind does not
follow? I never asked for anything but your friendship,
young man, and if I have that, I can with equanimity go to
any death the gods may devise. I have had a long, full life,
full of good friendships with people both old and young. I
can leave this life without regrets." Impulsively, the older
man embraced the younger. When he stepped back, there
was a strange expression on Kimala's face, and the young
prince's eyes were wet.

"Now," Akhilleus said with a smile, "you'd better get
away from me before Ramogi arrives. If he prevails, he'll
be your master."

"I'm not so sure of that, Mtebi," Kimala said, taking
pains to use the right name. "If we are not well governed
in the months to come, I do not want to be in the position
of having to enforce bad laws. I might just move on. See a
bit of the world. There's so much I don't know."

"You know as much as a man needs to," Akhilleus
said. "Just follow your heart, wherever it leads you. It's
wiser than your mind—or anyone's." He put out a great
gentle fist and struck the young prince an affectionate
blow on the chest. "Always the heart, my friend. The
evidence of the senses clouds the mind, and eyes and ears
can lie and often do. But your heart will always speak
truth to you. Remember that, won't you? Whatever may
happen here today." His smile darkened, then vanished.

"Now, go. And whatever gods there may be, may the
day go as they wish it."

III

When the two combatants finally appeared and were
led to the center of the field by Kimala, the watchers on
the periphery cheered lustily, shouting words of encouragement or derision to the men who were preparing to
battle to the death. But as Kimala retired to the edge of
the circle to stand at the head of his elite guard, the shouts

died, one at a time, leaving the scene in a strange and terrible silence.

Ebana's heart sank as she watched Akhilleus circle slowly to his own right, bent over in a half crouch, his eyes intent on the younger man's face. *He looks so old, so tired*, she thought. But no—that was deceptive. His mind was still sharp and alive—and cunning. She had taken note of how Akhilleus had observed Ramogi carefully when the younger man had handed spear and sword to an attendant. *Good*, she'd thought, he'd caught it. *Ramogi is right-handed*. And she'd sent Akhilleus a message with her mind, hoping that somehow her thoughts would become his: *Go to your right, Akhilleus. Stay away from his stronger side!* Either he'd heard, or his thoughts had coincided with hers. For now, as he circled, feinting, he stayed well clear of the hand with which Ramogi naturally handled weapons.

She looked around her quickly, fearful of missing anything. She nudged Musuri. "I think . . . Musuri, where are Obwano and Uranga?"

The old soldier's attention was absorbed by the combat. "Why, they're right here, by my si—" But then he turned to her, after quickly cocking his head to both sides. "You're right—they're gone. And I ordered both of them to stay right here, by my side, in case I needed them." He cursed under his breath. "You stay here. I'm going to look around."

"You're not going to watch?" she said.

"It will go as it will, whether I watch or not. You can tell me about it afterward. For once I'm going to find out what's going on." He squeezed her hand and slipped out through the crowd.

In the middle of the circle Akhilleus eyed Ramogi, feinted twice—and then struck. His old hand shot out like the head of a striking snake, his huge fist hitting home, catching Ramogi just under the eye. The blow should have knocked Ramogi to his knees, but the younger man was as strong as a bullock. Even though his head was jerked back violently, his instincts took over for his momentarily dulled mind as his hand reached out and closed with a crushing grip on Akhilleus's wrist.

Akhilleus grunted and twisted the hand free with some difficulty. The younger man had a grip like a crocodile's jaws! Before Akhilleus could completely recover, Ramogi let out a roar of rage and charged.

Akhilleus gave ground, feinted, and spun to one side. Ramogi's mad rush went past him—and Akhilleus's foot snaked out to trip him up. Ramogi stumbled forward, landing painfully on his outstretched hands . . . but his lightning reflexes saved him again. Tucking his head under, he rolled and came up on his feet, dusty and humiliated. And the angry, confused reactions of his mind once more gave way to the instant reactions of muscle and sinew. His body feinted with the left hand—and his right fist whipped out to strike Akhilleus on the left temple.

Akhilleus almost went down from the sheer numbing force of the blow. His head swam; he could dimly hear, as if underwater, the dull roar of the crowd around them. In an instant, Ramogi came at him again. He held up his hands to guard his face as Ramogi rained blow after blow on his forearms . . . and, step by step, he gave ground.

You'd better get hold of yourself, he thought, shaking his head. Ceasing his backward motion suddenly, he dropped his guard. Ramogi, unable to stop himself, came at him still—and ran into a battering-ram blow that caught him square on the end of his nose. Akhilleus could feel the bone crack. Ramogi staggered back onto all fours. . . .

Now was the time for the kill, but Akhilleus, to the crowd's surprise, stepped back calmly, hands at his sides, fists still balled loosely. He smiled benignly down at his opponent, the very picture of calm confidence despite the bruise that was already beginning to show on his own face.

The calm demeanor of the older man again drove Ramogi into a red rage. His hands trembling with uncontrollable anger, he scrambled to his feet.

But as he did, the onlookers could for the first time see the wreckage Akhilleus's blow had made of Ramogi's nose; bright red blood poured thickly down his lip into his open mouth. There was a gasp of astonishment from the great throng—and then, to Ramogi's astonishment, hoots of derision. "Look! The old man has first blood!" "What's the matter, Ramogi? Can't you handle a graybeard?"

Ramogi wiped his face with the back of his hand—and charged again. This time his long arm got through Akhilleus's guard. His fist struck Akhilleus on the cheekbone. Akhilleus staggered back, and Ramogi came on still, hammering at the older man's face. Now Ramogi was in charge. Feinting at Akhilleus's chin, he came up hard with the other hand and dug his rocklike fist into Akhilleus's belly.

The blow knocked the wind out of Akhilleus for a moment. He grabbed the young man's arms, pulled him close, and held on tight, trying to get his breath back, feeling not only his own sudden weakness but the untapped brute strength in the young man's torso as he struggled to get free of the bear hug Akhilleus had clamped on him. *Gods!* Akhilleus thought. *I was once strong like that. Where did my strength go to?*

He tensed himself—and suddenly released Ramogi, quickly stepped back almost to arm's length and punched again, right in the middle of the terrible mess he had already made of Ramogi's nose. His opponent cried out in sudden pain—and Akhilleus immediately knew he had won at least a partial victory. Men of Ramogi's tribe were trained to endure pain in stoic silence. Akhilleus feinted at Ramogi's nose again, then darted to his right to hammer one hard blow on Ramogi's left kidney.

The punch did not look like much, but Akhilleus knew that it had been the most painful blow yet struck by either man. Ramogi's face was convulsed with pain, and as he cautiously circled the slowly backtracking Akhilleus, his steps were labored and clumsy.

Akhilleus looked into Ramogi's glazed eyes and saw the anger and desperation of a man who was slowly and systematically being made to appear a weakling and a fool by a dotard twice his age. He saw rage compounded by impotence, humiliation, and pain.

Now's the time to look out, he thought. *A wounded animal is capable of anything. . . .*

"There you are, you son of a whore!" Musuri said, his powerful grip closing on Obwano's arm. "I told you to stick by my side, in case there's trouble."

But the face Obwano turned to him was not the face

of a man caught in a forbidden act. It was full of fear and concern. "Yes, but Musuri—I noticed Uranga was gone. You yourself told me to keep my eyes open, and . . . Look, Musuri! There he is!"

Musuri's head jerked to one side. He looked where Obwano's long black finger pointed. "Sacred name of Moloch," the old soldier said. "We're too late."

As he spoke he could see Uranga reach out and slip one of the confiscated swords from a scabbard carelessly worn by the last man in Kimala's elite guard. The noon sunlight glinted on the blade.

Slowly, doggedly, Ramogi pursued Akhilleus, driving him always to his own right. Ramogi's blows rained on the old man's forearms as before . . . and always Akhilleus gave ground, fending off the blows. Just once, as Ramogi pressed forward, Akhilleus's long leg lashed out to kick Ramogi in the knee, but landed only a glancing blow. Akhilleus recovered quickly and gave ground again, thanking his lucky stars that he'd managed to land that kidney punch a few moments before. Without it, Ramogi would be the one doing the kicking now—and Ramogi's legs were in better shape than his own, even allowing for the long march southward from Egypt.

Suddenly he noticed that he was moving into dangerous ground. From the corner of his eye he could see that Ramogi had been steering him to the edge of the crowd, near where Kimala stood silently at attention, at the head of his elite guard. *Careful*, Akhilleus thought. This close to the edge of the great circle there was less room to maneuver. . . .

Slowly, cagily, the old man gave ground, trying to move away to one side, toward the center of the great ring. But the young man, pursuing him, moved him toward the periphery of the arcing line of soldiers and onlookers.

This will be my only chance, thought Uranga. *Better strike straight and clean.* Hands trembling, face drenched in sweat, he watched Akhilleus back toward him, one flat-footed step at a time. *He's tiring*, he thought. *Here he comes; now . . . one step . . . two steps . . . wait . . .*

Now!

The sun flashed on the blade as the assassin lunged out of the crowd at Akhilleus's unprotected back, just as Musuri's still powerful voice, gruff and raw from a lifetime of issuing commands, shouted: *"Akhilleus! Look out!"*

Akhilleus wheeled—by luck, the right way.

The blade slid across his rib cage, leaving a light red line of blood.

Akhilleus's hand reached out and grasped Uranga's wrist in a grip like that of one of the great apes of the Mufumbiro. The sword fell to the ground.

Akhilleus's grip increased in pressure, forcing Uranga to his knees. The assassin squirmed and cried out in pain. Akhilleus twisted the arm and turned to look at Ramogi.

The assassin saw the direction of Akhilleus's gaze—and saw a possible way out. "Akhilleus!" he groaned. *"He did it! He* paid me to kill ou!"

Akhilleus stared at Ramogi. Beyond Ramogi he could see the perfect shape of the circle of faces begin to dissolve into an irregular mass as the crowd pressed forward. Kimala's men leaped into place around the combatants and the trapped assassin, forcing the crowd back at spear's point.

Ramogi's eyes darted back and forth. He would not look Akhilleus in the eye. "I do not know this man," he said. "I had nothing to do with—"

"You *both* lie," Akhilleus said suddenly, in a voice that carried to the farthest reaches of the now-silent crowd. "You, Uranga. You were paid to kill me in Egypt. I have known ever since we entered the lands of the Sudd. My eye has followed you everywhere."

"No, Akhilleus! It was Ramogi! He said—"

"It was Ramogi as well, wasn't it? He paid you to do what you were already disposed to do. Isn't that it, Uranga?" Still the killing grip increased, until Uranga howled in pain. Behind Ramogi the spearmen stood, weapons at the ready and pointed now at the back of the son of Bukango.

Finally Uranga's voice, distorted with pain, rasped, "Yes, Akhilleus! *Both*—Harmin in M-Memphis . . . and R-Ramogi here—"

Suddenly Ramogi reached out and snatched a spear

from the hand of one of the flanking guards. He drew back, ready to hurl it at Akhilleus . . .

. . . and just as abruptly something struck him from behind, knocking the weapon from his hands. Akhilleus glanced down and saw the head of a tribal spear protruding from Ramogi's belly. And, as his eyes rose, he saw the spearman behind Ramogi yank hard on the weapon. The spearhead disappeared—and blood sprang forth from Ramogi's stomach. The light went from his eyes and he fell to his knees, as if in silent supplication. But after a heartbeat or so, his thighs, too, refused to hold him up, and he fell forward heavily, on his face.

Ebana fought unsuccessfully to get through the crowd. Finally one of Kimala's soldiers recognized her and barked out an order. In a moment the mass of onlookers parted to let her through, and Kimala himself, after having his men seize Uranga, was restoring the crowd to some semblance of order. Ebana, embracing Akhilleus despite the messy, muddy concoction of sweat and ash that coated his body, once again felt his comforting arms around her, and it was the finest feeling she had ever had. "Akhilleus!" she said. "You're a lion!"

He chuckled, patting her back and looking over her head at Obote, who was regarding him with a thoughtful look on his wrinkled old face. "Actually," he said, "I'm a leopard. At least that was my father's clan. We're distantly related to Ngo, of the Bunyoro, on my father's mother's side." He smiled at Obote. "My memory fails me, Obote: Am I related to you in any way? Have I perhaps that signal honor?"

But Obote did not answer. Instead he spoke sharply to Kimala. "You will call a council of all the chiefs," he said. "Immediately!"

There was no hut in the kraal of Bukango that could accommodate all the chiefs of all the tribes. The council met outdoors, under the warm African sun, on the gentle slopes above the point, with the earth falling away from them to the deep blue of the Great Lake below. The air was clear, and the skies above were free of clouds. Akhilleus and Ebana, sitting together at the edge of the big circle, felt the soft breeze on their naked skins and thought they had never been so comfortable. *At peace at last,* Ebana thought. *And safe after many dangers. It's almost as if we were . . . at home.* The thought shocked her. Home? Here?

As Obote stood and spoke, she watched Akhilleus's face, understanding nothing except the one fact: They were safe here. That, at least, was sure.

"It is time to select a king to reign over us," Obote said, looking around him, "over all the tribes here represented. I would like to suggest—"

"I beg your indulgence," Akhilleus said, getting to his feet. "I apologize to the noble Obote. But before the tribes cast their votes, I must speak—with the kind permission of the chiefs."

"Certainly, Mtebi," Obote said. "We hear you. Continue." He sat down, eyes on Akhilleus's face.

"Thank you, noble and wise Obote," Akhilleus said. He looked around the circle of upturned faces. "Thank you all: chieftains of the Karamojong, Iteso, and Bagisu in the east. Lords of the Bagwere, Basoga, and Baganda on the shores of the Great Lake to the south of our kingdom. Leaders of the brave Bunyoro, Batoro, Bakonjo, Banyankole, Bakiga, and far-flung Banyarwanda in the great mountains of the west. Wise and judicious chiefs of the Acholi and Madi and Alur and Lugbara and Kakwa in the north, where the Great River flows toward the sea you have never seen. I honor you all and beg to speak.

"Bukango, on his deathbed, asked me to reign. I have won this right in combat with his son, Ramogi. But—" He paused, eyes sweeping the circle again. "How do I say what I must? Particularly when it means that I must bid farewell to you all, to this great nation that cries out to my blood through the souls of the countless ancestors whose bones lie buried in this ancient land?"

"Farewell?" Obote said. "But, Mtebi—"

"Farewell," Akhilleus said again, sadly. "You forget I am a son of Magimbi, a grandson of Lokosa, to whom honor was everything, whatever the price. I gave my word to the Great King of Egypt; to break this word would make me less, infinitely less, than the son of my great forebears. And should such a man, who is less than a man, rule? Should such a man reign?"

"But if you go—"

"Besides," Akhilleus said, his voice unwavering, "I am grown old. I will die soon. Perhaps I will die before I reach Egypt. This will not matter if I die on the path of honor, keeping a word freely given. If I should stay, I would still die—and the chiefs here gathered would have to gather again, and do at that time what I suggest they do now: name a young man, who will reign long, without interruption, without contention. A young man of proven wisdom and valor, a man who knows—as I no longer know, to my sorrow, having been away so long—the ways of all the tribes, not just his own. A young man born to lead, but who put aside this privilege in order to learn what a wise leader must learn of the ways of men if he is to command both their heads and their hearts."

He paused for no more than an instant, but was pleased to note that every eye had already fallen upon the slightly embarrassed subject of his words. For a moment he thought of naming the man, but his words had already wrought the effect he had desired, for, almost to a man, the chiefs, in what seemed a single voice, spoke the name that had been on his lips.

"*Kimala*."

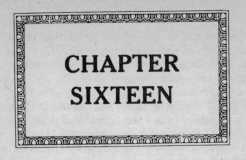

CHAPTER SIXTEEN

THE FAYUM

I

The high road ran south from Memphis, keeping close to the Nile and at times intersecting the long afternoon shadows of the very early pyramids commanding the heights along the way south to Lisht. Not far beyond the Egyptian army encampment the road passed the great masonry dam Khufu had built centuries earlier on the Wadi Garawi to impound water for the quarry workers engaged in building his own great monument and tomb. At royal Lisht itself it skirted the city and continued southward, turning west near the access road to the first true pyramid ever built, at Maidum.

From here, the traveler's attention was drawn less by the great monuments that wealthy kings and nobles might build—although an occasional tomb or temple could still be seen on the heights as the road climbed—than it was by the actual source of that prodigious wealth. And when, the heights once gained, the road began winding down into the great fertile lowland called the Fayum, the origin of much of those boundless riches became immediately evident.

Earlier dynasties and their kings had built cities, pyramids, and temples. The Twelfth Dynasty kings, however, had built waterways, changing the face of the land forever. In a generation or two, the region had become able to feed many more hungry mouths than before, and the population had more than doubled. Out of this sudden population boom the Twelfth Dynasty kings and their overseers had built a great civilization.

The immense lake, many leagues across, that was the heart of the Fayum, was fed by a stray arm of the Nile that left the main channel of the river far to the south, near Asyūt. This arm paralleled the river for many days' ride, then suddenly turned westward through a narrow opening in the rocks below the pyramid of Sesostris II and between the settlements of el-Lahun and Kom Medinet Ghurab.

This abrupt turn of the Nile's western arm marked not only a natural east-west boundary between the fertile Fayum lowlands lying to the west of Lisht and the near-desert of the upriver Nile shore, but for good measure marked a political boundary separating the realm of Memphis from that of the Thebaid in the south. The three nomes that lay between these two political regions constituted a prize that had passed back and forth between the two factions in Middle Egypt for centuries; and in the days before the coming of the Shepherd Kings, it had been possible to say that the possession of this region—the Fayum and its links to the main Nile—meant supremacy over the entire Nile Valley.

The Twelfth Dynasty kings had made the most of the fact and had launched a campaign, lasting many decades, to reclaim for cultivation as much of the Fayum as possible. When they had begun, the great lake—called Moeris—had covered most of the lowlands, leaving only its southern shore free for cultivation. But the Twelfth Dynasty kings had planned, then put into execution, an intricate system of canals and dikes unlike any in the known world. Canals now diverted water from Lake Moeris, reducing it to a fraction of its former size and liberating vast areas of rich bottomland once flooded, now fit for farming. Other canals and dikes harnessed the annual spring flooding of

the Nile, controlling its excesses. Still others were used
first to flood lands not previously planted, then to drain
them. As a result, the Fayum lands brought in two crops a
year instead of one, and produced in an average year twice
the volume of olives, beans, and grapes that even a rich
sector of the delta could provide. Where once had been a
vast lake surrounded by semidesert vegetation, the Sesostrises and their heirs had made a garden—one which
teemed with wildlife, and whose skies, in season, were
black with birds: ibises, pelicans, cormorants, herons,
cranes, flamingos, geese, and ducks of every description.
On every side there were canals, ponds, flooded fields,
and spacious villas built by the owners of the land, palatial
country houses where, even in the days of the Shepherds,
life could be lived on a gracious scale that would be the
envy even of kings of other nations.

Here, too, along with the stately homes of the lords of
the land, were smaller, but still beautifully appointed,
second homes of the nobles and ranking functionaries of
the court; of retired generals who had, after the custom of
the more ambitious in the army, married well; of wealthy
traders who, when their caravans carried them to distant
lands, wanted a safe place to leave their families; and of
such men as Shobai.

In happier days, during the first months after the
birth of the twins, Mereet had grown homesick for the
delta. She had never taken entirely to the life in Memphis,
where Shobai's increasingly lucrative work kept him for
most of the year, and had not cared to make friends with
the wives of the army men Shobai met in the course of his
duties. She had not been any more disposed to the butter-
fly life of the social world at the court of Memphis than
she had been to its provincial equivalent in the delta, and
although the twins had kept her quite busy at first, as the
months went by Shobai had more and more often come
home to find Mereet depressed and lonely.

Finally he had spoken to her and learned for the first
time how distasteful to her was the bone-dry country
around the capital, how desperately she missed the rich,
water-girt life of the delta. Inquiring among his wealthier

friends, he'd learned that the Fayum offered a life compatible with Mereet's memories of the delta. The young officer Hori, raised in the Fayum, had in particular painted for Shobai's mind's eye a breathlessly lyrical picture of the great oasis, with its rich greenery, azure lakes, and teeming wildlife. Secretly Shobai had put aside money, made his purchase with the aid of sympathetic and judicious friends, and, at the first opportunity for an extended holiday, had taken Mereet to her new second home.

He'd been amply repaid for his thoughtfulness; her boundless delight in the place, her happiness, had been everywhere evident. Even he, deprived of one sense by his blindness, had noticed a very considerable difference, if in nothing more than the slower, more leisurely, more natural pace of life in the watered land. And when the time had come to go back to Memphis and go to work again, he'd been as regretful as she. On the journey back to the city, they'd spoken of taking another, longer, holiday as soon as the first opening in Shobai's work schedule presented itself. But that opportunity had never come: The Shepherds had pressed on, battered the Egyptian armies back, and Shobai had been called to full-time service arming the new drafts that kept streaming in from the Upper Egyptian provinces. And their dream of returning together to their little villa had never come to fruition.

Heket, walking up from the pond with the naked, sun-browned twins, could see Shobai all the way from the road. He sat on a stone bench, under the grape arbor, in dappled sunshine. As she drew nearer, she could make out, even at a distance, that same neutral, unfathomable expression he wore so much of the time, and her mind read into it what she already knew was there: a burden of unutterable sorrow, the same sorrow she had seen and felt in him ever since the black day when they'd taken his wife away.

What misfortune! You would think that, being as highly placed as he was, he could find out what had happened to her. But either the guards who had come for Mereet on that terrible day had been kidnappers posing as soldiers, or someone in the court was lying. Or perhaps

THE LION IN EGYPT

both. Who could say? The upshot was that nothing could be done. She had disappeared from the face of the earth.

There was, however, the one chance that she was in the hands of the Shepherds. Shobai had thought he'd heard her cry out once, back on the river, as he was sailing upstream, and Hori had seen a woman struggling in the hands of a Shepherd guard on a boat going downstream—but Hori had never been able to say whether the woman was Mereet, and had privately confided to her, Heket, that he thought Shobai's mind had played tricks on him when he had sworn the woman had called out his name before the Shepherds took her below. "It's the sort of thing one's mind does at such times of stress," he'd said. "He wants to believe she's still alive."

Poor man! But now she forced the sadness from her and patted the children's bare rumps. "There's your father, children. Go to him, now."

Teti and Ketan ran, squealing, to the seated man, laughing and trying to climb up his powerful legs. "Father! Father!" His blank expression was transformed to one of delight as he picked up both of them, a child in each arm, and hugged them close.

"Children!" he said, sitting them up on his forearms. "Well, I'll wager I can tell where *you've* been today. Your hair's still wet."

"Father!" Teti, the girl-child, said. "I can swim! Heket showed me—"

"I can swim, too!" Ketan said. "But I fell down and bumped my leg! It made blood!"

Shobai hugged them both close, kissing them one after the other. "There, now," he said. "You'll be fine. Here," he said, handing them both to Heket. "You'll want to dress them. There's a bit of a breeze. It must be nearing sundown. How long is that from now?"

"Perhaps an hour, sir," she said, taking the twins up. "I'll go put on dinner, if you like, sir."

"Yes, do that," Shobai said. "I'll just sit out here in the grape arbor for a while. It's the most pleasant place to be at this time of day, with evening coming on." She started to go, but turned back when he said, "Oh, by the way—when was Hori due back?"

"Oh, sir, I forgot," the servant said, crestfallen. "I'm so sorry. The messenger came an hour ago. Hori will be delayed. It had something to do with the royal guards."

"Squabbling over the food, I suppose. They've disrupted the market so badly it's a wonder the farmers haven't just quit and taken up some other line of work. You work and work, and grow food to sell, and then some court functionary takes it away and gives you worthless government scrip for pay. You can't even barter it with your neighbors." He sighed again. "Now, if one could only think it was going to the army, or to feed the poor."

"Small chance of that, sir. Anyhow, Hori said that he wouldn't be until tomorrow night. He said to leave a light burning for him."

"Then we'll be sure to do that," Shobai said. "Now run along and get the children ready for dinner and bed."

"Yes, sir. Will you be wanting to put them to bed yourself, sir, like last night? And perhaps tell them a story?"

He shook his head. "No. Not tonight, I think, Heket." An afterthought, however, made him raise his head. "Let me kiss them good night now. Could you bring them here, please?"

She did so, and as she watched him kiss them both and hug them affectionately in his massive, gentle arms, she found herself weeping. He put them down and stroked their hair once again. "Good night, my darlings," he said, his tone serious but strangely faraway. "Now, run along. And, Heket . . . call me as soon as dinner is ready, please."

The sight of him lingered in Heket's mind for a long time as she toweled the children down and put them in their warm nightdresses, preparatory to putting the soup back on the fire. *The poor man,* she thought. *He seems so sad, so resigned. It's almost as if . . .*

Then, when the thought finally took form, it sent a cold chill down her spine, as though someone had walked on her grave. *It's as if he were saying good-bye to them once and for all.*

*   *   *

Shobai stood perfectly still and alert, one hand on the arching arbor. A light breeze had struck up, cool and soothing. It stirred the graying hair at his temples. He heard it sigh softly through the grape leaves overhead.

He's out there somewhere, he thought. *He's here at last. I can feel it, as surely as I feel the breeze. He'll visit me tonight. But when?*

II

From the heights above, el-Lahun was the strangest city Ben-Hadad had ever seen. "It looks like a senet board," he said to the girl seated behind him on the horse. "Baka told me about the planned settlements that the Sesostrises made out here, but I'm so used to towns with paths laid out by a cow that I didn't believe him."

"It doesn't seem right," Tuya said. "Everything in straight lines, like a cemetery. Square corners. And, look— the quarters of the city are walled off from each other."

Ben-Hadad spurred his borrowed horse, and they began winding their way down the hillside. Behind them, Anab lingered, gazing out across the Fayum toward the great lake. "Come on, Anab!" Ben-Hadad called back impatiently, as Lion scampered down the slope between them.

Tuya's eyes were on the city below. What a strange, utterly foreign-looking place! She wouldn't like to live there at all. It would be much too easily policed by the guards, with walls separating the one quarter from the next. She peered at the towering acropolis in the center, with its temples and temple outbuildings, walled off from the spreading villas of the eastern quarter—plainly a rich man's area, with its vast mansions constructed around central courts—and the slums of the west, obviously the homes of the service community. The Twelfth Dynasty kings certainly had been innovators. Nothing like this had ever before been seen in the Egypt she knew.

"Ben-Hadad," Anab said, pulling up alongside them

when they had reached the roadway below. "I just can't see Shobai settling there can you?"

"No," Ben-Hadad said. "But I was thinking that perhaps someone in the city would know where to find him. His name is fairly well known in Upper Egypt these days, it appears."

"Well, we can ask," Anab said. "But I just wonder what kind of information we're going to get from the kind of people who'd live in a place like *that*."

Ben-Hadad chuckled. "I know what you mean. But if my travels have taught me anything, it's that people are pretty much the same everywhere, once you get past the barriers of language and custom." Again he spurred the horse forward. After a few steps the animal's gait changed into a trot, then a canter.

The road underfoot was blessedly regular. That was one of the advantages of a town built near a pyramid complex: The roads had to be kept in good trim, and the priestly caste who ruled the city had sufficient backing at court to get funds to maintain the arteries connecting city and pyramid fields. Consequently, the three riders, with Lion running beside them on his short legs, made good time to the city gate. There they stopped but did not dismount, speaking down to the two guardsmen. "Excuse me," Ben-Hadad said. "We're looking for the home of Shobai, the armorer. I'm told he has property in the area."

"Shobai? Oh, you mean the big blind fellow," the younger of the two guards said. "He's way over by the lakeshore. You've still got quite a way to go. Have you come from the east? From the Nile Valley?"

"Yes," Ben-Hadad said.

"Please," the guard said, "if you've any news of the fighting . . . I have family in Memphis."

Ben-Hadad frowned. "I wish I could tell you," he said. "Some of the people in the city were moved south before the attack. Some wouldn't leave, and some couldn't."

"But—have the Shepherds—?"

"The Shepherds took Memphis," Anab said. "The Egyptian lines are just south of the city."

"Are you sure? Unas would never willingly abandon the city to—"

"Unas is dead," Ben-Hadad interrupted. "He died the death of a brave soldier—killing Vahan, general of the Shepherds, in single combat. The army retired to a more easily defensible position, without too many losses. But— Baka's back. I don't know if you remember the name. . . ." He watched their faces closely. Could Baka have been by here before him? He observed them, and guessed not. "He was a general in the delta wars," he added. "If anyone can help them, he can. He's already sent back an order for reinforcements from the court guards."

"Did you hear that?" the young guard said to his mate. "If I could only—" He turned back to Ben-Hadad. "The Shepherds—do you think they'll be able to break through our lines?"

"Not if Baka gets his reinforcements," Anab said. "He's a brave, resourceful soldier, and knows the Shepherds and their ways. Besides, the enemy has new, untried leaders. Not only did Vahan die in the battle, but his second-in-command died with him." There was pride in Anab's voice as he went on. "They've no one in charge with a tenth of Baka's experience and ability. If you've thought of joining him, go ahead! He can always use good men on the lines!"

"I may just do that," the young guardsman said. "And you three—the gods go with you, eh? Just stick to the road; it'll lead you all the way to the lakeshore. Once you're there, ask for Shobai. They all know his name."

"Thank you," Ben-Hadad said, impatiently spurring his horse on. But as they rode away, his heart sank. All too obviously Baka, coming by here before them, had not stopped to ask directions of these men. He must have known from the first where it was that he was going—and now he had a lead on them that they could never make up in time to save Shobai.

"Will that be all, sir?" Heket said after they had eaten. She stood in the doorway, looking down at Shobai, who sat quietly before the dying fire. The warm glow of the coals picked out his still-handsome features, as well as the old scars below the clean white cloth he wore over where his eyes once had been. His great shoulders were slumped, whether from fatigue or sadness she could not say. Since he had come to the Fayum from Memphis, he had shared few, if any, of his thoughts with her. Although she had attempted to solace him, as Mereet had bid her to do, he seemed to prefer solitude.

"What?" he said, coming out of his reverie for a moment. "Oh . . . yes, thank you. You can go to bed now, Heket. I'll just sit up a bit. It feels good by the fire. You might check the children before you retire."

"Yes, sir. I always do. Good night, sir."

But still she lingered at the door, looking at him. He had aged so in the last few days, she thought. He had suddenly gone from middle age to an old man. It was most distressing to her; there didn't seem to be a thing in the world she could do about it.

Defeat did that to you, she thought. Having to accept the inevitable, and knowing that what had hurt you was something you could not change, no matter how hard you tried. She shook her head sadly.

Well, it wasn't her affair, and there was little she could do, no matter how much her heart went out to him. She had work to do on the morrow, and it was time to turn in. The children would get her up all the earlier in the morning, since she'd put them to bed before their usual time.

She padded down the hall of the little house, holding the candle high, watching the strange shadows bounce off the walls, her footfalls silent against the mats on the earth floor. . . .

Then she stopped. She held her breath and peered into the darkness.

Was there someone out there? Was someone approaching the house?

She listened intently for the sound of footsteps. But there was nothing except the light breeze that had struck up at nightfall, when the wind in the valley had changed direction. Even the night birds whose cries had echoed across the little vale an hour before were silent now.

She started to move forward again—and once more

became aware of another presence out there, somewhere. But again there was no specific sound she could make out.

"Who's there?" she said in a tremulous voice. There was no answer but the wind.

Shobai sat tranquilly for a long time, until the unseen red coals had turned to white, until the fire had become half embers. His mind sought oblivion but could not find it; there was no peace within him. After a time he reached behind him for the cithara he had brought with him all the way from Ugarit, where his many years' career as a wandering bard had begun.

Absently he tuned it—finding now, without thinking about it, not the standard tuning of the port cities but the old tuning of Ur. It was a tuning that he and Hadad had learned from Kirta in their childhood. Somehow it seemed to his unthinking fingers the proper set of intervals for the present time, and they quickly brought the gut strings to pitch.

His fingers began to play idly upon the strings. Presently a sequence of chords emerged, and then it became a definite tune. Again without conscious thought entering into the process, he found himself singing softly and melodiously the Twelfth Dynasty dialogue between a man and his spirit:

> Death is before me today
> Like a sick man's recovery,
> Like going outdoors after confinement.
>
> Death is before me today
> Like a well-trodden way,
> Like a man's coming home from warfare.
>
> Death is before me today
> Like a man's longing to see his home
> When he has spent many years in captivity . . .

Then he realized what it was that he had been singing, and he thrust the cithara from him with a bitter curse. What sort of nonsense was this, coming from him, Shobai,

a man who had never given up, even in the darkest days
of his life? Who had remained defiant even after he'd been
enslaved in the Shepherd camp, beaten and starved, chained
naked to the stake in all weather? Who'd managed to carry
on even when he'd been blinded and his brother killed?
Was this Shobai, sniveling and waiting for death to end his
cares for him?

Well, one thing was sure: Whether or not he asked
for death, it had at last come to find him. And while it was
cowardly folly to beg for it, as the man in the song had
done, it was no folly to begin preparing oneself for it.

Consciously, this time, his hands once again reached
for the cithara and began stroking its strings softly,
delicately.

I suppose, he thought, *that if my life had gone
differently, I might be making my peace with the gods just
now.* What gods? Well, whichever ones happened to reign
in the country he happened to be in at the time—Osiris,
Baal, whoever. But it seemed that his ability to believe in
a specific set of gods had diminished the more he had
traveled, the more he had seen of the world. And he had
been a traveler for a long time—for all his life, it seemed;
it was part of his profession. He wondered if any of his
forebears had ever given full credence to any of the reli-
gions men lived by. Somehow he doubted it. The men of
no nation were also the men of no religion.

Yet there was—he had taken note of this many times
in his travels—something to be gained from the beliefs he
and his people had put aside, and he had never made
sport of men's beliefs, anywhere. What matter if they
were a well that the Children of the Lion had never been
able to drink from? Quite obviously it was a well that
slaked the thirst of others: of most of the rest of mankind,
for that matter. Faith was something that made people
strong in times of stress, of loss. It healed wounds that
would respond to no other medicine. He had often envied
others their ability to find solace in belief. But no matter
how he envied them, he had never been able in good
conscience to join them.

And now? Now, when life's last hours had come upon
him, what comfort had he to draw upon? What weapons

had he to fight off the dark with? Alas, here he stood empty-handed, and empty-hearted as well. When they had taken Mereet away they had taken away the one solace life had left him.

Except . . .

He put the cithara down and rose from his seat, making his way around the fire to the door in the hall, his movements as confident in the near-darkness as they would have been at midday. He paused at the door of the children's room and stood listening to their deep breathing.

The thought of the twins—of their future, of the life they would live without him—simultaneously tore at his heart and comforted him. At least he would have left them a good life, one cushioned by the money he had placed on deposit for them in the hands of responsible persons. They would have kind and sheltering treatment, grow up knowing who their forefathers had been, and what their heritage was. They would both—the boy *and* the girl—get the training in the making of arms that he had got in his own youth. It was flying in the face of tradition, to be sure, training a girl in a profession only men had held all these centuries—but the omen had been unmistakable, and its message had been clear. Both children had been born with the birthmark; both were Children of the Lion. His decision had not come easily, but once it had come it had been clear and irreversible. Both Teti and Ketan would get the training, would carry forward the ancient family tradition.

In any case, he thought, he would be spared the fate of poor Belsunu, the earliest ancestor he knew anything about, who had gone to his lonely grave in Canaan never knowing that his own son, Ahuni, lived. He had gone into the great darkness thinking himself the last of his line. What a loneliness his must have been!

But his own loss would be quite enough. The children were all he had left now, and as he bent over their beds to tuck the covers around their sleeping bodies, he found his hands trembling, his knees shaking, his face wet with sudden tears. "Good-bye," he said. "Good-bye, my little ones. How I would have loved to have known you through the years to come, as you grew tall and strong and lovely."

He stooped to kiss each of the sleeping faces. Then, feeling old and bent and broken, he stood and moved slowly to the door. "Good-bye," he said again in a low whisper, barely audible. "Good-bye."

As he reentered the hall he could instantly feel the change. He was no longer alone in the front of the house. There was another presence. The blind—he knew this by now, for all that he had denied it in his sighted days—had a new sense given them to make up for the loss of sight. He had never been able to define it, but he had been able to use it almost from the first. He *felt* the new presence in the house as surely as he felt the light breeze that swept softly in through the now-open front door. Just as surely, he knew who the presence was. And—it was the strangest feeling he had ever experienced—the sudden panic in his heart flared once and then went away, to be replaced by a great tranquillity that neither feared death nor welcomed it, but accepted it once and for all.

Between them the white coals glowed; Shobai could feel their warmth. And, quite as palpably, he could feel the presence across the fire from him. He bowed formally, his voice low and calm as he spoke: "Welcome to my house. I've been waiting for you."

Baka, his knuckles white around the handle of his army-issue sword, took in a deep breath and looked at the hulking, blind giant before him. *Strike now and be done with it!* he thought as the hot flash of rage ran through him. He stepped forward, raised the sword . . . and then slowly lowered it. He looked at Shobai's great slumped shoulders, at the huge, gentle, patient hands, scarred all over from the forge, and at the placid face, barely visible in the dim light of the dying fire. And something within shook him, shook him the way wind in the forest might shake a brown leaf ready to fall. "W-where is she?" he said hoarsely.

The blind giant's face remained expressionless. "I . . . I wish I could tell you," he said. "Even if it meant that

you would take her away from me." His hands made futile
gesturing motions. "I'm sorry," he said.

"I don't understand," Baka said sharply. "She's gone?"

"One day some men came, men in guards' uniforms.
They took her away—apparently she knew they were
coming. But when I asked at court, no one knew anything,
and no one admitted having sent soldiers after her. Then,
when Unas forced me to retire from the front, I heard a
cry on the river, and my companion said he saw a woman
being subdued on a boat headed downstream, a boat
manned by Shepherd guards. I—I do not know if it was
Mereet or not."

For a moment Baka, hearing yet unwilling to believe
what he heard, tensed, his hand again tight on the sword's
handle. He tried to speak, but could not. His heart beat
fast and his hands trembled, whether with rage or disappointment or some other emotion he could not have said
at the moment. "Then—then we have both lost her," he
said in a voice barely audible in the still room.

Shobai waited for Baka to speak again, but no words
came. "General," Shobai said finally, "you must be weary,
traveling all the way from Memphis. There's a chair beside you."

Baka stared uncomprehending. Then, weak-kneed,
he sank into the seat offered him. The sword slipped from
his hand to the floor. He stared at the blind man, hardly
seeing him at all.

III

The two men had sat silent for a long time. After the
first rush of talk about Mereet, they had lapsed into stillness,
leaving only the dying fire to sputter and crackle between
them. Once Baka rose to put a fresh log on the fire, and to
poke at it with the sword he had raised in anger a short
time before. As he did, a strange expression, almost a
smile, crossed his face.

"This sword—my sword—has seen much fighting. Perhaps too much. I've been a fool, as you know, a fool to think that I could beat back the Shepherd Kings single-handed. Men think that everything depends on their prowess with arms—and all the while their women are waiting and loving, giving birth to children . . . children like your Teti and Ketan—*her* children. But we do not own our children, do we? They belong to . . . to . . ."

Shobai smiled. "To all of us—to no one—or maybe just to themselves. Yes, to themselves. I think we have learned that much, my friend."

After a long pause, Baka nodded, and he was about to reply when Shobai suddenly raised a cautioning hand, rose to his feet, and moved to the door. Sensing that something was wrong, Baka rose, too—then stopped, as Shobai opened the door and stood on the threshold, listening intently in the darkness, motioning for silence.

It was a long time before Baka could hear the sound of horses' hooves—quiet and muffled at first, then louder.

Shobai turned back to him. "Did you have someone coming with you—or following you?"

Alarmed, his sword still in hand, Baka pushed his way out the door, to stand outside, away from the light around the entry. By now the horses—two of them—were clattering to a halt. Baka could see three figures dismounting—one of them rushing forward toward the dim light in the doorway. It was Ben-Hadad!

"Baka!" Ben-Hadad stopped in his tracks, looking first at one man, then the other. "Thank heaven we've found you in time!" he blurted out, breathless with excitement. "Baka, you can't kill him! I-I'll stop you! You'll have to kill me first!"

"And me!" Anab came into view, the light making his ugliness even more bizarre.

Before Baka could register his amazement, Tuya came forward as well—ready, too, it seemed, to prevent bloodshed. "Tuya . . . Anab," he said, "and Ben-Hadad—what in the name of—?"

But Ben-Hadad had already rushed past Baka and was standing before Shobai—though, in his astonishment at finding him alive, he did not know what to say. "S-Shobai?" he managed at last. "You are Shobai of Haran?"

"Your accent," Shobai said softly, unbelieving. "Your voice. It's Hadad's. It's his. Exactly as I remember it." He reached out tentatively, unsurely, with one hand, looking, for once, like the blind man that he was.

Ben-Hadad, tears in his eyes, took the huge, callused hand in his own and, without taking his eyes off Shobai, said to his companions, "Tuya, dearest . . . Anab—this is my uncle."

"*Shobai!*" Heket's voice, frightened yet almost scolding, came from the doorway, where she stood, lamp in hand, the sleepy-eyed twins peeking out from behind her cloak.

Shobai, tears running freely down his scarred cheeks, turned to her. "Come, Heket," he said. "Bring the children here. We're all together at last. All the Children of the Lion."

In the excitement of the reunion of uncle and nephew, as Shobai and Ben-Hadad tried in their enthusiasm to make up in one night for the many years of estrangement, and Heket bustled about serving the guests wine, figs, dates, and cheese, Tuya was forgotten. For a time she had tried to keep up with the entangled family tales, and had even been fairly successful. But when Lion arrived—as Ben-Hadad had predicted he would—she had joined the children as they tried to induce the dog to play with them. And in the end, after the twins had been sent back to bed—without the dog, Heket had insisted—she had drifted away to the dark steps outside. From there, gazing down the steep hillside, she could see the pale light of the moon reflected on the still waters of Lake Moeris.

Refreshed by the cool night air, she drew about her the shawl Heket had given her against the chill, and looked out on the moonlit valley. How peaceful it was here! How inexpressibly remote from the world of war, pillage, and cruelty she had left only hours before! One could hardly believe it was the same country, her poor, long-suffering Egypt.

She had never known the country at peace, of course. Most of her own young life had been lived in the shadow of the invaders, and even before that the nation had been almost constantly at war with itself. In the Black Lands of the delta, there had never been adequate protection for the average citizen against the marauding bandits and revolutionaries who roamed the countryside, looting, raping, killing. But here it was different. The almost eerie quiet of it all, the unwalled, undefended homes along the lakeshore, the unguarded farms and vineyards, and—

"It is lovely, isn't it?" a voice at her side said. "Peaceful, quiet—it might as well be a scene from the next life, for all the resemblance it bears to what we know of this one."

"Baka!" she said, turning to him. "You startled me."

He smiled at her. "Wait until you see what it's like by the light of morning," he said. "You won't believe any place could be so beautiful."

He paused, and neither of them spoke for a long while as they gazed out over the moonlit lake. "When I first heard that Shobai was to be found in the Fayum," he said, "I cursed the notion that such beauty should be wasted on a blind man, and most particularly on a blind man I had sworn to kill." He grunted, and shook his head. "What a fool I was," he said. "What a fool I remain."

"You're not a fool," she said. "A fool would indeed have killed him when he found him."

"Perhaps," Baka said. Looking up, she could see his sharp profile silhouetted by the cold rays of the moon. "How could I know beforehand that the man I had come to kill would turn out to be a better man than I can ever hope to be?" He chuckled to himself, without humor. "He wasn't afraid of me. He was waiting for me—prepared for torture, death, anything. He was at peace with himself. And his only sorrow was for Mereet."

"Mereet?"

"Yes," he said in a weary voice. "His only concern was for her. And for letting me know what there was to know of her. He *knew* what I'd suffered, thinking of her, and he'd suffered the same himself; but he wouldn't share his grief with me, realizing it would be too great a burden for me to bear. Instead, he . . ." His words were choked off, his hoarse voice breaking when he tried to speak. He closed his eyes for a while and seemed to master himself. "You've seen the children?" he said.

"Yes. They're beautiful."

"The girl . . . she's just like Mereet. I . . . when I met Mereet, she was hardly more than a child herself. Her features were delicate that same way, with that lovely, straight little nose. . . ." He shook his head savagely and turned away from her.

Tuya moved to his side, embraced him with both arms, and laid her face against his chest. "Baka," she said, "what will you do now? Where will you go?"

His hands, cold and stiff, touched her absently. "With Unas gone, they'll need an experienced commander," he said. "As much to protect them against Harmin and his swinish intrigues as to lead them against the Shepherds." She could feel the tightness, the anger, in him now. "That treacherous bastard—he's a worse enemy than twenty Shepherd generals. I have to go to Lisht, to head off his plotting, and then I . . ."

The unfinished sentence drew her attention. She stepped back and looked up at his face in the moonlight. "There's more, isn't there? You have to find her, if she can be found?"

"Yes."

"And if you find her? What then, Baka?" Seeing the desolation in his eyes, she took his chill hands in hers and pressed them to her heart.

"Why . . . if she's still alive, I'll have to return her to him, won't I? And to her children? What else can I do? After that . . . well, my path lies elsewhere. There's still a war to fight, as I said. And I've the fighting habit." He looked down at his hands, pulling them free of her grasp. "Look at them," he said. "They were once the hands of a scribe, soft and uncallused, like a woman's. Now they're hardly fit to hold a pen. Better a sword or spear or battle-ax. It's strange. Once you've offered them up to the arts of war, they're hardly good for anything else."

"No, Baka . . ."

"That's the way it is. We don't choose our destinies; we are chosen by them. To think otherwise is to defy the unchangeable edicts of the gods. I had notions about what I wanted to be. The gods had other ideas, and they made a killer of me. I'd be a fool to try to oppose their will."

"No! No!"

"You're as big a fool as I, girl. Can't you see? The
gods have you and your young man in as firm a grip as
they have me." She drew back, startled at his tone. His
face was set in a bitter smile. "Shobai, too. In a month he
and Ben-Hadad will be back on the front lines with me,
making weapons to kill Shepherds with. And you'll be . . .
where will you be, girl? You're carrying his child, aren't
you?"

"Yes," Tuya said, and for the first time, for some
reason, she was frightened by the thought.

Her consternation must have been evident. Baka smiled
grudgingly, trying to cheer her. "There are worse destinies to have. He's a fine young man, one who loves you—
and the war won't change him, as it did me. It's all I'm
good for now, no matter what I may have planned for
myself when I was young. And I'd better get back to it."

"Baka, don't go. Please, we need you here."

"Don't talk nonsense." He detached himself gently
from the hands that gripped his arms. "How could anyone
need me more than the soldiers at the front?" He stood
apart from her, loosening his sword belt to rebuckle it
higher. In the new position it looked smartly military once
again. "Besides," he said, "the blind man has done all he
can to look for her. But I haven't. And I still have friends
on the other side of the lines. If I can get a message
through to them, I can continue the search."

"Do you think you can find her?"

"Perhaps. Which reminds me: Ben-Hadad spoke of a
friend of his who was kidnapped up in Canaan and sold to
the Egyptians, or at any rate to an Ishmaelite caravan
bound this way. Tell him I'll ask around. Maybe someone's
heard at court."

"I will. And, Baka—?"

"There you are," a new voice said from inside. Pushing the thick door open, Anab stepped out into the night.
"Baka, you're not leaving, are you?"

"Yes. I have to get back to the army."

"Good! I'll go with you."

"You? But, Anab—"

Tuya interrupted him, winking at Anab. "He knows

what he's doing, Baka. Besides, you're going to need someone at your back, if the intrigues of the court are as bad as you say they are." She put an arm around Anab and hugged him with genuine affection. "I can't think of a better man than Anab to have alongside you when things get rough. He's as brave as a lion! Why, he saved my life twice. First he—"

Anab pulled Tuya aside. "That's enough of that," he said.

She would not be deterred, however. "That's how you can tell the brave ones, isn't it?" she said. "They won't let you brag about them. Take him along, Baka. You won't regret it."

Baka looked from her to the man with the ruined face. "All right," he said. "Although I warn you: The months to come will test your mettle, Anab—and mine, too, and everyone else's. We've got an army to rebuild, so—" He stopped and looked at both of them. "But of course you won't have heard. The messenger reported only to me."

"Messenger?" Anab said, buckling his sword.

"From Nubia. The emissary Akhilleus, a black man, stopped at Kerma on his way south. He made peace, after others had failed time and again. He even signed a treaty with them whereby they'd provide troops for the war— fierce Nubian fighters, already trained and proved in battle. They'll be sending us ore as well, to help us re-arm."

"Ore? What kind?" Tuya's voice was excited.

"Why, copper and tin from the eastern desert, I think," he replied.

"And iron ore?" she said.

"Iron? I don't recall his mentioning . . . You don't believe that tale of Shobai's, do you?"

"Baka, you weren't listening. He knows how to smelt the ore. He's made iron swords."

"So I've heard. And—I *wanted* to believe. But . . . I can't count on miracles. In any case, the messenger didn't mention iron specifically. But if Ben-Hadad and Shobai can make me such weapons, so much the better. In the meantime, I'll have my hands full keeping the Shepherds north of the line while we wait for the reinforcements we've been promised. My guess is that the Shepherds won't bother with us for the next few weeks. They've got some reorganizing to do, what with Vahan and Sahag gone. For that matter, so do we, and there's no time to waste. So get your horse, Anab, if you're coming with me. We've got an appointment in Lisht. Tuya—take care of Ben-Hadad. We'll need him, iron weapons or not."

They embraced. Anab edged away, but Tuya went to him and impulsively threw her arms around his waist and kissed him. "Oh, Anab!" she said. "I'll miss you so much, after all we've been through together! Look out for him, Baka, will you? I'd be heartbroken if anything happened to either of you." Her eyes were wet with tears.

Anab stood speechless, his hand to his cheek where she had just kissed him. "I . . . I can't get used to having people care about what happens to me," he managed at last. "G-good-bye, Tuya. And good luck."

When they had left, she stood listening to the retreating sound of the horses' hooves. Then, with a sigh, she went back to the door. But instead of entering, she stood framed in the open doorway, looking in at the two of them: at Ben-Hadad's beaming face as he listened to his newfound uncle talking, at the happiness that shone through Shobai's scarred face as he spoke, warming to his subject. ". . . better yet, we've reopened trade with Canaan, and the mines at Timna, south of the Dead Sea, are producing again! They're shipping ore out through the Gulf of Aqaba and from there across the Red Sea."

"Timna!" Ben-Hadad said. "My master, Ishmerai, said the Timna hillsides were so rich in malachite, and the sandstone that held it was so soft, that one man could mine sufficient ore in one day to yield enough copper to—"

"Ishmerai, you say? I met a man by that name once, many years ago. A smith from Succoth, I think, although it was in Ashkelon that I met him."

"Yes!" Ben-Hadad said. "That was Ishmerai!" He looked up, the happiness shining in his eyes, to see Tuya, and his ready smile embraced her as well. "Come, Tuya—sit by me." As she sat down cross-legged, his powerful arms held her close. "Oh, Tuya, I'm so happy! And—how strange it is. I've never been so far away from Canaan, from all the people I used to know. And yet"—he hugged her all the closer—"I've never felt so much at home."

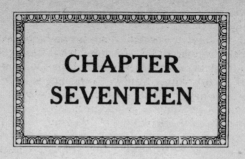

CHAPTER SEVENTEEN

CENTRAL AFRICA

I

No one in all the lands that the great Lokosa had put under one control had ever heard of a man being offered a crown and then refusing it. The first thought of the chiefs and their wondering people was that Akhilleus must be mad. No one, however, who had heard the big man speak could be induced to call him anything but wise. All the reasons the son of Magimbi had given for his refusal of the honors due him were indeed sound, and one—the giving of his word to the Egyptian king, and his unwillingness to break that word—bore upon the question of honor, which was high in every man's mind in the Land Between the Mountains.

Thus Akhilleus—"Mtebi" to all now, including those who had at first opposed him—was accorded special treatment during all the solemn ceremonies and festivities surrounding Kimala's investiture, and the chiefs vied with one another for the opportunity to show honor to Magimbi's eminent son and to his regal consort. Even old Musuri became the guest of honor at lesser gatherings, and was

370

both pleased and annoyed after several of these to find himself the recipient of the favors of selected virgins eager to bear a child of the seed of the old soldier who had traveled in so many lands and fought in so many wars. Musuri, knowing the potency of local custom and the unwisdom of flouting it, complied in every case, but he did not invite new encounters of this kind.

Now, however, as the ceremonies came to an end and it became time for resuming the ordinary affairs of the Land Between the Mountains, Akhilleus announced his imminent departure. A final feast was held in his honor, with all the tribal chiefs and leaders of the army in attendance.

The feast went on long after sundown, with dancing, singing, speeches, and much drinking and eating. Finally, as the crowd thinned, Akhilleus found himself alone with Kimala by the warm coals of the fire, with the nearest listener far away. He yawned, and as the yawn ended it turned into a warm smile. "Well," he said, "I'd better turn in. I'm going to leave in the morning, Kimala. Watch over my people for me, will you, my friend?"

"In the morning?" Kimala said. "But we were going to—" He laughed and sat back, looking at the older man. "That was my youth talking," he said. "Youth never wants to say good-bye. But you must do what you must do, and it is for me to understand and to help. You're going back the same way you came?"

"Yes. Even to taking a side trip to the great waterfall. I'll always think of it as the strongest spirit of the land, with its mighty waters pouring over the cliff to smash the rocks below."

"I understand. I go there sometimes myself. The river, it's the strength of this land."

"And of so many others," Akhilleus said. "I wish I could take you with me, Kimala, and show you it all. But your place is here, bringing peace and plenty to this lovely land of ours."

"Yes. But I'll escort you as far as the country of the Kakwa."

"We'll see. Incidentally, a troop of your young bloods

will petition you in the morning for permission to go with
me as mercenaries."

Kimala raised an eyebrow. "I did not know this.
From which tribe are they?"

"From many tribes. They approached me today. And
if you do not object, I'd like to take them with me. The
trip will be long and perilous, with possible danger even
at the end of it. In Egypt, you see, there are many men
like Ramogi."

Kimala's eyes narrowed in concern.

Akhilleus smiled. "I think, though, that if I had a
handpicked group of your compatriots at my side, I would
not fear so much for my safety."

"For *your* safety?" Kimala's smile was wise and
understanding.

Akhilleus chuckled. "Well, perhaps they'd also make
good seed corn for . . . oh, let's say an army of my own."

"One subordinate only to you, with no loyalty to the
Egyptian king?"

"Or to any of his underlings. You must remember,
one of those underlings paid Uranga to assassinate me on
the way here. That's hardly calculated to ensure my loyalty."

"*Hmmm.* Did you not tell me that Egypt was cut in
half, with the invaders occupying all the lands between it
and the Great Sea of which you spoke?"

"Yes. And naturally I'm less friendly with the invaders than I am with the Egyptians. Yet . . . the Egyptian
leaders—including the king—are not wise men. Perhaps I
could still have fought for them if I hadn't come back here
and learned what I have learned even in my dotard's
years."

"Dotard? Was it a dotard who bested Ramogi?"

"Oh, I can still play the younger man for a bit now
and then—that's not what I'm talking about. Look, Kimala—
I've already lost an empire, an empire on the Great Sea. I
was a merchant prince, rich enough to buy and sell whole
nations, if I'd wanted to. I had eighty, ninety, a hundred
ships plying the trade winds, and that's a bigger navy than
most countries could boast when I was trading. And now
I've given up a kingdom. Something in me does not want
to be anyone's subordinate anymore."

"Not even the king of Egypt's?"

Akhilleus smiled and put a confidential hand on Kimala's shoulder. "As I go north, Kimala, I think I'm going to raise an army. But I do not think I am going to march into beleaguered Egypt right away. I am going to stop in Kush, by the fifth cataract, many weeks' march up the river. And from there I am going to send emissaries to the Egyptian king. There is a city named Meroë, just above the rapids. I was well received there when I passed through—and I am well received in Kerma as well, where my wife has influential kin."

The wind changed, and it stirred the coals. Kimala waved away the smoke and looked Akhilleus in the eye. "You will have the balance of power in the region," he said. "Defender and invader alike will have to deal with you."

"Exactly. I fully expect to have trade established with both countries within a year. Trade routes exist through the western desert, with oases scattered no more than a day's march apart. Perhaps by this means I can make contact with what remains of my trading enterprise. It will not have broken up in my absence, I think. The people I left in charge were exceptionally able—and honest and loyal. They won't, it's true, be in any hurry to want me to resume control—but they will see the good sense in opening up new trade routes with Kush."

"But what has Kush to offer? You told me it was arid country, poor in resources."

Akhilleus leaned forward. "Poor now—yes. But in Memphis there's a blind weapon-maker, an old friend of mine. I knew both him and his father. And his father, before he disappeared, taught him a secret that will change the whole world."

Kimala appeared skeptical.

"Look," Akhilleus said, handing over his bronze sword. "This weapon was made by the blind man's father, many years ago."

"It is a beautiful weapon."

"I am glad you appreciate it. I am going to give it to you tomorrow, as a parting gift. In fact, I am going to make a little speech about it for my new volunteers."

"But—"

"No, hush, don't interrupt me. What I want to say is this: Imagine a weapon that could cleave this one in two with ridiculous ease. A blade as much harder than this, as this is harder than—oh, your arm, for instance."

"And where is one to come by such magical weaponry?"

"The blind man can make it. From the black metal I asked you about when we were in the Mufumbiro foothills."

"His father taught him this?"

"Yes. The black metal is called iron. All Egypt is poor in it—but not Kush."

"Ah. And are you to claim this from the native people by divine right?"

"No. I'm going to buy it. The hills where the black metal is found are thought worthless. I'll buy it all, and I'll build a new empire on it, one bigger than the one I had at sea. And I'll buy it for trinkets worth hardly more than the dirt we're sitting on."

Kimala pondered his words. "You'll be at the Egyptians' rear—and safe from the invaders at the same time. But your plan will take much time to carry out."

"I plan to live long enough to see it through. If not—" He shrugged. "First I'm going to bring the blind man south with me. He's in danger at the front, in any case, if one can draw any conclusions from the recent attempt on my own life."

"And what then, Mtebi?" Kimala asked.

Akhilleus stood up, filled his huge chest with air, and stretched, his great arms outspread like the branches of some enormous tree. It seemed to Kimala that as the old man did so, the years fell away from him rapidly—to fifty, to forty . . . "Ahhh," Akhilleus said. "The air of this place is wonderful. I'd forgotten. Totally forgotten. I suppose that in all those years I'd deliberately blotted out the memories. They must have been too painful to recall. But the moment the Nile came boiling out of that narrow defile, falling in one great, leaping cascade to the rocks below . . . I knew I was home. And I knew that coming home like this was going to be the most important thing I'd ever done—or most likely ever would do."

Kimala stared up at him intently. "You've changed

even since you've been here," he said. "I'm not sure how I'd describe it. I think that when you came into our land for the first time, you were still searching for something, and you weren't even sure what it was. But now . . . now, Mtebi, I think you've found it. Even if I'm still not sure what it was that you found."

"You're wise beyond your years," Akhilleus said, beaming down at him. "And a good thing, too. You've a great kingdom to govern, and it will take all the wisdom you can muster to do so." He looked around him, at the thinning ranks of the revelers, at the dark forest outside the ring of light. "What did I find?" he said. "Part of it was purpose, as you say. But I think I also found out who I really was. I mean, beyond the business of being little Mtebi the slave, and then Akhilleus the galley rower, and then Akhilleus the pirate and the rich man and the mountebank." He smiled at the darkness. "As we grow old, we shed skins, like a serpent, sloughing off an old, faded one for a brilliant new one, which in turn will grow old in time. But . . . but who is the person underneath all those skins, Kimala my friend?"

"I don't know," Kimala said. "Truly, Mtebi, I've no idea what kind of snake I am. And I'm still growing my own new skin."

Akhilleus chuckled and shook his grizzled head. As the wind sang softly in the leaves above, he reached up with his great arms and took hold of an overhanging bough. "Who knows?" he said. "You may never need another such skin. That is a reward—or a curse—of very long life, I suppose. But Bukango, he lived long enough to know. He may even have learned almost as soon as he assumed the crown. And I believe, Kimala, that he knew he had to grow into that crown—and he was capable of doing so."

Kimala nodded thoughtfully. "But what did you learn of your capabilities, Mtebi?"

Akhilleus's smile was open and accepting and eager, a young man's again. "I learned that I am smaller than the smallest fire ant in the trees," he said. "And that I am larger than the biggest bull elephant. I learned that I am all men, the weak and the strong, the old and the young, and that nothing a man is or can become is foreign to me:

the brave and the cowardly, the true and the traitorous, the wise and the foolish. There is no man so remote from me at this moment that I do not understand him, and sympathize with him, and even in a way accept him."

"I think I understand a little of this," Kimala said.

"Then you are a wiser man than I was at your age. But that does not surprise me." The smile that he aimed at Kimala now was of boundless affection. "In time you may well come to be called the greatest of them all, greater even than Lokosa himself. But in time, too, you and I will die and be forgotten, as completely as our remotest ancestors are forgotten. Yet there will remain the fact that we knew each other for what we were, that we met and learned from each other." He released the bough overhead and held out his arms to Kimala. "Come to my arms, my brother. My son. My true and noble friend."

Kimala stood up, and hesitated for a moment. Then he moved into Akhilleus's bearlike arms. "My father," he said, shaken, moved as he had never been moved before by anything in his young life.

In the morning the caravan gathered, augmented now by the stoutest, most robust young troop of mercenaries Musuri had ever had the pleasure of commanding. The old soldier's eyes shone with pride as he called them to attention and inspected them, his approval of their sharp turnout showing in his flinty-eyed smile.

Akhilleus had talked Kimala out of his offer to accompany the party to the edge of the kingdom. "The proper place for you just now is here," he said. "The people need to know they have a leader again, and they need to be reminded of it daily. Stay close to them. Be sure to—ah, but here I am advising you, who already know better, you who are so wise so young."

"Good-bye, Mtebi," Kimala said. "If I could keep you here with me, I would. But I think you go to a greater destiny than any you could know here, and I would not hold you from that."

Akhilleus gripped him by the biceps, smiled, and said, "Or perhaps it's just another skin for me to grow into before I die." His shrewd old eyes were mere slits now, and the gold in his teeth gleamed. "And if there's a single thing in the world that will make an old man feel young again, it's a new challenge to meet."

Ebana came to his side. "Challenge?" she said. "What challenge, you old elephant? You mean making it all the way home without falling down and breaking any bones? What are you bragging about now?"

Her tone was the old bantering one, but there was love and respect in it as she slipped an arm through Akhilleus's and smiled at Kimala. "What sort of nonsense has this man of mine been feeding you?"

Musuri joined them, interrupting. "Ready to go, Akhilleus," he said. "Just awaiting your order to start."

Akhilleus looked at Kimala. "I haven't told her," he said with a shrug. "Perhaps I should." He raised his long arm high, and in the line of soldiers and bearers stretched out behind him, every eye was waiting for the signal. The other arm hugged Ebana close and then released her. " 'Queen of Kush,' " he said. "It has a fine ring to it at that."

"What the devil are you saying—?" she began. But then his great arm swept down, and the rest of her question was buried in the cheer that arose, not only from the long line of soldiers and bearers in the caravan, but from the huge crowd Kimala had assembled to see them off. And now to the cheers was added the sound of drums, dozens of them, high-pitched and low, in many rhythms, all of which seemed, strangely, to blend compatibly with one another. To this combined rhythm they set off, heads held high. As they did, the mercenaries of Kimala's old command who had joined the caravan began to sing an ancient marching song of Akhilleus's people. It was a young man's song of joy, of voyages into foreign lands, of terrors braved, of conquest—and of farewell. And, perhaps, of an eventual return.

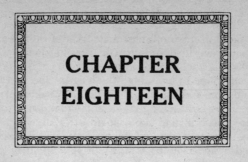

CHAPTER
EIGHTEEN

LISHT

I

In the street, the general Harmin paused before the broad foundations of the new palace Madir had ordered to be built for the Lord of Two Lands. The newly dried bricks were stacked in orderly rows, waiting for the construction to continue. Across the avenue, in a shallow canal diverted from the Nile, heavily tanned laborers and slaves were hard at work making mud bricks.

As he watched the antlike movement of the workers, Harmin shook his head and his lip curled downward in a sneer. "Waste of time," he muttered to himself. *Imagine, building a palace in this backwater!* Why, even as recently as a year ago, anyone who had mentioned the idea of moving the capital from Memphis to Lisht would have been laughed out of court! And now . . . Harmin surveyed the scene before him with unconcealed distaste.

Thebes, of course, was a different story. He could easily envision splendid new royal apartments there, not far from the river . . . maybe even on his own land. He had no doubts that someday Thebes could rival Memphis itself—perhaps even surpass it as the greatest capital in the world, now that the barbaric Shepherds were in control of the old royal city and would, in all probability, let it go to neglect and ruin.

"Oh, well." Harmin sighed heavily and continued on his way, not bothering to picture in his mind what the finished palace here at Lisht would look like. He had seen the architects' plans, of course, and had acted duly impressed, all the while thinking: *All for the greater glory of Madir.*

But now, as he turned to mount the staircase on his way to the vizier's customary early morning divan—held these days in a converted temple—thoughts of Madir made him grow edgy, uneasy. *If only that fellow Yusni had succeeded. . . .*

He barely bothered to nod as he passed the armed guard who stood, spear at the ready, before the doorway leading to the inner garden in which he would await Madir's call to his private chamber. As he moved from shade into the sunlit space between the twin palms in the atrium, his mind raced.

They had been lucky—extremely lucky—that Yusni hadn't talked—*and* that Unas had conveniently died in battle, before their assassin could do his work.

It had all been too easy . . . so far.

And now there was this troublesome business with Baka. Imagine—sending a messenger with thinly veiled threats to him, Harmin, general of all the pharaoh's armies! The gall of the man!

Harmin stopped pacing the courtyard and deliberately calmed himself. He must appear composed when called before Madir. As for Baka, he could be taken care of in good time—especially if today's interview went smoothly. And why shouldn't it? he reminded himself, smiling confidently. Hadn't Madir let him ram through his latest plan, almost without comment? Why, only two days after he'd presented his idea of reorganizing the army with himself, Harmin, actively in field command—effectively eliminating Baka, of course—the vizier's reaction had been openly supportive, including the present invitation to discuss the matter further and smooth out the details. And

the invitation had been couched in the most friendly terms
. . . almost *too* friendly for Madir. Again Harmin felt a
strange uneasiness.

Was Madir growing senile? He was, after all, twenty
years older than himself. That must be it! After all, there
came a time in every man's life when he suddenly went
from vigorous middle age to dotage. This was a time for
retirement, for handing over power and responsibility to
the younger, the better qualified. And, Harmin knew, a
wise man, in such cases, would do well to handpick his
successor and strike some sort of deal that would assure
his own continued safety and health in exchange for present support.

Well, Madir had shown ample signs of sagacity and
self-knowledge in the past. Perhaps now would be no
exception.

How should I handle it? he wondered—and almost
instantly he knew. Magnanimity was the key. He'd greet
Madir with great respect, with ample evidence of his
esteem. When the offer was made, he'd hesitate about
accepting, pleading his own inadequacy in the face of
Madir's magnificence and universally acknowledged com-
petence. All the time both of them would know it was all
show—but Madir would appreciate his having gone through
the motions. Old men did, when it came time for them to
step aside. . . .

"The noble Madir will see you now, sir." The inner
guard bowed and saluted, ushering him through huge
double doors into the great man's presence. Harmin, in
tune with his previous thoughts, greeted his superior as
gracefully, as respectfully, as he knew how. His final bow
was deep and protracted.

"Rise, Harmin," Madir said from his perch on the
vizier's throne, high atop a dais at the rear of the room.
"Let's not stand on ceremony, you and I. We've been
through too much together over the years. Stand easy, my
friend. Shall I have wine brought? Olives, perhaps? Dates?
Approach the platform, please. Don't overdo the formality."

"I thank the noble Madir," Harmin said. He noticed a
papyrus scroll in Madir's lap. "But—I fear I interrupt
pressing business. Shall I come back later?"

Madir's thin face smiled warmly. "No, no. As a matter of fact, the 'business' I have here concerns you. You might be interested in hearing of it." He clapped his hands. A servant entered from a side door, bearing a tray with wine and two golden cups. "You can put that down here beside the noble Harmin and withdraw. There's a good fellow!" The slave moved away silently. "Wine, Harmin? Surely you'll reconsider. No? Well, let me make a long story short. What I have here"—one bony hand indicated the scroll—"is a report on your activities as leader of our armed forces."

Harmin's face went stark white. "I—I can expl—"

"But, please—no false modesty!" Madir's voice grew almost unctuous. "You'll be pleased to hear that I have depositions from two of your generals, and that they had nothing but the most flattering things to say of your performance." He paused a moment. "Well, almost nothing. A trifle here and there. But nothing of any significance. For instance—"

"W-which generals?" Harmin said, thinking of Unas. "Because, my lord, I meant to tell you . . . Unas was plotting treason. If he had lived, he was to have stood trial before the Council within the month. I had the most unimpeachable testi—"

"Oh, have no fear," Madir said reassuringly. "I did, to be sure, have a report from Unas, but knowing your reputation, I disregarded it as the envious prattle of a spiteful underling." He shrugged his frail shoulders, as if pleading innocence of any suspicious thoughts. "But let us not speak ill of the dead. Whatever unsavory schemes he may have plotted went into the grave with him. Besides, there's no use dwelling on his failings, is there? After all, while he lived, he did give good service. Even you must admit that, my dear Harmin."

Magnanimity, Harmin thought. *Keep it magnanimous.* "I understand," he said hoarsely. "Of course."

"In any case, this isn't from Unas," Madir said, again indicating the scroll in his lap. "It's from the man who replaced him." He clapped his hands again, twice this time. "I took the liberty of bringing him here. I was sure you would want to meet him." He smiled as Baka, with an ugly young aide at his side—a skinny man with a curiously paralyzed face—stepped into the room. They were followed by two guards.

"*Baka!*" Harmin said, his voice tense with wariness. "My lord—here's the real traitor! He, like Unas, wants to—"

"—to replace you, my dear Harmin," Madir said. "And a good thing, too. If they hadn't brought the matter of your own depredations to my attention, why, who knows? You might even have succeeded in your treasons."

"*M-my* treasons?" Harmin stammered. "But—"

"Yes—your treasons," Baka said, fixing him with a cold, mocking smile. "First, the matter of my own betrayal, back in the delta. We traced it to you through Eben. He was only too glad to implicate both you and the priest Hapu."

"Eben? Hapu? I don't know what you're talking about!" Harmin's gaze flickered uneasily back and forth from Baka's deathly grin to Madir, who remained cool and impassive high above them on his pedestal. The two armed guards had discreetly moved forward to flank Madir . . . and, Harmin noted with increasing panic, their uniforms were not those of the army's palace guards, but those of Madir's handpicked, fiercely loyal bodyguard. Instinctively he backed away. A quick glance behind him, however, confirmed his worst fears: Two more heavily armed guards stood before the double doors, which were now closed and barred.

Madir cleared his throat noisily. "Well, Harmin," he said, "you'll have ample time in prison to consult your errant memory. While you're waiting to die, that is. Perhaps we can even arrange for you to share a cell with your friends Eben and Hapu. Which reminds me—we also traced to you the hiring of the assassin who was to have murdered Akhilleus, my emissary to Nubia. Did you think I didn't know about that, Harmin? Why, that alone would have assured your—"

It was too much. With a grunt of rage Harmin reached inside his robe for a slim bronze dagger and lunged at

Baka, wanting only to remove the mocking smile on the soldier's cold face. The dagger flashed—but at the last moment a slim brown figure interposed itself between him and his target. Harmin felt his blade strike home, but on the wrong man. Baka's aide slumped, staggered, and fell. Then Baka's wiry muscled arms went around Harmin, wrestling him to the ground, and Madir's guardsmen, rushing to the center of the room, ringed Harmin's livid face with sharp spear-points.

Madir wasted no time. "Take him to the dungeon," he said. "I don't want to see him anymore."

As Harmin was dragged off, still at spear-point, he got off one shouted curse before an unseen hand smothered his choked cry.

Baka had not risen from his knees. He bent over the fallen Anab, looking once—no more—at the fearful wound he had sustained. "Anab, my valiant friend," he said gently. "Once again I owe you my life. I . . ."

But Anab's own life was ebbing fast. The half face contorted as he tried to smile, but the effort and the pain turned his last expression into an unreadable grimace. "B-Baka . . ." he said. A great, rattling sigh came from the parted lips, and then the sightless eyes just stared, the two halves of the ruined face at last matching each other in their impassiveness. Baka, head bent, was silent for a long while.

Then, slowly, wearily, he stood up, his face drawn. "You saw," he said to Madir. "Blind, unthinking courage. This from a man who admitted he lived most of his life a coward, afraid of every shadow." He sighed, visibly trying to compose himself. "The struggle in which we are all engaged, it—it makes unlikely heroes." He looked down once more to the fallen body of his friend and shook his head. "I'll ask your leave, my lord, to have him sent across to the next world with appropriate honor and ceremony. Necessity made a man of him, and I'm sure he would have proved his mettle daily as time went by."

"I understand," Madir said. "And your request will be granted." He nodded to the remaining guard, who gently picked up Anab's lifeless body and carried it away.

Baka and Madir, alone now, did not speak until the guard's departing footsteps could be heard no more.

"You're right," Madir said then. "War does make unlikely heroes. You yourself were once a scribe, were you not? I can see you still, in my mind's eye, a retiring, scholarly sort, drilling pupils in their lessons. And here you are before me, a soldier, and a great one. No—don't deny it," he said, descending from the dais to take Baka's elbow. "The test of a soldier is not what he can do in a safe position with a superbly outfitted army, well-trained and fit. It's what he can do with ragtag irregulars, on the run, outmanned and outweaponed."

"I've had some luck," Baka said.

"Luck? Luck helps only the competent, and is wasted on others. Don't deny what I'm saying, my friend. And don't make light of your own heroism by refusing the generalship of my armies now, because I won't accept your refusal."

"I—I see," Baka said. "If you'll give me leave, however, to bury my friend first . . ."

"Of course," Madir said, putting an arm around Baka's shoulder. "But when the arrangements are complete, we must sit down together and discuss this war. In the meantime, whatever you need to strengthen the front-line army, just say the word. There's going to be no more raiding of your resources for the palace guards. If you need fresh drafts, new weapons, just tell me. From this moment on, address all messages to me directly. Make your runners known to the guards, and they'll be shown in to me without delay." He patted Baka's shoulder. "We've missed you, you know. If you'd been with the army these past months, we'd never have had to abandon Memphis to the Shepherds."

"This may or may not be so, my lord," Baka said. "Nevertheless, I believe we can turn the present situation to our advantage, and use the fall of Memphis as a rallying point for the new drafts. If we can train a fresh force in time, before the Shepherds have replaced the leaders they've lost, I think we can drive them back into the delta before the flood season comes. After that . . . well, we might have a bit of a standoff for a while . . . that is, unless this Akhilleus you mention can get us the mercenaries and the supply of ore I've been told he's promised us. Then—who knows?"

Madir smiled benignly and steered him toward the door. "Who, indeed? There is only one man I know of who could foretell the future—a young foreigner named Joseph. I wanted him for my court, but I'm afraid he was taken by the Shepherds. But, come—I've an audience prepared for you with the Lord of Two Lands himself, who will want you to tell him what life is like in the delta these days. We've kept an eye on your activities all this time, you know—even from here. I wasn't fooled by this 'Benu' fellow for long. The Phoenix, indeed! Although I must admit the name was appropriate, rising from the dead as you did."

Baka allowed himself a weak smile, which died as he again grew pensive. Finally he spoke. "My lord, there's also the matter of . . . well, I don't know how to say this . . ."

"Of your wife? Mereet, I believe her name is?" Madir again patted Baka's shoulder reassuringly. "Once the battle lines have stabilized, perhaps I can put my spies to work. Of course, if we do find her, there will be problems . . . problems you'll have to settle for yourself."

Baka was well aware of Madir's notorious network of informers, but still he was unprepared for this. As they left the reception room and passed through the double doors, he stopped abruptly and closed his eyes for a moment as Madir continued slowly down the great hall. He let a dozen paces separate Madir's words and his own. Then, opening his eyes and taking a deep breath, he said, "Right you are, my lord."

Madir patiently waited for Baka to catch up with him, but when Baka spoke again, it was of military matters, and Madir willingly let the previous subject drop. In any case, he had yet to learn what had become of Mereet—or, for that matter, of Uni and that remarkable young diviner. More than likely all three were dead at the hands of the Shepherds, although he couldn't be sure. *Well*, he thought, *all in its own time*. For now there was strategy to plan and an empire to rebuild, and for once he had a strong, reliable man at his side to help him with the job. The thought made his heart beat strong in his breast, made him feel young again. . . .

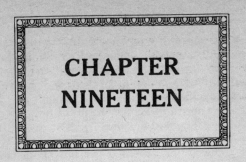

CHAPTER
NINETEEN

THE NILE DELTA

I

They left the main channel of the Nile at Heliopolis, transferring to a larger boat that plied the many lesser streams that cut their way through the delta to the sea. Standing by the starboard rail near the bow, Mereet watched disconsolately as the fields of olive trees and date palms passed by. Their course was, she estimated, roughly north-northwest, and . . . of course! She should have realized it! Soon they'd be moving into the country she'd been born in! If they followed the swiftest channel from here all the way to the sea, they'd pass Tanis, and . . .

But no—they'd never get that far. Surely the ship was bound instead for Avaris, the new capital the Shepherds were building. That had been what she'd overheard when the captain and the mate were talking, back in Heliopolis.

But how strange to be returning home this way, after so many years! She, who'd been the pampered daughter of a wealthy magistrate, back before the Shepherds had come: her home a palace, her inheritance the ownership of a prosperous school for scribes and lands many days' march

across, lands that produced enough fruit to feed an army
. . . Now here she was, coming back to a land where her
father's name wasn't even remembered and where she
possessed nothing, nothing in all the world, not even the
dear husband and children she'd left behind. And instead
of being an owner she was now one of the owned—a slave.
A slave of the Shepherd invaders.

She closed her eyes and felt the salt tears coursing
down her cheeks. She pressed her lips closely together
and tried to force the dark thoughts from her mind. From
now on it would be better to forget the past, to live always
in the present. It was the only way to keep her sanity—

A soft, masculine voice interrupted her thoughts.
"You're thinking about the past again, aren't you?"

She opened her eyes and wiped them with her hands.
Blinking away the tears, she turned and met the gaze of
the young man who, along with her, had been released
from the prison at Memphis. His eyes were warm and
sympathetic, and his face was sober and calm. What was
his name? Yussuf, or something like that? A foreigner's
name—but his accent was slight, almost nonexistent. A
patrician, somehow, despite his foreign origin. Well, that
was not unusual for a slave: They came from everywhere,
from every walk of life. Someone had even said something
about this one's being a king's son. Yet here he was, a
slave like herself. She sighed. "Yes, I'm afraid I was. It's
hard not to, isn't it?"

"Why should you want to forget?" the young man
said.

What was his name exactly? Ah, yes: Joseph.

"My people have a tradition of remembering," he
said. "Everything. We always say that the dead remain
alive so long as memory lasts. And if I forget the home I
left behind, how can I ever hope to find it again?"

"But—it hurts so," she said. "I left babies behind,
and a loving husband who needed me—" She stopped,
glancing around hastily. "Forget I said that," she whispered.
"So far none of the Shepherds seems to know who I am. I
want to keep it that way if I can."

Joseph looked at her thoughtfully, nodded. "Perhaps
I should relay that to Uni down below . . . although he

doesn't seem to be in a mood to talk to anyone these days. So . . . your husband would be a man of importance to the Egyptians, then? A man, perhaps, who could be forced to betray his fellows if it were known that his wife was a prisoner of the other side?"

She looked about her again. "Something like that. But do me a favor and forget it, will you, please?" She looked at him curiously. "You must indeed be a diviner, as I heard some others mention," she said. An edge of bitterness crept into her voice. "Tell me, my clairvoyant friend: Will I ever get home again? Will I see my babies?" Her voice cracked, and she stifled a sob.

"I don't know," Joseph said, perfectly serious. "I have no control over what visions are granted me by the God of my fathers." He turned, leaned on the rail, and looked out over the distant bank slipping past them. "I did have a vision of my own future," he said. "Last night I dreamed something about cattle—a vast herd of them. Some of them were fat, and some were lean. I'm certain that fact had great significance, but I am not sure what. Sometimes it takes a number of dreams before the first one begins to become clear. I do know one thing, though."

She put both hands on the rail and looked at him questioningly.

"I know that I won't be a slave much longer. I'll be a free man soon. Then I will begin to rise. In time, only one man will stand higher in all the kingdom. And even he will have to listen to my word before he does anything." His tone was uncomfortably matter-of-fact.

Mereet scrutinized him, looking at the strong, slim young body in its simple kilt and papyrus sandals, at the upright stance, the reddish-haired head atop the long neck, and the steady eyes, dark and serious. His words had sounded almost childish—wishful thinking of the most foolish kind. But now, facing him, she could not bring herself to say the scoffing words that hung on her tongue. Perhaps he did have something of a diviner about him; perhaps this unnamed god of his had, after all, spoken to him in some incomprehensible way; perhaps his words would prove true in the long run. He certainly had the look of a man born to rise in the world.

But then a wave of contempt at the thought swept through her, and she turned away. What nonsense! Surely this was nothing more than the bravado of untested youth. Surely this was idle talk that the facts of life would soon enough drive from his head. After all, the Shepherds regarded people not of their own blood as little more than cattle. Why should they free this young foreigner and give him an opportunity to rise? Why should his destiny be any more favored than hers, or that of the thousands of other slaves currently in thrall to the overlords of the land? Why should—?

"I see you don't believe me," Joseph said. "I understand. I would hardly believe it myself, this gift of mine, if it hadn't proved true so many times before. I know that some people resent my gift. Some even hate me for it. My brothers did. They sold me into slavery. But I understand their ire and their jealousy, and I forgive them. Someday I'll have a chance to do so in person. That, too, I know as sure as I'm standing here. And I also know that . . ."

His words trailed off strangely, and she shot a sharp glance at him. When she did she was shocked to see his body stiffen and his eyes roll back up into his head. His mouth hung open, and his hands, gripping the rail, began to shake uncontrollably.

Mereet momentarily panicked, then realized he was having some sort of fit, like that of people with the falling disease. She tried to steady him with her hands, and was astonished to feel his body as rigid as a day-old corpse. His breath was coming in gasps, and under his now-closed eyelids his eyes were trembling rapidly.

From the stern, one of the Shepherd guards shouted at her harshly: "You get away!" he said in crude Egyptian. "You do not touch!"

"He's having a seizure!" she cried back, trying to loosen his rock-hard grip on the railing. "I'm afraid he's going to hurt himself—"

Just then Joseph's body relaxed and he almost fell down. Her arms held him until he could get control of his legs and stand erect. "I . . . where am I? Who are you? If I . . ." He shook his head, trying to clear it. "Oh. Oh, yes.

I'm on the boat going downriver. And you're the wife of the blind man who—"

"*Shh!*" she said, putting a hand over his mouth. "I don't know how you know that, but be quiet about it."

Again the Shepherd guard shouted out a harsh warning. Joseph pulled her fingers away from his mouth and motioned her to stand back, so as not to anger the guard further. "Don't worry," he said. "They can't hear us. And—I won't tell. But . . . it's coming back to me. What . . . what happened to me just now, that's the way it strikes me sometimes when I have a vision."

"I wondered about that," she said, solicitude still in her tone. "Are you sure you're going to be all right?"

"Yes," Joseph said. "And—Mereet. That's your name, isn't it? I saw you with your children again. In my vision. You and the blind man, your husband and both children, the boy and the girl."

"The boy and girl? How could you know?"

"They're twins, aren't they?"

"Yes! But—how? No one could know that but . . ."

He went on as though he had not been interrupted. "I saw all four of you together. The boy and the girl were already as tall as you. They were robust and healthy, and the girl seemed nearly as strong as the boy. Then I . . . then the father was no longer there. But in his place there were others: There was a man. Does your husband have kin? A younger man, powerfully built, with curly hair?"

Mereet's brow wrinkled. "Hadad?" she said. "My husband's brother? But . . . he's dead. Years ago, when I was a child—"

"Yes! But he had a son! And the son has come all the way from Canaan to . . . to . . . ." Joseph seemed stunned, as if unable to believe where his own words were leading. "Mereet, you may not believe this, but—"

"*You!*" the guard bellowed again. "I tell slaves to get away from each other! Seaman—take slaves below! Put at opposite ends of ship!"

Strong hands closed around Mereet's arms, and she felt herself being dragged backward. A second sailor was hauling Joseph to the forward hatch to take him below.

THE LION IN EGYPT

"Joseph!" she called to him. "Don't forget me! When you come to power—don't forget!"

Joseph, in the seaman's burly arms, did not resist. But as he was carried away, he nodded to her once and smiled, then called back to reassure her: "You'll see them again—"

But a rough hand went over his mouth and silenced his words, and Mereet, her single garment in disarray, her bare feet kicking, was wrestled down into the hatchway and thrown into the darkness below. The last sound she heard before the hatch cover crashed down was the lonely cry of a gull, flying high overhead.

EPILOGUE

The sun had gone down hours before, yet with the full moon high in the east, it was almost as light as dawn on the hillside where the tents were pitched. The fire had gone out, but the coals glowed red. Lit from below, the gaunt, bearded face of the Teller of Tales had for a moment an uncannily demonic cast to it as he paused, his eyes wide yet seeming to look nowhere.

But now the scarecrow figure stood and drew itself up to its full height; the wizard's hands gestured, and the tale teller spoke once more to the rising wind:

"Go now," he said. "Go to your tents, my children, and sleep. With the morrow, I shall return. And when next I speak it will be to tell you of the rise of Joseph, son of Jacob, to high position and great power in the land of Egypt. You will hear how the despised slave became vizier to the great king of Egypt, of how he saved the nation when famine swept through the land, and of how he brought to Egypt his father Jacob and the brothers who had sold him into bondage.

"You will hear," he said, "of the beautiful Mereet, and of her long struggle to escape her captors and find her way back to her home and family. You will hear, too, of blind Shobai, and of how he trained both his children, boy and girl alike, and his brother's son, Ben-Hadad, in the ancient craft of the Children of the Lion, making arms to bring peace to Red Land and Black Land. . . .

393

"And you will hear of the black giant Akhilleus, mightiest of men, and of how he came back from the dark lands of his forefathers to forge a kingdom of his own in Kush and bring, for however short a time, peace to the troubled lands of the Great River."

There rose from the throats of the crowd a quick sigh; but the old man raised his hand once again. "Yet you shall also hear," he said in an ominous voice, "of evil voices, voices of treachery and dissent that rose within the ranks of the fighters for freedom, once more setting brother against brother, even as the dread famine descended on the land."

"Now!" a young voice in the crowd cried. "Tell us now!"

But the old man placed his sorcerer's hands together and bowed, then backed into the shadow of the hills above. "Tomorrow," he said. "Tomorrow . . ."